CHRISTINE FEEHAN

The Shadows of Christmas Past

SUSAN SIZEMORE

POCKET STAR BOOKS

New York   London   Toronto   Sydney

This book is a work of fiction. Names, characters, places and incidents are products of the author's imagination or are used fictitiously. Any resemblance to actual events or locales or persons, living or dead, is entirely coincidental.

An *Original* Publication of POCKET BOOKS

 A Pocket Star Book published by
POCKET BOOKS, a division of Simon & Schuster, Inc.
1230 Avenue of the Americas, New York, NY 10020

Rocky Mountain Miracle copyright © 2004 by Christine Feehan
A Touch of Harry copyright © 2004 by Susan Sizemore

ISBN: 0-7434-8296-4

First Pocket Books paperback printing November 2004

10 9 8 7 6 5 4 3 2 1

POCKET STAR BOOKS and colophon are registered trademarks of Simon & Schuster, Inc.

Cover design by Lisa Litwack; Photo of horse © Pat Powers/ Index Stock Imagery/ Picture Quest; title type by Ron Zinn

Manufactured in the United States of America

For information regarding special discounts for bulk purchases, please contact Simon & Schuster Special Sales at 1-800-456-6798 or business@simonandschuster.com.

❧ contents ❧

ROCKY MOUNTAIN MIRACLE

Christine Feehan

🌿 dedication 🌿

This book is dedicated to Sheila Clover, a woman I admire very much.

🌿 acknowledgments 🌿

I have to thank Dr. Lisa Takesue of Main St. Veterinarian Clinic for her unfailing patience when I asked veterinarian questions and, most especially, Tory Canzonetta, a federally licensed trainer at Destiny Big Cat Sanctuary, a last-stop haven for exotic cats. Visit the website at www.destinybigcats.com and see the beautiful tigers and other cats! Tory rescues exotic cats and keeps them safe and healthy. She gave me so much information and opened her heart and sanctuary to me for research.

I love to hear from readers. Please feel free to visit my website, www.christinefeehan.com and join my members-only private e-mail list to receive free screen savers, view teasers, and receive new-release announcements of my books.

chapter 1

COLE STEELE COULD HEAR the screams coming from the room down the hall. He knew those nightmares intimately, because the demons also visited him every time he closed his own eyes. He was a grown man, hard and disciplined and well able to drink his way through the night if necessary, but Jase was just a young teenager. Guilt edged his anger as he made his way through the dark to the boy's room. He should have done something, to spare his half brother the horrendous legacy of his own past.

In truth, he hadn't been in touch with his father for years. It hadn't occurred to him that his father would remarry a much younger woman and produce another child, but he should have considered the possibility, not just dropped off the face of the earth. Cole shoved open the bedroom door. Jase was already fully awake, his eyes wide with the terror of his memories. Something twisted hard and painfully in Cole's chest.

"I'm here, Jase," he announced unnecessarily. He wasn't good at soothing the boy. He had been born and bred in roughness and still had a difficult time being gentle. Worse, Jase barely knew him. He was asking the teenager to trust him in spite of his reputation and the rumors of attempted murder flying freely through the town. It was no wonder the boy regarded him with some suspicion.

"I hate Christmas. Can't we just make it go away?" Jase asked. He threw back the covers and paced across the room, the same edgy tension in his teenage body that Cole had in abundance as a grown man. Jase was tall and gangly, like a young colt, all arms and legs, looking a bit like a scarecrow in flannel pajamas. He had Cole's dark hair, but his eyes must have been his mother's, as they were a deep, rich brown. Right now, his eyes were wide with terror, and he turned away to hide his trembling.

Cole felt as if he were looking at himself as a youngster, only Jase had poured himself into books and Cole had become a hellion. Cole knew what it was like to hide the bruises and the terror from the rest of the world. He had grown up living in isolation and hiding, and he still lived that way, but he would be damned if this boy would endure the same.

"Did he shoot your dog for Christmas?" Cole asked bluntly. "That's what he did for me the last time I wanted to celebrate the holiday like my friends. I haven't ever wanted a Christmas since. He also beat the holy hell out of me, but that was insignificant next to the dog."

Jase faced him slowly. The horror was still all too stark in his eyes. "I had a cat."

"I'll bet he said you weren't tough enough and that only sissies needed pets and Christmas. He wanted you to toughen up and be a man. Not get attached to anything."

Jase nodded, swallowing an obvious lump in his throat. "He did a lot of things."

"You have burn marks? Scars from cuts? He liked to

whip me with a coat hanger. And when I didn't cry, he took to using other things."

"I cried," Jase admitted.

"I did too, at first. He was a mean son of bitch, Jase. I'm glad he's dead. He can't touch you anymore. I'm not going to lie to you and tell you the nightmares go away because I still have them. We both lived in hell and he had too much money for anyone to want to believe us." Cole rubbed his hands through his thick black hair. "He was sick, Jase. I got out, changed my name thinking he'd never find me, and stayed as far from him as I could possibly get. That's no excuse. I should have kept tabs on him. Maybe I could have gotten you away from him."

Jase shook his head. "He never would have let me go."

"You know what they're all saying, don't you? They think I had something to do with his death."

Jase nodded, his eyes suddenly wary. "I've heard. Why did you come back?"

"I was named your guardian in his will. It was the first I'd heard of you. I didn't know you existed until five months ago. I knew he must have done the same thing to you and your mother that he did to me and mine. I thought I could protect you, at least until you're old enough to live on your own. I figured I would be a better guardian than anyone else the court might appoint or that our father had named if I didn't accept."

Dawn was creeping in through the huge plate-glass window. Cole watched the sun come up. It was cold, and the ground outside was covered with several feet of snow, turning the hills into a carpet of sparkling crystals. "You hungry?"

"Are you cooking?"

Cole managed a lazy shrug even though he really wanted to smash something. It was always there, that volcano inside him, waiting to erupt. The thought of his father, the time of year, it wasn't all that difficult to bring rage to the surface. "I thought we'd go into town and give them all something more to gossip about."

Jase met Cole's eyes squarely. "They say you killed the old man and that you're planning to kill me next. Sixty-four million dollars is a lot of money, twice as much as thirty-two."

"They do say that, don't they?" Cole said. "And don't forget the ranch. It's worth twice that easily, maybe more with the oil and gas deposits. I haven't actually checked into how much yet." His eyes had gone ice-cold, a piercing blue stare that impaled the boy. "What do you say, Jase? Because in the end, you're the only one that counts as far as I'm concerned."

Jase was silent a long time. "I say I'm glad you came back. But I don't understand why he left us the money and the ranch when he hated us both so much. It doesn't make any sense." He looked around the enormous room, frowning. "I keep expecting him to show up in the middle of the night. I'm afraid to open my eyes because I know he's standing over the bed, just waiting."

"With that smile." Cole's voice was grim.

Jase nodded, a small shudder betraying the fact that he wasn't as calm as he tried to seem. "With that smile." He looked at Cole. "What do you do when the nightmares come?" He punched his fist into his pillow. Once. Twice. "I hate this time of year."

Cole felt a sharp pain in his chest and the familiar churning in his gut. His own hand balled into a fist, but he tamped down the smoldering anger and hung on to control for the boy's sake. "I drink. I'm your guardian, so I have to say that's not allowed for you. At least not until you're a hell of a lot older."

"Does it work?"

"No," Cole said grimly. Honestly. "But it gets me through the night. Sometimes I go to the workout room or the barn. I hung a heavy bag in both places, and I beat on them until my hands hurt. Other times I take the wildest horse we have and go out into the mountains. I run the hills, using the deer trails, anything to make me so tired I can't think anymore."

"None of that works either, does it?" Jase had tried physical activity as well, but he was finding that talking quietly with his half brother was helpful. More helpful than anything else he'd tried. At least one person believed him. And one person had gone through the same torment. It created a bond in spite of the ugly rumors that surrounded his tough, harder-than-nails half brother.

Cole shook his head. "No, none of it works, but it gets you through the night. One night at a time. He's dead, Jase, and that's all that matters."

Jase took a deep breath. "Did you kill him?"

"No, but I wish I had. I used to lie awake at night and plan how I'd do it. That was before Mom died. Then I just wanted to get out." Cole studied the boy's face. "Did you kill him?" He concentrated his gaze on the boy. Every nuance. Every expression, the way he breathed. The flick of his eyes. The trembling of his hands.

Jase shook his head. "I was too afraid of him."

Cole let his breath out slowly. He had stayed alive using his ability to read others, and he was fairly certain that Jase was telling the truth. Jase had been in the house when someone had shot Brett Steele right there in his own office. He wanted to believe that the boy wasn't involved in Brett Steele's death. Cole wasn't certain how he would have handled it if Jase had admitted he'd done it, and for a man in Cole's profession, that wasn't a good thing.

"Cole, did he kill your mother?" For the first time, Jase sounded like a child rather than a fourteen-year-old trying to be a man. He sank down onto the bed, his thin shoulders shaking. "I think he killed my mother. They said she was drinking and drove off the bridge, but she never drank. Never. She was afraid to drink. She wanted to know what was happening all the time. You know what he was like, he'd be nice one minute and come after you the next."

Brett Steele had been a sadistic man. It was Cole's belief that he had killed for the sheer rush of having the power of life and death over anything, human or animal. He'd enjoyed inflicting pain, and he had tortured his wives and children and every one of his employees. The ranch was huge, a long way from help, and once he had control over those living on his lands, he never relinquished it. Cole knew he'd been lucky to escape.

"It's possible. I think the old man was capable of paying everyone off from coroners to police officers. He had too much money and power for anyone to cross him. It would be easy enough for a medical examiner to look the other way if there was enough money in bribes. And if that didn't work, there were always threats. We both know the old man didn't make idle threats; he'd carry them out."

Jase met his brother's stare directly. "He killed your mother, didn't he?"

"Maybe. Probably." Cole needed a drink. "Let's go into town and get breakfast."

"Okay." Jase pulled a pair of jeans from the closet. They were neatly hung and immaculately clean, just like everything else in the room. "Who do you think killed him? If it wasn't either of us, someone else had to have done it."

"He made a lot of enemies. He destroyed businesses and seduced as many of his friends' wives as possible. And if he killed anyone else, as I suspect he must have, someone could have known and retaliated. He liked to hurt people, Jase. It was inevitable that he would die a violent death."

"Were you surprised he left you the money and guardianship over me?"

"Yes, at first. But later I thought maybe it made sense. He wanted us to be like him. He had me investigated and found I spent time in jail. I think he believed I was exactly like him. And the only other choice of a guardian he had was your uncle, and you know how much they despised one another."

Jase sighed. "Uncle Mike is just as crazy as Dad was. All he talks about is sin and redemption. He thinks I need to be exorcised."

Cole swore, a long string of curses. "That's a load of crap, Jase. There's nothing wrong with you." He needed to move, to ride something hard, it didn't matter what it was. A horse, a motorcycle, a woman, anything at all to take away the knots gathering in his stomach. "Let's get out of here."

He turned away from the boy, a cold anger lodged in his gut. He detested Christmas, detested everything about it. No matter how much he didn't want the season to start, it always came. He woke up drenched in sweat, vicious laughter ringing in his ears. He could fight the demons most of the year, but not when Christmas songs played on the radio and in every store he entered. Not when every building and street displayed decorations and people continually wished each other "Merry Christmas." He didn't want that for Jase. He had to find a way to give the boy back his life.

Counseling hadn't helped either of them. When no one believed a word you said, or worse, was bought off, you learned to stop trusting people. If Cole never did another thing right in his life, he was going to be the one person Jase would know he could always trust. And he was going to make certain the boy didn't turn out the way he had. Or the way their father had.

The brothers walked through the sprawling ranch house. The floors were all gleaming wood, the ceilings open-beamed and high. Brett Steele had demanded the best of everything, and he got it. Cole couldn't fault him on his taste.

"Cole," Jase asked, "why were you in jail?"

Cole didn't break stride as he hurried through the spacious house. At times he wanted to burn the thing down. There was no warmth in it, and as hard as he'd tried to turn the showpiece into a home for Jase, it remained cold and barren.

Outdoors it was biting cold. The frost turned the hills and meadows into a world of sparkling crystal, dazzling the eyes, but Cole simply ignored it, shoving his sunglasses onto his face. He went past the huge garage that housed dozens of cars—all toys Brett Steele had owned and rarely ever used—to go to his own pickup.

"I shouldn't have asked you," Jase muttered, slamming the door with unnecessary force. "I hate questions."

Cole paused, the key in the ignition. He glanced at the boy's flushed face. "It isn't that, Jase. I don't mind you asking me anything. I made up my mind I'd never lie to you about anything, and I'm not quite certain how to explain the jail time. Give me a minute."

Jase nodded. "I don't mind that you've been in jail, but it worries me because Uncle Mike says he's going to take you to court and get custody of me. If I lived with him, I'd spend all my life on my knees, praying for my soul. I'd rather run away."

"He can't get you away from me," Cole promised, his voice grim. There was a hard edge to the set of his mouth. He turned his piercing blue gaze directly on his young half brother. "The one thing I can promise is I'll fight for you until they kill me, Jase." He was implacable, the deadly ruthless stamp of determination clear on his face. "No one is going to take you away from me. You got that?"

Jase visibly relaxed. He nodded, a short jerky gesture as he tried to keep his emotions under control. Cole wasn't certain if that was good or bad. Maybe the boy needed to cry his eyes out. Cole never had. He would never give his father the satisfaction, even when the bastard had nearly killed him.

It was a long way to the nearest town. There had been numerous guards at the ranch when his father was alive, supposedly for security, but Cole knew better. Brett had needed his own private world, a realm he could rule with an iron fist. The first thing Cole had done was to fire all of the ranch hands, the security force, and the housekeeper. If he could have had them prosecuted for their participation in Brett's sadistic depravities, he would have. Jase needed to feel safe. And Cole needed to feel as if he could provide the right atmosphere for the boy. They had interviewed the new ranch hands together, and they were still looking for a housekeeper.

"You, know, Jase, you never picked out one of the horses to use," Cole said.

Jase leaned forward to fiddle with the radio. The cab was flooded with a country Christmas tune. Jase hastily went through the stations, but all he could find was Christmas music and he finally gave up in exasperation. "I don't care which one I ride," Jase said, and turned his head to stare out the window at the passing scenery. His voice was deliberately careless.

"You must have a preference," Cole persisted. "I've seen you bring the big bay, Celtic High, a carrot every now and then." The boy had spent a little time each day, brushing the horse and whispering to it, but he never rode the bay.

Jase's expression closed down instantly, his eyes wary. "I don't care about any of them," he repeated.

Cole frowned as he slipped a CD into the player. "You know what the old man was all about, don't you, Jase? He didn't want his sons to feel affection or loyalty to anything or anyone. Not our mothers, not friends, and not animals. He killed the animals in front of us to teach us a lesson. He destroyed our friendships to accomplish the same thing. He got rid of our mothers to isolate us, to make us wholly dependent on him. He didn't want you ever to feel emotion, especially affection or love for anything or anyone else. If he succeeded in doing that to you, he won. You can't let him win. Choose a horse and let yourself care for it. We'll get a dog if you want a dog, or another cat. Any kind of pet you want, but let yourself feel something, and when our father visits you in your nightmares, tell him to go to hell."

"You didn't do that," Jase pointed out. "You don't have a dog. You haven't had a dog in all the years you've been away. And you never got married. I'll bet you never lived with a woman. You have one-night stands and that's about it because you won't let anyone into your life." It was a shrewd guess.

Cole counted silently to ten. He was psychoanalyzing Jase, but he damned well didn't want the boy to turn the spotlight back on him. "It's a hell of a way to live, Jase. You don't want to use me as a role model. I know all the things you shouldn't do and not many you should. But cutting yourself off from every living thing takes its toll. Don't let him do that to you. Start small if you want. Just choose one of the horses, and we'll go riding together in the mornings."

Jase was silent, his face averted, but Cole knew he was weighing the matter carefully. It meant trusting Cole further than perhaps Jase was willing to go. Cole was a big question mark to everyone, Jase especially. Cole couldn't blame the boy. He knew what he was like. Tough and ruthless with no backup in him. His reputation was that of a vicious, merciless fighter, a man born and bred in violence. It wasn't like he knew how to make all the soft, kind gestures that the kid needed, but he could protect Jase.

"Just think about it," he said to close the subject. Time was on his side. If he could give Jase back his life, he would forgive himself for not bringing the old man down as he should have done years ago. Jase had had his mother, a woman with love and laughter in her heart. More than likely Brett had killed her because he couldn't turn Jase away from her. Jase's mother must have left some legacy of love behind.

Cole had no one. His mother had been just the opposite of Jase's. His mother had had a child because Brett demanded she have one, but she went back to her model-thin figure and cocaine as soon as possible, leaving her son in the hands of her brutal husband. In the end, she'd died of an overdose. Cole had always suspected his father had had something to do with her death. It was interesting that Jase suspected the same thing of his own mother's death.

A few snowflakes drifted down from the sky, adding to the atmosphere of the season they both were trying so hard to avoid. Jase kicked at the floorboard of the truck, a small sign of aggression, then glanced apologetically at Cole.

"Maybe we should have opted for a workout instead," Cole said.

"I'm always hungry," Jase admitted. "We can work out after we eat. Who came up with the idea of Christmas anyway? It's a dumb idea, giving presents out when it isn't your birthday. And it can't be good for the environment to cut down all the trees."

Cole stayed silent, letting the boy talk, grateful Jase was finally comfortable enough to talk to him at all.

"Mom loved Christmas. She used to sneak me little gifts. She'd hide them in my room. He always had spies, though, and they'd tell him. He always punished her, but she'd do it anyway. I knew she'd be punished, and she knew it too, but she'd still sneak me presents." Jase rolled down the window, letting the crisp, cold air into the truck. "She sang me Christmas songs. And once, when he was away on a trip, we baked cookies together. She loved it. We both knew the housekeeper would tell him, but at the time, we didn't care."

Cole cleared his throat. The idea of trying to celebrate Christmas made him ill, but the kid wanted it. Maybe even needed it, but had no clue that was what his nervous chatter was all about. Cole hoped he could pull it off. There were no happy memories from his childhood to offset the things his father had done.

"We tried to get away from him, but he always found us," Jase continued.

"He's dead, Jase," Cole repeated. He took a deep breath and took the plunge, feeling as if he was leaping off a steep cliff. "If we want to bring a giant tree into his home and decorate it, we can. There's not a damn thing he can do about it."

"He might have let her go if she hadn't wanted to take me with her."

Cole heard the tears in the boy's voice, but the kid didn't shed them. Silently he cursed, wishing for inspiration, for all the right things to say. "Your mother was an extraordinary woman, Jase, and there aren't that many in the world. She cared about you, not the money or the prestige of being Mrs. Brett Steele. She fought for you, and she tried to give you a life in spite of the old man. I wish I'd had the chance to meet her."

Jase didn't reply, but closed his eyes, resting his head back against the seat. He could still remember the sound of his mother's voice. The way she smelled. Her smile. He rubbed his head. Mostly he remembered the sound of her screams when his father punished her.

"I'll think about the Christmas thing, Cole. I kind of

like the idea of decorating the house when he always forbade it."

Cole didn't reply. It had been a very long few weeks, but the Christmas season was almost over. A couple more weeks, and he would have made it through another December. If doing the Christmas thing could give the kid back his life, Cole would find a way to get through it.

The town was fairly big and offered a variety of late-night and early-morning dining. Cole chose a diner he was familiar with and parked the truck in the parking lot. To his dismay, it was already filled with cars. Unfolding his large frame, he slid from the truck, waiting for Jase to get out.

"You forgot your jacket," he said.

"No, I didn't. I hate the thing," Jase said.

Cole didn't bother to ask him why. He already knew the answer and vowed to buy the kid a whole new wardrobe immediately. He pushed open the door to the diner, stepping back to allow Jase to enter first. Jase took two steps into the entryway and stopped abruptly behind the high wall of fake ivy. "They're talking about you, Cole," he whispered. "Let's get out of here."

The voices were loud enough to carry across the small restaurant. Cole stood still, his hand on the boy's shoulder to steady him. Jase would have to learn to live with gossip, just as he'd learned to survive the nightmare he'd been born into.

"You're wrong, Randy. Cole Steele murdered his father, and he's going to murder that boy. He wants the money. He never came around here to see that boy until his daddy died."

"He was in jail, Jim, he couldn't very well go visiting his

relatives," a second male voice pointed out with a laugh.

Cole recognized Randy Smythe from the local agriculture store. Before he could decide whether to get Jase out of there or show the boy just how hypocritical the local storeowners could be, a third voice chimed in.

"You are so full of it, Jim Begley," a female voice interrupted the argument between the two men. "You come in here every morning grousing about Cole Steele. He was cleared as a suspect a long time ago and given guardianship of his half brother, as he should have been. You're angry because your bar buddies lost their cushy jobs, so you're helping to spread the malicious gossip they started. The entire lot of you sound like a bunch of sour old biddies."

The woman never raised her voice. In fact, it was soft and low and harmonious. Cole felt the tone strumming inside of him, vibrating and spreading heat. There was something magical in the voice, more magical than the fact that she was sticking up for him. His fingers tightened involuntarily on Jase's shoulder. It was the first time he could ever remember anyone sticking up for him.

"He was in jail, Maia," Jim Begley reiterated, his voice almost placating.

"So were a lot of people who didn't belong there, Jim. And a lot people who should have been in jail never were. That doesn't mean anything. You're jealous of the man's money and the fact that he has the reputation of being able to get just about any woman he wants, and you can't."

A roar of laughter went up. Cole expected Begley to get angry with the woman, but surprisingly, he didn't. "Aw, Maia, don't go getting all mad at me. You aren't going to do anything, are you? You wouldn't put a hex on my . . . on me, would you?"

The laughter rose and this time the woman joined in. The sound of her voice was like music. Cole had never had such a reaction to any woman, and he hadn't even seen her.

"You just never know about me, now do you, Jim?" She teased, obviously not angry with the man. "It's Christmas, the best time of the year. Do you think you could stop spreading rumors and just wait for the facts? Give the man a chance. You all want his money. You all agree the town needs him, yet you're so quick to condemn him. Isn't that the littlest bit hypocritical?"

Cole was shocked that the woman could wield so much power, driving her point home without ever raising her voice. And strangely, they were all listening to her. Who was she, and why were these usually rough men hanging on her every word, trying to please her? He found himself very curious about a total stranger—a woman at that.

"Okay, okay," Jim said. "I surrender, Maia. I'll never mention Cole Steele again if that will make you happy. Just don't get mad at me."

Maia laughed again. The carefree sound teased all of Cole's senses, made him very aware of his body and its needs. "I'll see you all later. I have work to do."

Cole felt his body tense. She was coming around the ivy to the entrance. Cole's breath caught in his throat. She was on the shorter side, but curvy, filling out her jeans nicely. A sweater molded her breasts into a tempting invitation. She had a wealth of dark, very straight hair, as shiny as a raven's wing, pulled into a careless ponytail. Her face was exotic, the bone structure delicate, reminding him of a pixie.

She swung her head back, her wide smile fading as she

saw them standing there. She stopped short, raising her eyes to Cole's. He actually hunched a little, feeling the impact in his belly. Little hammers began to trip in his head, and his body reacted with an urgent and very elemental demand. A man could drown in her eyes, get lost, or just plain lose every demon he had. Her eyes were large, heavily lashed, and some color other than blue, turquoise maybe, a mixture of blue and green that was vivid and alive and so darned beautiful he ached inside just looking at her.

Jase nudged him in the ribs.

Cole reacted immediately. "Sorry, ma'am." But he didn't move. "I'm Cole Steele. This is my brother, Jase."

Jase jerked under his hand, reacting to being acknowledged as a brother.

The woman nodded at Cole and flashed a smile at Jase as she stepped around them to push open the door.

"Holy cow," Jase murmured. "Did you see that smile?" He glanced up at Cole. "Yeah, you saw it all right."

"Was I staring?" Cole asked.

"You looked like you might have her for breakfast," Jase answered. "You can look really intimidating, Cole. Scary."

Cole almost followed the woman, but at the boy's comment he turned back. "Am I scary to you, Jase?"

The boy shrugged. "Sometimes. I'm getting used to you. I've never seen you smile. Ever."

Cole raised his eyebrow. "I can't remember actually smiling. Maybe I'll have to practice. You can work with me."

"Don't you smile at women?"

"I don't have to."

COLE STEELE WAS BACK *AGAIN*. The bar was jammed, bodies welded together as they moved to the rhythmic beat of the music Maia Armstrong provided on the drums. The band was hot tonight, she could feel the music pounding inside of her exactly the way it needed to be to keep the house rocking. She tried not to see him, tried not to notice his body stretched out in a chair in a sexy, lazy sprawl. The music was usually all that mattered, all she thought about when she played. She could lose herself in the primal beats, the familiar feel of her hands on the sticks, whirling them in her fingers and finding that perfect pocket of sound.

Music took her far away from the terrible things she saw every day. The things that kept her on the move, town after town, knowing she could never really settle anywhere. Music was her solace. Cole Steele changed all that. What was he doing there? Had he already gone through all the women in the more upscale bars in town?

He was stinking rich and so sinfully sensual he should be locked up. He wasn't just the local bad boy; he was a hard, dangerous man, one that wielded absolute power. He knew it too. It was in the arrogance stamped into his very bones. He sat there watching her through hooded eyes, intent, focused, his hand absently stroking the long neck of his beer bottle. He looked so *sexual* to her. It wasn't a charade, he was really that way, his body hard and hot and ... Maia groaned inwardly. She was *not* falling for a bad boy. She had too much sense and too much self-respect. And he had far too much money and drama for her even to consider such a folly.

She wasn't going to look at him, wasn't going to let him get to her. A man like Cole Steele left fingerprints on a woman, took away her soul, and never returned it to her. Once he left burn marks—and he would—they would never fade. She refused to allow her gaze to stray his way, although she could feel the weight of his heavy, brooding stare. Instead, she picked a table near the front and flashed a high-wattage smile at the nearest man, wanting to focus anywhere but on the dark devil watching her.

Cole shifted his legs into a more comfortable position in an attempt to ease the relentless ache in his body. His fingers tightened around the neck of the beer bottle, nearly crushing it. Maia didn't need to be smiling at any other man in the room, not when she should be smiling at him. She didn't want the others, wasn't interested in them, but he could see her heightened awareness of him. She wasn't adept at hiding it.

Cole knew he was going to have to change his strategy completely. He might even have to eat his words and actually learn to smile at a woman. He'd wasted nine nights coming down to the El Dorado Saloon after hearing that Maia Armstrong, the traveling veterinarian, often sat in jamming on the drums in the evening. He was either losing his touch or his mind. There were a dozen women who'd made it plain they were willing to go to bed with him, so why was he so damned fixated on the one who refused to give in to him? With a series of storms coming, most likely bringing severe blizzard conditions, this was going to be his last chance to persuade her for a long while.

She'd noticed him all right. He'd made it abundantly clear he was interested. He'd managed half a dozen conversations with her. She was always polite, but she kept a distance firmly between them. He tapped his finger on the small round table as he watched her. Why was he so fascinated by her? Her smile could light up the entire room, and her laugh was contagious. He shouldn't have noticed, but it was nearly impossible not to. Especially when she was turning that smile on another man.

He dreamt of her. Ever since he'd seen her in the diner the nightmares that always plagued him during the Christmas season had been replaced with highly erotic dreams of her. Even Jase was beginning to tease him about her, knowing Cole only left the ranch in the evenings to see her. Cole absently stroked the neck of the beer bottle, wishing it were her skin beneath his fingers. He'd made up his mind he was going to have to be aggressive with her tonight. Subtle wasn't working at all. He'd had plenty of time to study her. It was his business to read people. Maia Armstrong was no pushover with men, but she detested public scenes. She wouldn't fight it if he didn't push beyond her limit.

A woman leaned close, blocking his vision, deliberately bending over him to give him a better view of her ample cleavage. He stared up at her with hard eyes and a distinct scowl. "You're blocking the view."

The woman flushed, but slid into the chair at his table. "You like this band?"

He glanced at her. Once. A curt dismissal. He stared at her until she got up and stomped away. His rude behavior would only add to his carefully cultivated reputation of being a complete bastard. What did it matter? His reputation had been blackened a long time ago. Maybe he really had become a complete bastard, but the truth was, he rarely found anything he wanted, and he wasn't going to tolerate anyone's interfering with his getting it. His gaze returned to the woman playing the drums.

Maia Armstrong intrigued him. It was as simple as that. He'd investigated her, of course. He investigated anyone and everyone who touched his life, or Jase's. She was the new veterinarian and played in a band in the evenings. She never took a permanent position in any town, but traveled, often filling in for other vets. She had taken the place of the local elderly vet who, because of failing health, had been forced to give up his practice before he could find someone to buy him out. Already, she was popular and very well thought of by everyone who had worked with her.

There were rumors about her. Some said she possessed magic. The majority said mysterious things happened when she was around animals. She managed to save the hopeless and was fast earning a reputation with the ranchers for being able to handle the wildest stock. The rumor persisted that she was able to cast spells, on both animals and men, and Cole was beginning to think there might be some truth to it. He was obsessed with her.

He took a long, slow pull of his beer, never taking his gaze from her. The band was finishing their set. He knew their music now, knew Maia's habits. He also knew she was very aware of his reputation, both as a lady's man and as a dangerous felon. She didn't like gossip, probably because so many people gossiped about her, and he was fairly certain she wouldn't make a scene when he made his move on her. He calculated the odds, just like he calculated everything in his life.

The drum built to a crashing crescendo, and Maia set her sticks aside and swept back stray tendrils of hair that had escaped from her intricate braid. Her skin was damp, glowing, her smile satisfied. She'd liked the way the music sounded, and it showed in her expression. Maia was never closed off to the world the way he was, and Cole found even that intriguing. He had positioned himself perfectly, making it impossible for her to get to the bar without walking past his table.

Cole caught her wrist as she swept by him, pretending, as she did each night, not to notice him. He shifted in his chair so that she was suddenly wedged between his outstretched legs, imprisoning her. "Have a drink with me."

Maia could hear her own heart thundering in her ears. Up close he was overpowering. He looked all male, his blue eyes dark with a desire he didn't try to hide from her. In fact, he wore his sensuality easily, with complete confidence, a devil in blue jeans and sin in his heated gaze. She knew the rumors. She knew what the town suspected Cole of doing. Murder. He'd been in jail. There was a tattoo on his upper arm, which he'd obviously gotten in jail and didn't bother to try to hide. His body was hard and fit; but sometimes, when he didn't think anyone was watching, she saw something sad and tragic in his unguarded expression. And that was truly dangerous.

The last thing she wanted to do was to add to the rumors flying around him. She couldn't imagine how difficult it was to be the favorite subject of the town's most malicious gossips. He couldn't possibly have done a third of the evil deeds attributed to him. Maia patted his dark head, a deliberate show of camaraderie for the patrons in the bar. At the same time, she wanted to let him know, very politely, that she wasn't playing his game. She leaned close to him, put her lips against his ear. "The lady sitting on the barstool to your right is devouring you with her eyes. You have an easy score right there to take care of any urgent . . . er . . . needs you may have."

Cole felt her warm breath against his ear, the whisper of her lips against his skin. When she leaned into him he inhaled the scent of her. Peaches and rain could be very intoxicating. His fingers around her wrist kept her connected to him. "I want you to have a drink with me." His voice was huskier than he intended, and her close proximity had more of an effect on him than he'd anticipated. His heart pounded, and he could feel his blood surging hotly through his veins.

Maia sucked in her breath sharply. Cole Steele was used to giving orders, used to having them obeyed, and he certainly knew his effect on women. His voice was almost mesmerizing. She could feel the hard column of his thighs pressing against her legs, as his thumb stroked over her bare skin where he held her arm.

Maia tugged a little on her wrist, not making it obvious to the curious onlookers. "I don't think that's a good idea." She smiled to take the sting out of her refusal.

"You never told me your name."

"You know my name." Mentally she kicked herself. She

was engaging with him when it was the last thing she should be doing. How in the world did the man manage to be so potent? He was the most sensual man she'd ever encountered. Her hormones were already in overdrive, just as they'd been for the last few days. And, of course, it had to be for the resident bad boy.

"What is it going to hurt to sit at my table and have a beer with me?"

"Because that isn't what you want from me. Let go." She stood waiting, looking down into his brilliant eyes. Cold eyes. Eyes that had seen things no one should ever witness. Maia sighed, trying desperately not to see those things, not to see or feel or react to the pain swirling so deep in their vivid blue depths. "Please."

Cole removed his hand instantly. Maia made herself walk when she wanted to run. Her heart was beating too fast. He was frightening in his intensity, and she was very susceptible to the man he hid behind his remote mask. She knew a hurt creature when she saw one. Man or animal, her entire being reacted to them. Cole Steele was one of those creatures, and he was just too darned dangerous for her to get involved with.

"Sounded great tonight," Ed Logan, the bartender said in greeting. He pushed a frosted glass toward her and leaned close, lowering his voice. "Keep away from him, Maia. He's bad news."

She tilted the glass, savoring the ice-cold water as it went down her throat. Her gaze strayed toward Cole Steele. His gaze was on her. Hot. Intense. Drifting over her body possessively. She turned her back on him, leaning against the bar. Immediately she was all too aware that her movement left Cole staring at her bottom, encased in tight jeans. It was all she could do not to shift positions immediately. "I have no idea what you're going on about, Ed."

"He's got a look about him. He's on the hunt for a woman, and it's rather obvious he has his sights set on you. You don't play with a man like that and win."

"You're such a sweetheart, Ed. I'd marry you myself if you weren't already taken. You can stop worrying. Cole Steele is so far out of my league that I don't even want to play. He'll settle his sights elsewhere fast enough. He'll get bored and move on to greener pastures."

"Just so you know to be careful. People are saying bad things about him. Most probably aren't true, but I know men, and he's dangerous."

"At least to women," she agreed. "Seriously, Ed, I can look after myself."

"He made a whole lot of enemies in this town when he came in five months ago and fired the crew that was working out at the ranch. Times are hard and in the winter everyone needs work. No one knows why he did it, and he isn't saying, but there's hard feelings."

"A man doesn't fire everyone without a reason, Ed," Maia pointed out. "Especially not a rancher with a spread the size of his. He needs them. Maybe a few head of cattle were missing. It happens all the time."

Ed shrugged his shoulders and picked up an empty whiskey glass, dismissing the subject of Cole Steele. "Loretta said to tell you to drop by anytime. And if you don't have plans for Christmas dinner, you're invited to that as well."

"You tell her thank you. Lucky you to have her."

Ed nodded. "I can't get over you managing to save that

dog of hers. She loves that mutt, and I was certain there was no hope after the car hit it, but you pulled it off."

Maia patted his hand. It hadn't been Loretta who fell apart when the little Jack Russell terrier had darted out in front of a car. Big Ed had been sobbing so hard he couldn't speak when he and Loretta had brought the dog to her.

She turned away and immediately felt the impact of Cole Steele's piercing gaze. It should have made her cold, but she felt heat spreading dangerously to every part of her body. She braced herself to get past him a second time. The jukebox was playing, and a few couples were swaying on the dance floor to a sultry love song. It might be more prudent to cut across the dance floor, but doing so would brand her a coward in her own eyes. Or maybe she was feeling reckless.

He stood up, a lithe, male movement of grace and sheer power, blocking her path. Cole towered over her. With his wide shoulders and muscular body, he made her feel intensely feminine. His hands found her wrists, his grip firm, but not hurting her as he drew her arms around his neck, fitting her body tightly against his hard, masculine frame. His arms caged hers, his thighs pressing against her until she was forced to walk backward to the dance floor. Immediately she was engulfed in flames, a wrenching desire spreading through her body and making her weak with need. His heavy erection was pressed tightly, unashamedly, against her stomach, spreading flames over her skin.

She said nothing. She refused to cause a scene by fighting him publicly, and in any case, she'd definitely wanted this. She wasn't a child who lied to herself. She'd deliberately chosen to walk past him to give him another opportunity to claim her. She closed her eyes and drifted with him on a tide of sexual awareness, on arousal, on heat and flames and lust all mixed together. It was a unique experience for her. Maia felt her body melting into his.

Cole bent his head to the invitation of her bare neck. With her hair braided, it left her vulnerable to the brush of his mouth against her pulse. She fit perfectly in his arms, as if she'd been made for him. He felt the urgent demands of his body, but more than that, there was an unfamiliar longing that rose and lodged deep where he knew he wasn't going to be able to remove it easily. Maia Armstrong left her brand on him, and he hadn't even made love to her. Or maybe he was; he'd never actually made love to a woman before, and maybe that was what he was doing.

She stole his breath. Took his animal hunger and turned it into something altogether different. Cole's arms tightened around Maia, urging her body even closer to his, wanting to imprint her into his bones. He had come to her to rid himself of demons for a night or two, but with her body fitting into his, something was softening inside of him, and for the first time since his childhood, Cole was terrified. He wanted to let her go and walk away, to be safe in his isolated world; but he couldn't let go of her warmth or the promise of magic in the curves of her body pressed so tightly to him.

Cole became aware that the last notes of the song were fading away. He was completely confident when it came to women. He was a highly sensual man and knew how to make a woman need him. It always came easy to him. "I want to go home with you," he said shamelessly.

Maia pulled out of his arms, refusing the stark hunger

and dark intensity that drew other women to him so easily. She flashed her powerful smile, the one he felt all the way down to his stone-cold heart.

"Pheromones are nasty little devils, aren't they?" Maia asked. "They strike at the most inopportune times."

He couldn't let her go. He saw it in her eyes that she was just going to turn and walk away from him. "Then come to the ranch with me." Was that really bad boy Cole Steele acting desperate? What the hell was wrong with him? He should go straight to the woman at the end of the bar who was devouring him with her eyes and walk out with her. It would serve Maia right. He knew she wanted him. She couldn't hide her reaction to him.

"You're afraid of me," he taunted her.

"Do I look stupid to you?" She stepped back cautiously, making certain she could walk without trembling. "Any woman with half a brain would be afraid of you. You have trouble stamped on your forehead and packaged not so subtly there in the front."

"Nice of you to notice, since you're the one causing the trouble." He made it a challenge.

"Nice to know I can," she replied, in no way perturbed by the accusation. "Go away, Mr. Steele. You're way out of my league."

The jukebox music shifted into another moody, sensual song, and Cole reached out to pull her back into his arms. "What puts me out of your league?"

She tilted her head to look up at him, which was a major mistake. His eyes were such a deep blue, almost metallic, and he looked at her with dark desire. With hunger. With possession and determination. There was a ruthless edge to his mouth and a need in the depths of his gaze she couldn't avoid. Her breath left her lungs in a rush. "Everything. Money. Experience. Life. I don't want to get singed, let alone burned. You come with far too high a price tag."

His eyes were locked on hers, and she couldn't break away, held captive in spite of her resolve. It was the fleeting glimpse of the hurt animal, the shadows of pain and betrayal he hid behind his cool, icy demeanor that kept her from walking off the dance floor. She slipped her arms around his neck and allowed her body to sink into the heat of his.

His chin rubbed the top of her head. "All this time I was thinking you were the one with the high price tag."

"You probably think all women come with price tags," she muttered against his chest. She turned her head to lay her ear over his heart.

"Don't they?" he asked. "Usually it isn't all that difficult, but you, lady, present a problem."

Maia listened to the steady rhythm of his heart. "I refuse to be a problem for you. You're the one insisting on dancing with me. I told you no."

"I didn't hear you say no."

"Really?" She smiled against his shirt. "I could have sworn the entire room heard me. I thought I was very emphatic about it."

"No, you definitely didn't say no."

"Well, I should have. My guard must have been down." She laughed softly, and the sound played right through his body.

"You're dangerous."

"Funny. That's what everyone says about you," Maia said.

Cole bent his head once more to the temptation of her bare neck. She was warm satin. He tasted her, teased her earlobe with his teeth. Before she could protest his action he lifted his head to distract her. "Why did you stick up for me in the diner the other day?" he asked. "Everyone believes I killed the old man. Why don't you?"

Maia shivered, tried to pull her suddenly scattered defenses back around her. His mouth had sent small flames licking over her skin. "You were cleared as a suspect. It's all they talk about sometimes, and it gets annoying. You were a thousand miles away when your father was murdered, but they want to believe you did it." She burrowed closer to the warmth of his heart without realizing she was doing it. "You inherited all that money and the ranch after you left home and turned your back on your father. And then you dared to fire everyone. It's human nature I guess. They want you to be guilty. And it gives them someone to talk about."

"I still might have had it done," he pointed out. His hands traced the contours of her back, slid down to her waist and over her hips.

"It was wrong of them. I felt bad for the boy. What is he? About fourteen, fifteen? He just lost his father, and they want to spread gossip about his guardian. It's malicious, and it makes me angry."

"He's fourteen, and he hated the old man." Cole heard the contemptuous words come out of his mouth. He never revealed anything private to anyone, least of all a complete stranger or a woman he had sex with. What the hell had gotten into him?

They weren't even dancing anymore, just holding one another and swaying, their bodies moving in a perfect rhythm. His arms tightened around her, and he drew her hips closer to him. The rest of the room seemed to have fallen away, leaving them wrapped in a world of two. Maia looked up at his face. Something fluttered in her stomach. His head began to descend toward hers, inch by slow inch. She could see lines etched into his face, the shadow on his jaw, his long eyelashes and the intent in his hungry eyes.

"Don't you dare."

"I have to."

"I said no. Very decisively." Maia pulled her head back to keep his lips from touching hers. She'd be lost if he kissed her with his sinful mouth. She was taking no chances.

"You are a such a coward. You're running."

"Like a rabbit," she confirmed.

"You haven't asked me why I was in jail. Is that the reason you won't take me home with you?"

His hands were making slow circles along her spine. His erection was pressed tightly against her stomach. She ached in places she didn't know could ache. "I haven't asked why because it isn't my business," she said, breathing a sigh of relief when the song ended. "I have to play."

Cole let her slip out of his arms because if he held her any longer, he was going to throw her over his shoulder and take her out of there to any place he could have her to himself for a long, long time. He managed to make it back to his seat without breaking anything. He took a long pull on the beer. It was warm and did nothing to cool the fire racing through his veins.

Cole watched her through half-closed eyes, already staking his claim on her, making certain the other men in the bar knew she belonged to him. No woman had ever gotten to him before. She seemed lost in her music, unaware of him when he was burning for her.

His cell phone beeped, and, scowling, he glanced down to identify the caller. "What is it, Jase?" Cole demanded, his eyes on Maia. If she smiled one more time at the lunkhead in the front row, he was going to have to smash his beer bottle right over the man's head.

For a moment there was silence, then a harsh, tearing sob. "I trusted you. You knew I cared about him. You knew Celtic High mattered to me."

Cole went still. "What are you talking about, Jase? Calm down and tell me what's going on."

"The bay. He's all torn up. What'd you do to him?"

"I didn't do a damned thing to him," Cole bit the words out in anger before he could stop them. "I'll have the vet there in an hour." It was over an hour's drive to the ranch, but he could shave off minutes. He couldn't blame Jase for accusing him. The kid had been taught not to trust anyone, but it still hurt. Much worse than that, Cole couldn't help his own suspicions. He'd investigated the kid's past, looking for red flags, cruelty to animals, anything that might indicate the old man had passed on his sick genes, but he'd found nothing. Still, the doubt crept in.

"He's in too much pain," Jase said. "He'll have to be put down. I can't do it. I tried, but I can't do it." He was sobbing openly. "He went through a fence and he's really torn up. There's wood sticking in his chest and stomach, splinters buried in his belly and legs. Some of the cuts are down to the bone. I can't put him down, Cole."

"Listen to me, Jase. I'll be there in an hour with the vet. Get Al and the other hands to help you. Take Celtic High to the big barn where all the equipment is. The vet will need light to work on him, and that's the most sterile environment we have. Tell Al to keep that horse alive."

"But, Cole," now Jase sounded like a young child seeking reassurance, "he's suffering."

"I didn't do this, Jase. I wasn't even there."

"I found your work glove in the snow by the fence." Jase sounded apologetic. "I don't know what I was thinking. I knew you went to town."

"I'll be there in an hour," Cole repeated. "Get Al and stick close to him until I figure out what's going on."

Maia watched Cole's face as he talked on the phone. He gave very little away with his expression, but something was wrong. She saw the way his hand tightened around the neck of the beer bottle. He'd been absently stroking it, almost seductively, and now he gripped it as if he wanted to throttle something. Cole abruptly broke the connection and shoved the cell phone into his pocket, stood up and looked directly at her.

At once her heart began to accelerate, pounding in her chest. His gaze was cold, hard, and very direct. He began to walk toward her with long strides, a ruthless stamp on his features and purpose in every step. For the first time, she faltered in her playing, losing the rhythm that was so much a part of her. The band ground to a halt. There was a sudden silence in the bar.

"Come on. I need you out at the ranch. Let's go." Cole's voice brooked no argument.

Maia studied his harsh expression. He reached out and caught her arm, nearly pulling her off her stool. "I said now."

A murmur of protest went around the room. It didn't deter Cole in the least. He crowded closer to her.

Maia glanced around the bar, a quick appraisal of the situation, then her gaze was back on his face. Implacable resolve. He didn't care that others might come to her rescue. He was perfectly prepared to fight, and worse, he might win.

His fingers tightened around her arm. "You don't want me to carry you out," he warned.

"You don't want me to slap your face either," Maia said, her gaze flicking coolly over his face. "Let's go."

"DON'T EVER DO THAT AGAIN," Maia warned. She paused just outside of the bar to take a deep, calming breath of the night air. "I know something upset you, and believe me, that's the only reason I'm out here with you right now. I am not the kind of woman you can order around."

Cole looked down at her, at the smoldering anger he saw in her eyes. It was snowing large flakes, falling softly and mutely between them. He reached out, his fingers curling around the nape of her neck, and pulled her toward him, his mouth taking possession of hers before she could protest.

She expected his kiss to be as wild and dominating as he was, but it was just the opposite. His mouth was incredibly gentle on hers, soft but firm, a whisper of fire, his lips brushing at hers with a disarming tenderness. He lifted his head, his blue eyes nearly dazzling her.

Cole could feel his heart thudding hard, too hard. There was a curious melting sensation in the region of his stomach, and his body reacted instantly to the close proximity of hers. He knew immediately he had made a big mistake. Maia Armstrong was no ordinary woman, and he was going to get burned if he didn't regain some control, and fast. His fingers massaged the nape of her neck, brushing caresses in her soft hair. He was renowned for his control, yet she seemed to turn him inside out. His careful defenses didn't work with her.

Maia managed to pull away from him. "If this emergency is some sham to get me to your ranch for more of *that* . . ." She glared at him and wiped her mouth with the back of her hand, desperate to remove his taste. His kiss had felt like a brand, making fire race from his lips and tongue to her belly, lower still, so that she'd felt her body go liquid with desire for him. *And he'd barely touched her.*

"*That* was an apology. And stop trying to wipe it off." He caught her wrist, pulling her hand away from her mouth, satisfaction mixing with something else in his eyes, something that could have been alarm. He led her across the parking lot. "I'm used to giving orders and getting things done. We have to get to the ranch immediately and telling you to come seemed like the fastest way to accomplish that."

Maia bit down hard on her lower lip. She should have stopped him, slapped him, done anything besides participate. She touched her mouth. It was still burning. She'd definitely participated. Where was her pride? Her outrage? The man was more dangerous to her than she'd realized. With an effort, Maia found her voice again. "You might want to give me the particulars." She sounded a little husky. "What type of animal, and what's the injury?"

"A horse. Jase's favorite horse Celtic High, although he won't admit it. Unfortunately, there's a blizzard coming, a bad series of storms that could hang you up for days. I can't trailer the horse out during the storm, so I'll need you to come with me now. I can only promise that if it's at all possible, I'll have the roads cleared for you to return."

Maia glanced upward at the rapidly falling snow. "I thought the storm wasn't supposed to hit for several hours."

"It's early. We've got to move fast to stay ahead of it."

"I'll need my rig. I can follow you out," Maia said, switching directions, the professional taking over. "I have the drugs and everything I need in the sterile packs. I have to call the service and let them know and get Dr. Stacy to take over while I'm gone. He's able to work on an emergency basis. If we're lucky, we'll beat the storm."

"I'll drive. We keep the road to the ranch plowed, but it can get rough in spots," Cole said, easily keeping pace with her. "And there's no way to plow during a blizzard. Jase said the bay went through a fence and that it has multiple injuries, gashes down to the bone and splinters of wood embedded in it. He said he thought the horse was suffering and should be put down, but he couldn't do it."

"And you want me to save the horse even if it can't ever be ridden again?" Many ranchers put down a horse that was no longer a working animal.

"Absolutely. Whatever it takes, as long as the horse isn't suffering," Cole said. "We've got a big ranch. He can live out his days there."

Maia nodded. "Okay then. And maybe we'll be lucky, and it won't be as bad as it looks. Horses can sustain heavy injuries, and if you keep them from getting an infection, can come back quite sound." She glanced back toward his truck, white from the fall of snow. "I'm used to driving in the snow. You don't want to leave your truck here."

"I have plenty of vehicles at the ranch, including a helicopter. And no one's going to touch my truck." His gaze met hers squarely.

Maia couldn't prevent the small shiver that went down her spine. Cole was right. Maia knew most of the townspeople feared him. There was always that dangerous edge to him he couldn't hide, and he didn't bother to try. Recognizing there was little use in arguing, she pulled out her cell phone and made the call to her service. The snow fell into her hair and down the neckline of her shirt while she gave the necessary instructions.

As she pushed the small phone back into her pocket, she reached for the driver's door just as Cole did. Maia pulled her hand back to avoid contact. "My rig," she said.

"But I'm driving. I know the road, and the storm is coming in far faster than we thought. It'll be safer with me driving because I know every rut and curve in that road." Cole swept the snow from her hair, sheltering her with his body from the worst of the flurries. "We don't have much time. Give me the keys."

Maia paused, her hand gripping the keys. "Why were you in jail?" She didn't want it to matter, but it did. She wasn't about to become another victim because she was too stupid even to ask.

Cole yanked open the door on the driver's side, swift impatience crossing his face. "Not rape, if that's what you think. I don't abuse women." He slid behind the wheel and slammed the door with unnecessary force.

"Oh, really?" She hurried around the vehicle to slide in beside him, handing him the keys. "All those poor women you take to bed must feel pretty abused when you never call them again." The moment she closed the door she felt trapped. He was potent up close, intensely male. His shoulders were wide, and his chest thick and well muscled. She could smell the faint scent of his aftershave. And his kiss lingered on her lips.

His gaze dwelt on her face for a long moment as he turned the engine on. Immediately "White Christmas" blared out of the speakers, filling the Toyota Land Cruiser with music. Cole winced and turned it off.

"We need to get one thing straight right now, Maia," he said. "When I take a woman to bed, she *never* feels abused. And I detest Christmas music."

"That's two things," she pointed out, furious at herself because she was tantalized by the very thought of going to bed with him. He was far too arrogant and sure of himself for her liking. *And he was a bad boy. Trouble. The kind of man a smart woman stayed away from.* "And I love Christmas music."

"You would."

"What does that mean?" He'd dragged her off before she could grab her jacket, and the temperature had dipped sharply leaving her cold and shivering. Maia switched the heater to full power and rubbed her arms for warmth.

"It means you're one of those sappy women who get all gooey around little kids and animals and you love the holidays. You probably give the garbageman a present." With something close to impatience, Cole tossed her his jacket. "Put it on until it gets warm in here. And you do, don't you?"

"There's absolutely nothing wrong with giving the garbageman a present. He works hard." She took the jacket only because she was freezing, "Why?" she asked.

"Why what?" He kept his eyes on the road, picking up

speed and heading out of town, pushing the speed limit as well as the margin of safety.

"Why do you detest Christmas music?" Maia watched him closely. His expression didn't change, but the tension in the Land Cruiser went up a notch.

"Doesn't everyone detest Christmas music?" he countered.

"No, most people love it. It's a happy time of year."

"Is it?" His voice was grim. "Maybe to you. To me, it's a damned nightmare."

"I take it you don't buy gifts for your lady friends," she teased.

He glanced at her then, his gaze ice-cold as it moved deliberately over her body. "I might be willing to come up with a gift or two for you if that's what it takes."

Maia locked her fingers together to keep from smacking him and turned her face away to stare out the window at the white world around her. If not for the injured horse and the thought of the boy waiting for them, she would have told Cole Steele to go to hell, pushed him out of her truck and driven back to town.

Cole felt the silence cut between them like a knife. He preferred quiet. He was never uncomfortable with it. Yet with Maia, he found himself wanting to reach out to her, to bridge the gap he was creating between them. He was fighting for the life he was familiar with, the one he knew and could survive in. He didn't trust things like laughter and warmth, had never thought about having them for himself until he'd pulled her into his arms and held her against his body. His body had demanded hers, and that should have been enough. No-entanglements sex was all he ever wanted, yet he didn't think it would be enough with Maia. She touched him in ways that were unexpected, intriguing, and frightening all at the same time.

He turned off the main highway onto the private road that led to the ranch. The snow was heavier than he'd counted on, but he knew every twist and turn. The snowplow had cleared the road before he left for town, but already, the surface was covered with a thick white blanket. He peered out at the snowflakes bursting at the windshield. Maia suddenly tensed and pulled back, making herself smaller in the seat, throwing up a hand to shield her face. A huge owl nearly slammed into the window, wings outstretched and flapping, head back, talons extended as if going in for the kill. It had come at them swiftly and silently, an apparition swooping out of the blinding snow.

The wicked talons reached straight toward Cole's eyes with only the glass separating them. Beside him, Maia gasped. He swerved, nearly losing traction, a string of curses erupting from him until he felt the tires grip and hold. The owl just cleared the top of the vehicle, and Cole breathed a sigh of relief. The bird had been so close he had been able to see individual feathers on its body.

Maia huddled inside Cole's jacket, closing her eyes, trying to calm her pounding heart. The owl had shrieked a warning to her, risked its life to caution her to go back. She glanced at Cole's face, the lines etched deeply there. The owl had flooded her mind with quick, flashing images of violence. It happened so fast, Maia hadn't gotten a clear glimpse of the animal's projection. Only the ominous warning. She took a deep breath and let it out slowly, trying to sort out what the bird was striving to communicate. Darkness. Horses moving. Men. Flashes of lights that could have been rifle fire. None of it made sense.

"That's never happened to me before," Cole said. "Maybe it was confused by the storm. Owls see and hear so well, I imagine accidents would rarely happen."

"He was in hunting mode."

Her voice was so low, Cole barely heard her. He flicked a quick glance her way. She looked pale, her eyes clouded with fear.

"I'm a good driver, Maia. I'll get us there."

She didn't answer. Cole sighed. She was doing him a favor, coming out to the ranch in the middle of what was rapidly becoming a mean blizzard. He should have been more polite. She'd probably worked all day, and she had a long, cold night ahead of her, trying to save the horse for Jase.

"I shouldn't have said that about buying you." Cole glanced at her. It was always so easy with women. He looked at them, they fell into his arms. They had sex, they went home, and he didn't think about them again. That was how it was supposed to work, but Maia seemed to blow his carefully constructed barricades all to hell.

For a moment he thought she wouldn't respond. She didn't turn her head to look at him, but stared out the window at the flurry of snowflakes. "Why did you?"

"You get under my skin, and I don't like it," he answered truthfully. "I've never met a woman like you."

"You've met a million women like me. It's just that none of them ever stood up to you before." Her voice was low and half-muffled by his thick jacket, but it found its way into his body, past his skin and muscle to his very bones.

She turned back toward him, and his breath left his lungs in a rush. He wasn't used to anyone having that kind of effect on him, and it shook his usual calm. He kept his expression carefully blank, his warning system shrieking at him that he was in trouble. "You're an interesting woman. Anyone else would have jumped on the fact that I admitted you get to me, but not you. You have to be different."

"It wouldn't serve any purpose to discuss it. I'm not going to sleep with you. I don't do one-night stands. I'm not at all into casual sex." She managed a small smile. "But I'll admit you're a terrible temptation."

He glanced at her, felt the wheels slide in a particularly heavy drift of snow, catch, and propel them forward. She flung out her hand to grab the dashboard, but she didn't tell him to slow down.

"I always get what I want, Maia." He said it with complete confidence. He didn't know if it was her cool refusal, the warmth in her small smile, or the stark intensity of his desire for her, but he was determined she wouldn't elude him. Even when he knew he was risking more than he should.

"Well, want something else. I don't have a lot of energy to put into fighting with you. You're the kind of man who normally sets my teeth on edge."

"And that would be why?"

"You're arrogant, bossy, too rich for your own good. Sexy as hell, but you know it, so you don't even bother to be polite. There are a lot of willing women out there, Steele, go after one of them. I told you, straight up, I'm not a one-night-stand kind of woman. That should be enough for you."

"It should be, shouldn't it?" His gaze slid sideways toward her for a brief moment. Her hands were twisted together to keep them from trembling. The vehicle slid several times, but he kept it on the road. "I'm a good driver, Maia," he reiterated. "Relax. I won't let anything happen to you."

She tensed again, pushing back into the seat and bracing one hand on the dashboard. He tapped the brakes, slowing the Land Cruiser just as several deer leapt in front of them. The snow nearly coated them, giving them a ghostly appearance, eyes shining, tails flicking in alarm. Cole swerved again, barely missing the high embankment. The deer were gone as silently as they appeared. Maia's breath was audible in the close confines of the car.

"I don't know what the hell is going on tonight. Usually the deer are bedded down and under cover during a storm."

Maia huddled inside the jacket. The images were more vivid this time, but still jumbled. Fists pounding into flesh. Blood on the grass. On the rocks. Her mouth was too dry to speak. She could feel a bead of sweat trickling down the valley between her breasts, but she shivered with cold . . . with fear.

Cole slowed the Land Cruiser, anxiety creeping into him. "Maia, are you all right?" He couldn't really take his eyes from the road, just small glances at her, but she was definitely frightened. "I know it looks bad out here, but I know the road. This is a good rig. The drifts are so high on the embankments, we can't possibly get lost, even with the road covered. You must be used to animals rushing out in front of the truck with all the driving you do." What he wanted to do was stop the truck and pull her into his arms.

Maia felt suffocated by the snowy white world enclosing them. "Maybe we should turn around." The panic in her voice made her wince.

"We're closer to the ranch than to town. I can't leave Jase out there alone, not with a wounded horse. I hope he listened to me and got Al to help him. By now, the ranch hands will have gone home to avoid getting caught in this blizzard." He reached out to comfort her, but she shrank away from him, and he gripped the steering wheel, angry at himself for the gesture. "Is that what you really want? To turn around?"

Maia made an effort to pull herself together. What could she say in her defense? That animals were warning her away from the ranch? He'd have her thrown in a padded cell. "No, of course not. I take it that this horse is very special to Jase."

"He won't admit it, but yes," Cole answered. "If it's at all possible, save the horse for him. The cost doesn't matter. And if you could make Jase a part of it in some way, maybe have him assist you in treating the bay and caring for it afterward, that would be great."

There was something elusive there. Maia heard it, but couldn't grasp it. "Have you always been close to Jase?"

"We met when I was given guardianship over him. We had different mothers, and I didn't know he existed until I was contacted by the private investigators the lawyers hired to find me."

"How could you not know you had a brother?"

Cole shrugged. "I checked out of that life a long time ago. When the lawyers told me about Jase, I was shocked." He frowned. "The snow's really coming down. I left Jase out there with Al, my foreman, to watch over him."

"Weren't you afraid you'd get caught in town?"

"I knew the storm was coming, but I thought I had a couple of more hours before it really hit. I'd never allow Jase to spend the night alone there, so one way or another, I would have gotten back to the ranch."

Maia heard the note of honesty, of absolute determination in his voice, and she believed him. Cole was such a deceptive mixture. He'd come to the bar hunting for sex. He made no apologies for it and cared little what others thought of him. He exuded complete confidence, even a coldness, yet there were terrible shadows in his eyes. And there was Jase. He barely knew the teenager, yet he looked out for him with a fierce protectiveness she would never have credited him with having. She believed Cole would have tried to walk back to the ranch rather than leave the boy alone with just the foreman. Things didn't add up.

"Do you have children of your own?" she asked.

"What do you think?"

"I think you'd never let anyone get that close to you. You must have been terrified when you were named guardian to this boy. Why did you say you'd do it?"

"What is it they all say? So I can murder him and get all the money instead of sharing it with a kid."

"You don't even change expression when you hand out your nonsense. Don't worry, Steele, I don't want to know your deep dark secrets."

"You think I have secrets? I thought my life was an open book. Haven't the gossips given you the scoop on me?" The snow was nearly blinding him as he maneuvered the road. At the rate it was coming down, he wasn't certain they would make it to the ranch before the road became impassable. Even if he could call Al to bring out the snowplow, he wasn't all that certain it would do any good. They were no longer in front of the storm but in the thick of it.

"Don't you have secrets? Doesn't everyone?" Maia wanted to keep talking. She would have chosen to sit it out rather than continue driving. It was becoming difficult to see more than a foot in front of the truck.

"Even you, Doc? Do you have secrets as well? You're always laughing and seem so carefree, yet you move from place to place, no home, nothing permanent in your life. No boyfriend who'll get upset when you move on."

"Who said I don't have a boyfriend? And I usually fill in for the same vets, so I make a lot of friends along the way."

"You don't have a boyfriend, or you wouldn't have let me get away with putting my hands on you while we were dancing. You aren't that kind of woman."

Shocked, she turned toward him, but he was staring out the window into the driving snow. "A compliment. Who would have thought?" Maia burrowed deeper into his jacket. The inside of the car was warm enough, but his jacket gave her a sense of security. She could smell his scent, masculine and outdoorsy, the spice of his after-shave. He drove with the same confidence he did every-thing, and it helped ease her anxiety a bit, but they seemed to be enfolded in a white, silent world. She wished he'd play music just to keep her nerves from jangling. She had nothing else to hang on to but their conversation. And he wasn't comfortable with making small talk.

"Why don't you have your own practice?" Cole asked, flicking a quick glance her way.

Maia stiffened. Her eyes held a wariness that hadn't been there before.

"Maia, it was an idle question to keep the conversation

going. You don't have to answer. I detest people prying into my private life."

He heard her swift, indrawn breath, and saw her turn toward the passenger-side window. Cole was ready instantly for trouble, peering through the windshield to try to see what might be coming at him beyond the heavy shroud of snow. He spotted dark shapes running alongside them, slipping in and out of his field of vision. "What the hell is that?"

"Wolves."

He didn't dare take his eyes off the road to look at her. Cole concentrated on driving, alert for the moment the wolves would run out in front of the Land Cruiser. He didn't doubt it was wolves. Jase and he owned several thousand acres, and their ranch backed up to the national forest where wolves had been relocated.

"The wolves have always stayed away from my ranch and well back into the forest. What's bringing them out?" He glanced at her. Somehow she knew. "You've known the animals were there each time before we saw them, before they jumped out in front of us."

"How could I?"

He didn't listen to the words so much as her voice. It was strained and trembling. She was lying to him. She knew, but he couldn't figure out how. "I don't know, but you reacted, bracing yourself."

"I must have seen them."

A mournful howl rose, sending a shiver down Maia's spine. A second, then a third wolf joined in. A chorus followed them, long, drawn-out notes of warning. She bit down on her knuckles to keep her teeth from chattering.

"What are they doing?" Cole asked. "Why are they running alongside the truck in hunting mode? And the owl, it was coming in as if hunting, head back, talons extended, coming right at me." Even to him, it sounded completely ridiculous. Had he not been trapped in the middle of a snowstorm, he wouldn't have ever said such a bizarre thing, yet it felt right, not strange.

"I have a certain affinity with animals," Maia admitted. She sent up a silent prayer that he wouldn't ask what it meant. She didn't know what it meant. "Stop! Don't hit it." She flung out her hand to brace herself on the dashboard as he fought the Land Cruiser to a halt without even seeing what was in the road.

Before he could stop her, Maia was out of the vehicle, dragging a bag with her, disappearing into the swirling white flakes. Cole slammed his fist against the steering wheel, pulled a gun from where it was holstered in concealment on his calf, and checked the load before he shoved open his own door.

The snow swirled around him immediately, engulfing him in a white, silent world and as fast shifted with the wind to allow him glimpses of the animals and Maia. He heard the chuffing of the wolves as they surrounded the vehicle. Maia crooned to something in the distance. He began to move toward her, watching the wild creatures warily. Immediately the chuffing turned to warning growls. He froze, trying to peer through the heavy fall of snow. The wind blasted through the canyon, and he saw her crouched over something on the ground.

"Maia? I didn't hit it, did I?"

"No, it was injured earlier. I'll just be a minute. Get back in the Cruiser. The wolves are getting agitated."

"I'll stay here and watch your back."

She hissed her displeasure. Actually hissed. He heard it. "I can't protect you while I'm working. Get in the car and wait for me." It was a definite order.

The wind blew a blanket of snow between them again, and when it lifted, he could see the darker shapes slinking around them. He stayed where he was, afraid of disturbing the precarious balance Maia seemed to have. The next blast of chilling wind revealed her straightening and backing away from the shape on the ground, clutching her bag in her hand. She walked quickly toward the Cruiser as the wolf jumped to its feet, shook itself, and hurried off.

The moment he slid in beside her, her gaze went to the gun in his hand. "Good grief. I thought you couldn't carry a gun once you'd been in jail."

"Ranchers need guns." He shoved it back into his leg holster and glared at her. "The next time you decide to take a stroll with a bunch of wolves in a blizzard, let me know ahead of time." He wanted to shake her although she was already shivering uncontrollably and covered in white and that instantly made him feel protective of her.

"I'll do that." She didn't sound as tough as she would have liked with her teeth chattering. "Is that heater putting out any heat?"

"Yes, you should warm up again in a minute." He was cautious as he began maneuvering along the road, alert for any more animals. "Are you going to explain what just happened?"

Maia pushed the alarming warnings out of her mind and shook her head. "I don't think there is an explanation. Do you want to tell me how you get away with carrying a gun?"

"I hide it."

"I'm not buying that. You wouldn't risk losing Jase over it. You're not even on parole are you? Is all the gossip untrue? Have you ever been in prison?"

He sighed. "Maia, I have a job. I'm good at what I do, and I'm good because I don't answer questions. Most people I just tell to go to hell, or look at them and they shut up. Why don't you believe what everyone else wants to believe and make it easy on me?"

She leaned back against the seat, for the first time relaxing. "Because it's all made up, and I prefer to hear the real story. What kind of job do you have?"

Exasperated, he glared at her. "It isn't going to happen."

She thought it was progress that he didn't tell her to go to hell.

"I'M GOING TO PULL YOUR RIG into the barn. You'll need all your equipment, right?" Cole asked.

Maia nodded as she climbed into the backseat. "Keep looking straight ahead while I change into my scrubs. I don't have a lot of clothes with me and I don't want to get everything filthy."

"I do have a washing machine."

"Since I only have what I'm wearing and my scrubs, I'm not taking any chances," she said.

He glanced at her in the rearview mirror. She was shocked to see humor creeping into his eyes. It wasn't much, and it faded fast, but it was there. "I managed to keep this thing on the road through animals running out in front of me and a blizzard, but now you're asking just a little too much. I'm not exactly a saint."

Maia wiggled out of her jeans and dragged her familiar soft cotton, drawstring pants over her hips. "You will get us into an accident if you don't watch what you're doing." She tossed her shirt aside and pulled her loose top over her head, showing the minimum amount of skin. "And I'll bet no one has ever accused you of being a saint." She whistled as Cole honked the horn in front of a large building. "Nice setup."

The doors swung open to allow him to drive inside. The barn was huge and very clean, obviously used as a hospital for the animals on the ranch when needed.

Jase Steele waited anxiously as they parked the Cruiser in the huge barn. Maia saw his face, puffy and swollen from shedding tears he thought no one would see. The boy was unable to hide his relief as Cole unfolded his large frame from the Land Cruiser. "It's bad, Cole," he greeted.

"Let the vet take a look, Jase," Cole advised. For one moment he thought about hugging the kid, but he couldn't quite find a way to do it. Instead, he handed the teenager one of the packs. "We'll need your help."

"I would have put the horse down, Mr. Steele," Al Benton said, "but the boy refused to let me."

"Were you able to tell how this happened?" Cole asked, choosing his words carefully.

Al scowled. "Someone had to have run him into the fence, Mr. Steele. His rump had a couple of welts on it."

"Who was around?"

"All the hands were already gone when Jase called me."

Cole let his breath out slowly. Al hadn't been with Jase. That didn't sit well with him. Doubt tickled at his brain, even though he didn't want to think the boy could have done such a thing. It made him feel like a monster even to entertain such a notion. He ticked suspects off in his mind. Al, the ranch hands, Jase. The ranch hands were working away from the main house and shouldn't have been there. He shook his head to rid himself of the persistent doubt about his younger brother. If he was lucky, it was a legitimate accident. Maia was already walking briskly toward the horse, and he trailed after her, grateful for the distraction.

"The wounds are down to the bone, Mr. Steele. The horse isn't going to be any good for work," Al said.

Maia flashed a brief smile in the foreman's general direction "Let's not draw any hasty conclusions. I haven't had a chance to assess the damage yet." She glanced at Jase. "You did great getting him in out of the snow and putting him in the stocks so he can't move."

"Al helped me," Jase said. "He's been quiet." He patted the horse's neck, his hand trembling. "He didn't give us any trouble at all."

"What's his name?"

"His official name is Celtic High, but I call him Wally." His gaze shifted toward Cole, then away.

"Let me see what I can do for him." Maia put her hand on the horse's neck as she moved around to look into its eyes. Her stomach somersaulted. Images crowded in fast and ugly. Brutal, mean memories of an animal watching helplessly as a boy was beaten and taunted and cruelly punished for nonexistent crimes. The images were harsh and jumbled together. The animal's sorrow and pain, both physical and emotional, beat at her.

She saw through the horse's eyes, memories of young Jase hiding repeatedly in his stall, only to be dragged out again and again while the animal could do nothing to help him. She felt the familiar lurching in her stomach, the sweat beading on her body and the strange dizziness that always accompanied revelations the animals passed to her. It was her greatest gift, and a terrible curse. She could do nothing to help the children and animals she saw coming through her practice. She could only remain silent, just as the animal was forced to do, and move on, move away.

"Maia?" Cole's hand went to her back to steady her. "Put your head down."

She kept her hands firmly against the horse, forcing herself to see what the animal was willing to share. Something stinging his rump. The shadow of a big man in the snow, raising his arm and slamming it down with purpose. Repeated lashings across the hind legs and rump until the horse ran without thought into the fence in a desperate effort to escape the terrible blows. Too big to be Al or Jase. Wide enough shoulders to be Cole, but the horse displayed no nervousness near him.

"Maia." Cole gripped her hard. "You're as white as a sheet. She was sweating too, and her gaze was filled with a kind of horror. It had nothing to do with the gaping wounds or the blood. He knew it was something else, something entirely different.

Maia shook her head, letting go of the horse's neck and stepping back. "I'm all right." She couldn't look at him. Couldn't look at Jase. Who had done such things to the boy? Who had kicked him? Broken bones? Killed pets in front of him? *He's fourteen, and he hated the old man.* She remembered the icy cold of Cole's voice when he'd made the statement. But Brett Steele was dead. Who had cruelly tormented the horse until it had rushed headlong into a strong fence, nearly killing itself?

Maia forced herself to appear normal. "I'm not the best traveler." She used her stethoscope to check the horse's heart, lungs, and bowel sounds, which gave her some time to compose herself before she faced the Steele brothers.

"If you don't need me, Mr. Steele," Al said, "I'll be heading back to the house before it gets so bad I can't make it. My wife's called a hundred times already worried."

"Yes, by all means, Al," Cole's gaze was on Maia's pale face. He didn't take his hand from her back. He could feel the small tremors running through her body. "Be careful. This storm looks bad. I take it all the animals are bedded down in sheltered areas?" His tone implied they'd better be.

"Yes, sir. It was all taken care of before I let the hands go home." Al turned back. "I know this isn't the best time, but Fred, my wife's brother, came by again looking to get his job back. He's a good hand, Mr. Steele. He's got a couple of kids. It's not like there's a lot of work this time of year."

Jase whipped his head around, his face still and white. The horse suddenly moved, reacting to the boy's sudden tension. The movement flooded the animal with pain, but the bay rubbed its head against Jase in an attempt to comfort him. The gesture immediately brought the teenager's attention back to the animal.

Cole's fingers, on Maia's back, pressed deeper into her skin. There was heat there, a touch of anger. "I told you no, Al. No one who worked for Brett Steele will *ever* work for me or for Jase. I know he visits you, but I don't even like the man to set foot on this property. I've looked the other way because I know family's important to you and your wife, but I don't want to see him and I don't want him to go anywhere on the ranch other than to your home. Is that understood?" His voice was ice-cold and carried a whip.

"Yes, sir."

"And I don't want you to bring this matter up again." It was a distinct threat. Even Maia recognized it as such. She glanced at Jase, who was stroking the Bay's neck. She touched Cole's wrist. Gently. Reminding him he wasn't alone. Lines etched his face, and he looked quite capable of anything. Even murder. If she could see the buried rage rising up to swirl so close to the surface, so could Jase.

Cole let his breath out slowly, trying to relieve the anger boiling up in him. Al kept hammering away at getting his brother-in-law a job, but one look at Jase's pale face told him the man had been present during one or more beatings. He felt like smashing something, preferably Al's face for bringing up the subject yet again and putting that look back on the boy's face.

"Yes, Mr. Steele," Al said and turned and walked away.

Cole looked at Maia. "You ready to do this?" What he wanted to do was thank her, but the words stuck in his throat. Jase looked as if he couldn't take much more.

"Al wanted to put him down," Jase said. "He kept telling me it was best. I knew the horse was suffering, Cole, but I couldn't let him go."

"I told you to hang on," Cole said. "Let's see what the Doc has to say."

Maia took the horse's head in her hands a second time and looked into his eyes, acknowledging pain and memories, giving brief reassurance. She didn't care if the Steele brothers thought she was a nutcase, the horse deserved some comfort before she went to work. When she was certain the animal understood what she was going to do, she began her inspection, her face carefully blank as she evaluated the damage. "Left hock has a three-inch laceration with bone exposed. Right hock, most wounds are superficial abrasions. We have a left front dorsal forearm laceration through the muscle down to the bone, approximately five inches long. We have major splintering from the fence around the laceration, one piece fairly large." It looked like a stake to her, but she was very matter-of-fact, aware of Jase watching her every expression. She put her hand on his shoulder. "We can deal with this if you're willing to help out. First I need to give him painkillers and start him on antibiotics, then we'll get to work."

Jase watched her preparing syringes, his eyes wide. "What are you giving him?"

"Four different types of painkillers. All of them do something a little different. We don't want him to feel anything while I work on him, but he has to stand, so we can't exactly knock him out. He'll be sedated though, Jase." Maia gave the shots deftly, using her fist to strike and numb the muscle before jamming the needle in. "The last two shots are for tetanus and a good dose of penicillin."

Jase crooned to the horse as she administered the rest of the shots. "He's been so good. He hardly moves, and it must hurt so bad."

"The shots will numb everything for him," Maia assured. "Our next step is to get the wound sites as sterile as possible. That's imperative. We're going to flush the site, and remove the debris and splinters, including the large one. Horses can lose a lot of blood, Jase, and still be fine." She worked quickly as she explained, mixing a liter of saline with Betadine. Without giving Jase any time to think about it, Maia grasped the small stake with both hands and pulled the large piece of wood from the horse's chest.

"The barn's well lit, great in fact," Maia said, to keep the boy focused on her and not on the blood. She filled a syringe with the mixture of saline and Betadine. "I need you to begin flushing, Jase. You have to squirt this all over the wound sites. We'll flush all three sites, and I'll clean them, then suture them. This one here"—she indicated the hole where the stake had been—"we might leave open to drain."

Jase took the syringe from her and aimed it at the gaping wound on the horse's foreleg and chest. The flood of saline and Betadine removed dirt, debris and even splinters. "Is this right?"

Maia noted his hand was much steadier. "That's exactly what I need. We want the area really, really clean." She soaked gauze in Betadine and washed the area thoroughly, making certain to rid the wounds of all foreign objects. "What I'm doing is clipping the skin so we can suture the clean edges. I've flushed it again with Betadine and deadened the area with lidocaine, so really, Jase, he isn't feeling any of this."

Cole watched her hands, fingers deft and sure, as she used stents to keep the skin loose as she sutured the wound. She worked with obvious skill. It took a long time to close the five-inch gash to her satisfaction.

"This is a drain. I don't want to close off that hole in him. It's too big and we want to encourage it to drain. We'll have to really watch that area for infection." Maia spoke patiently to Jase. Her voice was very calm and her hands steady. "I'm also putting a second drain in the gash as well. The stents will keep the skin loose, and I think it will heal nicely, but I'll want you to check this area several times a day for any signs of infection."

Jase nodded, looking very solemn. "I'll do it, Doctor."

"I'm Maia Armstrong, Jase."

He nodded again, ducking his head a little to avoid her

gaze. "I can sleep out here with him and sort of keep watch."

"It's too cold," Cole said abruptly.

Maia glanced at Cole from under long lashes. He felt her reprimand all the way to his toes. The woman knew how to give a look. She turned her high-wattage smile on Jase.

"That won't be necessary, Jase, although it's so good of you to offer. He'll be fine out here, and I want him to stay quiet."

Every now and then she spoke softly to the horse and to Jase, instructing him to flush the wound on the hock a second time before she worked on it. When he was finished she used gauze soaked in Betadine to clean it again, removing the last of the dirt and splinters.

"Is he going to be all right?" Jase asked.

"We'll see. We have a long way to go." She crouched beside the horse, working close, without fear or hesitation, as she closed the second gash. She didn't seem to be aware of time passing or the temperature in the barn dropping.

"I'm going to put antibiotic paste on him, Jase. You can't let this stuff touch your skin, so we use tongue depressors to smear it on. Primitive, but it works." She straightened, stretching a little as if her muscles were cramped from crouching so long beside the horse. "We'll have to take his temperature every day, and he'll need antibiotics injected into the muscle twice daily. Have you given shots before?"

Jase nodded. "A couple of times. Cole's been teaching me. Before, I didn't really go near the animals."

She smeared the paste on liberally. "Don't worry, soon

you'll be an expert in giving horses shots. You're a natural."

"Do you really think so? I thought about working with animals a long time ago. I like being around them." Jase glanced at Cole, clearly nervous by the admission.

Maia ignored the significant rise in tension and continued applying the antibiotic paste. "I think you're good with animals. You have to read them, their body language, the look in their eyes. I think you have a real affinity for that."

"What do I have an affinity for?" Cole asked.

Maia laughed, the sound unexpected in the large barn. White vapor drifted around them from the simple act of breathing. She sent a mischievous smirk in Jase's direction, winking at him. "Trouble, Mr. Steele. I think you're a magnet."

Jase made a strangled sound, trying to suppress his laughter. Cole turned away from them. It was the first real laugh he'd heard from the boy, and the sound flooded him with warmth. Maia had a way of bringing Jase out of his shell, and Cole was grateful to her, even though he wished he'd been the one to make Jase laugh.

"You got that right, Doc," Jase agreed.

Maia crouched once again beside the horse. "What I'm doing now is putting pressure wraps on three of his legs to help prevent swelling. I considered putting a stack wrap on his left front, but we'll see how he does. I think he'd just rub it off. I want to keep a careful record, Jase. I'll put this chart out here, so if you happen to take his temp or administer his penicillin when I'm gone, we'll have a record of everything."

"I'll do it," Jase promised.

"I think we're just about finished. We'll let him rest."

Maia stretched, yawning as she did so. "I hope you have some extra clothes you're willing to share, Jase. I didn't bring much with me, and I have a feeling you may be stuck with me a while. I'll need to wash my scrubs, and I'd really love something to sleep in."

"Sure, Doc," Jase said, eager to find a way to repay her. "I'll find you something. And you won't have to worry about getting lost in the snow between the house and barn. All the walkways are covered and enclosed."

She smiled at him. "That's handy. I really think he'll be fine. If we weren't in the middle of a full-blown blizzard, I'd trailer him into the clinic, but I have all my equipment with me. I think we're prepared to handle anything that comes along."

"Will I be able to ride him eventually?"

"Let's make it past the infection stage and see how everything heals," Maia hedged. "He had some nasty injuries." She patted the horse's side. "He wants to get better, and that's more than half the battle right there."

"Did he tell you that, Doc?" Cole asked, his eyebrow raised.

"Well, of course. And he's rather fond of Jase as well. I'm surprised a man as sensitive as you didn't catch all that." She grinned at him and blew on her hands to warm her aching fingers.

His heart lurched uncomfortably. He couldn't help tucking stray strands of hair behind her ear. She looked tired. "Jase, you need to shower and hit the sack. I don't want you staying up all night." Cole took her hands and began to rub them between his own.

Jase glanced at his watch. "I haven't eaten, Cole. I need food. Sustenance. Something like pizza."

The moment he said the word, both brothers reacted, expressions shutting down, wariness creeping into their eyes. They had already compared experiences of their father's reaction when as a boy Cole had stayed after school to have pizza with his friends. Jase had done the same thing. Brett Steele believed in absolute control and his punishments had been vicious.

"I know how to make pizza," Maia said into the silence. "If you have the ingredients, I can make it." Deliberately she pulled her hands away from Cole and clapped Jase on the shoulder. "You do have flannel pajamas, don't you?"

"You're bribing him," Cole pointed out, taking direction from her. Maia seemed to know naturally what to say and do with the boy, where he was still floundering, feeling his way, knowing he was out of his depth. "Jase, don't give up your flannels. I think she's hungry enough to make pizza for us anyway."

"Well, I am, but I had planned on making *you* cook," Maia said.

Jase snorted. "Don't even go there, Doc. Cole's cooking is downright ugly."

"Hey, traitor." Cole managed to ruffle the boy's hair. His affectionate gesture startled both of them. He dropped his hand quickly and Jase suppressed a small grin. "A beautiful woman comes along, and you side with her."

"I show good sense, you mean," Jase bantered back. "She can cook."

Maia's smile widened. "I'm an *awesome* cook. And I love flannel, so I can be bribed."

"I have a flannel shirt," Cole said. "If we have to pay for our four-in-the-morning supper, I'll contribute to the cause." He took Maia's arm. "You're falling down you're so tired. And if you continue to shiver from the cold any longer, you're going to rattle your teeth loose. Let's get up to the house."

Jase patted the horse good night and hurried after them. "Thanks, Doc. I know it wasn't easy doing all that work."

"I like being a veterinarian. I really think you should give it some thought, Jase. School's hard, and you have to be at the top of your class to get in, but I'll bet you have the brains for it."

"He's a great student," Cole acknowledged immediately.

"I had tutors most of the time," Jase admitted. "My father didn't want me to go away to school."

She'd bet he didn't. The wrong person might see his bruises. And a man like Brett Steele wouldn't want to lose control of his prized possessions. His own sons. She stole a quick glance at Cole's darkly etched features. He'd managed to escape his father's world, but now he was trapped all over again. What had that done to him? He was removed from everyone, keeping a distance from the rest of the world, yet trying desperately to keep the same thing from happening to Jase.

She sensed that Cole had to let Jase inside of him. Into his heart. His mind. He had to allow himself to love Jase, to care about him. Obviously he felt affection and a need to protect the boy. And that made him vulnerable. Brett Steele had effectively tied Cole to him, to this place so haunted with his chilling ghost. The elder Steele was certain that his money and his influence would enable him to reach his sons from beyond the grave. Cole was trying to find a way to fight back, to give Jase a life. He just didn't seem to understand that he and his brother would have to save themselves together, that it was a package deal.

"Do you go to a regular school now?" Maia shivered as Cole flicked a switch and the barn went dark. He waved her through the open door to the covered walkway. The floor was constructed to drain the water away from the center as the heating coils embedded in the concrete path melted the snow. Drifts of snow were piled high on either side, cutting the wind.

"Cole wants me to go to a private school, but I don't mix too well with other kids." Again Jase glanced nervously at his brother as if he feared he was revealing too much and would be reprimanded.

"You might like it if you try it," Cole said with no inflection. "You wouldn't have any trouble academically. You're really smart, Jase, and you know it."

"That doesn't make me socially acceptable," Jase muttered.

"Is anyone ever socially acceptable?" Maia asked.

Cole made a snorting sound of derision. "I'll bet you were the most popular girl in school. Prom queen. Cheerleader."

Maia winked at Jase. "What do you think?"

"I think you should have been if you weren't," Jase said honestly.

"You don't have to find me flannel pajamas, and I'll still make you a pizza," Maia declared. "That was a nice thing to say."

"I said it first." Cole crowded closer to her, keeping his body between her and the elements as best he could. She was wearing only the thin scrubs and couldn't control her continuous shivering. "You're making me crazy, Doc." He put his arm around her and pulled her closer to the heat of his body.

"I'm a mess," she said, drawing away. "I'll need that washing machine."

He pulled her back to him, slipping his arm around her waist so that she fit even closer. "I don't think you know how cold you are, Doc. You're turning blue. You look good blue, but it clashes with your spunky attitude."

"I'm not spunky." This time she stayed near the intense heat pouring off his body. Warming her. It felt good, and she was chilled to the bone. He smelled masculine. She'd never smelled a man before, but inhaled deeply, taking him into her lungs and trying not to rub her head against his chest like a cat. It wasn't just the way he felt and smelled, it was the way he made her feel. "No one says spunky anymore."

She'd never been so physically close to a man before. She moved around too much to form really close relationships with people. She'd certainly never experienced such tremendous physical attraction before. Cole Steele made her feel ultrafeminine, completely aware of herself as a woman—and him as a man. "The word 'spunky' is definitely out," she affirmed.

As the walked, her body moved against his in a perfect rhythm reminiscent of dancing. She could feel her color rising, or maybe it was her blood pressure, as she remembered the feel of his body pressed so tightly against hers when they'd danced together. The last thing she needed was to be trapped for any length of time on his ranch with him. She had no idea if her self-control was that strong.

Cole raised an eyebrow at his younger brother. Jase

grinned at him, genuine amusement on his face. "I'd have to agree with Cole on this one, Doc. You are one spunky woman."

Feeling deeply unsettled by her attraction for the larger-than-life man walking so close to her, Maia was grateful when Cole opened a side door to the main house, and they were in the snow room. Jackets were hung on the walls, and boots lined the floor. Both men removed their shoes, and Maia did the same. It was cool in the room, but far warmer than outside.

The inside of the house was so warm she felt the blast of heat on her cold skin. The entryway was tiled, but warm on their feet. She looked up at the archways and high ceilings, her breath catching. "Good grief. You live here? This is a modern-day miracle."

Cole and Jase exchanged a long look. Jase cleared his throat. "I'll find you some warm clothes." He hurried off while Cole pulled a blanket from the back of one of the deep, oversized couches and wrapped it around her. "How about I make you something hot to drink, and I'll cook tonight." He glanced out the series of glass windows making up the front of the house. The snow was steady with no letup. "I think you're going to be here a few days, and you'll get the chance to make Jase your famous pizza another time. Right now you need to warm up."

Maia couldn't argue with him. She was shivering uncontrollably. "I'd love a hot shower." Just the idea sounded like ecstasy.

The thought of Maia naked in the shower was enough to give Cole heart failure. "Sure." His voice was husky and she gave him a sharp glance. He put his hand over his heart. "You're killing me."

"Good. It's about time someone did. All those women come way too easy for you. It isn't good for you, you know."

"What? Women? You make me sound like a gigolo. There haven't been all that many." Why was he defending himself? It was her smile, the way it lit her eyes, the way her soft mouth curved. Inwardly he groaned. His mouth tightened. His jaw hardened. Why did he have to be so intrigued by everything she said and did?

Maia pinned him with her gaze, a small smirk escaping over his reaction. "There *were* that many women. Point me toward the shower and the bathroom had better have a really good lock on the door. I did mention I'm proficient in several forms of martial arts, didn't I?"

"I knew we were compatible. So am I."

She heaved an exaggerated sigh. "Of course you are. What was I thinking?"

MAIA THREW OFF the goose-down quilt and sat up. It was impossible to go to sleep. She was so tired she wanted to scream in frustration, but the house seemed to whisper to her. Evil, haunting whispers she couldn't ignore. The pain in the house ran deep, was soaked into the walls and floors and ceilings. She pressed her hands over her ears, trying to drown out the whispers and finally gave up, leaping from the bed. It wasn't because she was psychic that she could feel the pain radiating out off the walls, it was because it was so intense *anyone* would have felt it.

The blizzard had to stop soon, or she would be going out of her mind in this place. Maia wandered through the spacious hall and down the curving staircase. The front of the house was mainly glass, and the snow reflected light from every source, illuminating the interior of the house with soft silver light. The house was beautiful, but it was a cold beauty, almost cruel. It gave her the creeps. Shivering, she made her way toward the kitchen. Something to warm her up might help her sleep. If it weren't so cold, she would go out to her Land Cruiser and sleep there.

"What are you doing up?"

Maia whirled around, her heart in her throat. Cole Steele was sprawled out on the overlarge couch, long legs stretched out in front of him and a bottle of Jack Daniel's on the table. Her gaze jumped from the bottle to his face. In that one, unguarded moment, she caught a glimpse of a man ravaged by pain, by unspeakable horror, and she knew the truth. Jase had not been the only one to be abused. Cole had suffered the same torment as Jase, and it explained a lot about the man he had become. Wary. Dangerous. Solitary. It was a miracle that he had come back to take care of his half brother.

Cole wrapped his hand around the neck of the bottle, his gaze all at once hot as it drifted with too much interest over her body. "I asked why you were still up." There was a dark sensuality that called to everything feminine in her.

"Ghosts live in this house, but you already know that, don't you?"

His fingers tightened around the bottle. Without taking his eyes off her, he lifted it to his mouth and took a drink. His shirt was open, leaving the heavy muscles of his chest bare. There was rage in his eyes. Too many memories and none of them good. "Yes," he answered abruptly, studying her over the rim of the bottle. "When they get to be too much, I drown them. Do you want to join me?"

Maia shook her head, resisting the need in him. So much darkness and intensity, and Cole was very tempting. She healed hurt animals, and right now, he was far too close to being one. His way of forgetting was to drink, to have sex with a woman . . . any woman. "Hot chocolate for me. I presume you must keep a supply of chocolate on hand with Jase around."

He nodded and turned away from her, setting the bottle carefully on the table and staring out the huge glass panel to the pristine snow endlessly coming down. He looked utterly alone, and her heart stilled. Maia glanced around the enormous room, with its cathedral ceilings, and the curving stairway that went off in two directions. The house should have been alive with joy and music and Christmas decorations. There should have been logs in the fireplace and the fragrance of cinnamon and pine wafting through the air. Instead there was a boy alone in his room struggling to find a way to survive and a man drowning his demons in alcohol.

She shook her head. The pain and suffering in the house was overwhelming for someone as empathic as she was. And it made her angry on a level she'd never experienced before. Cole and Jase Steele existed, yet they weren't really living. The ghost lived, and he ruled with an iron fist in the house.

Maia thought it over as she made the chocolate. The house itself was the most beautiful thing she'd ever seen, yet it was bleak and as empty as the life Cole Steele seemed to live. Earlier, in the kitchen, Jase had laughed with her, teasing her about his pajamas being too big when she rolled up the cuffs and generally acting like a happy boy. Her heart had gone out to him as he worked so hard at being normal when the very walls of the house shricked and wept for his suffering.

Cole had said little, never smiled, his blue gazed focused and direct, watching her watch Jase. Sitting in the kitchen chair, in his own home, he should have been relaxed, but instead, he had been on edge, wary, aware of everything around him. Now she knew why. She could have sat in that chef's dream of a kitchen and wept for both of them. Two men struggling to learn to come together as a family. Wary. Secretive. Ready to push everything and everyone away—including each other. Everything, healer and woman and compassionate human being responded to the intense pain in both of the Steeles, but a part of her, her instinct for self-preservation, wanted to run away and hide. She had no idea what to do to help either of them.

With a small sigh of resignation, knowing she couldn't just ignore it all, Maia added marshmallows to the chocolate and, picking up the mug, went to lean in the doorway to the living room. Cole's head was in his hands, his body tense, hair damp as if he'd just woken from a night terror—or still remained locked within it. She dug her fingers into the doorframe to keep from going to him. He wouldn't accept comfort, unless she offered sex—and she wasn't about to offer herself up as a sacrificial lamb.

"Go to bed, Maia," he muttered without looking up. "It isn't safe when I'm like this."

She took a cautious sip of the hot chocolate. Waiting in silence. Cole turned his head and looked at her, and her heart jumped, nearly melted. "Why are you doing this to yourself?"

The careful, expressionless mask was back in place, but he couldn't hide the pain revealed in his eyes. It remained there. Alive and ugly and so ingrained she wanted to comfort him. *Needed* to comfort him.

"You think I do this to myself?" There was controlled violence in his voice.

A shiver of fear went down her spine, but Maia persisted. She gestured around the house. "You keep this house a monument to the pain and suffering he caused.

You live inside his world, and you expect somehow that you and Jase can overcome it. He's all around you, alive, here in this house, and you don't do anything to get him out of here."

"Who do you mean by *he?*" he asked suspiciously. He stood up, tall and lethal, a man who worked hard to stay in shape, to train himself to be the weapon he'd become. A man who despised pity and refused sympathy, preferring to remain alone rather than risk trusting anyone. Few knew about his past, he'd come clean with a soft version for his superiors at work, but never a woman. He didn't need a bleeding heart trying to stake a claim on him.

Maia's heart began a frantic pounding. She was very aware she was isolated from help, possibly for days. Cole looked capable of anything. She forced a shrug, trying to look nonchalant. "The ghost, of course. You admitted you have one."

He shook his head as he took an aggressive step toward her, bare feet making no sound in the thick pile of carpet. "Don't dodge the truth. Someone's been talking to you. What did they say?"

She took another sip of chocolate. The cup was shaking so she steadied it with her other hand. "I know something happened to Jase, yes. It's not all that difficult to figure out. And"—she indicated the bottle with her chin—"that says it happened to you as well."

He spat out a string of ugly imprecations, taking a second step toward her. "You don't know anything about us. Big deal, I'm having a drink. Don't feel sorry for me, Doc, I don't need it."

Despite her fear—or maybe because of it, Maia burst out laughing. "I definitely am feeling sorry for *me,* not you. Everyone has to live with demons, Steele. Some are worse than others, but we all have them. It's your choice how you deal with them. Drink yourself silly if that's what floats your boat. Personally, I'd drive the ghost out of my home. Reclaim it from him. Exorcise him, if you will." She looked around the house. "It's beautiful here and you've allowed it to become a mausoleum, cold and ugly with something cruel living in it. I can feel it. You can too. And so can Jase. I don't know why you want to keep it alive, but, hey"—she shrugged—"it's nothing to do with me."

Her heart hurt for him. Ached for Jase. But Cole Steele was never going to accept compassion from her. It would seem too much like pity to him. And if she had sex with him, which he so obviously wanted, it might get him through the night, but he'd still have to face his nightmares again and again.

"You're damned right it's nothing to do with you." Cole crossed the room, to stand in front of her. The top two buttons of his jeans were carelessly unbuttoned as if he'd pulled them on hastily and exited his bedroom as fast as he could.

Maia refused to be intimidated. She knew he was being blatantly sexual on purpose, hoping to scare her away or get her into his bed. The knowledge gave her the confidence to walk right past him and she set her mug on the coffee table.

Using her most casual voice, as if they were conversing over a trivial matter rather than one that cut so deep, she said, "It doesn't matter, Cole. We just believe in handling things differently. It doesn't mean I'm right, and you're wrong, it just means I wouldn't do things your way, and you wouldn't do them my way."

His cool blue gaze drifted over her. "What would you do if you lived here with ghosts?"

It sounded taunting, like a challenge.

She raised an eyebrow, turned to look around the spacious room. "I wouldn't let him drive me out or ruin my life. I'm mean like that. If I could actually have a home, no one would take it from me."

Maia wanted a home, but for some reason wouldn't stay too long in any one place. Cole filed the information away for future use. "Give me an example. Jase hates Christmas. It wasn't a nice time of year for him. He doesn't even like to hear the music, it brings on nightmares. If I cranked up "Jingle Bells," I'd just be making things worse for him." And for himself. He'd looked death in the eye a thousand times, courted it, spit at it, and he'd never so much as broken a sweat. But the thought of hearing Christmas music, seeing decorations, reliving nightmares every moment scared the hell out of him.

Maia nodded. Cole might be telling the truth about Jase, but in the scenario he was describing his and his brother's names were interchangeable. She took a deep breath and let it out. She wasn't a psychiatrist, and she didn't have anything but her instincts to go on, but she knew someone had to reach out to Cole Steele before it was too late. He shut out the world, preferred to live in isolation, but Jase had provided him with a small window of opportunity to get his life back. What Cole would not do for himself, he might be willing to do for Jase, and heal them both in the process.

"Everyone is different in how they handle these things, but the truth is, Christmas comes every year. Jase is going to have to face it year after year. And the season seems to come earlier every year. What happens if he wants to get married and have children? It doesn't mean he can't have a great family life without celebrating Christmas; but if he falls in love with someone like me, someone who loves Christmas, it might be difficult."

Someone like me. Cole's heart did a funny somersault. Maia did love Christmas, and he could see with her sunny, outgoing, giving personality, she would. She was happy and cheerful, and she wanted a home. Families celebrated things like Christmas. He nodded, feeling more alone than ever. "I've considered that. I just don't know how to go about getting him to enjoy the season. If we go into town, and he looks at all the decorations, that's enough to trigger the nightmares."

"It started here, didn't it? With his father?" She asked it carefully, not looking at him, not taking a chance he'd see the knowledge in her eyes. She was treading on very dangerous ground. Cole would be lethal under the right circumstances, and she didn't want him to feel as if he had to defend himself.

"Yes." He bit the words between his teeth. It wasn't talked about. Jase wouldn't be happy she knew he'd been abused, any more than Cole wanted her to know. There was a sense of shame in being a victim, even if you were a child and couldn't stop it.

"Jase has to feel his father's presence here all the time, especially if you both leave everything the way it was. *I* feel the man's presence. How could you not? If I was making the decisions, and I was going to keep the ranch, I'd change every single room. I'd redecorate, even use rooms for different things. I take it Christmas was never celebrated here?"

"God, no," Cole said. "The old man hated Christmas."

"Do you know why?"

Cole shrugged. "I'm guessing his old man hated it, but whatever his reasons, he used it to hurt everyone. He was at his most dangerous then. He seduced women, even brought them home in front of his wives. If anyone made the mistake of turning on the radio where he could hear a Christmas song played, and I'm talking the housekeeper or one of the ranch hands, he'd play it over and over and beat the hell out of Jase or his wife."

Or Cole and his mother. Maia sat down in the wide, cushioned chair. She deliberately chose a single chair rather than the couch to keep a safe distance between them. Cole made her feel vulnerable. There was too much pain and suffering, and she was a healer. When she felt pain, she responded. She forced herself to remain calm, to breathe in and out when she wanted to scream with anger at the destructive monster who had caused so much suffering in his own children. "So in effect, that man is still dictating what goes on in this house."

Cole passed his hand over his face, as if to wipe away the memories crowding in. "I fired everyone. The ranch hands, the housekeeper, anyone that was here and had to have known what was happening to him, but it didn't help much. I keep Jase with me when we interview people, and I listen to his input. He has a say in whom we hire and whom we pass on. I want him to feel safe here."

"How can he when that man is still in this house? Brett Steele is everywhere, in every room. And he's still the boss. He forbade you to enjoy such a simple thing as a Christmas season, and you don't. So he wins. Even from the grave, he wins."

Cole swore savagely, making Maia wince. She stared out the window to the heavy snowflakes, waiting for him to regain control of his temper.

"I'm sorry, Steele. You asked, and I gave my opinion. I'm no professional, and I'm sure you must have sought counseling for Jase. I shouldn't have said anything when I don't have any experience."

He waved a dismissing hand. "I wanted your opinion, or I wouldn't have asked. I've considered what you're saying myself. I guess I just wanted you to say there was another, easier way. I've taken Jase to counselors; he doesn't trust anyone. He refuses to talk to them."

"There has to be a really good professional who could help him."

"Maybe, but I haven't found the person. I can't blame Jase. He tried to get help when his father was alive, and no one listened. In all fairness, they didn't dare listen. Money talks, and the old man had a lot of power. He could destroy a business easily and did if his son befriended someone or talked out of turn. Jase's trust is a fragile thing right now. I'm not going to force him to see anyone until he knows he can count on me."

"And can he?" Maia asked quietly.

"If I never do another thing right in my life, I'll do this. Yes, he can count on me. He's coming first in my life. I've put my job on hold until he's squared away."

Maia's gaze met his. "What job?"

Cole sprawled out in the chair across from her. "Does it matter?"

"Sure it does. Do you like what you do? Do you miss working?"

"I like the isolation of it. It's comforting. I know the

world and the rules, and nothing is ever a surprise." Cole was astonished the words slipped out. Maybe he'd had more to drink than he'd realized. He pushed the bottle away with the tips of his fingers.

"I guess I feel the same way about my job," Maia said.

Cole regarded her through half-closed eyes. She was always surprising him. There was something soothing and right about having her in his house. He could never imagine anyone else ever being there, but somehow Maia just fit. "Why do you travel so much? You should have a home."

She flashed him her smile. The one that could knock a man off his feet even from a distance. He'd wanted that smile turned on him; yet alone in his house, with demons surrounding him and alcohol buzzing in his veins, it was all too dangerous. She was so beautiful, curled up in the chair, her bare feet tucked under her. And the question had to be asked, what was under those thin, flannel pajamas? He'd never considered flannel sexy before, but he was looking at it in an entirely new way.

"What? Stop looking at me as if you're the big bad wolf." She shook her head. "I guess you can't help yourself, you're always in hunting mode."

Instantly his expression closed down. His gaze was watchful, shrewd. "I don't like games, Maia. What the hell are you talking about?"

He was thinking conspiracy theory. She sat across from him, weariness plain on her face, no makeup, no guile, and he was actually considering the possibility that she had somehow set up the injury to the horse and was out to get him, using Jase. Had he gone over the edge? To be paranoid of the veterinarian? *She traveled all the time. Was a stranger in town, but was able to gain the trust of those around her fast.* Nonetheless, the little voice that was always asking questions and compiling data persisted.

Maia saw the wariness in his eyes. The sudden alertness. There was danger, but she couldn't figure out what button she'd pressed. Talking with Cole Steele was like walking through a minefield. It was no wonder he preferred one-night stands. No talking, just get down to business and he was safe. "I'm sorry, I didn't mean to upset you. I was referring to your penchant for hunting for women in bars. I was just about to say when you're not treating women like sex toys, you're really an okay human being, but I've changed my mind. You're a very difficult human being."

His eyes went cold and hard. "What the hell does that mean? I don't treat women like sex toys."

"Of course you do. It's *exactly* what you do. You troll the bars for women willing to get you through the night, no strings attached. Hopefully you're also a safety boy."

"Safety boy?" he repeated, unable to believe what she said.

"I hope you at least protect all those women; otherwise, there's no hope for you at all." She turned away from him, shrugging her shoulders carelessly when she didn't feel careless at all. She was beginning to be pulled into the drama in the Steele home, and it frightened her. She didn't want to care about them, or worry about them. She couldn't afford to get involved with someone like Cole Steele.

"I'm not about to pick up a disease or get someone pregnant, if that's what you mean. And I don't give a damn what you think about me."

His voice was as cold as ice, but he was smoldering with anger. She could tell.

Maia stared out the glass window, watching the snow coming down relentlessly. It was much safer looking at the snow than looking at him or around at the ice-cold beauty of the house. "I was stating a fact, not making a judgment; but you obviously have an entirely different set of values, so of course you wouldn't see it that way."

Cole could feel his temper rise. No one managed to get under his skin the way she did, although he couldn't deny her accusation. He had gone into the bar several nights running with the sole intention of sleeping with her in the hopes of getting through the Christmas season. Looking at himself through her eyes wasn't a pretty sight, and the revelation was difficult to take.

"How do you know how I'd see anything?"

Maia turned her attention back to him, her too-cool gaze sweeping his face. "I don't, Cole. And I don't want to know anything. Whatever your suspicions of me are, I'm not looking for a husband, a lover, money, or anything else. I do my job, and I get out of town."

Cole could feel his stomach churning. She'd given him an out. He should go the hell to bed, walk away and leave her alone. But something held him to the chair. Held him under her gaze. He wished it were sex. Wished it were the intense physical attraction he felt for her. He didn't want it or need it to be anything else. He scrubbed his hand over his face, trying to rid himself of the demons that refused to let go.

"The first lesson I can ever remember learning was never to trust anyone at all. Not my mother, certainly not my father, not the housekeeper or any of the hands. It didn't matter how nice or friendly they seemed. They would report everything to him. They would stand there watching when he killed something I made the mistake of caring for. They stood in silence when he beat me with his fists or a whip or a hanger or whatever else happened to be handy." He waved his hand to encompass the ranch. "This was a prison. There was no way to get away from him. He had his security force, who watched our every moment."

He was half-angry with himself the moment he revealed one of his darkest secrets. He'd told her by way of apology for his paranoid conspiracy theories. Or maybe to prove to himself he wasn't as far gone a human being as he believed he was. Whatever the reason, he couldn't take it back no matter how much he wished he could.

Maia was silent, careful to keep her expression from reflecting the horror and compassion in her mind. She couldn't blow the moment by speaking, by saying or doing the wrong thing. Cole Steele was telling her something she doubted he'd ever admitted to anyone. He might have glossed over a difficult childhood, but he'd never spoken the details aloud to another human being. She picked up the mug of chocolate, now cool, wrapping both hands around it.

"Don't think I'm telling you this for sympathy," Cole said harshly. "It's important for you to know what Jase has had to deal with. I don't want him to become like me. I want him to be normal. This is about Jase. You understand? Just Jase."

Maia managed to nod, blinking rapidly to keep tears at bay. Cole Steele was a lost man fighting desperately for his younger half brother. She swallowed the lump threatening to choke her. Who was going to save Cole?

"He responded to you. You're the first person I've ever seen him do that with. He has that distance between him and everyone else, but he laughed with you. Actually laughed. Jase needs something I can't seem to give him."

"You're giving him exactly what he needs right now, Cole. Stability and a sense of family. After so many years, you said he's, what? Fourteen?" At Cole's nod, she continued. "Jase is afraid to trust anyone completely. He wants to, but it's ingrained in him not to. Time will take care of that. As long as you don't let him down, he'll count on you and learn to rely on your relationship."

"Men like Al's brother-in-law, they wanted to pretend what went on here at the ranch was all right, just something they had to put up with to keep their families going, but they were part of it, holding Jase here, watching what the old man did to him. I don't want them anywhere near Jase, with their smirks and patronizing bullshit."

Maia heard the suppressed rage in Cole's voice. The men he'd fired were luckier than they knew. Cole was capable of extreme violence. "Jase isn't ever going to get over this completely, Cole. It doesn't work that way. The things we've experienced become part of who we are. It can make him a stronger, better person, but he won't ever forget it or be able to get away from the consequences, the impact on his personality."

Cole leaned back in his chair, allowing his breath to leave his lungs. "Who are you, Doc? Where do you come from?"

"I'm no big mystery, Steele. I grew up in a small town. My parents were killed in a car accident when I was about sixteen, and I went to live with my only relative, my grandmother. She was an awesome woman, and I hope I learned a lot from her. I loved animals, got decent grades, and decided I'd be a veterinarian. I was about halfway through school when my grandmother died, and I discovered she had a bit of money put away. It enabled me to buy my own equipment, and the rest is history."

"Your entire life in a few short sentences." He saluted her.

Maia smiled at him. "I told you it wasn't a big deal. Now, *you* are different. You're surrounded by mystery and intrigue."

"It's what women find appealing."

"Really? I thought it was your brooding loner image. I guess it ties in though, I can see that. Are you going to give tips to Jase on dealing with women?"

Cole shook his head. "Jase is going to find a really nice woman someday and have a family. He'll have two kids and come home every night to someone who loves him." He sighed. "He's not excited about going to a regular school. I was hoping he'd go to a private one or even the public school, but he's always had tutors, and he isn't comfortable with anything else."

"He isn't comfortable not being with you. In effect, this ranch has been the only place he's ever been. Didn't you say your father kept him prisoner here? Or close to it? He's staying in his comfort zone. We all do that. We stay with what we know."

Cole tried not to wince. She was lashing him, and she wasn't even aware of it. If anyone stayed in his comfort zone, it was he. Cole didn't duck the issue. He was an adrenaline junkie, and he kept the rest of the world at a distance. She was just sitting there, looking beautiful, pointing out his every flaw, and through it all he had the most incredible urge to kiss her until neither of them could think anymore. "Isn't it about time you tried to get some sleep?"

Maia glanced at her watch, deliberately ignoring the flare of desire in his eyes. "You're right. It's already morning. It doesn't look like we're going to get much of a break from this storm."

Cole stood up, waited until she'd rinsed out her mug and climbed the stairs to the long sweep of a landing. "Good night, Doc, thanks for everything you've done."

Maia smiled at him over her shoulder. "Anytime, Steele."

chapter

6

"JASE," COLE SAID casually, "the doc's out with the horse right now, so there's no rush. Before you go out to check on him I want to run something by you. I need a little advice."

Jase sat down at the kitchen table across from his older brother. "What is it?" They'd slept in late, and he was anxious to make certain his horse had gotten through the night without a problem.

"The doc." Cole pushed his hands through his hair, leaving it spiked and disheveled. "I checked the weather, and it looks like we'll be socked in for at least a week."

"She'll have to stay here?" Jase couldn't prevent the grin from spreading across his face. "I don't mind. I think the doc's all right."

"She loves Christmas, Jase, and she'll be stuck here with us probably through the twenty-fifth. She'll miss it." Cole didn't look at the boy, but stood up and paced across the room in a restless, edgy movement. "She came out here doing us a favor, she's stuck working; in fact she's already out with Celtic High"—he glanced briefly at Jase, assessing his expression—"I mean Wally. I don't know, what do you think we should do?"

Jase rubbed his hand over his face, subconsciously copying his older brother's gestures. "Anything to eat around here?" He looked around the room, anywhere but at his brother. "I'm starving, and it smells good in here."

"You're always starving. She made breakfast burritos for us. You just scoop up the eggs and wrap them in the tortilla. The tortillas are still warm."

Jase made his burrito, took a healthy bite, and sat there chewing, contemplating. "I don't know, Cole. What do you think? She's really nice. Maybe we could put up a tree or something."

Cole had his back to the boy, and he closed his eyes, his gut kicking up a protest. His ear was finely trained, tuned to catch the slightest nuances, and he could hear the combination of hesitancy and hope. "We've never done that before, either one of us. It might be interesting. The old man would turn over in his grave."

"As long as he stays in it," Jase said.

Cole turned back to face him. "I saw the body, Jase. He's dead." Cole didn't admit he had insisted on seeing the body. He wouldn't have believed anything or anyone would ever manage to kill Brett Steele. The man had seemed invincible, a monster with such power he could live forever. *Jase had been in the house when the old man had bought it.* Cole tried to push the thought away. *Jase wasn't capable of murder—not even of a monster like their father, was he?* That niggling doubt persisted no matter how hard Cole worked at keeping it at bay.

"Who do you think killed him, Cole?"

"It could have been anyone. He had a lot of enemies," Cole answered honestly, feeling relieved that there were other suspects. "I think the question we need answered is *why* someone killed him. Did it have anything to do with us? The ranch? The money? Anything that could affect us."

"I didn't think of that. Why would it have something to do with us?"

Cole shrugged. "I don't know, but it bothers me that all these rumors are so persistent, the ones about me trying to do you in. Al mentioned you were helping him feed horses the other day, and you leaned against the fence in the corner and it gave way. If he hadn't grabbed you, you would have gone over that small cliff. You often lean up against that section when you watch the horses run. I've seen you do it."

Cole had personally gone out to inspect the fence. Someone had deliberately loosened the post from the cement. The fall wouldn't have killed Jase, but it might have broken a bone or two. What had been the point? Any of the new hands could have done it. Cole had hired them out of Jackson Hole, but that didn't mean they might not be friends with the former crew. Al had even mentioned that his brother-in-law, Fred, had been around that day.

"Al said the fence was old and needed repairing."

"Maybe. But now there's this incident with Wally. Don't you think it's strange my glove was found by the fence? I haven't been out there in a week, and my work gloves are always in my truck. I don't believe in coincidence. The old man was murdered, and, even though these incidents seem unrelated, I'm not so certain they are."

Jase sagged in his chair. "I was thinking the same thing." He looked at Cole, fear in his eyes. "But I was thinking maybe it was him. I know it's crazy, Cole, but what if he found a way to come back? I read a couple of books on the subject, and some people believe a spirit can linger after death, especially if the death was violent."

"That's a load of crap, Jase. He's dead and gone."

"Then why does it feel as if he's still here? I swear I'm afraid to do anything. I even look up when I go into all the rooms, looking for the cameras he had to watch us all the time." Jase looked about to cry.

"I destroyed the cameras and all the tapes, Jase. I did it right in front of you. We cleaned him out of here." Cole cleared his throat. "Maybe we should try a Christmas tree and a few decorations. Let's take the house back completely. He can't dictate to us what we can or can't do. If you're still feeling him here, it's because we haven't made the house ours." He tried not to wince as he repeated Maia's logic. "So it's really up to you if you want to try to celebrate Christmas this year. I'm game if you are."

Jase shrugged, trying to look casual. "Well, maybe we should do it for the doc. I'd hate for her to be out here looking after Wally and missing something she loves."

Cole kept his expression carefully blank. He wasn't about to take away the boy's courage by letting on that the very thought of trying to celebrate the holiday scared the hell out of him. He knew what he was getting himself into. Brett Steele had been particularly cruel at Christmas, and the number of Cole's nightmares increased in direct proportion to days of celebration. "Since I've never actually had a Christmas, we might need a little help in figuring out what we're supposed to do."

"You know how pathetic that makes us, Cole?" Jase asked. "I can't go to school with a bunch of other kids and pretend my life is okay. I know you think I should, but I'm never going to be like them. I don't want to have to pretend anymore."

Jase took every occasion to remind Cole he objected strenuously to going into a classroom. Cole sighed. "I want you to have friends, Jase. You don't want to end up being a loner. If you don't get out there and mix it up with your peers, you'll never be able to."

"Is that what happened to you?" Jase asked, belligerence creeping into his tone.

"As a matter of fact, yes. I grew up the same way you did, remember? You aren't alone in this. I wasn't allowed friends either. I had tutors right here on the ranch. If I liked one of the hands too much, he was sent packing. I don't have friends, and I don't make them. It's a hell of a way to live."

"I don't want to go to school," Jase said stubbornly.

Cole was happy the boy was at least telling him how he felt. That said he had grown comfortable enough with Cole to do so. In the first few weeks they'd been together, the boy had rarely offered an opinion on anything. "Let's do this, Jase. We'll start with this Christmas thing for the doc. If we can manage to get through it without the two of us going nuts, maybe we can move forward from there."

Jase nodded. "I don't mind trying for the doc, but I'm not promising about school." He scooped up more eggs and rolled them in a tortilla. "She's a pretty good cook, isn't she?"

"I thought so."

"You like her don't you, Cole?"

Cole went very still inside. He tried a casual shrug. "What's not to like?"

Jase pushed his fork around the table. "Have you gone into the old man's office since he died?"

Cole's head went up alertly at the boy's tone. "A couple of times, not recently."

"He has a couple of maps of the ranch that I wanted. I was going to put them in my room, but they're gone. They were in his desk drawer."

"What do you mean, 'gone'? No one's here but the two of us. I didn't touch the maps, didn't even know they were there."

Cole felt a twinge of alarm. It was a silly thing, a missing map meant nothing at all, so alarms shouldn't be going off, but he'd long ago learned to pay attention when a small detail was out of place. "Jase, are you certain the maps were still there after Brett was killed? Someone could have borrowed them."

Jase nodded. "I looked at them a week or so after he died."

Cole drummed his fingers on the table. "That was before I fired Justine and Ben Briggs. It didn't occur to me they might take anything. I wouldn't know it if they did. They worked here for years, so they'd know more about what was in the house than either of us. They could have robbed us blind, and we wouldn't know." But why would they take maps and not the Ming vase or the artwork worth thousands? Or any of the other priceless objects decorating every room of the house. "You're certain of the time line?"

"Cole, I was terrified to go into his office. I waited a week after he died, then when I pulled the maps out, I couldn't make myself take them to my room. I folded them carefully and put them back in the drawer in his desk."

Cole decided the kid looked scared. "Jase." His voice was very gentle. "Brett Steele is dead, and his ghost can't do a damned thing to us. It certainly didn't remove maps from his office. You have to stop reading those books."

"I didn't think about Justine or Ben taking anything," Jase admitted with a small sigh of relief. "That makes more sense."

"Why were you interested in the maps, Jase?"

Jase pushed the last bite of burrito around on his plate with his fork. "The ranch is so big, and I hated that all the workers knew every canyon and peak and I had no idea what they were talking about. They'd be talking about the cattle being in some canyon; I'd ask where it was, and they'd laugh at me. I hated that. I hated feeling so small and stupid all the time. I was the boss's son, and they knew more than I did."

Cole swore savagely under his breath, his back to the boy. Every little hurt added more to Jase's feelings of inadequacy. The old man had purposely made him look small in front of the ranch hands, belittling him and correcting him, even publicly humiliating and punishing him every chance he got. Cole knew without Jase's telling him, because he'd received the same treatment.

"I'll find you maps of the ranch, Jase," he promised gruffly. "Even if I have to draw them myself."

"Thanks, Cole." Jase stood up and carried his plate to the sink. "Has the doc been up a long time?"

Cole inhaled the scent of fresh coffee. "Yeah, she's been up a while. She's out there with that horse of yours. Go on, I'll take care of cleanup this morning." Cole waved the boy out, not wanting to face Maia yet. She'd disarmed him without even trying, filling the house with the fragrance of breakfast, giving him an unfamiliar sense of warmth and home. He sat there for a moment contemplating that. He'd never felt as if he'd had a home before.

When he woke up that morning he'd been instantly aware that Maia Armstrong was in his house. Not just any woman, but Maia Armstrong. He never let a woman spend the night with him, and he always left their houses immediately after sex. With Maia, everything seemed different, but he couldn't put his finger on why. It wasn't the fact that he'd awakened with a hell of a hard-on from the erotic dream he'd had about her, instead of waking from the usual nightmare, tangled in his sheets with a gun in his hand. It was because she'd brought a sense of home to the monstrosity of a house he occupied.

He had awakened looking forward to the day and he hadn't experienced that feeling very often. He had lain there, staring at the ceiling, his heart pounding and his mouth dry, terrified that Maia Armstrong could do that to him. Make him happy by just being in his house. By making a building seem like a home just with her presence. By removing the endless nightmares and replacing them with dreams of her. Her smile. She had a killer smile. Her eyes went soft, almost mesmerizing. The sound of her laughter. It seemed to vibrate through his body, wrap around him until it squeezed his heart and lungs.

He swore out loud, jumping up fast enough to knock over his chair and turning around in the huge kitchen without a real purpose. She was getting under his skin. He should have found a way to seduce her last night and get it over with; instead, he'd revealed intimate, private details he never should have admitted. She had ammunition to use against him, and he'd given it to her. "Oh, you're good, lady," he said. "What are you after?" He picked up the chair, slamming it against the table.

Immediately he was ashamed of himself. What was he thinking she wanted? Him? She'd made it clear she had no intention of sleeping with him. His money? That would entail some kind of a relationship with him. He threw a plate into the soapy water, avoiding the dishwasher. Suds and water splashed over the edge of the sink. He needed a damned housekeeper, not a girlfriend.

"Cole!" Jase burst threw the kitchen door, slamming it back on its frame so hard it nearly bounced. "Come quick. The doc fell and hit her head."

Cole rushed past him, his heart in his throat. "How the hell did that happen?"

"I don't know, I found her on the walkway. There's ice all around her."

"Ice?" Cole sprinted along the covered walkway. There was snow piled high on either side and more flakes were coming down rapidly. The walkways had been specifically constructed with a wide overhang to keep any water from running down onto the surface for the very purpose of keeping ice from forming. The latticework and snow, piled so high on either side, kept the wind and drafts at bay, forming a warmer tunnel for them to use in going back and forth between the various buildings.

Maia lay sprawled on the ground, one hand at the back of her head. Cole could see the bright red blood staining the white snow underneath her. He crouched beside her, catching her hand gently and drawing it away from the wound. "Let me see."

She looked up at him, her wide eyes dazed and slightly

unfocused. "I just slipped. It wasn't icy when I came out here, and I didn't notice the surface."

Cole felt the lump on her head through the mass of thick dark hair. It was sticky with blood. He studied the walkway. There was no dripping water that could have caused the snow to ice over the way it had. The surface was slick with a layer of ice, almost as if someone had sprayed water over it. He studied the latticework. A few drops of ice clung to the wood just about level with his waist. "Don't move, Doc, just lie still while I take a look at you." *Jase was the only person around.* He swore silently. He didn't want to think the boy could in any way be like their father, but his own past and his job gave him a suspicious nature. He had to eliminate Jase as a suspect. There were ranch hands—even Al—living on the ranch and even in a blizzard one of them could have arranged the "accident."

He glanced once more at Jase. The boy looked so anxious, every instinct Cole possessed told him he couldn't possibly have sprayed the water on the walkway to make it icy.

"The fall just stunned me for a minute."

"Did you get knocked out? Jase, was she out for any length of time?"

"She swore a lot," Jase reported.

"Did she now? I wasn't sure you knew how to swear," Cole said, looking down into Maia's eyes. It was a big mistake. A man could lose himself there. He couldn't look away from her. He bent his head and brushed a kiss across her mouth to break the spell.

Her eyelashes fluttered, and she managed to glare at him. "I work with animals, believe me, I know how to swear. And was that another apology?"

"Sheer desperation."

"You do look a bit desperate," Maia conceded, struggling to sit up. "And I didn't lose consciousness. I think I knocked the wind out of myself, and my head hurts pretty bad, but if you'll help me up, I'll be fine."

"I'm going to lift you, Doc. Just put your arms around my neck. Jase, watch your step, the surface is icy, and we don't need another accident."

"I've never seen the walkway ice over before," Jase said. "Maybe there was rain or slush coming down with the snow."

"Maybe," Cole conceded, but the temperature was far too cold for rain or slush, and they both knew it. "Just stay close until I can take a look around, Jase." He lifted Maia into his arms, holding her against his chest. Her skin was cool after being outdoors for so long. She was heavier than he expected, her muscles solid and firm. He felt the tension in her the moment he cradled her close. The same faint fragrance of peaches and rain he'd noticed the night before clung to her skin and hair.

"I can walk," she protested. She tried to hold herself rigidly away from him. "I'm ruining your shirt." Maia felt silly being carried by Cole Steele. If her head hadn't been throbbing with enough intensity to make her teeth ache she would have insisted on walking.

"Relax, Doc, I have a lot of shirts, and there's only one of you. I don't give a damn about the shirt."

"That's a good thing, because it's a mess already." She tried to move her head to keep the blood from dripping onto his shirt.

Cole made a single sound of impatience and she subsided, trying to relax against him in spite of her embarrassment. Jase skirted around the ice and hurried ahead to open the door. "I'll get blankets," he called over his shoulder.

Cole carried her to the oversized couch, placing her with care in the middle of the cushions. "When you went to the barn this morning, you're positive there was no ice on the walkway?"

Maia looked up at the concern on his face. His voice was low, obviously to keep Jase from overhearing. "It was easy to get to the barn. I remember thinking everyone should have a walkway like that. Most ranches in the outlying areas use rope or cable as a guideline when it's snowing."

"We've got cable up in places," Cole said. He took the ice pack and washcloth from Jase as the boy hurried up to them. "Thanks, Jase. The doc's going to be fine. She just looks a little pale. Women do that to give men heart attacks."

Maia laughed. Cole should have known she would in spite of her injuries, but he wasn't at all prepared for the sound filling the space around them. His space. It was always there, between him and everyone else, but she didn't seem to see it, and she put things there like her laughter. She was definitely getting under his skin, and it made him edgier than usual.

"Well, I don't think you should, Doc," Jase chastised, his hand over his heart, "because I was really scared."

"I'm sorry, Jase. I didn't see the ice. I guess I wasn't looking. And just for your information . . . Ow!" Maia pulled her head away and glared at Cole as he dabbed at the cut on her head. "That hurts."

"Stop being such a baby." Cole was extraordinarily gentle as he wiped away the blood. There was an unfamiliar lump in his throat. All the while he was turning over possibilities in his mind. Had someone sprayed the walkway with water in order to cause Maia harm? Who could have done such a thing? He needed to take a closer look at Al and his wife. Find out if anyone had been visiting. Perhaps Fred had stayed with them instead of going home to his family.

"Does it really hurt, Doc?" Jase asked, frowning at Cole.

"I'm fine," Maia assured. "He's being gentle. I feel a little stupid falling on my head." She wasn't going to mention the bruises all over her backside. Cole's face was very close to hers, and she could see his long lashes, the bluish shadowing along his jaw, the tiny lines etched into his weathered features. His gaze met hers and her heartbeat accelerated instantly. "You're lethal." She didn't mean to say it aloud. She had to blame the bump on her head. It knocked out her good sense.

"Yes I am," Cole warned. "Don't forget it."

Maia looked up at Jase and burst out laughing a second time. "At least I'm not the only one saying dumb things. Your horse, by the way, is doing great, Jase. No temp, the drains are working, and I gave him his antibiotic shots, so he's fine for the time being. I didn't feed him, so you'll have to do that. And I want to move him to a small enclosure where he can get around without hurting himself. The trick is to get him to walk enough to keep the swelling down, but not so much that he pulls out the sutures or does more damage."

"I still have to feed the other horses this morning," Jase said. "I told Al I'd do it so he wouldn't have to risk driving in the storm. We knew the storm would be bad, so I'll take care of the stables, then let Wally into the small round pen inside the big barn. I can feed him there, unless you just want him to exercise a couple of times a day."

"I'll feed the horses, Jase," Cole said. "Give me a few minutes with the doc here to get her settled, and I'll go make the rounds."

"I don't mind, Cole," Jase objected. "I can do the job."

Cole scowled and opened his mouth to make it a command, but Maia deterred him, touching his wrist with her fingertips. When he glanced at her she shook her head slightly and turned her head to smile up at Jase. "Actually, I was hoping you'd stay with me for a little while so we could come up with a plan for Wally." Her smile widened until it lit her eyes. "I think the name suits him. He likes it."

"Did he tell you that?" Cole asked, his voice edged with sarcasm.

"As a matter of fact, he did. What do you say, Jase? Let the grouch feed the horses this morning, and we'll map out a plan of action for Wally."

"You may as well plan Christmas for us too." Cole made the suggestion to forestall Jase's protest that the horse wasn't anything special to him. His heart jumped, slamming hard against the wall of his chest in protest. He would have taken the proposal back, but the boy suddenly looked hopeful.

Maia's fingers tightened on his wrist. He hoped to hell she had no idea what the turn in the conversation cost him. Cole refused to meet her eyes, instead busying himself with getting the matted blood from her hair so he could see the wound.

"You sure you didn't try ice-skating," he said gruffly as he looked at the laceration.

A faint smile softened the lines around her mouth. "I've always wanted to learn, but it wasn't my intention."

"I can take her ice-skating if she wants to go," Jase volunteered. "There's a pond that freezes over every winter. It's great for ice-skating."

Cole glanced at the boy's face. He was staring at Maia as if she were a goddess. He sighed and leaned down, his mouth against her ear, his lips brushing her skin. "Tone it down before the boy asks you to marry him." The faint scent of peaches in her hair triggered a heat flash that seemed to spread through his veins straight to his belly and centered in his groin.

She turned her head so that her mouth was brushing against his cheek. "Really? I didn't realize I had such an impact."

Her voice vibrated down his spine. He could have sworn her finger stroked his wrist but when he looked down, her hand was lying there motionless. Innocent. Her lips were feather-light, soft and full. Cole felt the burn right through his skin. He jerked away from her. She was reducing him to a smitten teenager. Jase could fall under her spell, but he was damned if he would. It was supposed to work the other way around. He certainly wasn't mesmerizing her. And she sure wasn't falling into his bed. Maia looked up at him, her eyes wide and beautiful, and the breath left his lungs in a rush.

Cole backed away from the couch. "I think you'll be fine. Jase, get the doc an aspirin and stay with her while I get the chores done."

"And you're really fine with decorating the house, or maybe even getting a Christmas tree?" There was a note of fear in Jase's voice.

Cole felt the echo of fear in his gut. "Sure. Sounds like a plan." He turned away from them. A woman who appeared soft and gentle but had a core of steel. A boy, lost in his past and trying desperately to find security and a home. Cole shook his head. How the hell had he gotten into such a mess? He needed familiar ground. He was never afraid. He had nothing to lose, and when a man had nothing to lose, he didn't experience fear. He was letting some little slip of a woman scare the holy hell out of him.

Outside, he examined the ice-coated walkway. Someone had poured water over the snow to form the icy surface. The hose was buried in the large snowbank on the outside of the walkway, but he could see the hose had been stuck in one of the latticework holes and sprayed onto the surface. Small droplets of water had frozen on the lattice.

Was it Jase? It didn't feel right to him. Jase seemed to be genuine. A nice kid who needed a family. Could he be as sick and disturbed as their father? They were in the middle of particularly harsh blizzard. No one else was in the house or around the ranch that Cole was aware of. He studied the ground near the hose. The boot impressions in the snow were large—too large to be Jase's—and led back toward a door that opened into the barn. Someone had opened that door and spied on Maia while she worked on the horse. Jase hadn't been wet or covered in snow when he'd come running in.

If Maia had gone out early to tend the horse and the walkway had been fine, then only Jase had gone after her. It was possible Jase had shot the old man. He'd never been ruled out as a suspect. He didn't want Jase to be guilty, but the evidence wasn't stacking up in the boy's favor.

Brett Steele had been found in his office, dead from a single bullet smack in the middle of his forehead. Cole shook his head. Jase had found the injured horse. He could have easily driven the horse into the fence and then gone to get Al, making a show of being upset and blaming Cole. Jase claimed he found Cole's glove in the fence.

Cole straightened and took a cautious look around. His alarms were shrieking at him. Something was terribly wrong, and he knew he was in danger. Maia Armstrong could very well be too. And Jase.

He shook his head, vowing to find out who was sneaking around the ranch and why as he trudged through the snow to the stables to feed the horses.

He patted an outstretched neck as one of the horses greeted him, then tossed a flake of hay into the last feeding bin.

He ran his hand along one of the horses' backs, bent closer, and noticed a girth mark near the horse's belly. It could only mean the horse had been ridden recently, within the last couple of days. Cole leaned down to pick up a foot, examining the hoof. Dirt and debris were caked in the shoe. Very slowly he lowered the hoof to the stable floor, a slight frown on his face. Al hadn't said anything about taking the horses out.

Cole closed the door to the stall and went to examine the saddles and bridles. A large saddle was set to one side, slightly off kilter, but it didn't mean anything. A rifle scabbard was hooked to the saddle, and it had a mud pattern splattered across it.

A muffled footfall alerted him. Cole eased back into the shadows of the tack room and drew the gun from the holster strapped to his calf. Only the munching of the horses as they chewed hay and the sound of their continual restless movements in the stalls broke the silence. Cole didn't make the mistake of moving. He had endless patience when needed. A shadow stretched across the wall, a man holding a pitchfork out in front of him. Cole stepped out into the open, his gun rock steady, an extension of his arm.

Every vestige of color drained from Jase's face. He dropped the pitchfork and backed against the stall. "Don't shoot me."

Cole swore savagely. "What the hell is the matter with you? I *could have* shot you. What were you thinking?" He shoved the gun out of sight.

"I came out to help you," Jase defended, his face tight with fear and growing anger. "What are you doing with a gun?"

"None of your damned business," Cole snapped. Jase turned and ran out of the stable, disappearing from Cole's line of vision.

Cole crushed down the need to throw something. He should have identified the intruder before coming out of hiding with his gun. He knew better than to let his highly tuned instincts take over completely. Dammit. He was going to have to explain the gun. How did you tell a teenager your entire world was made up of conspiracies, and you siphoned through them one at a time to get to the truth?

chapter 7

COLE ENTERED THE LIVING ROOM to find Jase pacing furiously back and forth across the room. The boy cast a dark, furious look at his brother. Maia looked up and met Cole's gaze, lifting her hands palm up in inquiry. Jase stopped pacing abruptly and stood breathing heavily, his hands on his hips.

"You could have killed me! Maybe you want to kill me just like everyone says," Jase burst out. He glared at Cole. "Maybe you tried to kill the doc just so she wouldn't find out about you."

"Jase!" Maia said firmly. "That's enough. You're afraid and angry, but don't say things you can't take back."

"He didn't put a gun in your face. He's been in jail. Everyone knows he's been there," Jase continued, breathing hard, his young face twisted with fear and hurt.

"Come sit down over here," Maia patted the couch beside her. "I can tell you whatever Cole may have done or not done in his life, he wouldn't do anything to hurt you. Someone is trying to drive a wedge between the two of you." She didn't look at Cole. She couldn't bear to see the hurt in his eyes she knew would be there. He stood motionless, a man apart, isolated, hurt beyond reason and unwilling to risk himself further.

Jase flung himself onto the couch beside Maia, tears glittering in his eyes. "I hate this. I hate my life." He included Maia in his glare. "I hate that you stick up for him. You don't even know him. You don't know whether he killed our father, or whether he hurt Wally and tried to hurt me. You don't even know whether or not he covered that walkway with ice in order to hurt you. Everyone says he's after my share of the money, and maybe he is." A sob escaped, and his chest heaved as he tried to hold the emotion in.

"That's enough," Cole's tone was low, but it was a whiplash.

"That doesn't even make sense, Jase," Maia said softly. "I knew about the gun. If you went into the stable and startled Cole, of course he pulled the gun. Someone hurt your horse. Naturally Cole would be worried about all of our safety."

Jase rubbed at his eyes with his knuckles, looking four instead of fourteen. Cole let out his breath slowly as his younger brother's expression became somewhat mollified.

"Cole, you need to talk to Jase. I can leave the room if you want me to, but he needs you to share your life with him. You're helping whoever is persisting in these rumors about you trying to kill Jase. You're enabling whoever is attempting to keep you from trusting one another by remaining silent about your past. If you want this to work between you, you have to trust one another, and the only way to do that is to get to know each other." Maia held her breath, waiting for Cole to tell her to go to hell.

There was a long silence. She stole a quick glance at his face. His rugged features were very still, expressionless. He stared over her head at the wall behind them. A muscle jerked in his jaw, the only sign that he'd heard her. She could feel Jase trembling, could feel the tension in his body winding tighter and tighter. With a small sigh, she twisted her fingers together. What could she say to convince them?

"I saw the shadow of a man holding a pitchfork and thought someone was stalking me. I didn't know it was you. I yelled at you because I was afraid I could have hurt you accidentally. I didn't hurt the horse, and I sure don't want your money."

Jase looked a little embarrassed. "Maybe I didn't mean everything I said. It just reminded me of . . . things."

"I know what you mean," Cole said. "He shoved a gun in my face more than once too. I'm sorry I scared you."

"That's all right." Some of the tension began to drain from the boy's body.

"I was in jail, Jase." Cole took a deep breath, let it out. His fingers curled involuntarily into a fist. "I work for the DEA. I went into prison undercover to stop a very large drug ring involving guards, inmates, and the supply trucks. I've worked undercover most of my life. It's an isolating job and makes you very distrustful of everything and everyone around you." He made the confession in a rush, wanting to get it over with, half-horrified that he was letting them both into his life. "I don't tell people what I do. It's habit, and it's kept me alive over the years."

Maia kept her lips firmly pressed together, astonished, not by what he'd said, but that he'd admitted it. Cole Steele was not a man who'd easily reveal the details of his life. She wanted to console him, put her arms around him and hold him close, but neither Jase nor Cole could allow a show of compassion. Beside her, Jase was trembling, uncertain how to react to his brother's revelation. Tension coiled around Cole, his face a mask without expression. Only his eyes were alive, turbulent and raw with pain.

"You're some kind of a cop?" Jase asked. His voice cracked, making him sound younger and even less sure of himself.

Cole nodded. "I have a small apartment in San Francisco that I rarely use. Most of the time I'm on the road, sent undercover to various countries. Sometimes it's here in the U.S. We carefully cultivated my reputation and network in the drug world. When the old man was investigating me, the P.I. raised a red flag, and we fed him the details of my life just the way we do everyone who investigates me. I was using a different name, and the private investigators just assumed I'd covered my tracks to be rid of the old man. They bought my undercover role and took it at face value. So now Cole Steele has the same background as my persona at work."

"And you didn't want me to know?"

Cole flinched inwardly at the hurt in the boy's voice. "I wanted to wait until we knew each other better, Jase. Things have been so bad for you. I'm not used to being around anyone for an extended period of time. I had to know if I could be someone you could count on."

"But you let all those people say that you were here to kill me."

Cole nodded. "And I'll continue to let them say it. I don't care what people say or think about me. I'm only concerned with what you say and think."

"I tried not to think they might be right, but I found your glove by the fence. And sometimes, when you look really mean, you look a little bit . . ." Jase trailed off.

The knot in his gut tightened. Cole refused to look at Maia. "I've seen the resemblance. I always carry a gun, Jase."

"I guess I'm not supposed to tell anyone."

"I'd rather you didn't," Cole said.

"Are you going to go away again?"

Maia felt the boy beside her, stiff and awkward. She could feel fear rolling off him and immediately locked her gaze with Cole's. Pleading with him. Hurting for him. Did he realize how important that single question was? The relationship between the two brothers was so fragile.

Cole felt the impact of Maia's eyes. He swallowed his first careful answer. He had promised himself he would change the boy's life. He couldn't very well do it from a distance. His leave of absence might turn out to be far longer than he'd anticipated. "I'll stay as long as you need me, Jase. Or want me. It's up to you."

Jase jumped to his feet. "All right then. I won't say anything." His voice was gruff, covering his emotions. "I'm sorry I believed those people, even for a minute."

"I think you were smart to be careful, Jase. After what we've been through, we need to build our relationship on solid ground."

Jase nodded and practically ran from the room.

Maia guessed he was close to tears. "I'm sorry," she said. "I didn't mean to intrude on such a personal moment with Jase. I couldn't figure out a way to leave gracefully in the middle of it all. I won't say anything about your life to anyone."

"I never thought you would." And he hadn't. That was the strange part. It never once occurred to him she might reveal the truth about what he did. And did that mean he trusted her? Cole turned away from her to stare out the window at the driving snow. "We have a problem here, Doc. More than one, and I'm going to need your help."

"You don't think the ice got there naturally, do you?" Maia said shrewdly.

"No I don't. And I don't think a ghost is running around the ranch turning on hoses and arranging accidents with the horses."

She studied his face. He wore an expressionless mask, but there was something frightening about the expression in his eyes. "It's Jase, isn't it? You're worried about him."

Cole glanced toward the door. "Yeah, I'm worried."

Maia sighed. "It was definitely a human driving Wally through the fence."

He spun around, his gaze sharp as it raked her face. "What makes you so sure?"

She pulled the ice pack away from her head. "If I told you, you'd want me locked up in a little cell. Suffice to say, I just know."

He stalked across the room and crouched down in front of her, his face inches from hers. "Not good enough. Tell me."

Maia pushed at the wall of his chest. "Stop invading my space. I don't know you well enough to tell you. I don't know anyone that well." She couldn't think straight with him so close. He was the most sensual man she'd ever met. His eyes were just so intense, his features etched with need.

"I told you about the DEA."

"You told Jase, not me. I just happened to be in the same room."

"I told *you*. You know damn well I was telling you." He pulled away from her, a flash of irritation on his face. "I don't even know why I wanted you to know, but if I'm going to come unraveled around you, the least you could do is open up a little."

"You aren't asking for a little. You had me investigated before you ever made your big move on me, didn't you?"

"Hell yes. I'd investigate the pope if his life touched Jase's life." He stood up and put the length of the room between them, his eyes alive with the suppressed rage that was always swirling so close when he confronted his own demons.

She stared up at him for a long moment. "You investigated Jase too, didn't you?"

"I'm not about to apologize for it either, Doc. You have no idea what our lives were like." He stopped abruptly, going very still, watching her expression. "Or do you? How do you know things?"

Maia hesitated. She was going to ruin her chances of ever being a permanent veterinarian anywhere if she told him.

"It's important. Do you really know things? Would you know if Jase drove that horse into the fence? Or if I did it?" How could she know?

Maia caught a glimpse of the fear in him, and it all fell into place. He suspected Jase of being like their father. It made sense. "It wasn't Jase. The man was too big." She didn't want to continue, but she couldn't let him think such a monstrous thing.

"How do you know?"

"The animals."

The room went totally silent. Maia shifted deeper into the cushions, trying to avoid seeing the look she knew would be in his eyes. She pressed her fingers into her eyes in an effort to relieve the headache that continued to pound.

Cole studied her face for a long time. "You mean they really do talk to you?" he asked, trying hard to keep skepticism from his voice. She was being serious and waiting for him to scoff at her. Maia Armstrong had secrets; it was there in her eyes, in the way she avoided looking at him, and he intended to find out what they were.

"Not exactly," she hedged. "Look, do we have to do this? Is it really necessary?"

"You know things about me no one else knows. Hell you know more about the Steele family than most people do. What are you afraid of?"

"I'm a veterinarian, Steele. You think people are going to want some nutcase treating their animals? And that's what they'll call me." She didn't have to tell him anything. She could stare him down, tell him to go to hell, be stubbornly silent. Maia was capable of all of those things. So why was she sitting there like some sacrifice, waiting for the axe to fall?

"No one is here but the two of us." Cole was back in front of her, crouching down, his hand on her knee. His piercing blue eyes caught and held her gaze as if to give her courage. "How do the animals talk to you?" Could it really be possible? There was no getting around the fact that several animals had run out in front of his vehicle as he drove through the blizzard to get to the ranch, and each time she had known they were there before they could actually see them.

Maia shook her head, but couldn't look away from him. There was no escaping Cole Steele and his brother, or their pain, shrieking at her from the depths of their being.

"Telling you the truth about working for the DEA wasn't so bad once I did it. It was actually a relief to tell you the truth. I don't talk about the old man and my childhood, but now you know, and I don't have to worry that somehow I'll slip up and you'll find out things that I've kept hidden away."

"It isn't the same thing, Cole."

"Just say it, Maia. You know I'm going to badger you until you do."

It was the way he said her name. A caress. A silky, satin tone that brushed over her skin and slipped inside of her. Disarmed her. He always called her "Doc" and somehow by using her first name it created an intimacy between them. A trust. "I see their memories. I don't know how, but I've always been able to see things they've seen. The memories come to me in images, very vivid and, most of the time, very distressing."

He caught her chin in his hand, forcing her to look at him. "Why would you be afraid to tell me?"

Maia pulled away from him, shrinking back against the thickly upholstered couch. "Most people would just think I was crazy." She shook her head, her gaze avoiding his. "I know it sounds crazy." Why had she even admitted it? What was wrong with her? She knew better than to say anything. Cole Steele of all people. What was she thinking?

"Tell me what Wally saw."

Maia's gaze jumped to his. Held there. "A young boy dragged from the stable, kicked, beaten around the head and shoulders. Something thin and long hitting the child over and over. The boy screaming. The man was about your height, but thinner. Once he dragged the boy out by his hair. He slapped him repeatedly in the face." She swallowed, rubbed her hand over her face as if to clear away the memories. "The boy was Jase and the abuse didn't just happen once." She pressed her fingertips against her eyelids again as if she could shut out the vision. "I hate that I know these things because there's never anything I can do about it."

Cole's palm curved around the nape of her neck, his fingers massaging the tension out of her. "It never occurred to me that animals would be witnessing crimes."

"Just because they can't talk doesn't mean they don't see things."

Cole turned over her revelation in his mind, over and over. It was a fascinating premise. Could it be true? He had his hand on her, could feel the tension running through her body. She was waiting for him to scoff at her, yet the idea that she could really "see" memories of an animal was bizarre. She could easily have guessed the things that had happened to Jase.

"What about the attack on the horse? Who drove him into the fence?"

"A large man, tall with wide shoulders. It couldn't have been Jase. He's small and thin, and Wally likes him."

"Tall like me, you mean," Cole said, his voice cool.

"Yes, but Wally likes you too." It sounded so stupid. Utterly ridiculous. Maia shook her head, her face flaming. "I know it sounds weird. Go ahead, tell me I belong in a mental institution."

The pad of his thumb absently stroked her pulse. Each brush sent small tongues of fire licking over her skin. Electricity seemed to leap from his skin to hers. She forced air through her lungs, waiting for him to react. Waiting for his condemnation.

"Who told you that you were crazy?" he asked quietly.

She flinched. She tried not to, but she couldn't prevent her reaction. "Does it matter? It does sound crazy."

"I think so."

She lifted her chin, her turquoise eyes blazing into his. "A man I dated. Another vet. I thought we were close, and he asked me how I managed to figure out what was wrong all the time with wild animals, and I was dumb enough to answer him."

"And he said you were crazy?"

"I don't blame him. Unfortunately, he told everyone at the clinic, including the pet owners, and I was out of work. That I did blame him for."

Cole leaned in close and brushed his lips, feather-light over hers. Her heart somersaulted. "He was the idiot, Maia." He pulled back slightly, blinking so that her attention was drawn from his mouth to his lashes. He was so masculine, but for those incredible eyelashes. She wanted to touch his face, to feel his skin. Cole Steele was totally mesmerizing, and she could see why women fell so easily under his spell.

"You're way out of my league, Steele. Sit over there somewhere and stop touching me." She pointed to a chair across the room.

"Am I getting to you?" A ghost of a smile flickered over his mouth for the briefest of moments.

Maia's heart stuttered in reaction. She'd never seen him

smile, and she couldn't actually call the curve to his lips a smile, it hadn't lit his blue eyes, but it was enough for her to know if he ever did, she would melt. "Yes."

Cole didn't move, his gaze going hot as it moved over her face, focusing on her mouth. "It's about time."

"Stop that." His mouth was only a scant few inches from hers. She could feel the warmth of his breath. His body leaned into hers, his chest bumped against her knees. His palm was still curled around the nape of her neck, and his thumb swept over her jaw. Her stomach tightened. "You're dangerous." Her voice came out in a whisper. An ache.

"I thought I was, but I've changed my mind." His lips brushed a second time over hers. Teasing. A caress that wasn't quite a caress. "I've decided you're the dangerous one. I tell myself to stay away from you, but I just can't seem to do it." His lips tempted hers again. Firming. Coaxing. His tongue stroked across the seam of her mouth. His teeth tugged on her lower lip.

Maia gasped and let him in. Let him stake his claim. His mouth pressed firmly against her, hot and moist and all too expert. Somehow he wedged his body between her legs, pulling her close, his arms strong as they wrapped around her. Her body went boneless, the heat leaping like a wildfire between them.

His fingers snagged in her hair and she yelped. They pulled apart, staring at one another, Maia gulping for air. His fingertips moved gently over her scalp. "I'm sorry, I got carried away."

"I'll say you did!" Jase's voice was stern.

Cole turned to find the boy leaning his hip against the doorway, his arms across his chest, a frown on his face.

"Would either of you like to tell me what's going on?" Jase asked straight-faced, effectively reducing his older brother to a teenager caught necking.

"I'd rather not," Maia said, trying not to laugh.

"I have absolutely no idea what's going on," Cole admitted. "But, whatever it is, it's her fault." He couldn't stop looking at her, mesmerized by the warm laughter in her eyes, the curve of her mouth. She hadn't lived a perfect life, he had felt the sadness, the wariness in her when she talked about the strange ability she had of reading images in the minds of animals, yet she still found joy in life. She made him want to laugh with her. He wasn't certain he was capable of laughter, but he felt himself wanting to be.

"Hey now, don't you go blaming anything on me," Maia objected. "Honestly, Jase. He started it." She rubbed her mouth. "At least I think he did, I can't remember now. But he's such a flirt."

"He said he doesn't have to smile at women," Jase reported. He was trying desperately to make up for the accusations he'd leveled at his brother earlier. Unsure of himself, he followed Maia's lead, teasing Cole.

Maia's eyebrow shot up. Cole sank back on his knees, groaning aloud. "Jase. That was a brotherly confidence you weren't supposed to share." He looked at Maia. "We're still trying to get the hang of being brothers. Neither of us knows a lot about it yet, but I'm certain that was confidential."

"Brotherly advice?" Maia asked.

"Something like that," Cole admitted.

Maia shook her head. "Don't listen to him, Jase. Women like men to smile once in a while. They can only take brooding hunks for so long, then they get bored."

"You didn't look bored to me," Jase pointed out, abruptly switching sides.

Maia laughed again, and the sound wound itself around Cole's heart and warmed his insides.

"*And*," Jase added, "it's rather sickening to hear my brother referred to as a hunk."

"She did call me that, didn't she?" Cole said with evident satisfaction.

"No one said you weren't a hunk," Maia's blue-green eyes darkened as her gaze drifted over him with deliberate inspection. "But just because I noticed that you were hot doesn't mean I liked you kissing me."

Jase snorted. "She liked it.

Cole nodded. "Yeah, I know."

"So did you." Jase grinned at him mischievously.

"Way too much. The doc is one of those dangerous women your elders are always going to be warning you about."

Maia shoved at Cole with her foot. "I love the way you manage to turn the tables on me. I'm injured here. You're supposed to be soothing me, not stirring things up."

Cole raised his eyebrow at her, his eyes going dark. "I don't think I'll touch that." He went back up on his knees to examine the back of her head. "The ice seems to have done its job and stopped the bleeding and the swelling."

"Well good thing, since you weren't paying attention," Maia scolded.

"I had better things to do." Ignoring her wince, he pushed the matted hair from the cut. "I don't think it needs stitches."

Maia jerked her head away. "Since I'm the only one capable of stitching anything, I should say not."

"I can stitch a wound if I have to. I sewed up my arm once," Cole said.

Jase and Maia exchanged a long frown. Maia wrinkled her nose. "Don't tell us anything else. I'm going to have nightmares."

"I ran into a guard down in Colombia. He had a big knife. He wasn't supposed to be there, and I got careless."

Maia reached out and pushed up the sleeve of Cole's shirt to reveal a jagged scar about three inches long. "You aren't making it up."

"I don't make things up." Cole got to his feet with a sigh of regret. It was time for all of them to return to the real world. "Jase, did you and Al go riding the other day? The day Wally was injured?"

Jase shook his head. "No, the hands took care of the cattle, and Al stayed with me working around the ranch house. We saw the fence over by the corrals leaning and we repaired that. I nearly fell actually, but Al caught me before I went down the hill. The post was rotten or something and gave way. I discovered Wally a couple of hours later when I came back to the ranch house to put away the tools. I called Al, and he came right away."

Cole sighed. Someone had taken the horse out earlier. Either Jase was lying to him or something he didn't understand was going on. "I didn't like the look of the walkway this morning, Jase. It's too much of a coincidence to have the horse injured and the walkway iced and the fence post give way when you leaned against it. I don't like any of it."

"What are saying?" Jase asked.

Maia could see the fear creeping back into the boy's eyes and it saddened her. For a few minutes, he had been a normal teenager, teasing an older brother.

"I'm just saying we're stuck here until this series of storms passes, and I want you to be careful," Cole said. "We should stick together when we go outside."

"Cole, who else is on the ranch? You told me no one was here other than the three of us," Maia said. "Is it possible you're being . . ." She broke off when his gaze swept over her face. The dark hunger was gone. His eyes were back to ice-cold, piercing blue.

"Paranoid? Maybe. But it's how I stay alive. I don't know what's happening, and until I do I just want to err on the side of caution." He stood beside Jase, clapping a hand briefly on his shoulder. "That doesn't mean we can't have fun, or do the Christmas thing, it just means we stick closer together if we go outside. We can share the work and keep an eye on the doc when she's looking at the horse for us."

"I came down here to tell the doc that my mother's things are in the attic," Jase said. "There's a chest up there that might have a few Christmas ornaments in it."

Cole glanced at Maia's face, trying to get something from her. He wasn't certain what it was. Reassurance maybe. Courage. The thought of decorating the house turned his stomach.

"I'd love to see some of your mother's things, Jase," Maia said with her usual warmth. Her gaze was on Cole, watching his face closely, reading too much.

He presented a stone carving to the world, a man invincible, one who had no fear, yet she seemed to see through the barrier between him and the rest of the world. The one woman he wanted to impress. The *only* woman who got under his skin and threatened to turn his carefully ordered world upside down was the one who saw him vulnerable.

Maia sighed. "Jase, you ever notice Cole can look scary?"

"I told him he did," Jase said, with a triumphant grin toward Cole. "Just last week I told him that."

"He does it when he's losing a battle."

Cole raised an eyebrow. "I don't lose battles. Don't be telling the boy a thing like that." A part of Cole stood off to the side, observing the banter, the way Maia seemed to be able to bring them all together when there was always such a distance between him and everyone else. A distance between Jase and everyone else. He wished he knew how she did it.

No one had ever teased him before. Even his coworkers refrained from venturing into personal territory with him, but Maia had no problem giving him a bad time. He reached out, tucked a stray strand of hair behind her ear before he could stop himself. He wanted to touch her, to feel her skin. He ached for her. Cole pulled himself up short. He was beginning to want more than her body. He found himself looking for her smile, listening for her laughter, watching the expressions chase across her face.

Jase's rude snort of derision dragged him from his thoughts. "You've got it bad, Cole. You're a goner."

Cole couldn't take exception when he heard the laughter in the boy's voice. It was genuine and even affectionate. Maia had managed to put it there somehow. He turned away from both of them, a lump in his throat. "I'm denying everything," he managed to get out. His voice was husky, and he knew if he looked at her, Maia would have a small knowing smile on her face.

"What are we going to do with the doc?" Jase asked.

"She can just sit there holding the ice pack, and we'll go up to the attic and get this box you want. I finished feeding the horses before I came in. Al's got the cattle under shelter with plenty of feed, so we're good for a few hours. We may as well start figuring out what we're supposed to do about Christmas."

Maia's laughter came again. "You sound like a man about to be hung. Christmas is *fun*, Steele, not a funeral. Jase, the man has such an Eeyore attitude."

Cole swung around. "*Eeyore?* You just called me *Eeyore*."

Jase burst out laughing, joining Maia. The sound drifted through the ranch house, dispelling the cold, barren feeling and replacing it with a warmth that had never been there before.

chapter 8

COLE DUSTED OFF THE BOX before he brought it down to Maia. Jase had obviously managed to remove things he'd treasured and conceal them before his father could throw them out. It said a lot about the boy's courage. He'd only been ten when his mother had been killed. He must have been terrified to defy his father and gather her things. The housekeeper would have reported it had she seen him, and there were the cameras to avoid, yet the boy had managed to keep a few precious items. As Cole placed the box carefully in front of Maia, he realized his genuine affection for the boy was growing. And that was frightening.

He couldn't warn Maia how much the contents of the box meant to Jase because the teenager was right beside him, anxiously watching his every move. He could only hope she would notice as she seemed so aware of every little nuance involving the boy.

"This is wonderful, Jase," Maia said, warmth and enthusiasm spilling over into the room. "Like discovering a treasure box. How ever did you know it was up there?"

Cole let his breath out. "He managed to put up there when he was ten, right after he lost his mother."

Maia looked up at the gruff note in Cole's voice. "I'll be very careful going through it, Jase, don't worry." She slipped off the couch and sat tailor fashion on the floor beside the box. "Do you remember what you put in here?"

Jase sank down beside her. "Yeah. I never went up to the attic, although I thought about it a lot, but I was afraid the old man would catch me and throw it all out." He glanced at Cole fearfully as if he might be revealing too much.

"That was smart," Cole said. "If he caught you, there would have been hell to pay. While you're looking over what we have, why don't I fix us something to eat. How's the head feeling, Doc?" He needed her to look at him. He had to know Jase was safe with her, but he had to get out of the room before that box was opened.

His blue gaze met and clung to hers. Maia sat very still, letting the heat in his eyes wash through her. She saw into a part of him he tried so hard to hide. Ravaged. Damaged. A man struggling to overcome his own past in order to save a boy. She didn't want to see it because it only drew her deeper into the lives of the Steeles and she didn't want that. She'd disclosed too much to him already. Kissed him when she should have resisted. She ached for the boy he'd been and the man he'd become. "A bit of a headache, nothing serious," she answered.

Jase watched Cole leave the room. "He says it's okay to celebrate Christmas; I don't think he really wants to."

"Maybe he needs to celebrate it, Jase," Maia said. "He's a grown man, and he's quite capable of deciding what he does and doesn't want to do. If he's given you the go-ahead, then he must want to celebrate the holiday as well. And isn't it about time? Christmas is a special time of year.

I love the way it brings everyone together. It's a time for family. Cole never really had a chance to have a family before, but now he has you." Carefully, she began to open the box.

"Do you have a family waiting for you to get home?"

"Not anymore. I was an only child. My parents died when I was sixteen, and I went to live with my grandmother. I lost her a few years ago. No cousins, no aunts or uncles. I'm pretty much it."

"That must be awful for you not to have someone to be with when you love it so much."

Maia smiled at him. "I would prefer to have a huge family, but since I don't, I find ways to celebrate."

"My father hated Christmas," Jase began in a rush. "He was really mean around Christmas, and he forbade us to ever have a tree or presents or decorations. If Mom gave me a present, he threw it away and he . . ." Jase trailed off. "Mom was like you."

"She loved Christmas?" Maia pulled open the flaps of the box, nearly holding her breath, careful not to look at Jase.

"Yeah. She used to sneak me presents, and when we were alone she'd show me the decorations her mother had given her. They'd been in her family a long time. She loved the ornaments and always wanted them on a tree. She used to tell me we'd put them on a tree together someday, but we never did. If she'd tried to do that, my father would have smashed them . . . and her."

Maia took a deep breath and let it out slowly, praying she could come up with the right words for Jase. The pain and horror and guilt of a young boy being the cause of his adored mother being "smashed" by his abusive father were in Jase's voice. Despair and helplessness, love and regret were in his eyes. She was determined to find a way to heal the pain in the boy she was growing so fond of.

"We can do it for her, Jase. This was her house too, wasn't it? We can give it back to her. If you tell me the things she loved, we can redecorate and make it your mother's home the way she wanted it. The way it should have been." Maia leaned toward him. "You asked me how I celebrate. Well, I always do something fun, but I want to do something for someone. Let's do it for your mother."

"But she's dead."

"You think about her every day don't you?"

Jase nodded.

"Then she'll never be dead. It doesn't matter whether you believe in another life after this one, Jase, only that she's alive through you. She wanted to celebrate Christmas and we can give her this. If you want to do it. As long as you're comfortable with it." Without waiting for an answer, Maia looked into the box. Everything was carefully wrapped in paper. She could tell the tissue was old and that Jase's mother had been the one to preserve many of the items originally. Jase had simply done what his mother had taught him. Several tissue-wrapped items lay on a folded quilt. She lifted the first one out of the box, brought it to her lap, and gently began to unwrap it.

Beside Maia, Jase audibly drew in his breath, his body tensing as she slowly drew back the tissue paper to reveal the treasure it protected. The ornament was beautiful, a shimmering star, platinum and covered with glass sparkles that reflected light from every angle so that it seemed to shine on its own right there in her hand. She held it up.

"I remember that star," Jase said. "She took it out and held it up just like you're doing. She said when she was young her mother always put it near the top of the tree closest to the lights so it would shine all the time."

"Where are we going to get a tree? We might have to improvise," Maia said.

Cole had been listening just outside the entryway, unable to stay away. He sighed, knowing she was drawing him deeper into unknown territory. He moved back into the room to stand in front of her. "We'll manage a tree, Doc. There's bound to be a break or two in between storms."

"You'll really get a tree, Cole? Bring it in the house?" Jase asked.

"Sure. We can put it in front of the window. I doubt if you have enough decorations for a big one, but we can improvise."

Maia put the star carefully to one side and reached for a second ornament. "We'll have fun making ornaments. And I checked out the kitchen. You're certainly not short on food supplies. We can bake all kinds of things and probably cook a traditional Christmas dinner as well."

"I like the sound of that," Jase said. "I'm hungry all the time."

"He's a bottomless pit," Cole confirmed. "We bring in more groceries than we do feed for the stock."

Jase was thin, even for a teenager. Maia could imagine that he was just beginning to trust enough and be confident enough in his relationship with Cole to regain his appetite. She leaned back against the couch as she held up the second ornament. It was an alligator with a red knitted scarf circling the neck. The jaws of the alligator opened and closed when she turned the tip of the tail.

"Why would someone have an alligator hanging on the tree?" Cole asked, taking it from her to examine it closely. "I thought you always had Santa Claus and things like that. This is pretty cool."

"Mom was from Louisiana," Jase reminded. "She used to pretend the alligator was going to bite my finger. She said it was to remind her of home."

"What else is in there?" Cole asked, curious. He had never really looked at any Christmas ornaments before, avoiding the decorated trees in the stores wherever he happened to be when the holiday rolled around. For most of his life he'd told himself it was stupid, hanging things on trees, but the little alligator evoking the memories of Jase's mother seemed different.

Maia handed him the next ornament, a crystal crescent moon with a small baby lying inside the curve of the moon and a little silver star hanging off the tip. It was dated fourteen years earlier. Cole turned it over and over. He looked at Jase. "This is commemorating when you were born. I wish I'd had the chance to meet your mother, Jase."

"Too bad we can't get to town," Maia said, struggling to keep tears from flooding her eyes. She might have lost her family, but when she had one, it had been wonderful. She'd been raised to feel secure and loved by her parents and grandmother. "This will be the first Christmas you're opending together as a family. We could have picked up an ornament celebrating that."

"I would have liked that," Jase said, taking the small crystal moon from Cole.

"The great thing about not having a tradition is, you get to start your own," Maia pointed out.

"We don't need to go to a store," Cole said gruffly. "I can carve an ornament for us. What do you think it should be?"

"Cole's a great wood-carver," Jase said. "You should see some of the things he's done. Something to do with a horse, Cole. Can you do that?"

"I can come up with something."

"Carve the date into it," Maia advised.

"Dinner's ready if you two want to eat something." Cole said to hide how uncomfortable he was with the way the conversation was going. Have someone take a few shots at him with a gun, and he was on familiar ground, but he was feeling his way with Jase, trying to give his brother a sense of security and home. He couldn't believe he'd opened his mouth and offered to carve a Christmas ornament.

He shoved his hands through his hair in sudden agitation. He didn't even know what a home was. Who was he kidding? He was beginning to sweat just thinking about night coming. They'd arisen late after staying up taking care of the horse, and now the afternoon was waning. He glanced out the window. The snow was coming down endlessly, large flakes that held them prisoner at the ranch. He hated the place. How could bringing in a tree and hanging a few ornaments change that?

Maia set the ornaments back in the box. "After dinner we should build a fire," she said, indicating the huge stone fireplace that was a showpiece along the center of one wall.

Jase drew in his breath audibly, his shoulders stiffening and his face paling.

Cole stood up. "I don't think there's ever been a fire in

the fireplace." He reached down and with his casual strength, pulled her up. He drew her body close to his, bending over her to examine the back of her head. "You have quite a bump there."

"And a headache, but it will go away." She knew better than to look up at him with his face so close to hers, but the temptation was too much. Her gaze met his. His eyes had once again darkened. She put her hand on his chest to keep a few inches between her and the heat of his body. Just for protection. If she knew any incantations for self-defense, she would have been chanting them. "What's the use of having a fireplace if you never light a fire?"

Cole exchanged a long look with Jase, even as his hand came up to capture Maia's. To press her palm tighter against his heart. "Good question."

"You think we should try to light a fire?" Jase was breathing too fast, almost gasping for air. He actually looked scared, searching the living room as if someone might have heard them talking.

"Calm down," Cole said gently. "You're starting to wheeze. He's dead, Jase. Keep telling yourself that. This is our house now, and we can have a damned fire in the fireplace if we want to have one." He allowed Maia escape him. "You're right. We have a ghost in the house, and I want him gone."

Jase slowed his breathing, following Cole's direction until the wheezing was gone. "All right, we'll light the fire."

Maia followed them into the kitchen. Cole swept his arm briefly around Jase's shoulders. It was momentary, but he'd done it obviously without thinking about it and that pleased her. "I'm sorry if I'm stepping on everyone here," she said. "I'm not trying to push anything on the two of you. You're both obviously uncomfortable with having a fire. We don't need one. Please don't change everything for me. It's your home, do whatever makes you comfortable."

"Our father liked to brand things," Cole said. "Including people."

Maia winced at the grim tone. She stared in horror first at Cole, then Jase. "No way." She felt sick, actually sick.

The brothers nodded.

How did anyone survive such a childhood? Who was she to tell them how to get over it? Horrified at the things she'd said to Cole, she gripped the back of a chair, her knuckles white. "Please don't feel like you have to celebrate Christmas for me. Is that what you're doing?"

Jase shook his head adamantly. "No, I want to celebrate it for my mother. I thought a lot about what you said. She loved this house. He wouldn't let her have any of the things she wanted in it, but she would tell me what she'd put in spots if she had her way. She wanted cream-colored drapes in the library. She said they'd look great with the wood."

"Cream-colored drapes? I guess we're going to change the drapes." Cole raised his eyebrows at Maia. "You know anything about drapes?"

She laughed just like he knew she would. "Don't panic. We're grown-up. We can figure out how to fit drapes." Maia didn't feel like laughing, but Cole was trying to bring back levity for Jase's sake, and she was more than willing to help him.

Cole knew he could get used to the way the house felt with her in it. Jase set the table, and Cole pulled a chair around for Maia. "Sit down. You're looking a little pale. I'll see to the horse tonight. Maybe you should have let me put a couple of stitches in that cut on your head."

"I don't think so." She glared at him. "You come near me with a needle, and you'll find out how mean I can be."

Jase snorted. "You're a baby, Doc."

"Oh, like you'd let him sew up your head! I'd wind up looking like Frankenstein's mother."

Jase grinned at Cole. "She'd make a great monster, don't you think?"

"Great, just like the *The Nightmare Before Christmas*. I'm Sally."

Jase and Cole exchanged a puzzled look. Both shrugged, nearly at exactly the same moment.

Maia groaned. "Don't tell me you're both so deprived you never saw that movie? Good grief. Live a little. Rent it. I'll even spring for it."

"Yeah, she says that now with the snow coming down, but once the roads are clear, she's going to renege," Cole said. "Eat your steak."

"I don't eat meat, but the salad's wonderful," Maia said politely.

Jase took one look at Cole's face and burst out laughing. "I wish I had a camera."

"And why don't you eat meat?"

Maia made a face at him. "I told you why."

"I guess I could understand if animals talk to you all the time," Cole teased.

The tone was gruff, but Maia was pleased he'd actually managed to say something to kid her. She tried to keep a stern face, but she knew her eyes gave her away every time. When she wanted to laugh, it always showed.

"You wouldn't want to eat your clients," Jase added.

"Oh you two are a laugh a minute," Maia said. "You should take your little comedy act out on the road."

"She's getting grouchy. Must be the headache. Women, by the way"—Cole leaned across the table toward Jase, to impart his wisdom in a conspirator's overloud whisper—"get headaches a lot."

Jase's grin widened.

Maia lifted an eyebrow. "Really? I wouldn't have thought you'd get that reaction, Steele, but now that I've spent time with you, I can see it."

Jase nearly fell off his chair laughing, so much so that Cole rolled up a newspaper and smacked him over the head.

"It's not that funny, little bro."

"If I'm little, what's Maia? I'm taller than she is."

"Everything is taller than Maia."

Maia managed an indignant glare. "I'm not short. I happen to be the perfect height. Sheesh, not everyone has to be a moose."

"Now she's calling you a moose," Jase said. He was laughing so hard he was beginning to wheeze.

Cole reached out and put a calming hand on his shoulder. "She's going to kick off an asthma attack if you're not careful, and she'll be chasing you around the house with that needle she uses on the horse. Take a breath, Jase. Use your inhaler if you have to."

Although he was automatically breathing slow, deep breaths to aid his younger brother, Cole was watching Maia as well. She was clearly becoming distracted, trying to stay in the conversation, but bothered by something he couldn't hear or see.

"What is it, Doc?"

The smile faded from her face, and she turned her head toward the kitchen door. "Do you have a patio out there, a shelter?"

"Of course. Everything is connected by walkways to the house," Cole said. "That way, when it snows, there's no way to get lost."

Maia stood up, pushing back her chair. "I'll be right back."

Jase was startled out of his wheezing when she left the room. "What's she up to, Cole?"

"Lord only knows," Cole said, but he glanced toward the kitchen door. The sound of the wind and tree branches hitting the house could be heard, but nothing else.

"I like having her here," Jase confided.

"So do I." Cole realized it was true. He never spent so much time in anyone's company. Jase had been the first real commitment he'd made outside of his job. Maia brightened the house, brought warmth and laughter and a sense of home. His heart lurched at the idea. "Do you think any woman would make this place feel the way she makes it, or just the doc?" He kept his voice very neutral but found his stomach was tied up in knots. The kid mattered to him, even his opinion mattered, and that realization was almost as shocking.

Jase shook his head. "It's definitely the doc. I like her a lot, Cole."

Cole crumpled his napkin and threw it on the table. "Yeah, I do too."

Jase frowned. "You don't sound too happy about it."

"Would you be? Hell, look at us, Jase. We're about as dysfunctional as two men could get. You think the doc is going to be looking at me. I can't even make up my mind if I want her to." He shoved his chair back.

"She kissed you," Jase pointed out. "Do you think she kisses everyone?"

Cole's entire body tensed, every muscle contracting. The knots in his belly hardened into lethal lumps. "She'd better not be kissing everyone," Cole said. There was enough of an edge to his voice that Jase looked wary.

"Are you angry, Cole?"

"I just don't trust anything I don't understand, Jase. I don't altogether understand the doc or how she makes me feel." Telling the kid the truth wasn't as easy as he thought it would be when he'd first made the promise to himself. He hadn't counted on meeting Maia Armstrong and feeling so intensely about her.

"Well talk nice to her," Jase advised. "Otherwise, you'll scare her off."

"Scare whom off?" Maia asked as she came back into the room carrying her small bag. She was dressed in a thick coat and mittens. "If you're talking about me, Jase, your brother doesn't scare me. He's all growl and no bite."

"Where the hell do you think you're going?"

Jase groaned and shook his head, covering his face with his hands. "Do you ever listen? Even I know you can't talk to women like that."

"Thank you, Jase," Maia said. "You know, Cole, if you took a few lessons from your younger brother, you might develop a certain charm."

"Just answer me."

Maia sighed, color washing into her face. "I have to make a call."

"A call? What the hell?"

"You already said that. Didn't he say that, Jase? Yes, a call. I heard an animal, and I'm going to go see what's wrong."

"I didn't hear anything," Jase said, frowning slightly.

Cole ignored his younger brother, his gaze holding Maia to him. "Didn't you pay any attention to me saying I wanted everyone to stick together when we went outside?"

Maia winced a little at his sharp tone. "Yes, of course I did." Truthfully the moment she heard the call of an animal in distress she hadn't thought of anything else. "I'm just going out onto the patio. You can come if you want, but you'll have to stay quiet."

His blue eyes slashed her as she gave the order, but she didn't look away, staring right back at him, refusing to be intimidated.

Jase jumped up with determination. "I'm coming too."

"You just don't want to do the dishes," Cole said.

The two grabbed jackets and gloves from the rack just outside the door in the small mudroom as they followed Maia out. Cole hung back watching as she stood on the large covered patio looking out into the snow. She didn't call out, and he heard nothing, but she suddenly turned her head toward the north and stepped off the patio into the snow. He moved quickly, catching her arm.

"Maia, call whatever it is to you. You can't go out into this. Jase and I will hang back out of the way, but you stay undercover."

The storm had let up some, but it had dropped several feet of snow, and with the next serious storm approaching fast, he didn't want to take any chances.

"I'm not sure it will come to me with the two of you so close," she said.

"At least try."

She hesitated a moment, glanced at Jase, then complied, whistling softly as if calling a dog. The sound of the wind answered her. Snowflakes fell in a continuous soft drift, muffling sounds of the night.

"I'm going to have to go out to it," she persisted.

Cole retained possession of her arm. Something was moving just outside his range of vision, the fall of snow nearly obscuring it. "Stay here. I want you where I can see you at all times." He whispered it, straining to see beyond the veil of white.

Beneath his fingers, Maia suddenly tensed and stepped away from him, moving to the very edge of the patio. "She's coming in."

Cole felt the hairs on his body raise. He moved closer to Jase, shifting his body to place himself between the unknown and his brother. What he wanted to do was drag Maia back into the safety of the house. While the snow was white and seemed to sparkle everywhere, the clouds were dark and ominous with the continuing threat of the blizzard. He didn't know if that was what triggered his protective instincts or whether it was sheer self-preservation, but his warning radar was shrieking.

The mountain lion emerged out of the snowdrift, covered in flakes, ears flat, eyes alert and watchful. The yellow-green gaze settled not on Maia, but on the Steele brothers.

"Maia." Cole reached out and caught the back of her coat, giving it a small tug to try to bring her to him. "Jase, back into the house. Come on, Maia. This is dangerous."

"No," Maia kept her tone low and almost crooning. "She's coming to us. She's feeling threatened, and any movement on your part will have her running away. Just stay calm and don't move." As she spoke, Maia knelt and patted the patio beside her.

Nearly belly to the ground, the cat inched its way to her, using a freeze-frame stalking motion, never taking its gaze from the men. The cat crouched rather than stretched out, presenting its left side to the veterinarian, but obviously ready to spring away quickly should there be need. Maia put her hand on the cat's back, fingers sliding into the rich fur.

Cole pressed one hand to his heart and slid the other down to his calf, where his gun was stashed.

Maia allowed the images from the mountain lion to crowd into her mind. Something moving through the air, nearly over the top of her. A loud noise that had the cat snarling. Men and horses. The scent of man invading her territory. The sting in her side that spread pain through her body and slowed her down, accompanied by the sound of the rifle.

"She's been shot," she said quietly.

Maia took a deep slow breath. "It isn't as if I can keep her from going against her natural instincts. If you are going to watch this, please don't turn your back on her and don't stare directly into her eyes. I sometimes look them in the eyes, but I have some strange affinity for wild animals." She kept her voice crooning, as if talking to the cat.

"The wound is in her shoulder which is a good thing. I'm going to give her both Rompom and Ketamine to knock her out. Jase, it's always much harder with exotics, particularly large cats. Normally you have to dart them, and the problem is, they are very hard to dart down because there is no set dosage even if they're the same age and height, the normal criteria for dosing an animal or even a human. It's different with them because their adrenaline is pumping very fast. It's rare to take a large cat down with one dart." As she spoke she was preparing the shot.

"Maia." Cole didn't like her in such close proximity, yet she was moving with confidence.

"Please don't talk. This is very hard on her. She trusts me, but not you. You have to look at the body language of a cat to know what's going on inside of them." She set the dose of Ketamine aside and withdrew a second syringe. "This is yohimbe, Jase. You *always* have it ready when you're working with exotics. The danger is, they'll fight the drug until they finally drop, but then, as they relax, they can go into cardiac arrest. I think she'll be fine, she isn't fighting it, but we have to be ready. Yohimbe reverses the Ketamine. I'm giving the injection in the muscle and it will sting, so expect a reaction and don't move. Once she's out, you can get close to her."

Cole kept the gun hidden along his thigh. His heart was pounding in fear, and his mouth was dry, not for himself, or even Jase, but because the sight of Maia so close to the wild animal was terrifying.

Maia caught the head of the cat in her hands and leaned forward nose to nose, her face inches from the cat's teeth. She seemed to exchange breath with the animal, obviously communicating in some way, but Cole's fingers tightened around the gun. It took a tremendous effort to keep from aiming it at the animal. Maia put her hand on the cat's heart as if matching her own heartbeat with the mountain lion.

Maia pulled back to pick up the syringe. The cat yowled as she administered it. "I know, baby," she said softly, "it stings, doesn't it? Just go with it and get sleepy for me." She glanced over her shoulder. "I need to work fast, this won't keep her under for long."

"Can we help?" Cole asked, shoving the gun back into his holster.

"Remember how I mixed the Betadine and saline? You can do that while I give her fluid. It's going to balloon up at the site, Jase, but the lump will dissipate as the fluid is absorbed in the cat's body. I'm giving her a sub queue of lactated Ringer's solution for dehydration. It's hard to find a vein on the big cats, but they absorb liquid under the skin. I'm putting in the fluids right here in this area."

"Do you want me to put this in a syringe like we did for the horse?" Jase asked. He crouched quite close to Maia, almost nudging her out of the way.

"Yes. Use it to flush the wound site. The wound is on the trapezoid muscle, but it looks like the bullet just sliced it rather than penetrated." Maia turned her head toward Jase.

Cole could see they were nearly nose to nose. For some reason it put a lump in his throat. Something deep inside him shifted. Moved. Melted. He saw his young half brother, so starved for love and attention, turning to Maia. She seemed so willing to give the boy the things he needed. It came naturally to her. She imparted knowledge casually, and Jase soaked it up.

"You lavage it, and I'll debride the area. We want it sterile, just like with Wally."

"She's so big," Jase observed. "I've never seen a mountain lion other than in pictures before." There was awe in Jase's voice. Unable to help himself, just as curious as Jase, Cole crowded closer to see what they were doing.

"They're solitary animals, Jase," Maia explained. "The females are smaller than the males. This one probably weighs in around ninety-five pounds and most are somewhere between seventy-five to one hundred and twenty-five pounds, so she's average and healthy. A female will keep her cubs with her about year to a year and half. This one is still young, maybe two years old."

"Can I touch her?" Jase was already reaching out, his expression lit up with excitement. Cole had never seen him as fascinated or intrigued with anything. The boy moved even closer, actually bending over Maia to peer at what she was doing. She didn't seem to mind in the least, showing him what she was doing next.

"Sure, it's safe. She's out. Her eyes are open, but she's out." Maia squeezed ointment into the cat's eyes to prevent them from drying out. "She can't blink like this, so we have to do it for her."

"I've heard them scream before," Jase said. "It was like something out of a scary movie."

"Mountain lions purr, rather than roar like the other big cats do, and yes, they have a phenomenal scream," Maia said, guiding Jase's hand along the cat's back.

Cole watched the way her hands moved through the mountain lion's fur. He tasted envy in his mouth. Need. How did he become a part of such a thing?

Maia glanced at Cole over her shoulder. "You don't hunt them on this ranch, do you?"

"It's legal here in Wyoming," he said. His voice was strangling around the lump in his throat. "But since I've been here we certainly don't hunt them, and we wouldn't unless they went after our horses or cattle. Most stay in the high country." Forcing his mind to concentrate on details, he studied the cat, trying to determine, from the lacerated muscle, the angle the shooter had shot from. "How old is that wound?"

"It's fresh. Maybe twenty-four hours, a little longer, but not by much. Damn hunters. It's makes me so mad, they wound an animal and leave it to suffer."

"You're saying she was shot on this ranch yesterday or

the day before?" Cole's body touched hers, as he bent over her to get a closer look at the wound.

Maia glanced at him, recognizing the edge in his voice, the sudden alert interest. "She definitely was shot somewhere on the ranch.

"There was no one here but Al and me," Jase said. "I didn't hear a shot."

"It was probably miles from the ranch house," Cole said.

"I'm going to give her an injection of antibiotics, then we'll put them in her food and try to keep her here over the next few days," Maia deliberately changed the subject when she realized Jase was becoming agitated. She sent Cole a warning glance.

Cole shook his head. "Maia, this is a working ranch. You have any idea how dangerous that is? If you feed her, and you'll have to, she might want to come around here. And then we're going to have to shoot her anyway."

"I'll make certain she knows to stay in the high country."

He stepped even closer. "Fine. If I have to have it here, I want to pet it too." He felt stupid asking, but it was the chance of a lifetime. There was breathtaking beauty in the animal and a sense of raw power. The moment his fingers sank into the fur, he felt connected to it, and in some strange way, the mountain lion solidified his connection to Jase and Maia. He dropped his other hand on Maia's shoulder, needing to touch her as he took the unique opportunity to get close to a live mountain lion. Jase beamed at him. They exchanged a small grin. Maia was magic and mystery, and it was becoming difficult for Cole to focus his mind on anything else.

Maia's hand covered Cole's as he petted the cat's deep fur.

"Amazing. I've never had an experience like this." There was wonder in his voice, a boyish excitement, much like Jase's, yet there was that underlying dark sensuality he couldn't suppress. Seeing Maia with the cat, getting so close with Jase, just being herself seemed to bring it out in him.

Reluctantly, Maia pulled her hand away to reach for the needle. She had to avoid looking at Cole. Sharing the experience with him was a fantasy she'd always kept secret, sharing her love of exotic cats with a man she . . . Abruptly she pulled her mind away from the thought. "I'm suturing the wound, Jase," Maia continued. "If it were any older, there would be too much bacteria in it, but I'll leave a drain and use dissolving sutures. Hopefully we can keep as much air getting to it as possible."

"How'd you learn all this?" Jase asked eagerly. "This is what I want to do."

"I specialized in exotics as well as smaller animals. I actually interned in both Africa and Indochina," Maia said. "I may go back to specializing, but for the time being, the mobile clinic works for me."

Jase looked up at his brother, a grin on his face. "I know I could do this, Cole."

"I know you could too, Jase," Cole encouraged. Because Jase was so excited, the boy didn't even notice he was shaking with cold.

"Large cats can't be treated lightly, Jase," Maia said as she worked. "You always have to be aware that they are wild creatures, even the 'domesticated exotics.' You have to pay attention to body language all the time. And you have to be aware of what 'zone' they're in. I have a five-zone gauge I use to determine the risks of working with a wild animal. Things like bad weather, such as we have now, high winds, tornadoes, and such will drop them into the zone, and we're very much at risk. As she comes out from under the ketamine she'll be at her most dangerous because she'll be dopey and fearful. We don't want to be around for that."

"Where do you want to put her, Doc?" Cole asked, trying to be practical, trying to find a way to help, to be a part of what she was.

"Somewhere she'll be safe out of the storm and fairly warm, where I can easily check on her and feed her."

"We have the toolshed," Jase said. "It has heating coils in the floor although we never use them. We could lock her in there."

"You two get it ready while I finish up here. I wish I had a Fentanyl patch for pain, that would be the best, but I don't carry that with me. I'll have to use a combination of morphine and Valium instead. Hurry, she's going to start waking up, and she won't be a happy kitty."

Cole frowned. "I don't like you carrying any of those drugs around with you. It's too dangerous." He couldn't resist petting the cat a second time.

Jase and Maia exchanged a quick grin behind Cole's back, Maia rolling her eyes at his warning. She made no comment, knowing it was useless to argue with his protective bristling. She was a vet and needed the drugs. "Any ideas on how we're going to move her?" she asked.

"I can carry her," Cole said. "But she'd better not wake up and bite my face off."

"She won't. Let's go then. Is it far?"

"No. We'll use the main walkway, then have to use the cable to get to the shed, but it's only a few feet." Cole hesitated as he crouched beside the big mountain lion. "You're sure she's under?"

Maia took one last listen to the cat's heart and lungs. "Yes, let's go."

Cole would be lifting a deadweight and trudging a distance, part of it in deep snow. Maia didn't have to like it, but she couldn't think of any other way to transport the animal.

Using the covered walkway was easy enough, but Cole struggled a bit in the deep snow. Jase hurried ahead to get the shed ready and to kick on the heating coils. He snagged a couple of blankets from the barn and came running back with them as Cole staggered through the door.

"I feel her moving," he announced.

"Lay her down," Maia instructed, "and back off. We'll just let her be. You have something for water for her?"

"I have this old bucket," Jase said, and held it up.

"Good, we'll use that then. Come on, she's definitely coming around." Maia backed out and closed the door, leaving the mountain lion to wake up on its own.

She stretched tiredly. "I'm suddenly freezing."

"So is Jase," Cole said. "Let's get back to the house."

Cole stayed behind Maia, crowding her close as she followed Jase through the snow and the walkway back to the patio, where she collected her equipment. They entered the mudroom to remove jackets, mittens, and shoes. "I don't know about encouraging these wild animals to come around. What if that cougar decides Wally's an easy meal?"

"She won't," Maia said, trying to keep her teeth from chattering.

"That's the coolest thing I've ever seen," Jase said.

"I'd prefer you didn't mention it to anyone," Maia said.

"There sure is a lot of cool stuff I can't tell anyone," Jase groused.

She was shivering so much Cole pulled her against the warmth of his body and began to run his hands up and down her arms. "What are we going to feed her?"

"*I'm* going to need ten to fifteen pounds of beef or chicken for her daily. They eat bones and all, and they're *always* hungry. Jase, don't you go near her. She's a wild animal and injured, so she's unpredictable. I'll put her antibiotics in her food."

"What do you know about mountain lions, Cole?" Jase asked. "Do we have a lot of them around here?"

"We have our share, but honestly, I don't know that much about them at all."

"They are the second largest cat in the Western Hemisphere," Maia said, "and they're also the fastest. Unfortunately, they tire easily because their hearts don't match their size. They lose stamina in a long run and generally miss their kill nine out of ten times, which means a lot of hunting for them."

Cole stooped to pull off her boots. "I couldn't believe how powerful the animal felt to me. Just being in its presence was intense."

"Big cats are at the top of the food chain, so they have an 'arrogance' and mantle of power they wear like a second skin." Maia grinned at Cole. "Those of us who are drawn to them are often accused of being the same way."

"Great, are you saying I'm a predator? Or that you are?"

"Maybe parts of you are. You definitely have power, and you know it." Her smile widened. "I know I do."

"I was drawn to it too," Jase reminded, tossing his boots aside. "And I don't have any power at all."

"Sure you do. And there are people who believe animals come to you to give you messages. A mountain lion crossing your path is a sign you have power, and maybe it's time you should learn about yourself, strengthen and sharpen your own powers. That could be the message to you." Maia tried to get across to the boy that if he knew and could read the mountain lion, he could understand Cole and maybe himself a little better.

"Do you believe in that?" Cole asked.

Maia shrugged. "Cats fascinate and repel and inspire fear all at the same time in most people. Because of that, exotics are often labeled as magic or mystical."

"Don't you think people are fearful because they're in the presence of a predator, a natural killer?" Cole asked.

"Sure, subconsciously I'm sure they are, but it's that very energy that attracts people to the cats and gives them the mystique."

Cole opened the door to the kitchen and waved them through. "Does this kind of thing happen to you everywhere you go? Wild animals appearing out of nowhere?"

"Just about," Maia admitted with a small secret smile. She had turned a corner in the restaurant and run right into the Steele brothers. To her, they weren't that much different from the mountain lion. She rubbed at her arms in an effort to get warm. "I think my blood has turned to ice."

"Come on, let's get that fire built," Cole said, pulling her into the living room.

"Jase, would you get the doc a blanket? She's freezing."

Jase hesitated only a moment, clearly not wanting to miss anything, before he hurried off, taking the stairs two at a time.

"Cole," Maia waited until he turned to face her. He knelt in front of the massive fireplace, a log in his hand, his hair spilling across his forehead, and her stomach gave a curious flutter. "You don't have to do that."

"Actually I do. You're right, you know. It's silly not to use a fireplace just because the old man could be cruel. I'm hoping it gives the room a completely different atmosphere. Mostly I'm hoping Jase will like it."

"Someone should have done something about that man." Her voice was tight. She couldn't imagine how Brett Steele had gotten away with his vicious behavior for so long. How could the ranch hands and housekeeper look the other way?

"Someone did." Cole turned back to building a fire.

Maia studied him in silence, rubbing her chin on her knee as she watched him. His movements were all efficient, graceful. There were sharp edges to Cole's personality but none to his physical movements. He reminded her of the mountain lion, moving with fluid, sure strength. She loved just looking at him.

Jase hurried in with a down comforter she recognized from her bed. He tucked it around her, flicking a quick glance at the fireplace. Flames crackled brightly, casting shadows on the wall and window. Outside the glass, the light flickered across the snow so that flames leapt and sparkled in a strange, beautiful illusion. "Wow. Did you know it did that?"

Cole sat back staring out the glass at the phenomenon.

"No. The architect must have designed it that way." He scooted back until his back was pressed against the couch, close to Maia's legs. "It is amazing."

"Breathtaking," Maia agreed. "You know, we could easily cut some branches and make a wreath for the fireplace and door. That would bring in the smell of Christmas. I looked in the freezer, and there is a turkey. If we take it out now, we could thaw it in the refrigerator and cook it."

"You're planning on cooking it, right?" Jase said. "Because the thought of Cole cooking a turkey is scary."

"What exactly do you do in the kitchen, Steele?" Maia asked.

"He set off the smoke alarms three times already," Jase said. "And the food . . ."

Cole moved so fast he seemed a blur, dragging Jase to the floor in a wrestling move. Jase stiffened, letting out a squeak of terror in spite of the fact that Cole cushioned his fall. Cole froze. Maia launched herself from the couch, blanket and all, landing on Cole's back. "Jase, pin him! Pin him! You've got to get him in a headlock!"

"No fair double-teaming me," Cole protested, reaching up to hook Maia around the waist. "You're on time-out with that scalp wound."

"You're just afraid," Maia taunted. "You don't want to get beat up by a woman."

Cole rolled her in the comforter, careful not to flip Jase off him when the teenager did his best to put him in a headlock and hang on as Cole wrestled with Maia. She was like an eel and believed in using her skills, even in playing. She had no intention of surrendering easily, and what had started out as aid to Jase in learning to play turned into a challenge. She called out instructions to the boy, and he readily threw himself into the game, trying to get a lock on Cole's legs to prevent him from getting leverage.

Maia laughed so hard she couldn't get a good grip on Cole and found herself lying on her back, staring up into his blue eyes. Jase slipped off Cole's back to land beside her, laughing with her. Cole stretched across the two of them. "Consider yourselves officially pinned."

"You cheated," Maia accused. She turned her head to laugh with Jase. "He tickled me. In wrestling, there's no tickling."

"I had to end it fast. You shouldn't be playing around with your head banged up." Cole tried to use his toughest voice, but Jase and Maia only laughed harder, shoving at him, their eyes bright with fun. He found himself lying in a heap on the floor, his arms around the two of them with something hard deep inside of him slowly melting away. It had started when he saw Maia and Jase together with the mountain lion and now, playing in the living room with them, a dam seemed to be bursting inside of him. It was a frightening feeling, one he wasn't ready for.

"My head's just fine. It was just a little cut."

"Still, it's better for you to take it easy for a few days." His voice was gruff.

Maia's fingers tangled in his hair, and he felt a surge of electricity rushing from her to him. His body reacted, and he immediately slid away from the two of them. What had possessed him to start a game of wrestling with Jase? He sat back, eyeing Maia as if she were some kind of sorceress. He knew he was looking wild and crazy but he couldn't help it. She destroyed his control.

"What is it, Cole?" She sat up too, pushing her tumbling hair out of her eyes and looking up at him with concern. "Did I hurt you?"

"Not yet," he said before he could censor himself.

Jase sat up slowly, looking from his older brother to Maia, his smile widening as he did so.

Cole glared at him. "Don't say a word."

Jase held up both hands. "I wasn't going to say a word." He exchanged a slow smile with Maia before turning his attention to his mother's treasures.

For the next hour they examined the contents of the box, putting the ornaments aside and unfolding the obviously old quilt.

Maia took a shower and washed her hair, coming down once more dressed in Jase's clothes. They checked the horses together in the evening, and Maia frowned a bit over Wally, concerned he might be getting an infection. When she went to feed and water the mountain lion, Cole insisted on standing by with a gun. He had long since sent Jase to bed and stood guard over her by himself.

As they walked back to the house he shook his head. "This is crazy, Maia, you know that don't you? Having a mountain lion locked up in the toolshed on a horse and cattle ranch. We'll have to watch Jase every minute. He's likely to try to sneak another peek at that animal."

"She's trying to be good. She's wants to leave," Maia admitted, "but she'll stay a couple of days. I'd like a good seven days with her before she takes off, but I'm not going to get it."

"They really talk to you?" He pushed open the door for her and waited while she hung up her jacket and pulled off her boots. "Because after watching you with that animal, I think I'm ready to believe anything."

"It's not actually talking. More like images."

"You're frowning."

"It's just that I'm very concerned about what the animals keep showing me." Maia was reluctant to admit it for obvious reasons. "I feel silly telling you, but if I don't, and something happens, I'd blame myself." She sighed and moved away from him to go into the kitchen. The making of tea was a soothing ritual, and in any case, she needed to take the turkey from the freezer. "You already know I pick up images from animals, so there's no reason to pretend it isn't happening."

Cole followed, aware it was difficult for her. "I'd like to know."

"It's just that there's always violence involved. Wally and the deer are the only animals that revealed to me the violence toward Jase. The rest of the animals are showing me things that are happening away from the ranch house."

He toed a chair around and straddled it in the middle of the kitchen, watching as she filled the teakettle and set it on the stove. "What kinds of things?"

"Something flying above their heads. Men and horses moving on the ground. Rifle flashes in the night. I get bits and pieces, nothing concrete, but I think some men may have had a fight and someone was killed here on the ranch." She pulled open the freezer to remove the turkey, setting it in the refrigerator without looking at him. "I could be way off base, but something traumatic happened here sometime ago, and I think something happened here again very recently."

Silence stretched out between them.

She didn't want to see his face, to know he thought she was crazy. Why had she said anything? Would she ever learn? She was falling in love with him, and it was far too soon. Love wasn't supposed to happen so fast, rushing at her like an avalanche. She knew better. She spooned loose-leaf tea into the teapot, thankful the kitchen was a chef's delight and so well stocked with everything. Once again she was blowing her chances with a man she could care about because she admitted her affinity with animals.

Maia spun around. "You know what? I don't care if you believe me or not. This is who I am, and I'm not going to apologize for it." She pushed her hand through her hair in agitation. "I like animals better than people anyway."

His eyebrow shot up. "You don't like them better than you like me."

"Yes I do. I don't know what I was thinking." She glared at him, angry at herself for being so vulnerable to whatever he might think of her.

"You were thinking the animals might be warning us about something, and it was important." He tried his hand at teasing her. " Has anyone ever called you Dr. Doolittle?"

"No! And they'd better never do it either."

His blue eyes moved over her face with cool amusement. "You have a temper." Obviously he wasn't that good at teasing, but he liked her reaction.

"No, I don't. Well," she hedged. "Okay, maybe I do. But the fact is, I don't care whether you believe me or not." She couldn't tell if he was making fun of her or whether he really meant what he said—that he was worried the animals were warning them. It didn't seem possible that he could believe her.

"Yes you do."

His voice was low, a seduction of her senses that she felt all the way through her body. "I hate that you're so good at flirting, Steele. You've been a playboy for so long, you don't know when to stop."

He stood up, an act of aggression, and she recognized it as such, stepping back until she was pressed tightly against the sink, one hand up to stop him. "I'm tired of you calling me insulting names, Maia."

"I wasn't insulting you, I was stating a fact. You're too experienced, and you know it and you use it, and I just want to kick you for it," she defended.

He walked right up to her, his chest pressing into her palm until it was the only thing between them. She could feel his muscles beneath the thin shirt, the rise and fall of his breath, the steady beat of his heart. His skin radiated heat. "Back off, Steele."

"I'm about to apologize again. I seem to do that a lot nowadays."

There was genuine amusement in his voice. Real laughter even if his mouth didn't curve into a smile. It was in his eyes, in his voice. She felt it in his chest. *She* had given him that gift, and she knew it. There was seduction in the knowledge. She stared, fascinated at the warmth that replaced the ice in his eyes. He lowered his head until his lips were inches from hers. Until his breath was warm against her mouth.

He kissed her hard, taking her breath, devouring her rather than coaxing her. His arms swept around her, pulled her to him, fitting her body into his.

Maia melted into him, her body going pliant, her mouth answering with a ravenous hunger of her own. Her arms slipped around his neck, fingers tangled in his hair, and she gave herself up to his kiss. His hand slid up her back inside her shirt, fingers splayed wide to take in as much bare skin as possible. Heat spread, heat and hunger and need. His kiss deepened, and his hand closed possessively over her breast.

Maia gasped and arched into his palm. His mouth left hers, blazed across her chin, down her neck to nuzzle at her breast until she moaned a soft protest, her arms cradling his head to her. "Stop. We have to stop."

"Actually, I'd rather not." He kissed his way back up to her mouth, settled there with long, persuading kisses.

Maia kissed him right back but kept a hand wedged between them. "I'm not quite ready for this."

He groaned and rested his forehead against hers. "I am."

"Yes, well now I'm the one apologizing," Maia said. "I have to be certain of what I'm doing and what I'm getting into. I'm sorry, Cole. I'm just made that way."

"I like the way you're made, Maia, but dammit all, I want you in my bed."

"I do rather like the way you apologize," Maia said, touching her fingertips to her mouth, a faint smile appearing as he swore. She could still feel him burning on her lips. Could still feel his hands on her skin. She ached, her body tight and full and edged with need. She had to go upstairs, right away, or she was going to take her clothes off right there in the kitchen and give him more than he ever bargained for.

"Good. I have the feeling I'm going to have spend a lot of time apologizing to you."

"You're probably right." She removed the teakettle from the heat. "I'm going to bed now. Alone. It's the only safe thing to do."

"You're certain I can't change your mind?"

"No, that's why I'm leaving now before it's too late." She slipped past him and hurried away, leaving him standing in the kitchen with a rueful expression on his face. She was fairly certain it was a good thing he couldn't read her mind.

chapter

10

"COME ON, JASE, DOC, bundle up, and let's go looking for a tree. We have a couple hours of break in the storm, and this might be the best opportunity we have."

"What did the weather report say?" Maia asked.

Cole gave her a sharp glance. "Don't think you're escaping when you've got a mountain lion penned up in my shed and a horse in the barn and a teenage boy looking for a huge meal. I don't have the time to clear the road and let you out even if I were so inclined, which I'm not."

"You'll do anything to get out of cooking, won't you?" Maia said, her grin as contagious as always. She slipped into her jacket and pulled on gloves. "I'm definitely going with you. I'm very particular about trees."

Jase and Cole exchanged a long, amused look, then groaned in union. "You would be," Cole said. "We'll take the snowmobiles and head out toward the upper ridge. The fir trees are thick there, and we can top one of them."

"Why are we just taking the top of the tree?" Jase asked.

"We don't want to kill the tree," Cole said. "I like our trees. You can never have enough trees."

Jase looked out the window toward the tree-covered

mountain. "Guess not. We'd have such a shortage if we took the whole tree." He exchanged a grin with Maia.

"I did notice the trees on the ranch were getting thin from all the Christmas celebrations going on around here," Maia teased.

Cole opened the door to the mudroom and waved them through. "I can't believe how funny the two of you are. I let you spend a little time together taking care of that horse, and you develop a comedy routine."

Maia leaned in close to Jase, her arm slipping around his shoulders. "He's grouchy this morning."

"Yeah, it's the one cup of coffee syndrome. I've seen it before," Jase replied. "No one talks to him before the first cup of coffee, or he bites off their head. After the first cup of coffee he growls at everyone, but there's no biting."

Cole caught Maia around the waist, bringing her to a halt, his teeth scraping back and forth at the nape of her neck. "I bite after the first cup of coffee if you deserve it," he warned. His teeth nipped a little harder, sending chills down her back. His tongue swirled over the sting right before he pressed a kiss against it.

"Bite Jase if you're going to bite someone," Maia admonished, shoving at him.

"Ugg. That's sick, Doc," Jase protested. "Totally sick. Cole, don't you even try biting my neck."

A slow, mischievous grin curved Cole's mouth very slowly, giving him a young, boyish look. Maia's breath caught in her throat. Jase backed away from him, laughing, holding out a hand to stop his older brother's purposeful advance.

"Back off!" He dashed out into the snow.

Deliberately, Cole pelted his brother with several snowballs, packing the white flakes into round balls and heaving the missiles on the run. Maia sided with Jase, just as Cole knew she would, throwing snowballs with good aim, scoring several hits. She threw hard and accurate so he was forced to turn away from his intended victim to protect himself. To his astonishment, Jase tackled him from behind, throwing him into the snow and leaping off, running, his laughter carried away by the wind.

The sound stirred some long-forgotten emotion in Cole. He had to fight back a lump in his throat and blink to clear what had to be tears from his burning eyes. He got up slowly, keeping his back to the two of them, shaking with the tidal wave of intense feelings Jase and Maia roused in him. A dam really had burst somewhere deep inside of him, blown open by the happiness spilling over from a simple snowball war.

Or maybe it was so much more than that. Maybe it was all the things in his life he had now that he'd never had, never trusted, and never thought he wanted.

He watched Maia chase Jase through the snow. Her cheeks were red and her eyes filled with merriment, with happiness. He had all but forgotten those things until he found her. The boy was throwing missiles as fast as he could, but Maia clearly had him on the run. Cole could only stare at her, flooded with the knowledge that the intensity of the emotions she brought to him was the very thing he had feared from her. He loved her. It was too fast and too insane for someone like him to even consider, but he knew he needed her. And Jase needed her too.

Jase turned and streaked past Cole, skidding to a halt behind him so that a snowball landed with a splat on Cole's chest. The snow was dazzling white, nearly blinding him. He pushed sunglasses on his nose and settled them in place just as Maia plowed into him. Catching her in his arms, he fell backward, Maia landing on top of him. He rolled, pinning her beneath him.

Time seemed to stop, and he felt his heart somersault, his stomach tighten. She was so damned beautiful lying beneath him with her eyes so full of life.

Cole bent his head and kissed her. Hard. Hungry. Hot. Meaning it.

Maia stared up at him a long moment, the only sound their mingled breathing. She felt her heart stuttering hard in her chest. Little butterflies fluttered in her stomach. She was falling hard. Fast. She didn't even know if Cole was capable of loving her. It was frightening to think how much she cared when she didn't have the slightest idea of his real feelings. Needing space, she scooped up a handful of snow and plastered it against the side of his head. "Cool off, Slick, we're hunting for a tree."

Cole studied her face, the way she suddenly withdrew from him. He had to let her go, with Jase standing over them, but he didn't want to. He wanted to hold her to him. Instead, he made himself wipe at the wet snow trickling down his face. He raised his eyebrow. "You take all the fun out of things."

"I do my best." She shoved at his chest. "And we're getting that tree today. All the kisses in the world aren't going to change my mind."

Cole got to his feet, pulling Maia up with him. Jase sat in the snow staring at them as if they'd both grown new heads. "You going to sit there all day?" Cole asked.

"I just might," Jase said, and took the hand Cole

extended to help him up. He was grinning from ear to ear, and Cole resisted the urge to drop him back in the snow.

Jase moved ahead of them, bounding like a frisky colt through the snow to the garage housing the snowmobiles. Cole paused just outside the door, staring up at the second garage looming taller right alongside the first building.

"What is it?" Maia asked.

"I don't know exactly." But he suddenly wished he were alone, able to conduct an investigation.

"What's in there?"

"The helicopter and a small plane."

"Really? You have your own helicopter? Do you fly it?"

"Yes. I can fly both the plane and the helicopter. I was in the service for a while. It was the best way to get away from the ranch and have enough money to live. The old man could have destroyed or bought any company I chose to work for, but he couldn't exactly make the Air Force disappear."

"The things I'm learning about you are fascinating." She took a step toward the larger garage but stopped when Cole put a hand on her shoulder. He was looking around the countryside, his eyes flat and hard and ice-cold. She froze, taking her cue from him.

Cole caught the brief glint of light reflected from a ridge up above the house. He didn't make the mistake of staring into it, but a chill went down his back. It could have been a scope, but more likely it was binoculars. Deliberately he glanced up at the sky. "We'd better find that tree before the next storm hits."

Jase eagerly shoved open the garage doors to reveal several snowmobiles. "Come on, Doc, I'll race you!"

Maia felt Cole's hand on her shoulder guiding her

toward the snowmobiles so she went with him. "What is it?"

Cole was grateful she was always so alert and kept her voice low. She never seemed to panic. "I don't know yet. All these strange things the animals have been showing you, the things you've described to me, do you believe they're trying to convey something to you?"

"Absolutely," Maia said firmly.

"Keep Jase occupied for a few minutes."

"Don't do anything crazy."

Cole slipped into the shadows of the building, encouraging Jase and Maia to follow him inside. If someone were lying up along the ridge with a scope or binoculars, they wouldn't be able to see him go through the door of the covered walkway leading back to the house.

"I forgot something, Jase. We need a couple of tools. You check out the snowmobiles, make certain we have plenty of gas and they're running fine, while I go back and get what we need."

"Sure," Jase agreed.

Maia was silent, watching him with fear in her eyes. He couldn't help brushing a brief, reassuring kiss over her mouth as he passed by her. "Keep him in the garage," he whispered as he moved into the walkway.

He sprinted along the covered path, forced to take a roundabout route to keep from exposing himself to the ridge, but he made it back to the house certain he hadn't been spotted. Up in his room, he retrieved a rifle with a scope and binoculars. With the white sheet wrapped around him, he scooted on his belly onto the balcony, rolling into position.

He raised the binoculars to his eyes, scanning the ridge

for activity, keeping his own movement to a minimum. It took a moment to spot his quarry. Fred Johanston, Al's brother-in-law, lay on the ridge, watching the activity in the garage through a pair of binoculars. Cole lowered his glasses and scooted back into the house, carefully sliding the balcony door closed, not wanting to give away his position.

Fred Johanston was up to something, but what? There was no way he'd inherit the ranch should both Jase and Cole die. He had no hope of being Jase's guardian. What was he up to? Cole didn't have much time. He didn't want to tip off Fred that he was on to him. Hurrying through the house, back outside, he took even more care to keep out of sight of the ridge, but he took several weapons with him.

He'd already committed to taking Jase and Maia on a hunt for a Christmas tree, and if he abruptly changed plans it could alert Fred that Cole was on to him. Better to act as if nothing were wrong and figure things out the way he always did, methodically, slowly, putting the pieces of the puzzle together until they fit perfectly. Now that he knew they were under surveillance, he could take the appropriate steps to keep them safe.

Maia looked up as he hurried in through the side door, his weapons stashed safely in a small toolbox. "Everything all right?"

"The snowmobiles are gassed up and ready to go," Jase said.

"Well, put on your gloves and pull down your hat over your face. The doc and I are going to race you."

"No we're not," Maia said.

"Awesome," Jase said. "I'm the king on a snowmobile."

"The rules are, we go out the door full throttle, head for

Moose Creek, and you have to zigzag through every open field or you're disqualified."

"Piece of cake," Jase said. "You'll never catch me."

"Don't be so cocky, kid," Cole reached over to zip the boy's jacket to his neck. "You're also disqualified if you take a spill."

"*Hello!* I don't suppose you heard me say no way," Maia said, tugging at Cole's arm. "We are *not* racing."

"I can't believe you'd be afraid of a little speed, Maia," Cole said. A mischievous almost grin slid over his face.

Maia glared at him with suspicion. "If I thought you could do that on purpose . . ."

"What?" He sank down onto the snowmobile and patted the seat behind him. "Climb aboard, and let's go get that tree."

Maia slid behind him and wrapped her arms around his waist. "You aren't going to tell me what's going on, are you?"

"I don't know yet," he said truthfully, "but we're going to be very careful."

The ride through the snow was wild and exhilarating. The two snowmobiles flew over the snow. A few flakes fell from the clouds, reminding them they didn't have much time, but they still played, Jase and Cole racing across the pristine fields toward Moose Creek. Maia's laughter rang in Cole's ears and found its way into his heart. She rested her head against his back and urged him on when Jase was inching ahead of them.

All the while, Cole made every effort to keep trees and slopes between them and the ridge. He encouraged Jase to play, deliberately forcing the boy to zigzag through every open field so it would be nearly impossible to get off an accurate shot should Fred have the desire. Cole hadn't seen a rifle, but he'd seen the saddle and blanket and the scabbard, and he was certain it had been Fred who'd taken the horse out. And it must have been Fred who shot the mountain lion the same day he'd run Wally into the fence. But why? What possible reason could he have? He certainly couldn't expect to get his job back that way. Revenge? Could it be that simple?

Jase brought his snowmobile to a halt in front of a particularly tall fir tree, pointing. The branches were full and the tree's needles were thick. "This one's a beaut! What do you think, Doc?"

"He would ask you," Cole said, helping her off the machine. In the thick of the trees they were well protected. Snow was beginning to fall again, and the wind was picking up. He glanced up at the sky. "I think this one's going to have to be it, Jase. We've just about run out of time. The storm's coming in fast."

There was a lot of laughter and just as much argument as Cole and Jase decided what was the best way to top the tree. Maia stood back watching, laughing at them, but all the while she could see that Cole was extremely alert, his eyes restless, constantly moving. He was wary, extremely so, and he exuded a powerful aura of danger. He was hunting, she knew, but had no idea what he was looking for.

The tree was tied to a sled and secured behind Jase's machine. That told Maia Cole wanted to be mobile or he would never have risked allowing Jase to pull the tree. They made their way back at a much more cautious and sedate pace. It was far colder with the snow flying at their faces in spite of their warm coats. The snow fell steadily, a sign that they were in for another long storm.

Maia was happy to see the inside of the house. It was

warm and felt welcoming with the fire in the fireplace and Jase's mother's quilt along the back of the couch. She'd put cider on the stove to simmer, and the fragrance wafted through the rooms. "Much better," she said and smiled at the teenager.

He was too busy struggling to get the tree inside the house, maneuvering it with Cole giving orders and both staggering and tripping until Maia nearly fell over laughing. "I wish I had a camera. You two are not very good at this."

Cole glared at her. "I don't see you helping, and this was your idea."

"I'm suffering the effects of my scalp wound from yesterday," Maia said.

"You were able to wrestle yesterday." He walked his end of the tree around, keeping away from the windows, always conscious of the watcher on the ridge. He glanced outside. The snow was relentless, falling steadily in a soft, silent monotonous way that packed on feet rather than inches. Cole seriously doubted if anyone could be out in the whiteout. The tension immediately drained from his body.

"Fine," Maia said. She took the toolbox Cole had insisted on carrying along with the tree. "I'll find the perfect position for you. The two of you just hold on to it while I study the situation."

"Study the situation?" Jase yelped in protest. "This is *heavy*."

"Yes, well," Maia waved a dismissing hand and settled herself on the couch, the toolbox at her feet while she examined every angle of the room.

"Oh, for God's sake," Cole said, exasperated. He shoved on his end until Jase went with him, standing the tree dead center in front of the window. "Right here. The damned thing is going right here, and we're *not* moving it."

In the end they moved it four times, Maia going from one end of the room to the other to study the positioning from every angle. Jase threw himself on the floor twice, laughing at his older brother's expression and pointing to him until Cole threatened to throw him out in the storm.

"That's perfect. Now we need wire and those pincher cutter things," Maia said. "We'll make a wreath."

"I thought we were going to eat, woman," Cole objected. "You have to feed men if you want them cooperative."

"You just ate," Maia protested.

"That was hours ago," Jase said. "Sorry, Doc, but I'm with Cole on this. I'm on empty."

"You two are bottomless pits! Fine, I need to make popcorn anyway."

"I love popcorn. Make the buttery kind," Jase said.

"*Not* to eat." Maia put her hands on her hips. "We string it and make a garland to wrap around the tree."

Jase and Cole exchanged a long look. "I think that knock on the head did more damage than we suspected," Cole told his younger brother. "We're not wasting the popcorn on the tree, Doc."

Jase shook his head. "What part of *starving* don't you understand?"

"Oh for heaven's sake. We'll make sandwiches, and you can eat them and leave the decorations alone," Maia said.

"I like the part about the sandwiches," Jase said, and took off for the kitchen.

As soon as she and Cole were alone, Maia caught Cole's arm. "What is going on? I know something is, so don't pretend you don't know what I mean."

"I'm not sure what's going on, other than I want us all to stick together," Cole said. "When I figure it out, I promise, you'll be the first to know."

"Is there something I can do to help?"

He framed her face. "You're doing enough already. There's no way to make it up to you, the things you're doing for Jase."

Her heart did a silly flutter as the pad of his thumb slid back and forth over her lower lip. She was beginning to think of various ways he could repay her if he really insisted on it. Maia knew she was incredibly susceptible to him. Jase was her savior, whether he was aware of it or not. She would never be able to hold out against Cole if the boy wasn't with them almost constantly, and once she gave herself to him, she knew it would be forever. It was a terrible realization that she'd fallen so deeply for a man she had known for only a few days.

She couldn't look into his eyes. There was need there and hunger and something so compelling she would never be able to resist. He was doing all the things he knew would cause him nightmares in order to give his younger brother a chance at a normal life. She was hurting him. She ached inside knowing she was the cause. Yet because he was a willing participant, she was falling deeper and deeper in love with him.

"I'm enjoying myself, Cole. This has been fun." Her voice was so husky with her awareness of him she was embarrassed. If his thumb touched her lower lip another minute, she was going to bite him.

"Maia." He bent his head.

She groaned, knew she was lost as she moved into the heat of his body. Her arms stole around his neck, and she instantly became a part of him. Skin to skin. Breath to breath. His hair felt like silk between her fingertips. And his mouth was a haven of fire and hunger that matched her own. She sank into him, his kiss sweeping her away just as she knew it would. She was just as demanding as he, matching fire for fire, hungry, almost greedy in her response.

His arms tightened around her, and his kiss was possessive, a man starved, claiming her, and she claimed him right back, pushing so close they didn't need the clothes separating them.

"Get a hotel room," Jase said. "Geez, this place is getting to be X-rated." He leaned against the wall, a cold piece of pizza in his hand, chewing as he regarded them with feigned disgust. His eyes were bright with happiness, and neither could fail to recognize the hope on his face.

Maia pulled her mouth away from Cole's, pressing her forehead against his chest, trying to find a way to breathe when her lungs felt starved for air. "He's getting hard to resist, Jase. I think we need to put some kind of warning label on him."

"You're just tired, Doc," Cole said, catching her chin, forcing her to look at him.

A woman could definitely get trapped in his blue eyes. She sighed. "That must be it, but just in case, kiss me again."

He didn't wait for a second invitation. He lowered his head to hers, his hand sliding around her neck, holding her still for his kiss.

"I could kiss you forever," she murmured.

Jase rolled his eyes. "Well don't. Think food instead."

Maia blushed, shocked she'd admitted it aloud. "He mesmerized me, Jase, it isn't my fault."

"That's not how it looked to me," Jase said. "You were definitely doing the kissing."

Maia pulled out of Cole's arms. "I'm going to go check the horse and the cat in that order."

"You're running," Cole informed her.

That intriguing trace of amusement flashed momentarily in his eyes. She had to look away from temptation. "Yes, I am, but don't go thinking it's because of your studly self. I'm running from having to cook. I'll make the popcorn, but the two of you are bottomless pits, and if I'm the one putting together Christmas dinner *and* baking . . ."

"Cookies," Jase interrupted. "Lots of cookies. And pies." He poked his brother. "She just zapped you, bro, put you right in your place."

"I thought you wanted to let that cat rest. Stop avoiding me and come into the kitchen. I'll do the cooking, and you do your strange thing with the popcorn." Cole took her hand and drew her into the kitchen. "I started on the wood carving by the way. I've actually found a couple of pieces of wood that might be perfect for a couple of them."

"I've never seen anyone carve before. Will you teach me?"

His gaze moved over her face. Dark. Brooding. Sexy. Maia backed into the table. "Maybe not." She waved at him. "Get started on your cooking."

"I'm making progress."

"You *were* making progress, but I've come to my senses again." She turned her back on him, rummaging through cupboards to find the popcorn. "Jase, find me a needle and thread please."

"Did you really go to Africa and Indochina, Doc?" Jase asked, stuffing potato chips into his mouth.

"Yes. It was beautiful. I loved it, but you have to be prepared for a lot of bugs."

"I'm going to do that someday," Jase said. "What you did for Wally was so great, but I couldn't believe how it felt to touch that mountain lion." He leaned both elbows on the table, chin in hand and studied her with his bright eyes. "I *have* to do that again."

"There's something incredible about a wild cat. Tigers and lions and leopards, all the exotics. You look them in the eye, and you just know we need to find a way to share our space with them. They're incredible."

"Do you want to go back there?" Cole asked, his voice tight.

There was a sudden silence in the room. Maia knew the Steele brothers were watching her closely. She turned her head, meeting Cole's gaze. Her stomach did a crazy flip. It wasn't often she could read his expression, but he was tense, expecting a blow. She forced a casual shrug. "If I want to work with exotics again, most likely I'd find a zoo somewhere. I'm a fill-in vet, so I can make enough money to start my own practice."

"Why don't you take over the one here?" Jase asked.

"Money, honey. I've got some saved, but not enough."

Popcorn began to sound off, a rapid gunfire of miniexplosions.

"Smells good," Jase said.

"I think you'd eat anything if it didn't move," Maia observed, laughing at him. "Leave my popcorn alone. And I'm putting you to work stringing it while Cole makes dinner." She tossed him the small sewing kit containing needles and thread. "Come on, help out, shark tooth."

chapter
11

THREE A.M. The small alarm clock beside Maia's bed blazoned the time in bright glowing numbers. It seemed she was always awake at 3:00 a.m. in this house. She wasn't used to the creaks and strange noises, although, she had to admit with a great deal of satisfaction, the aura of the house was undergoing a change.

She shifted restlessly in the bed, sighed, giving up on sleep, and threw back the covers. Cole had participated in decorating the tree, but he'd been thinking of something else. She'd watched him closely. He had made a dozen excuses to go outside. He'd checked the windows and doors in the house, and for the first time since she'd been there, he'd turned on a security alarm, after first changing the code. And that told her something. Cole was worried about an intruder other than the ghost of his father.

She was falling madly in love with him. She hadn't expected it, and the depth of the emotion was terrifying. She needed to get off the ranch. To go far away. She couldn't stop thinking about Cole. She dreamt of him. Longed to touch him, to take away the shadows always present in his eyes. She'd known from the first moment she'd laid eyes on him that she wouldn't walk away unscathed, but she hadn't counted on the intense attraction she felt for him. He never said a word to her about his real feelings. He never said a word about love or indicated that when she left he wouldn't be happy or even that he might want to see her again.

A sound penetrated through the walls, echoed down the hall. A cry of despair. A tortured protest. Maia stood for a moment, her hand to her throat, hearing the tormented groan of despair. If she went to him, she knew she would never be able to resist giving him what he needed, yet making love to him would only make leaving more difficult for her. She heard a string of curses. Unable to resist his terrible need, she hurried out of her room.

Cole's door was closed, but she pushed it open to see him raking his hands through his hair. His body still shuddered with the aftereffects of his nightmare. As she entered, he swept a gun from under the pillow, pointing it straight at her heart.

"Damn, Maia." He pushed the gun out of sight, struggling to slow his heart rate. "I told you it was dangerous to come downstairs when I'm like this. You think it's any safer in my bedroom?" Cole sat up. The sheets were tangled around his legs and hips, covering part of him but leaving his thigh bare. He knew it looked as if he'd fought a battle and lost.

"I don't care." She crossed the room to his side, pushing the hair from his forehead, her fingertips lingering on his face, tracing a path to his mouth. "I don't want you to be alone tonight, Cole." She knelt on the bed, the light from the snow spilling through the window to bathe her in silver.

Cole's breath caught in his throat, his lungs burned, and he could only stare as her hands went to the buttons of the soft flannel shirt covering her body. She slid each one open. Slowly. One by one. He caught brief glimpses of her body. A soft expanse of skin he ached to touch.

His fingers curled into two tight fists. "Not like this, Maia. You don't have to come to me feeling sorry for me because I had a damned nightmare." What the hell was he saying? He wanted her. Ached for her. His body was so damned hard, he was afraid he might shatter. "I don't want you like this." It was a total lie. He wanted her any way he could have her.

Maia flashed her killer smile, the one that sent his body into overdrive and caused him to turn into a jealous idiot if any other man was within several hundred feet of her. His breath left his lungs in a rush when she allowed the flannel shirt to slide from her shoulders to the mattress. The silvery light played over her body, caressing it lovingly. She looked like a temptress there, kneeling on his bed, her hair tumbling around her face, her eyes enormous and sexy and looking at him with hunger. Her body's feminine curves invited his touch.

"You're killing me."

She leaned forward, her tongue swirling over his chest. "I hope so."

The action exposed the enticing curve of her hip and buttocks. His hands trembled as he reached to cup her bottom, sliding his palms over her smooth skin. She did that to him, made him ache and tremble with the intensity of his hunger for her. He burned from the inside out, a rush of fire that engulfed his body and heightened his senses until he was afraid of losing his control.

Her tongue licking so delicately at his body nearly drove him out of his mind. She pushed the sheets away from him, exposing him to the cool air, but it only hardened his body more so that he was thick and bulging with his desire for her. Maia murmured something against his chest, her tongue tracing a path to his belly. Every muscle in his body contracted. His heart shuddered in anticipation.

"Maia, what the hell do you think you're doing?" His voice was strangled as his lungs labored for air.

"Exactly what I want to do," she said, and wrapped her fingers around his erection.

A groan exploded from his throat. He'd had too many erotic dreams of Maia in his bed, his hands on her satin skin. "You'd better know this is what you really want," he warned. Because he wanted her more than he wanted the sun to come up in the morning.

"I always know what I want." Her breath was warm and moist, and his heart stopped beating for one moment, then began to slam with alarming force in his chest. She did the same delicate licking that had driven him wild. Now it was beyond his imagination. He was going to implode if she didn't stop. Just when he was certain he couldn't take it anymore, her mouth closed over him, tight and hot and moist, drawing the relentless ache to a fever pitch.

His hands fisted in her hair, his hips coming off the sheets, thrusting in a rhythmic slide. He swore, the words tumbling out in an animalistic growl. His control was nearly shattered. His muscles clenched so tight he thought his jaw would break.

Maia lifted her head and smiled at him, satisfaction

evident. "Are you thinking of me yet? Of my body? Because I want you to know who's in bed with you."

"I know damned well who I'm with, Maia." He pushed her backward until she tumbled onto the bed, her legs sprawled, her body open to him. "I know *exactly* who you are. I feel like I've waited a lifetime for you."

His hands pressed into her hips, locking her there, pushing her thighs wider apart for him. "Every time I look at you, I think about what I'd really like to be doing. I want to feel you coming apart for me, Maia."

Before she could respond, he lowered his head as he brought her hips to him. His tongue slid over her heated center, teased and tasted before probing deeply. Maia writhed beneath his hungry mouth, bunching the sheet in her fists, sounds she couldn't prevent escaping, which only fed his voracious need to show her she belonged with him. He didn't have the words, so he used his body to prove it to her. His tongue stroked and thrust and cleverly pulsed until she was consumed with wave after wave of orgasm ripping through her. He sank his fingers deep, and she exploded again, crying out his name.

Cole lifted his head, kissed his way up her body to the underside of her breasts. The cool air was nearly Maia's undoing after his hot mouth. She ached, and still the pressure was relentless in spite of her orgasms.

"What are you doing?" she demanded.

"Making sure you know who you're in bed with. I don't want you ever to be satisfied with any other man." His teeth scraped back and forth on the sensitive flesh. Tiny little bites that drove her insane. "I want you to belong to me. All of you, Maia, not just your body." His mouth closed over her breast, tongue flicking her nipple, teeth teasing until she couldn't tell if the pleasure was so great it was painful.

He rose over her, pushing against her entrance, so that her body, so slick and hot reacted with a slow giving of way for his penetration. He paused for one slight moment, their mingled breathing the only sound, and then he thrust hard, driving the full length of him as deep into her as he could go. He discovered he loved her cries as much as her laugh. He thrust again, over and over, hard and fast, long, deep strokes, driving her higher and higher until she was clutching at his forearms, crying his name.

Sensation after sensation rocked her body, heat seared her until she thought she would have to scream for him to relieve the terrible ache. More. She wanted more. Everything he had, everything he was. She gave herself up to him, surrendering completely, her hips rising to meet the brutal thrust of his, every bit as hard, desperate for him to fill up every empty space.

"Maia, you're so damned tight," Cole's voice was husky, the words torn from his rigid throat. "Hot and tight and dammit all, you belong to me. Like this, baby, just like this." He plunged into her again and again, groaning with pleasure as her muscles pulsed and throbbed around him even more. Until her control was shattered and she burst into fragments, her body convulsing around his, tightening and squeezing and milking him dry so that he called her name aloud, his voice rough with sensuality.

Maia stared up into his face. The harsh lines were gone, the horror of his nightmares replaced with satisfaction. He looked like a well-sated lover, his body relaxed and his piercing blue eyes soft with contentment.

Cole propped himself up on his elbows, looking down

into her face, still trying to get his breathing under control. He could feel her body still rippling with aftershocks around his. "You're so beautiful you take my breath away."

Her laughter was soft, musical, tightening his body all over again. "That's not what took your breath away. And you lie so wonderfully. I'm ordinary-looking, but I don't mind if you want to delude yourself." Her hands slid over his body, traced his sculpted buttocks and hips. She could see a brand burned into his flesh on the back of his thigh. Her fingertips smoothed over the ridges with a small caress.

"I probably should sneak back to my room," she added.

He stiffened. "This is not a one-night stand, Maia. I told you that."

"You did not. I forget your exact words, but . . ."

He caught her hands, stretched them above her head, pinning her wrists to the mattress so he could bend his head and take possession of her lips. He sank his tongue into the velvet darkness of her mouth, his tongue tangling with hers, exploring, commanding a response. He bit lightly at her lower lip, her chin, blazed a path of fire from her throat to breasts.

For a moment he breathed in the sight of her bathed in the silvery light as it spilled across her breasts. Her nipples were peaked and hard, already roused. Her soft mounds were rising and falling with every breath she took, jutting upward toward his mouth. His body stirred to life, deep inside of hers, hardening impossibly. He bent to the offering, flicking her nipple with his tongue, feeling her response, the way her hips thrust upward and her body convulsed around his. He drew her breast into his hot mouth, suckling strongly, his tongue teasing her nipple, teeth scraping gently.

Maia gasped and moaned, her body tensing, her breasts swelling with the attention. His body began to move, long slow strokes that left her moaning and lifting her hips in an attempt to control the rhythm. Cole held her beneath him, pressing kisses between her breasts, nibbling at her chin and lower lip, using his mouth to bring her to another climax while his body kept a slow, lazy tempo.

"Cole." It was a protest. A plea.

He smiled. A genuine smile. He felt it welling up out of nowhere. Cole could make her want him, plead with him, make her body come apart. She didn't try to hide the way she felt such an urgent need of him, and that was more of an aphrodisiac than anything else ever could have been.

"Cole what?" he whispered against her mouth. Her muscles were already suckling at him, so tight and hot he wasn't certain he could keep the slow, languid pace he was setting. "What do you want, Maia?" The pleasure kept building and building inside of him, starting somewhere in the region of his toes, becoming an excruciating pleasure/pain in his groin and belly. There was fire in her tight sheath, her skin soft and inviting, her breasts thrusting up toward him with her arms stretched out above her head. An offering to him. Maia gave herself to him completely, and there was so much seduction in that knowledge.

"Hurry up. Now *you're* killing *me*." She lifted her hips again, deliberately tightening her muscles around him.

With a groan, Cole gave in, plunging deep and hard, unable to resist the hot furnace of her body. He couldn't resist kissing her, sucking on her lower lip. How often had he found himself staring, enthralled by the soft curve of her mouth? His tongue plunged into her mouth with the same urgency his hips drove into her. It could never be enough with Maia and he knew he never wanted it to be.

Stretched out under him as she was, helpless under the pounding force of his body, she still tried to reach him, to lift herself to meet him. Cole felt her body stretching to accommodate him as with each thrust he seemed to grow thicker and harder, nearly bursting with the pleasure she brought him. He held them there, on the edge of a great precipice for what seemed forever, then both went over, climaxing together, the force of it leaving them shuddering and limp, a fine sheen glossing their bodies.

Cole groaned softly and rolled his weight off of her when he could, but he kept his hand on her ribs, just under her breast, wanting to keep her in his room. "Just stay," he ordered softly. "I need you to stay."

It took Maia longer to catch her breath, to gather her scattered thoughts. "I've never felt that way before, Cole."

He turned his head to look at her. "That's a damned good thing, Maia. I'm looking to be number one in your life. Being a fantastic lover is one of the requirements."

She laughed, just like he knew she would. "Is it? I had no idea. Well, you definitely passed that test." She glanced at the door. "I hope I didn't scream. Please tell me I didn't."

"Unless Jase has a nightmare, he sleeps deeply, and his room is way down at the other end of the floor. We wanted to give one another a lot of space when we first moved in together."

"He's a good kid."

"Yeah, he is. All along I've been so worried that Jase might have killed the old man. I wouldn't have blamed him for it, but I didn't want him to have done it. I couldn't find a way to prove him innocent and even in some of our conversations, little things he said made me wonder."

"How awful for you both," Maia sympathized. She reached for his hand, twining her fingers through his. "Jase isn't naturally violent, Cole. If he killed his father, he would have done it in self-defense. And to be honest, I don't think he could have. He was too afraid of him. And it isn't in him to kill anyone."

"No, it isn't." Cole turned over, his arm sliding around her waist. "But it is in me, isn't?"

The sadness in his voice shook her. Sadness. Distaste. A note of fear. Maia framed his face with her hands, shifting so she could rise above him to look directly into his eyes. "You're *nothing* like that man, Cole. You're strong and yes, you could be violent if the circumstances called for it, but you're nothing at all like him."

"You don't know that, Maia."

"Yes I do. I saw your face when you touched the mountain lion, when I worked on the horse. I watch you with Jase, how careful you are. Even when you're trying to get him to play, you protect his falls. There's nothing in you that is cruel. Your father reveled in being cruel. It isn't in your nature, or in Jase's nature. You like to be the boss, but you're not out to control everyone. You encourage Jase to speak his mind and make decisions. That's not wanting control."

Cole slid his hands up her rib cage, cupped her breasts in his palms and leaned forward to rest his head against her soft flesh. Maia immediately cradled his head to her. "I read people, just as I read animals, Cole. I would never have allowed myself to become involved with you and Jase if for one moment I thought either of you was cruel to humans or animals. I have too much respect for myself."

She smiled. "I have a little bit of violence in me as well, and a great deal of self-preservation."

His arms tightened around her. "I see him in myself sometimes, Maia."

"He had strength of will, Cole, and he passed that to you. He must have had a way with women, and you have that attraction as well. Not everything about him was bad. Some of his traits are useful and, hopefully, both you and Jase have them."

He lifted his head, his blue eyes moving over her face, studying her features inch by inch. "You're a damned miracle, you know that?"

"Of course I do. Temper and all." She laughed, the sound happy and warm, filling the large bedroom.

Cole felt her laughter all the way to his bones. She had the power to shake him with that simple lighthearted sound. Her body was soft and warm and welcoming, but she was so much more to him. *She would always be so much more to him.* The revelation was no longer a shock. Maia seemed as much a part of him as breathing. She was the joy that had been missing from his heart. When he woke in darkness, she brought light to him. She brought out things in him he hadn't known were a part of him.

How could he tell her these things when they'd only been together so short a time? She wouldn't believe him. How could she? His arms tightened until she stirred in protest.

"You're going to break me in half, Cole," Maia said. "What's wrong?"

He forced himself to let his arms slide away from her, to lie back and lace his fingers behind his head. "I know you've told me about the images the animals have shown you several times, but would you go over it again in detail. Everything you can remember."

"Why?"

"You ought to be over being uncomfortable about it with me," Cole said. There was a soft growl in his voice, a deep note that seemed to vibrate right through her skin. "I'm just thinking about all the images the animals have been conveying to you, and I'm trying to put it together. Maybe the answer to the mystery of what's going on at this ranch is in those images."

Maia sat back, her hand on his chest, right over his heart. She knew he hadn't told her what had put the shadows back in his eyes, but if he wasn't ready to tell her, she wasn't going to force a confidence. "I'm going to let you get away with that just because I know you're worried about something happening on the ranch, and I want to be filled in, but I know that's not what you were worried about."

Maia waited, but Cole didn't respond. "Fine. The owl was very vague. Impressions of dangers, something flying overhead. Flashes of light. Horses moving. I couldn't get a very good take on it because the images seemed faded and far away." She shrugged. "I know that sounds dumb."

"The deer then."

"Blood on the grass and rocks. Fists hitting flesh. More impressions of danger."

"Were the images as vague?"

"Distant. And the wolves were even more so. Something overhead. Blood on the ground. The one I treated was injured sometime ago."

"Someone shot it?"

"No, I think it was kicked by a horse or trampled. The

bone was out of the socket, but I'm not certain how the injury actually occurred or how long ago. The poor thing had really suffered."

"All this time I thought my father's death had something to do with his fortune or the ranch or Jase. I couldn't figure out why he was murdered and how anyone other than my uncle would profit and only if he was named guardian, which he wouldn't be. Besides, he wouldn't want the responsibility."

"So if your father wasn't murdered for the inheritance, what was the reason?"

He shrugged, a small sigh escaping. "I'm not actually certain, but I think your animals were trying to tell you something. I'm working on a time line. Tell me how preposterous this sounds. I think your cat, the owl, and the wolves were showing you something that happened a while ago."

"*Maybe*. It was vague."

"Exactly. The memory wasn't fresh."

Excitement flared. "You're right. When Wally showed me the images of Jase as a boy being beaten, the memories weren't nearly as vivid as when he showed me how he was driven into the fence. I had a very difficult time making out the images from the owl and the wolves, but the mountain lion's images were much clearer."

"You're certain she was shot the day Wally was injured?"

"The wound would have been infected if more time had gone by. Yes, it was definitely fresh."

"Could she have been shot from someone in a helicopter?"

Maia shook her head. "No, she was above the shooter,

at least that's the way the angle of the wound appeared to me."

Satisfaction edged his expression. "That's what I thought too. So the event in which the helicopter was flying overhead could have taken place when my father was still alive."

"Well, of course there's no way of knowing for certain, but it's a realistic possibility," Maia said. "I'm lost, Cole. You obviously have an idea where all of this is leading, but I haven't a clue."

He kissed her, a brief hard kiss, his eyes alive with excitement. "That's because you don't think a like a criminal."

"I suppose that's a compliment. You have such a sweet tongue on you."

He showed her he did, kissing her again and making a thorough job of it.

Maia caught his shoulders and pushed him back down to the bed. "Talk. Explain."

"I think my father brought something onto the ranch, most likely something illegal. Some of the ranch hands were probably involved. They would have had to be. Most people didn't know it, but the old man could fly a helicopter. He employed a full-time pilot, but only because he liked to feel superior to everyone and give orders. He thought flying was a menial task."

Maia reached for his hand again. Cole didn't seem to realize how agitated he became when he talked about his father. It wasn't overt, but more a subtle tension rising, building and building until she felt he might explode with the force of a volcano. "I'm not certain I understand."

"Suppose he brought in something worth a fortune,

and some of the hands were in on it and expected to get a share. The old man goes out with his pilot and moves it from wherever it was originally stashed."

"You're thinking of a shipment of drugs."

"I always think in terms of drugs or weapons. It's my job. But yes, suppose the old man was running drugs out here. He has a few thousand acres. The ranch backs up to a national forest. Parts of our ranch are on the border. He could bring in drugs, and no one would be the wiser. Or diamonds. Anything. An illegal shipment worth a fortune."

"The horses and packs. The helicopter overhead. Maybe. It's a stretch."

"Not that big a stretch if you knew him. He would revel in working outside the law. He thought he was smarter and more cunning than anyone. I could easily see it. And if some of the hands were in on it and knew he had the shipment and he suddenly announced he was cutting them out, it would be a damned good reason for someone to kill him."

"Why would he do that?"

"Because he could. You would have had to know him. He liked the power of it all. Suppose he went with his pilot and moved the shipment somewhere the hands wouldn't know about it, and then he killed the pilot and left him behind with the stash."

Maia shook her head. "It doesn't make sense."

"You said someone was killed. I checked, Maia. The pilot went missing a few weeks before the old man was murdered. He was actually considered a suspect. No one's heard from him. The rumor was, he and the old man had a falling out, and he quit."

"So your father killed the pilot, but why?"

"Because the old man moved his stash, and the pilot knew where, so he had to die. Then he told the ranch hands he was cutting them out of the deal. He knew they couldn't go to the police, and they wouldn't want to lose their jobs, so he felt very safe. But one or more of them decided they didn't want to take orders from him. So they killed him in his office and went out to pick up the stash, only it wasn't there anymore."

"Because he'd moved it before he cut them out of the deal."

"I think that's what's going on, Maia. They didn't care who was named guardian because we didn't know about the stash. They could look around the ranch for it, and we'd never know."

"Until you fired them."

"That's right. I fired them, and I'd be very suspicious if they began hanging around the ranch. Jase told me some maps disappeared from the office. I didn't really give it all that much thought, but it makes sense. They're looking for whatever the old man hid."

"So they wanted you out of here at least long enough to do a thorough search of the ranch. That's why the rumors, to get you to take Jase and leave."

"And that's why the accidents. They knew the storm was coming. Jase was supposed to go into town with me that day, but he decided he wanted to hang out with Al. So they tried to injure him just enough so Al would have to drive him into town, and they could poke around. That didn't work, so they drove Wally into the fence thinking Al would trailer the horse into town. The storm was breaking too fast, and I opted to bring you home with me."

"Why push it? Why didn't they just wait?"

"Maybe they have a buyer, or they're getting anxious. Whatever it is, one of my horses was ridden the day Wally was hurt. I think while Al and Jase were tied up looking after him, Fred took the horse and went looking. That's probably when he shot the mountain lion."

"This is all speculation."

"Yes," Cole admitted. "But Fred was watching us when we went to get the tree yesterday. And I've got this gut feeling. I've never been wrong when I've had that feeling before."

"So why the ice on the walkway?"

"To get us out of here. If you or Jase or even I were injured, we'd have go into town to the hospital, and they'd be able to search without interruption."

"In a blizzard?"

"Four separate storms, Maia. It wasn't supposed to be this bad. And if we were trapped on the other side, the road wouldn't be cleared, and we'd have a hard time getting home."

"So how do you prove it?"

"I'm working on it." He reached out to cup her breasts again, thumbs caressing her nipples into hard peaks. "I'll think better in the morning. Right now, I want to spend the rest of the night getting to know every inch of your body intimately."

She felt her body respond immediately. "Sounds like a good plan to me."

chapter 12

"TOMORROW'S CHRISTMAS EVE, Cole, and I haven't had a nightmare since we ran into Maia in the restaurant." Jase shoveled scrambled eggs onto his plate and scooped up bacon to go along with it. "If the doc is a vegetarian, why is she all gung ho to cook us a turkey?"

"You'll have to ask her that."

"Have you had nightmares since we met Maia?"

Cole nodded. "Yeah. But they don't last long."

Jase paused in his frantic eating to look up at his brother. "If the tree really bothers you, Cole, I'll help you take it down. The doc will understand."

"No, the tree stays up. I can get through the night, Jase. I like the tree."

"I do too," the boy said, relieved. "I kind of like the whole Christmas thing. The doc makes it feel different. I'm not sure why, but she makes everything so fun."

"On Christmases past, I always felt an outsider looking in," Cole said.

Jase blinked and swallowed quickly. "That's it! That's how I always felt. Sometimes you're smart, Cole."

"Thanks, Jase." A trace of humor showed in Cole's eyes.

"You're welcome." Jase leaned his chin into his palm as he thoughtfully chewed a mouthful of food. "I've been giving a lot of thought to this, Cole. I think we should keep her. We need to keep the doc."

Cole's mouth twitched in an odd approximation of a smile. "Keep her? As in lock her up? I don't know that she'd be too happy with that, Jase."

Jase flashed an exasperated frown. "Do I have to spell it out for you? You need a wife. You really do. And I need a mom, and the doc is perfect for us, so ask her to marry you."

"You've been thinking about this for all of what? Five minutes? What exactly are we offering her, Jase?"

"Money. We've got lots of money. She likes the house, and she really likes kissing you, so maybe you should step up that part of it. I think she'll go for it."

Cole shook his head. "You need to do a little more thinking, Jase. You know we can't just buy her. Maia isn't like that. And I don't have all that much to offer her, but I'm working on it."

Jase's face brightened. "You are? I really want her to stay with us, Cole. She makes us feel like we belong."

"We do belong. Whether or not I can get her to stay, we're always going to be family."

"Good morning!" Maia entered the kitchen, her smile wide as she took in the sight of the two brothers eating breakfast. "You're up before me this morning."

Cole was not going to allow her to get away with putting distance between them. He'd made it damn clear last night he was making love to her, not having sex. And this wasn't going to be a one-night stand. Jase might have had the right idea. He needed to step things up.

Cole snagged her around the waist and pulled her into his arms, settling his mouth over hers firmly. Staking a claim as blatantly as he could. His hand curved around the nape of her neck, held her still while his teeth tugged at her lower lip and his tongue teased at the seam until she opened for him. Her body softened, seemed to melt right into his as he kissed her thoroughly. At once he pulled her tight against him, losing himself in her heat, in the rising tide of intense desire she brought with her.

Jase cleared his throat. "See? I told you she likes kissing you. Are you two going to be doing that all the time, because it's okay with me if you are, just not in the kitchen."

"Yes," Cole said decisively.

"No," Maia assured at the same time. They exchanged a long look. She laughed and rubbed Cole's jaw. "You're looking all serious and stubborn this morning, Steele. I was planning on making gingerbread for a gingerbread house and using the gumdrops in the cupboard for trees. No one can be serious when we bake for Christmas."

"Hey! Those are *my* gumdrops! I made Cole buy them for me, and I'm not giving them up."

"We need them for the gingerbread house. It's part of decorating for Christmas," Maia explained patiently. "We have to use whatever is available and gumdrops work."

Jase held up his hand. "We're not going to *eat* the gingerbread?"

"No, I'm going to make a really cute house and decorate it with frosting and whatever else I can find."

He shook his head. "She's crazy, Cole. You can't bake bread and not expect us to eat it. You're going too far, Doc. I can do without the cute house, but the stomach demands food and baked goods."

"You aren't getting into the spirit of the season, Jase," Maia pointed out.

"Yeah, and I'm not going to either if you deny me food." He stuffed more toast into his mouth. "And stay away from my gumdrops."

"Don't talk with your mouth full."

Cole poured Maia tea from the teapot he had steeping under a small towel. "Before you start baking gingerbread for houses, would you mind going out to the stable and checking out the horses. See if any of them pass on any memories to you."

Her heart gave a curious flutter. He'd made her tea the exact way she liked it, even adding a small amount of milk. "What are you planning?" She set the teacup on the counter, a slight frown on her face.

There was anxiety in her turquoise eyes. Cole caught her hand, holding it against his side. "It's no big deal if you can't find out any more details," he assured her. "I'm going to shake things up a little regardless and see what happens. I checked, and we've got a short window of opportunity. The weather should clear for Christmas Eve."

"I don't like the sound of that." Maia said. "Opportunity for what? And what are you shaking up?" She tightened her fingers around his. "You aren't going to do anything crazy, are you?"

She looked so afraid for him he bent down to brush the top of her head with a kiss. It was an amazing feeling to have someone worry about him. "I just want you to see if you can give us a little clearer picture, that's all."

"Clearer picture of what?" Jase asked, his eyes bright with curiosity.

Maia expected Cole to hedge, but he didn't. He let go of

Maia, to sit across the table from the boy. She picked up her tea and followed.

"I'm beginning to think all these accidents, with the horse, with you, Maia and the ice, even the old man's murder, are all connected. We promised one another we'd be honest. You're not a baby, and I don't intend to hide anything from you. I may be completely off base, but if I'm not, we have a problem on our hands."

Jase went very still. "You think it's Al?"

Cole drummed his fingers on the tabletop. "I don't know about Al. I hope not. He pulled you away from the fence that was giving way, and he's done a good job with the crew and given his best to the ranch."

"He's helped me a lot," Jase said, his voice tight. "No one ever took the time to work with me. I've learned about the horses and cattle, the hay, even repairing fences. He always answers my questions, and he never makes me feel stupid."

"I like the man too, Jase," Cole said. "I honestly don't know one way or the other, but if I'm right about all this, I don't think he could be in on it. If I'm right, his brother-in-law is the perp, and he tried to get you and Al off the ranch."

"I never liked Fred." Jase ducked his head. "I was sometimes afraid it was you, Cole." He confessed it in a soft rush of words. "I'm sorry. I tried not ever to think it, but I can't seem to trust anyone very much."

Cole's smile held no humor. "If anyone can understand, Jase, it's definitely me. I was having the same problem worrying about you. We'll make it through this and whatever else is thrown at us. Together. Maia's right. We can make our own traditions and become a family right here. We've come a long way just by taking back the house."

Jase nodded. "That's true. And it looks great. The doc threw a bunch of pillows on all the furniture in the living room, and it looks completely different. With the tree and Mom's quilt, I feel like the house is really ours."

Maia set her teacup on the table and stood up. "I'm glad you like it, Jase. I'd better get to work if you want me to check the horses in the stable too. I'll see to Wally first, check the horses, then feed the mountain lion. I don't want her scent on me when I'm around the horses."

"I didn't think about that," Jase said.

"You've always got to remember what you're doing around exotics, Jase. You can never become complacent. You can't ever turn your back on them. People have no business owning them and trying to turn them into pets. I've heard of a tiger being kept in an apartment building. It was rescued, but then what do you do with it? Zoos have little funding, and the rescue sanctuaries are full. It leaves euthanasia as the only choice. It makes me angry."

Her gaze met Cole's piercing blue eyes, and she shrugged. "I told you I have a bad temper. Anything to do with the mistreatment of animals brings out the worst in me. It takes so much to run the rescue sanctuaries, and half the time they don't have the funding they need to feed and shelter and provide veterinarian care for exotics."

"Why is it so much, Doc?" Jase asked. "You'd think people would pay to see the animals, and that would provide the money for their care."

"It would be nice if it were that simple, but it isn't. You need licensed people who know what they're doing, an enormous area, and all exotics have special needs. You can't return them to the wild like a lot of people mistakenly want you to do." Maia realized her voice was rising, and she blushed, holding up her hands in surrender. "I'll stop, it's the only safe thing to do."

Cole leaned over to brush her mouth with his. "I like you all fired up. I can see we aren't going to have any hunting on this property anytime soon."

She looked flustered, indignant, a little wary. Maia pulled away from him, glancing at Jase, who was grinning. "Is the weather really going to give us a break tomorrow?"

Immediately the smile left the boy's face. "Not that much of a break, right Cole? Not enough to get into town."

Cole's expression shut down completely. His shoulders tightened. He drummed his fingers on the table, watching Maia closely. "We could probably get you out if you really wanted to leave before Christmas, Maia. I don't want you to go, and neither does Jase, but if you have somewhere important to go, we'll do our best to get you there."

Jase shook his head hard, his lips pressed tightly together. Maia caught the glitter of tears in his eyes as he turned away from her. The room was suddenly filled with terrible tension.

"Somehow I can't see the two of you taking care of the mountain lion without me." She tried to keep her voice teasing to lighten the situation. Her heart was breaking for them both. A man and boy struggling to be normal when they didn't even know what normal was. She didn't need the pretense from them, and she didn't want it. Deliberately she poked Jase in the ribs. "You'd get eaten, although if Cole doesn't feed you every five minutes, the cat might be in danger."

"It would depend on how hungry I am," Jase said.

"Are you saying you would eat a cat?" Cole lifted his eyebrow, but inside he could feel the tight knots in his stomach beginning to loosen. She wasn't going to leave them. He had a reprieve.

"Ugg, you're a sick, sick man, bro. I wouldn't really."

Maia stood up, pushing back her chair. "I'm off to work; you both behave while I'm gone."

"Actually, we're coming with you," Cole said decisively.

Maia shrugged and picked up her bag. Frankly, she'd feel far better if they did come with her. If Cole was right, and his father had hidden something on the ranch that people felt was worth killing for, she didn't want to run into someone looking for it.

Wally looked much better, and there was no sign of infection. His temperature was normal, and he was moving around the enclosure much more comfortably. Maia fed him his antibiotics with his grain and hay while Jase talked to him at great length.

"He's a natural with animals," she told Cole, seeing the pride on his face as he watched his brother. "If he wants to be a veterinarian, he'll be a good one."

"He's a great kid," Cole agreed, leaning one hand against the wall near her head, effectively caging her between the wall and his body. "And he's smart, Maia. The old man was a complete bastard, but he had brains. Jase is serious about hitting the books. He hasn't gone to a regular school, but he's had the best of tutors. Brett Steele didn't want idiots for sons, and he made certain we were well educated."

"You don't have to convince me, Cole, I can see Jase is smart." She was fairly certain Cole had no idea how proud of his brother he sounded.

"I wanted to thank you, for saying you'll stay through Christmas. He really needs you here." Cole hesitated a moment. He could hear his own heartbeat. "I do too." Had he really said it aloud? Damn, he sounded pathetic. He stood there, blocking her way so she couldn't walk away from him, terrified of losing her when he didn't really have her. When had his feelings changed from wanting to go to bed with her to needing her in his life? How had she wrapped herself inside of him?

Maia stroked a hand down his chest. There were shadows in his eyes, a set to his mouth she didn't quite understand, and she was trained and always alert to read subtleties. More and more he reminded her of the mountain lion, wary, dangerous, in need but ready to strike out if threatened. "I want to stay," she admitted softly.

Desire mingled with relief flared in his eyes. It hit her then. Cole Steele, the invincible, the man always aloof and uncaring, the man with supreme confidence, had very little where she was concerned. She went up on her toes and pressed a kiss onto his chin. "I really wanted to stay and not just because of the cat."

"Or Jase. You're very fond of Jase," he prompted, needing to hear her admission.

She laughed, her eyes warming into a brilliant blue-green. It was all he could do not to sweep her up into his arms and carry her off. Who would have thought one person could impact his life this way, make something he thought he lacked come alive deep inside of him and thrive and grow into such intense emotions.

"You're such a baby. I'm *very* fond of Jase."

He waited. When she didn't continue he stepped closer until her soft breasts pushed against his chest and his hips aligned perfectly with her, pressing against her body. "That's not very nice."

There was a growl to his voice, a sensuality that sent fire zinging through her veins. It was impossible to resist him and she didn't even try. She moved her hips suggestively, a slight feminine enticement, her body soft and welcoming. "I wanted to stay to be with you."

"Was that so hard?" He lowered his lips to hers mostly because he had to, because if he didn't he might really lose his mind and carry her off. The shape of her mouth was incredibly sexy, especially when she flashed her dynamite smile. He was drowning in lust, but more terrifying than that, he could feel love and it was overwhelming. So much so that he dared not examine the emotion too closely.

Maia's arms encircled his neck, her fingers tangling in his hair. "You know it was," she murmured into his hot mouth. She loved kissing him. Loved touching him. She had no idea where it would lead, if anywhere. Her job kept her traveling constantly and Cole Steele wasn't exactly the settling-down type. She had left herself open for a tremendous amount of pain, and worse, she'd known it before she'd ever gone to his bedroom. It had been her choice. She'd made it willingly, hoping she would think her time with him had been worth it when she had to go.

For a moment she leaned against him, into him, wanting to cling to his strength. All the while he was kissing her, making it impossible to think straight. And she didn't really want to, she wanted the fire flashing through her veins and over her skin. And she wanted the warmth in her heart, filling her until she ached with it.

Jase banged Wally's stall gate closed with a little extra force to remind them he was still in the barn. Maia glanced at him to find him grinning from ear to ear. He shook his head at her.

"I know. He's just irresistible, but we won't mention it because he's already so arrogant we can't take it."

"Speak for yourself, Doc," Jase protested. "He doesn't do a thing for me."

"Come on, you two," Cole said. "I'm letting you clean out the stalls while I feed the horses just for that, Jase," he added.

Jase put his hand on his back and began groaning loudly as he followed them along the covered walkway to the stable.

Cole and Jase fed and watered the horses while Maia wandered around the stable, taking her time, trying to get a feel of the place. It was a beautiful structure, well lit and functional. The horse stalls were roomy, and each led to the wide ring in the center of the building where the horses could be exercised and worked in any kind of weather. Like everything else, the builders had spared no expense, and the setup was as good as it could get.

Maia leaned against the gate of a stall and talked softly to the occupant, waiting for the horse to come to her. She loved horses, loved the way they moved and the way they pressed their velvet noses into her palm when she murmured to them. They were always responsive. Most of the horses had memories of packing bundles along a mountain pathway to one of the larger buildings on the ranch. Two had memories of a young boy being beaten. The horse in the corner stall had vivid memories of being ridden hard, quartering the ground back and forth up in a mountainous area. A shudder ran through the horse when it recalled the sight of a mountain lion perched on a branch a distance away, the rifle burst, and the cat leaping to the ground and disappearing into heavy foliage.

"Are you picking up anything?" Cole asked curiously.

Maia nodded. "But I'm not certain what you're looking for."

"Landmarks, something I can use to identify the area they were in, rock formations, the type of trees, a mountainous area versus a valley or a meadow. We have a couple of thousand acres, and if we include the state and federal lands, we're looking for a needle in a haystack."

"I'll try again, but I can't direct them. I'm sort of a receiver." She felt she was failing him. The information was obviously important.

Cole's hand curled around the nape of her neck, his thumb sliding along her jaw. "Whatever you give me is more than I had to start with."

"Give me a little more time with this one." She indicated the horse in the corner stall.

Cole watched as she brushed the animal and spoke softly to it, spending another fifteen minutes lavishing attention on it. He waited to ask her about the images until after she had fed the mountain lion and checked it over thoroughly. She was mostly worried about infection. The cat stared at Cole and Jase the entire time, and they kept a good distance away at Maia's insistence, but behind her back, Cole had a weapon out and ready if the animal made one wrong move toward Maia.

"I'm telling her," Jase whispered, a grin on his face.

Cole shrugged. "She can learn to live with it," he said, his jaw set in a stubborn line. "Someone has to look out for her."

Maia stroked a hand through the cat's fur before leaving it to rest, backing out of the shed. "The two of you look as if you're up to some deep dark conspiracy." The truth was, the lines etched so deep in Cole's face were soft-ening, and every once in a while a faint smile would appear. There were times he actually appeared at peace. Even Jase seemed more relaxed and laughed often.

Her heart gave a funny little lurch. She felt a part of them, as if they were all connected in some strange way. As if she belonged. Maia had to look away, tears burning in her eyes. It was ridiculous to be so involved so fast. She could only put it down to the intensity of the Steele brothers' needs. The thought of leaving them was break-ing her heart, so she just couldn't think about it. She would have Christmas with them, and that would have to be enough.

"Whatever you're thinking about, stop," Cole instructed, his arm curving around her waist to draw her beneath his shoulder. "You looked so sad." He put his other arm around Jase's shoulders, pulling him closer as well. "I want you to help Maia inside with her baking. I'm expecting you to look after her, Jase."

Maia glanced up at his face quickly. He was moving them both back toward the house at a brisk pace. A small spurt of fear burst through her. "What are you going to be doing?"

"Just looking around a little more. I need for you to tell me if you have any other details for me." He reached past her to open the door to the mudroom.

Maia waited until they were back in the kitchen and she had control of her frantically beating heart. He wasn't going to go looking around a little; he was going to bait a trap for a killer. She feared he was the bait.

"You're shaking your head." His tone was very gentle. "Does that mean you don't have anything for me?"

"No, it means I don't want you to do this. Go to the police."

"I am the police."

Maia sank into a chair. "I know, but you don't have anyone to help you."

"Maia, I would never go into a situation without backup. I'm good at what I do. I trusted you with the mountain lion and the wolves. You'll have to trust me with this."

She flashed him a faint smile. "Should I stand out in the yard with a gun?"

"No, you can stay in here and have faith that I'm really not a nice guy at all." He sat down across from her. "What did you see that could help me?" He glanced at his brother, who was leaning against the counter, his face pale. "I'll need you to listen to her, Jase, and help me figure this out."

The boy took a deep breath and nodded, dropping into the chair next to Maia.

Beneath the table, Maia slipped her hand into the teenager's. "I didn't get much that made sense to me, but I can describe the area fairly well. It's definitely up in the mountains, where there are lots of trees. There are huge rocks and a formation that looks as if it's a fortress. I had the impression of a series of caves."

"Yeah, I've been there," Jase said. "I went one time when the old man was gone on a business trip. I snuck away from the men watching me and got lost. I found a trail off of the streambed, just past where the waterfall is. I followed it because the trail was a little wider than a deer trail and my horse had almost automatically turned on it, as if he'd been there before. I was pretty certain I could find my way back, and eventually I did."

"I remember those old caves. You didn't go into them, did you?"

"No, I was only about nine at the time and pretty scared of all the stories the hands told about bears and mountain lions."

"Which are true," Cole pointed out. He stood up and pushed back his chair. "I'm going to take the snowmobile out while the weather is holding." He glanced at his watch. "I've got about an hour and a half before the next storm breaks."

"I don't like you going out alone," Maia objected, shaking her head adamantly. "Let's just call the police and let them investigate."

"I agree, Cole," Jase said, trying to sound adult and firm. "I don't want anything to happen to you."

"I'm just going to take a look around," Cole said. "Nothing's going to happen to me. You both have to remember, the old man owned this town. The police, the school officials, even the counselors were afraid of him. They needed his money, and he had too much political clout to fight him. I don't know who at the police department I can trust. And if he was smuggling something, especially drugs, he's been doing it for years and getting away with it. That means corruption somewhere."

Maia put her arm around Jase. "An hour and a half, Cole. Give me a number to call, someone you trust, if you don't come back."

He studied her face, set in a determined expression, for a moment before scribbling a number on a tablet beside the phone. "Give me two hours, Maia. I'll be back, I promise."

"You'd better be," she answered.

chapter 13

 THE SNOW HAD BEEN FALLING for hours. Maia stared out at the white, silent world. It had seemed so beautiful, a sparkling crystal world, and now it appeared hostile and suffocating. The world outside her window was so white; even though it was nighttime, it appeared light. Through the swirl of flakes she could see the trees and shrubbery encased in ice. Long icicles hung from the overhang of the walkways and decorated the outbuildings. The corrals had layers of snow topping each rail. There was no movement, the world was silent and still as if locked in a frozen time frame.

Cole had come back from his snowmobile ride on time, but his entire demeanor had changed. He hadn't discussed anything with either Jase or her. He'd glanced at their baking project, an elaborate gingerbread house, nodded without really listening to them, and disappeared into an office to spend the rest of the evening on the phone. He was distant and almost frightening, his features expressionless, his eyes hard. He seemed so remote from her, almost as if he were a different person.

"Maia?"

She whirled around, her heart pounding, her hand

going protectively to her throat. There'd been no sound to give him away, but Cole stood in the middle of her bedroom wearing only a soft pair of jeans. His face was in the shadows, and he looked intimidating, a man possessing raw power, filling the room with his muscular build and the force of his personality.

"You aren't afraid of me, are you?"

Maia took a deep breath and let it out slowly. She knew wild animals, had been around them in various environments, and she was well aware that Cole's instincts were those of a trapped animal. She could almost smell the danger emanating from him.

"You've put on your DEA persona, the one you use to stay alive," she stated, her gaze meeting his steadily. "Poor Jase was frightened, and, yes, so was I. You become a different person, one neither of us is familiar with."

"Dammit, Maia."

She sent him a faint smile. "If it keeps you alive, Cole, it's all right with both of us. Whatever it takes to do your job, just do it and don't worry about us being a little uncomfortable with it. Jase told me you were this way when he first met you. I don't blame him for being intimidated."

"What do I do?"

"You put distance between yourself and everyone else, and you shut down your emotions."

"I work undercover, Maia. I can't be showing my emotions to the world, and if I discuss anything with anyone, someone might overhear me or be an enemy. That's the world I live in."

"It's the world you've *always* lived in. As an adult, you simply went out and found the environment most comfortable for you, the one you were familiar with, where you knew all the rules."

He pushed a hand through his hair, his only sign of agitation. "Am I going to lose you because you finally figured out who I really am?"

She smiled, her lips curving into a soft, amused smile that lit up her face. "I've always known who you are, Cole. I knew there was this side of you. It comes out at unexpected times, and it's disconcerting and intimidating, but it isn't anything I can't handle." She shrugged. "You don't know me very well. Most things don't throw me all that easily. I was raised to be my own person, to think for myself and follow my instincts. I can be afraid *for* you and not be afraid *of* you."

"Come here to me."

"You need to talk to Jase. He's too young to understand why you need to withdraw from him." She crossed the distance because she couldn't resist the dark sensuality of his voice. There was something in him she couldn't help but respond to, and tonight he wore that dark intensity she found so compelling.

"I will, Maia," he promised, drawing her into his arms. "I didn't like not having you in my bed."

"I've only been in your bed once, Cole," she pointed out.

"You were there all night. I've never wanted anyone in bed with me all night. I can't sleep because I'm always on edge and feel I have to be alert just in case. I didn't feel that way with you. I wrapped my arms around you and fell asleep. It felt right."

"You didn't do much sleeping."

His hand cupped her face, his thumb sliding over her

soft skin. "I'm planning on not sleeping much tonight either."

"Oh really?" She slid her arms around his neck and pressed her body against his. "That's a good thing. Are you going to tell me what you're up to with the snowmobile and phone calls?"

"Later. I'll tell you later." His teeth tugged gently at her ear. "Much later." He slid his hands under the hem of the soft flannel shirt she wore to find bare skin. His hands cupped her bottom, and lifted her to bring her more in line with his own body, holding her there for a moment, savoring the way she fit against him. Her soft body stilled the pounding in his head and tamed the roaring of his nightmares, the terrible memories he could never quite push into oblivion.

Her hands skimmed over his chest, her lips sliding over his neck, his jaw, her teeth nibbling on his lip until he was kissing her, losing himself in her heat. He drank her in, devoured her, needing to be closer to her to keep the demons at bay. "I have too many clothes on," he whispered into her hot mouth.

"Yes you do," she agreed, her hands dropping to the waistband of his jeans.

He felt the brush of her knuckles against his belly, over his hard arousal. Every thought went out of his head but his need to feel her body surrounding his. Heat and flame danced over his skin and invaded his veins, spread through his muscles. Whatever roaring beasts had threatened to consume him with rage and hatred fell quiet under the caress of her stroking fingers, under the assault of her hot mouth gliding over his chest. He was harder than he'd ever been in his life, more in need, his mind crowded with erotic images, with hunger and need that left no room for nightmares.

His hands slid over the curves of her hips, along her thighs, his fingers dipping into the moist heat of her body. He loved the way she responded to him, the way she gave herself so generously to him. She made it clear she wanted to touch him, needed to feel and taste him with the same urgency he felt for her. He slid the flannel shirt from her body and dropped it onto the floor before catching her up in his arms and carrying her to the bed.

"I'm not going to let you go, Maia," he warned, wanting to be honest, hating to be so damned vulnerable. "I can't let you just walk away from me."

Her fingers skimmed his face, caressed his shoulders, and moved down his back. "Who said anything about going anywhere, Cole? A little action would be appreciated."

"You want action?" His eyebrow shot up, his face darkly sensual.

Maia arched up to press her aching breasts against his chest, to rub the tips of her nipples across his skin while her teeth nipped at his chin. "I'm on fire here."

He felt it then, a wild rush of excitement coursing hotly through his body. She tightened every muscle, brought every nerve ending alive. He wanted to pound into her, drive so deep she could never get him out. *Brand her.* At once he stiffened. Pulled away from her, sitting up on the bed and wiping his face.

Maia sat up, her arms sliding around his waist. "What is it?"

He shook his head. "You shouldn't be here with me. The things I think about are wrong. There's too much violence in me. I don't want you to get hurt, Maia, not you."

"Do I look fragile to you? I want you just the way you are, Cole. I know what you are and who you are. You just have to figure out I'm quite capable of handling anything you can throw my way. You think you're rough with me, but you're not. You're strong, and the way your body is so frantic for mine only makes me want you more."

"Do you think I don't see the bruises on your skin from my gripping you too tight? Dammit, Maia, I thought I could find some way to be normal with you."

She laughed. "That's just silly. I have bruises every day from the work I do. I'd rather you put them there when you're giving me so much pleasure you're driving me out of my mind."

He should have known she would laugh. He turned his head and met her eyes. Desire, hot and intense and filled with some emotion he shied away from trying to identify. He couldn't stop himself from having her, not when she was so hungry for him. Cole spread her across the bed, coming down on top of her, his hands sliding over silken skin as his mouth settled over hers.

Her thighs tightened and she shifted her hips, aligning her body more perfectly to rub against him in temptation, a siren's call. His palm stroked over her breast, captured it to roll her nipple between his thumb and finger. Her breath caught in her throat, and she arched back, open to him, wanting him. His mouth left hers at the invitation, and he kissed his way over the creamy mound to settle there, fingers stroking and massaging while she cried out, unable to prevent the sound of pleasure from escaping.

"I need you, Maia," he whispered softly.

Maia trembled, shuddering with arousal, lifting herself

almost desperately into his mouth. "I need you too." Her hands skimmed over his back, caught at his hips to guide him into her.

His knee nudged her thighs wider apart so that he could easily settle there, pushing into her slowly, penetrating with a deep, long stroke that pushed through velvet-soft petals, forcing her tight muscles to open for him. Immediately he was bathed in tight, hot-silken heat. The breath left his body in a rush, and fire streaked from his toes to the top of his head. She did that. Maia. She did things with her body he still couldn't comprehend.

His hands pinned her hips, holding her firmly, giving him the ability to set the pace and control the ride. He needed that, needed to allow his own driving violence to well up slowly, to mingle with the passion and emotion he felt for her. He began to move harder, deeper, until he was plunging into her over and over as her breathless cries urged him on. Her fingers biting into his buttocks nearly drove him wild. He held on to his sanity as long as he could, pushing her higher and higher, holding off her release until she was writhing beneath him, every bit as desperate as he felt.

When it came, their release was shattering, her body gripping his so tight he thought he'd explode as they came together. They stared into one another's eyes for a long time, then he was kissing her over and over, greedy for the taste of her, needing her sweetness, afraid of saying or not saying the right words to her.

He held her to him, his hand stroking through her hair, aching to say something, anything to make her feel what he was feeling. "Maia?" His heart pounded in a kind of terror. His mouth went dry.

She turned her head and smiled at him. "I'm here."

Her smile always affected him. He dreamt of her smile now. Just as he dreamt of her body open and soft for him, a haven, a refuge he never wanted to give up.

He tried to say the words women needed. He wanted to tell her to stay forever. What did he have to offer her? He was consumed with rage at times. At those times he needed the rush of working undercover. He was driven to find and arrest men who thought themselves above the law, more clever and superior to all others. There were parts of him he was afraid of. A violence he sometimes dealt with by beating a boxing bag for hours, or racing a horse over a mountain trail. So many things he held in little compartments in his mind, deep where no one saw.

Until Maia. She looked through the emptiness in his eyes, somewhere beyond the shadows, and she seemed just to accept him. It was terrifying to think he could be wrong. And if he asked her and she turned away from him, he'd be lost.

Cole sighed. "I found the old man's stash," he confessed. He turned on his side, rising above her to prop himself up on his elbow. He could hear the regret in his voice and knew she would think it was because of his father. "I didn't want to know anything more about him. And I didn't want to have to tell Jase."

"Jase has you now, Cole," Maia said, placing her palm over his heart to comfort him. If anyone needed comfort it was Cole. He just didn't recognize it.

"It wasn't all that hard to find it. When I was a kid I used to go up to that large rock formation, and there was a series of caves. One of them was very small, but when you accessed it, if you crawled to the back, there was a larger chamber. I couldn't find it and I knew immediately the old man had covered it up. I knew approximately where it was, so it didn't take long."

"It was a shipment of drugs?"

"A large shipment. The remains of the pilot were propped up in the back against the wall of the cave like some macabre pirate skeleton left to guard the bundles. I should have known having oil wells, natural gas reserves, and a thriving cattle business wouldn't be enough for the old man. He needed to feel superior. He needed the rush of pitting his brains against law enforcement."

"Maybe you did know what he was doing, or suspected on some level as a child, Cole. You became a DEA agent. Subconsciously you may have been trying to find a way to separate and define yourself."

He bent his head to kiss her. "You say the nicest things, Maia. I don't know how you always think of the exactly the right thing to say to make me feel better when I'm feeling low, but you manage it."

She nibbled her way across his jaw to tease at his mouth with her teeth. "I say what I think, which isn't always a good thing, Cole."

"I have to go, honey. I checked with the weather service, and I've only got a few hours to pull this off. Follow me down to the kitchen. I want to show you how to set the alarm." He brushed backed her hair, kissing her again and again as if he might not stop, then pulled abruptly away.

Maia followed him to his room and sat on his bed. She sat up, watched him dress, clutching the sheet to her as if that might protect her from the sudden fear she was trying to suppress. He was dragging weapons out of every conceivable hiding place and shoving them into holsters, taping them to his back until she could only stare in horror.

He tossed her his own flannel shirt wishing he could stick around and enjoy her in it. "Come on, Maia. I have to go now." He couldn't look at her much longer and not feel the choking fear of losing her. Facing gunfire and possible death was nothing compared to the terror of being so vulnerable to another human being.

Maia followed him down the stairs, buttoning buttons as she went, trying to look casual and calm, wondering if Cole had felt the same way when she had attended the mountain lion. She listened dutifully to all his instructions, but when he turned away from her she caught his hand and tugged him back, reluctant to let him go.

"You're coming back."

"Of course." Cole kissed Maia hard. "Turn on the security alarm the moment I leave. All the doors and windows will lock automatically. You know where the safety rooms are. One upstairs and one down. Use them if you have to."

She clutched his fingers, holding him to her. "Don't do anything stupid."

"I'm never stupid, Maia, and I never forget details. Take care of Jasc. There's paperwork in the top desk drawer in case of emergencies. My boss has copies. I faxed them to him last night."

"Don't tell me that. Tell me you're going to come back to me all in one piece."

Cole leaned down to kiss her again. "Stay out of trouble and keep Jase occupied. I don't want either one of you to get any ideas about being a hero. When I'm out there, I'm going to treat everyone as the enemy. I can't be worried that you or Jase will get it in your heads to try to help. I might end up shooting one of you."

"I'm not stupid, Cole," Maia assured him. "I'll take care of Jase, but he's not going to like that you snuck out so early."

"He'd want to come, and I don't have a lot of time to spend arguing with him," he glanced at his watch. "The weather will be closing in faster than anticipated. I have maybe three or four hours at the most, then the storm will break again."

"You mean you don't have a lot of time to spend reassuring him," Maia corrected. She let him go because she had no choice. Cole Steele couldn't be anything other than who he was, any more than she could be. "Then I'll see you in three or four hours."

He slipped out the kitchen door into the mudroom to pull on the clothes he'd prepared and slung his pack and rifle over his shoulder before going outside. He wanted to be seen, but look like he was being cautious, wary of anyone who might be watching. He was a man with something to hide. The minute he set foot outside of the mudroom, he became that person, walking with deliberate stealthy intent, casting glances back toward the house as if someone might catch him leaving. He moved in stops and starts, hurrying across open space, stopping in the shadows and behind buildings and trees to look around. It wasn't until he was by the garage housing the snowmobiles that he was certain he was being watched.

The air was cold and dry, the wind coming at him in gusts. He pulled his knitted cap over his face to keep from being burned or frostbitten as he burst out of the garage, the snowmobile swaying wildly, then catching traction to skim over the snow. Maia was right, he realized, as he flew over the snow toward the trail leading into the higher mountains. He should have talked to Jase. If something did happen, this could look bad. He was deliberately setting it up to make others think he was taking the drugs for himself and selling the shipment to the highest bidder.

He shook his head, a frown on his face. That was straight from Maia's mind to his. She was even making him think like her. He had never thought to let anyone into his life to such an extent, but there was no keeping Maia out. She had managed to twist herself deep inside of him until he didn't want her out. She brought him alive in a way he'd never been before.

Cole scanned the surrounding areas, openly using binoculars, wanting those watching him to be aware he was leery. He was a man doing something illegal, and he knew it. He felt an itch between his shoulder blades and sent up a silent prayer it wasn't the scope of a rifle trained on him. He was counting on the fact that Fred and his people had murdered Brett Steele *before* they realized he'd moved the shipment, and they wanted Cole to lead them to it. He'd never had so much to lose before, and the thought of the danger didn't give him quite the same rush it always had.

He glanced at the sky before setting off again. The clouds were heavy and dark, but the weather was holding. He could have moved the stuff closer to the house, but it might have endangered Maia and Jase. This way, if anyone wanted to take the shipment from him, they had to follow him away from the ranch house, but with the weather so dicey, it was touch-and-go whether he was going to pull the entire thing off and make it back before the next storm hit.

He was able to maneuver the snowmobile up the trail

through the rock formation because the snow was so deep. It enabled him to move the sled he was dragging into position at the front of the cave before rolling back the rocks blocking the entrance. He had to use a pry bar as leverage to remove the boulders before crawling inside. This was the most dangerous part. While loading the snowmobile, he would be vulnerable. He was inside the cave and would have to crawl in places to drag out the bundles to stack onto the snowmobile. He wouldn't be able to see or hear an approaching enemy.

Cole worked steadily, sweating as he did so, aware of the least little noise, every moment feeling as though it might be his last. They didn't need him to bring out the shipment, only to lead them to it. He tried to keep his exposure down, keeping as much of the bare foliage between him and open spaces when he came out of the cave to add to the burden on the sled.

When they came, they came like wolves, slinking out of the forest to surround him, guns drawn, Fred leading the pack. He grinned at Cole. "Like father, like son. But I'm afraid that's my dope you're trying to steal."

"It belongs to you?" Cole asked, straightening slowly as he tied off the last bundle. "I don't think so. I don't see your name on it anywhere."

Fred held up his gun. "This is my claim, Steele. Keep your hands where I can see them."

"How'd you know about it?" Cole said, sounding disgusted.

"I helped bring it in before your old man got greedy and moved it. We did it all the time. I have the connections, Steele, you don't. I've got everything in place; you'd just lose it all. You should thank me." He laughed and cocked his gun, pointing it straight at Cole's heart. "You can go join your daddy in hell."

"Hold it, Fred!" The voice came from above them. Al lay stretched out in the snow, the rifle trained on his brother-in-law. "I'm not going to let you kill him, Fred. I don't know what this is all about; but I saw you watching him, sneaking after him, and you're not going to kill him."

"What are you going to do, Al?" Fred snarled. "Choose your almighty boss over your own family? Has he promised you a share if you side with him?"

Cole looked anxiously toward Al. He knew a couple of Fred's buddies were circling around trying to get position on him. The last thing he wa nted was his foreman to get killed. "What are you planning, Fred? We can make a deal."

"I had a deal with your old man. He double-crossed us. He sat there in his stinking office surrounded by enough money for a hundred men, but he was so damned greedy. He laughed at me, laughed at all of us. He dared us to go to the police."

"So you put a bullet in his brain."

"You should have seen his face when I pulled the trigger. He was good at killing, but he didn't want to die. I should know, I did enough of it for him."

"But you did it too soon, didn't you, Fred? You didn't know he'd moved the shipment."

Fred shrugged, glanced up toward Al, obviously waiting for his men to pick off his brother-in-law. He scowled, angry they were taking so long and Al still had the rifle rock steady on him. "I thought I'd have time to find it, but you fired us all."

Cole smiled at him. "Smart of me, wasn't it? How long

were you killing and running drugs for the old man? You the one who killed Jase's mother?"

"She kept trying to take the kid. He wasn't going to let her do that. She should have known better."

"So you arranged the accident? How'd you manage all this time to get away with it?" Cole made a small movement toward the snowmobile.

Fred brought his gun up. "Don't be stupid, Steele."

"Don't you be stupid, Fred," Al said.

"I've been getting away with things a long time. You just need a few key people in your pocket," Fred bragged. "Put the rifle down, Al, or my sister is going to be a widow. Do it now."

"You're under arrest. All of you. Put your guns down," Cole said. "Right now you're surrounded by federal marksmen with rifles trained on every one of you. Drop your weapons now." Cole sent Fred a grim smile. "I'm with drug enforcement."

"What the hell are you talking about?" Fred whipped his head around wildly looking for his crew. He caught a glimpse of several of his men down on the ground, others clothed in all white standing over them and holding rifles to the backs of their necks. "You've been in jail. What are you, a snitch?"

Cole walked across the scant feet of snow separating them and removed the gun from Fred's hand. "You bought a cover story, Fred." He pushed the man toward one of the officers. Flakes of snow were already drifting from the skies.

Al stood up slowly, rifle at his side. "This is going to kill my wife. I'm sorry, Mr. Steele. I had no idea what he was up to."

"He wanted you to think I drove that horse into the fence. It was to get you and Jase off the ranch so he could search it."

"I figured that out. He was watching you all the time. I didn't ever consider drugs might be a part of it. I just thought he was mad over losing his job."

"Thanks for coming after me."

Jase sat white-faced at the table as Cole told him about the drug shipment, the murder of the pilot and the boy's mother. The teenager went very still, tension and anger radiating from him. Abruptly he rose and without a word, ran out of the kitchen into the mudroom. They could hear him stamping into his boots.

Cole sighed and stood up. "I'd better follow him."

He looked tired and strained. Maia went to him, put her arms around him. "At least you both know what really happened to Brett. You don't have to wonder about it anymore. And neither of you has to worry about the other's having been involved in that violent act."

His hand slipped over her silky hair, but Cole didn't answer. There was no way to tell her how deep rage could go. How it could consume one and eat away every good thing until there was only nightmares and demons left in the world. Jase had to fight it the same way he did.

Maia watched him go before sinking down into the chair Jase had vacated, hands over her face, weeping for both of them. She cried for a long while, and, when they didn't return, she washed her face and went after them. It was instinct more than anything else that led her in the right direction. Before she reached the barn she could hear the rhythmic pounding of flesh against something solid.

"Jase!" Maia stopped in the doorway of the barn staring at him with horror. "What are you doing to yourself?"

Jase slammed his bloodied hands into the heavy bag repeatedly. "I hate him. He's taken everything from me. *Everything!*"

"Jase." There was a wealth of warning in Cole's voice.

Maia glanced at Cole, saw the misery and despair in his eyes as he crouched against the wall, watching his little brother rage at things neither of them could control.

"Stop it right this minute!" She used her most authoritative voice. It startled both men so that Jase dropped his arms to his sides and stood breathing heavily, small droplets of blood trickling down his knuckles to the floor. She moved into the barn, marched straight over to Jase, and took his hands in hers to prevent further action.

"He took your mother, and he took your childhood, Jase. You have a right to be angry about that," she said, turning his bloodied, swollen hands over to examine them much more closely. "But doing this to yourself is just plain stupid."

"Yeah, well you don't have a father who murdered and ran drugs and abused animals and every other thing he could get his hands on," Jase snapped, snatching his hands away. "He didn't beat you and brand you and humiliate you, and he didn't kill your mother."

Cole stood up, a flow of strength and power, instantly protective of Maia.

She didn't look at him as she stepped closer to them. "Jase," she kept her voice low and even. "You persist in thinking Brett Steele was normal. He was ill. I don't know if something made him that way, or whether he just deteriorated into his sickness. Power can corrupt. He was a genius. You both know that, and you inherited his brains and his strengths. He wasn't all bad. There were good traits in him. He can only destroy your life if you let him."

"What if I'm like him? I could be like him," Jase said.

Of course he would have the same fears as Cole. She glanced at the older man, and he immediately put his hand on Jase's shoulder.

"I thought the same thing, Jase," Cole admitted. "About me, about you. Hell, we share the same genetics. But you're nothing like him, even less so than I am. Look how good you are with animals. And you hit the books instead of turning out to be the resident bad boy. I'd put your sanity and your character ahead of those of anyone I know."

"What he did is no reflection whatsoever on you as a human being, Jase. You have your own life and your own responsibility to live your life in the best way that you can. Of course your childhood will impact your adult life, but you're aware of it and can take steps to counter any demons that arise. You're strong and you're smart and you can handle anything that comes your way."

Jase shook his head, tears glittering in his eyes, spilling over to run down his cheeks. His chest heaved, and his shoulders shook. "I don't think I can ever be okay again, Maia."

She gathered him into her arms, pressing his face into her shoulder while she held him. The teenager sobbed as if his heart was breaking. She looked desperately up at Cole.

Cole swept his arms around both of them. "We're going to make it, Jase," he reassured, rubbing the boy's neck, crowding close so Jase would feel his determination and strength. "We're going to be all right together."

chapter 14

"It's MIDNIGHT, officially Christmas," Maia announced. She rubbed the top of Jase's head as she set a tall glass of cider on the coffee table in front of him. "Merry Christmas."

Jase was much calmer, sitting in the living room and staring at the tall tree. His mother's ornaments adorned the tree, and he stared at the alligator. Maia twisted the tail and watched the jaws open and close around a strand of popcorn. She was rewarded with a faint smile from Jase.

"When do we get to open gifts?" he asked. His voice was gruff, husky with leftover tears, but he had his emotions back under control.

"Usually Christmas morning," Maia answered, curling up on the couch beside Cole. "Although some people open them on Christmas Eve." She leaned over to check the ice packs she'd placed on his hands. "Keep those there. It's a wonder you didn't break all your bones."

"I can't exactly drink my cider if I've got this stuff wrapped around my hands," Jase pointed out. There was a flash of a smile in the look he exchanged with Cole.

"Then you can just stare at the cider," Maia said, "but

you keep your hands in those wraps. You're lucky I didn't chase you around the house with a needle to give you a tetanus shot at the very least."

"You did," Jase reminded her. "Cole had to save me. You threatened to numb my knuckles too or something equally scary." He looked at his older brother. "Do you do that a lot? Go undercover and have guns pointed at you?"

"Yes." Cole refused to lie or gloss over his job to Jase.

"Have you ever been shot?"

"Twice, and I was stabbed a couple of times. Just like when Maia works with the animals, she has to watch herself, never forget even for a moment what she's doing; my job is the same. I can never get careless."

"How did you get all those agents here?"

"It wasn't easy. I couldn't go to the local police because I didn't know who was dirty or who could be trusted. I called my boss, and we set the trap fast."

"You took a big risk," Maia said. Cole had been away from them for the four hours he'd indicated he would be, and the agents had spent several more hours trying to get the prisoners and the shipment of drugs off the ranch. The storm had moved in slowly, and with Al and Cole working together, they'd finally managed to get everyone out safely. Maia had spent hours wanting to be alone with Cole, needing to touch him, to reassure herself that he was unharmed, but then Jase had broken down completely, and they had spent the remainder of the time consoling him.

"The weather was closing in, and it worried me that Fred was getting anxious. I didn't want either of you caught in the middle. And remember, I didn't know whose side Al was on. I'm glad it was ours."

"Are you going to go away, Cole?" Jase finally voiced the question that was preying on his mind.

For the first time, Cole hesitated. Maia and Jase regarded him with wide, fearful eyes. Cole leaned over the table toward his brother, avoiding looking at Maia. "Jase, I want to tell you I'm always going to be here, but that would be a lie. I have to work sometimes. I won't be working as much, but every now and then, I need to work." It was the adrenaline rush. It was the rage that swirled too close to the surface that was never going to go completely away. He hoped he wouldn't need it as much, but he knew he'd never be utterly free of his demons, and if Maia was going to agree to be in his life, he needed both Jase and her to know he would have times he couldn't help but leave them.

"You have money. You can have my money," Jase burst out.

"That's not what he means," Maia said gently. "He means when things are really bad for him, working undercover is a way of sorting it out."

Jase just stared at her, hurt and fear mingling together in his eyes.

"Like you pounding the bag," she added. "He goes undercover and becomes someone else for a while. Does that make sense?"

Cole wanted to protest, but she was right. It was a world he was familiar with. Lies and deceit and never getting too close. A world of violence, where explosive rage often had a legitimate target. He was going to lose here. He could see the handwriting on the wall, and it was killing him.

Jase subsided, shrinking back into the chair, making

himself very small as he turned to Cole. "Are you planning on putting me in a boarding school so you can go back to the drug enforcement work?"

"No! Absolutely not. Why would you think that Jase? I want you to attend a regular school, but not a boarding school." Cole shoved both hands through his hair. "This is crazy. My work has nothing to do with you going to school. If I have to leave on an assignment, I'll have someone who you trust stay here with you. Someone I trust that we're both comfortable with. I'm not going anywhere until that happens."

Jase took the ice packs off his hands and grabbed a handful of cookies. "Well, I'm not going to worry about it then. It's not like we have anyone else."

"I told you, we're getting a housekeeper. I just haven't found one yet." There was a warning note in Cole's voice.

Jase shrugged. "You scare everyone, Cole. I don't have to worry about anyone coming here to work in the house unless she's after your money."

Maia hastily covered her mouth with her hand and looked away from them. They sounded more and more like brothers every day.

"Don't encourage him, Maia," Cole said.

She didn't even wince at the hard edge to his voice. Her smothered laughter rang out from behind her hand before she could stop it. "I'm sorry, really I am, but you so deserved that one. You need to practice smiling in the mirror, Cole. It will help you win over the ladies."

"He doesn't have to smile at women," Jase reminded with a wicked grin.

"Put the ice packs back on your hands and stop eating so many cookies," Cole said. He reached under the coffee table and pulled out a small object. "Here's your Christmas present." His voice turned gruff and it embarrassed him, but he persisted with a dogged determination. "I don't know exactly how this is done, and I didn't wrap it, but I made this for you, Jase." His fingers remained wrapped around it, concealing the object. "You know I'll get you something nice from town once we can get out of here, but I wanted you to have something on Christmas morning."

"Let me see it," Jase said eagerly, holding out his swollen hand.

Cole placed the wood carving in his brother's hand. A snarling mountain lion was crouched protectively over a small alligator. The carving was intricate, each curve and line smooth and etched deep so that the figures seemed to be alive. Jase turned it over and saw the date carved into the bottom.

"It's the two of you, isn't it?" Maia asked, taking the carving out of Jase's hand to stroke her finger down the cat's back. "You and Jase. That's what it represents."

"It's all of us," Jase corrected. "You, me, my mom, and Cole."

Maia handed the carving back to him. "It's beautiful, Cole. You're an unbelievable artist. I had no idea."

"It looks so real," Jase said. "Thanks, Cole."

Cole let his breath out slowly, a small smile somewhere inside of him. Jase understood what he was trying to say with the carving, and more than anything else, that mattered.

"I have something for you too, Jase," Maia said. "It's not nearly as nice as what Cole made for you, but you might be able to use it." She pulled a book out from under the cushions of the couch. "It's a book on animal behavior. I learned a lot from it, and as you can see, it's been well used, but I thought if you were really interested in becoming a vet, you'd enjoy it."

Cole put his arms around Maia. He'd never heard her sound quite so vulnerable, her words spilling out too fast. The book had to have meant a great deal to her, and she wanted Jase to feel the same way.

Jase opened it, read what she had written, and smiled. "We did share a journey, didn't we, Maia? Look at this, Cole. Maia's mother gave this to her."

"I was about ten," she admitted. "All I could think about were animals. My poor parents had to put up with me constantly bringing home hurt things."

"You still do that," Cole said, "or maybe they just gravitate to you."

"Thanks, Maia." Jase nudged his brother.

"Jase and I have a present for you," Cole said. He pulled an envelope from his pocket and held it out to her.

Maia opened the seal slowly and took out the card. She blinked several times trying to make sense of the lettering. "I don't understand." Her heart was pounding out of control. She swallowed several times, before raising her gaze to Cole's.

"You own the clinic," Jase said eagerly. "It belongs to you. You don't have to go away now."

Cole gazed at her steadily, not blinking or looking away, compelling her toward the unknown. Maia blinked rapidly to break the spell. He was so deep inside of her she could hardly breathe without him. The feeling was too strong, too fast, and she didn't entirely trust it.

"But I can't take this. I can't possibly accept this." Maia

shoved the card back into Cole's hand. "You know I won't, Cole."

"You have to accept it," Jase said. "If you don't, you'll ruin the rest of it."

"The rest of what? There can't possibly be anything more. Are you two crazy? You can't go buying a clinic for me. I love you both dearly for the gesture, but I'm not going to accept it."

Cole sat there, staring into her eyes, his face hard and etched with lines of suffering. "The part where we ask you to stay. The part where I ask you to marry me."

Her heart sounded like thunder in her ears. For a moment she thought she might actually faint. He looked so alone, so prepared for her refusal of him that she ached with a need to give herself to him. She didn't dare look at Jase, but she knew he would have a similar expression of need on his face.

"Why, Cole?" She moistened dry lips with the tip of her tongue. "So when you need to go away you'll have someone you trust here with Jase?" It didn't matter that she loved him so much. She couldn't live with him knowing he didn't return her feelings. She knew she could love Jase always, be a good mother or sister and friend to him, but she didn't want to be a convenience. She had far more respect for herself than that.

Cole groaned inwardly. He should have known it would look like that to her. Maybe it was part of it, maybe it was all wrapped up in needs and hunger and longing for a home and a family. He took her hand, his rough fingers sliding over her soft skin, his thumb caressing her ring finger. "I don't want to be without you."

"How can you possibly know whether you do or you

don't, Cole?" Maia was going to cry. She hated crying, and her reaction was generally to strike out at whoever managed to cause the tears.

Cole felt her trembling. "I know because I know the difference between living in hell, and being alive in paradise. I don't want to lose what you've given me. I *feel* all the time when I'm with you. The entire range of emotions. Happiness, sadness, exasperation, even anger. All of it. I've never had that before. I want you to be happy, Maia. I watch every single expression that crosses your face. I watch you with Jase, with the animals. I think about you day and night. I want to go to bed at night with you beside me, and I want to wake up with you in my arms. I've never felt that way about anything or anyone before."

"You can't leave us, Maia," Jase burst out.

"Jase needs you almost as much as I do," Cole added, feeling on the verge of desperation. She was blinking back tears, and he had the feeling she was going to pull away from him at any moment. He slid a ring from his pocket, a circle of brilliant diamonds to slide on her ring finger. "Jase found the perfect Christmas present for me, and gave it to me ahead of time. I want to give it to you."

"Cole," she warned, shaking her head, looking down at the ring. She'd never seen anything like it, and it had to be worth a fortune. "Where in the world did you get this, Jase?"

"It was in the box with my mother's things," Jase said in a low voice.

"Oh, my God, you cannot give this to me. You have to keep it for the woman you marry," Maia said, turning her head to look at him.

It was a mistake. The boy had tears in his eyes. He

immediately reached out, putting his hand over hers and Cole's. "I gave it to Cole because it was all I had to give him. He needs you. He's different around you. Relaxed and happy, and he smiles. I'd never seen him smile until you came to be with us. And I need you too. Don't leave us, Maia."

She took a deep breath. It was overwhelming to be caught between the two of them, their dark secrets and their dawning hope. "There's more to being married and relationships than need. If I stayed, and it wasn't right, eventually it would all fall apart. You both know that." She wanted love. She deserved love. As much as she loved them both, she would not be cheated.

"Maia." Cole caught her chin and forced her to look at him. "I'll be the first to admit I don't have a lot of pretty words to make this right. I don't know the first thing about how to tell a woman she's my entire world, but that's what you are to me. You're not someone I want as a housekeeper for Jase, but if I could choose a woman to be a mother figure, a sister, a friend for him, then it would be you."

"What do you want for yourself?"

"I want a woman who loves me in spite of all my failings. A woman who understands when I have nightmares and do things she might be afraid of. I want you, Maia. I don't even know when I fell in love with you. I just know that I am in love with you."

For a moment she could hardly believe he'd said the words. She'd wanted to hear them so badly, she was afraid it was a trick of her imagination. The wild pounding in her heart began to subside and she could feel peace stealing into her. "Funny thing, Steele," she said, "I feel *exactly* the same way about you."

Cole sat in shocked silence, afraid to move or speak. Afraid of breaking the spell. Someone, a long time ago, told him miracles happened on Christmas. He was terrified of believing it.

"I'm very much in love with you."

Jase hissed out a breath between his teeth. "You two are making me want to pull out my hair! Cole, you should have told her you loved her right away. Maia just say yes, so I can breathe again. I'm having an asthma attack and trying not to die while you two figure it out."

"Yes," Maia said.

Cole dragged her into his arms and kissed her. She fit there, fit him. Understood him. He had no idea how it had happened, but the how and why didn't matter, only that she loved him.

A noise drew his attention and he turned to find Jase waving his arms, wheezing, desperate to breathe.

"You weren't joking," Cole said. "Where's your inhaler?" He searched through the pockets of Jase's shirt. Jase pointed frantically toward the kitchen, and Cole sprinted away.

"Calm down, Jase," Maia added, taking his hand. "It's going to be all right. We're all going to be fine."

Cole was back, handing the boy the inhaler and watching with a slight frown on his face as Jase used it. "Next time, don't be fixing my problems until you're safe, Jase. I should have been watching you more carefully."

Jase took a deep breath and smiled at his brother. "Someone has to look after you and Maia. You're really not all that good with the women, Cole. I know more than you do about romance. And you'd better smile at her *a lot*."

Maia laughed. The sound filled Cole with joy. He looked around the house. His home. It belonged to them now. Maia, Jase, and Cole. It was their home. The fire burned brightly and filled the room with warmth and comfort. The Christmas tree filled it with fragrance.

"You know, Jase," Cole said. "I think Christmas is going to be our favorite holiday."

"I think you're right," Jase said with complete satisfaction.

The two brothers looked at Maia, and she threw her arms around them. "I knew you'd see it my way," she said happily.

epilogue

FOUR YEARS LATER

Cole sat in his parked truck watching the people hurry along the streets, carrying brightly wrapped packages and waving cheerfully to one another. The stores were heavily decorated, as were the streetlights and even one or two of the trees in front of the shops. The tall fir in front of the veterinarian clinic was a masterpiece, with lights and ornaments and a blazing star on the top, courtesy of Maia.

He could hear music blaring out of the clinic, a wild rendition of "Jingle Bells." That was so like Maia. The clinic was closed, but people were going in and out carrying boxes of food and presents to cars. As always, she headed up the drive to take dinners and gifts to the less fortunate, and she'd managed to rally quite a crew to help her.

He couldn't wait to see her, to watch the way her eyes lit up when she first saw him, to see her smile blossom and hear her laughter. He ached to hold her, to feel her skin against his and he could already taste her kiss. Sometimes, when he was away from her, he woke up with the taste of her in his mouth. He'd been gone two months this time. It was the longest they'd ever been apart, and he'd felt every second of the separation. He'd never stay away that long again. He needed his family far more than he needed the outlet of his undercover work. He would still continue it, but he would not take a job where he would be separated from them for so long. He'd learned, in his long absence, that they were his balance and sanity.

A part of him was afraid of his welcome. Afraid that smile, the light in Maia's eyes wouldn't be there for him this time. His hands gripped the steering wheel, thinking about losing her, losing what he had because he could never quite rid himself of the demons that plagued him his entire life.

He heard laughter and turned his head to see the two little girls running up the street, clutching at Jase's hands, dragging him toward the clinic. Their dark hair, so like his, was shiny and bobbed as they ran. His three-year-old twin daughters had Maia's deep blue-green eyes and her smile. He loved the sound of their laughter. He still couldn't believe he had daughters. Beautiful twins who climbed all over him and kissed him every chance they got. Maia had given him that gift.

Observing Jase with his daughters brought a lump to his throat. His brother had grown into everything he'd hoped. He was tall and strong, his gangly frame filled out. He carried himself with confidence. The shadows that had always been present in his eyes were replaced with contentment. He had friends and did extraordinarily well in school. Maia had managed that as well. She'd had him working daily in the clinic with her, taking him on ranch calls and teaching him her craft, encouraging him in school and, more importantly, bringing him a sense of family.

Cole slid from the truck, knowing he was going to have to go in and face his fate. Unlike Jase, he knew he would never be rid of the past. He would awaken in a cold sweat, Maia in his arms, her voice soothing, her body soft and inviting, always ready to take away the nightmares. He loved her so much he ached with it, yet he couldn't always stay. No matter how hard he tried to hide it, Maia always saw the demons growing in him.

It was always Maia who put her arms around him and told him to go. "It's okay," she would whisper, kissing her way up his back to the nape of his neck. "Do what you have to do and come back to us." She never cried, and she never chastised him or made him feel guilty. She was Maia, offering him freedom with love in her eyes. And he always returned because he couldn't live without her.

But as he opened the door to the clinic, his heart pounded with fear. If she rejected him, his life was over. He knew that, knew he needed her more than most men needed their wife and lover. She gave him acceptance and understanding when he didn't have it himself. She taught her daughters that same acceptance and understanding of his shortcomings, and she'd taught it to Jase.

The music greeted him as the door swung open. Someone bumped into him, laughed, and called out a merry Christmas. He just kept walking through the outer office, down the decorated hall to the back room, where the operation of filling boxes was taking place. Dread was growing, a dark ugly feeling he couldn't stop. All around him were the signs of Christmas, of happiness overflowing. He walked with confidence, but deep inside, where no one saw, he was screaming inside.

"Daddy!" Ashley screamed his name and rushed him, a small dynamo, throwing her arms around one leg, effectively stopping him.

Mary cried out and followed her twin, twining her arms around the other leg.

Cole reached down for them, his heart nearly bursting as he picked the girls up and settled them on his hips, kissing them over and over, but all the time his attention was on her. On Maia. He heard Jase's greeting. Felt the boy clap him on the back, and he returned the awkward hug. But it was Maia he watched. Maia he waited for.

She turned slowly, as if she were afraid to believe it was true. Her gaze settled on his face. He held his breath. There it was. That slow smile of joy that lit up her eyes, brightened her face. Tears shimmered. The tears that were never there when he left but always there when he returned.

"You're home."

He handed the twins to Jase. "I'm home." He gathered her into his arms and found her mouth with his. She fit close to him, her arms winding tightly around his neck, her mouth every bit as demanding as his. He tasted her sweetness. He tasted acceptance. Desire. Most of all he tasted love. He felt weak with joy, with relief. Maia was his rock, his foundation. His very life.

"Get a room." Jase and the twins chimed in together, something they did often around Maia and Cole.

Maia laughed, resting her head on Cole's chest. "You made it home for Christmas."

"I'd never miss Christmas. Did you put up the tree already?" He held his breath again. It was silly to want to choose the tree, not when there were only three days left.

"We never break tradition," Jase answered. "It wouldn't be the same without you."

Maia just burrowed closer to him, her arms sliding around his waist. Cole looked at his brother over her head, and they smiled. They had a home. A family. And they had love. If that wasn't a Christmas miracle, nothing was.

A TOUCH
OF HARRY

Susan Sizemore

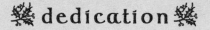# dedication

For Matthew Krause, who introduced me to Mission Wolf.

chapter

1

"Was that a coyote?"

"Coyotes don't come in black," Marj Piper answered the man in the seat beside her, as the ghostly dark form disappeared from the blaze of her headlights. "That thing is *fast!*"

She followed the creature's movements across the moonlit Arizona desert before darkness completely swallowed it. It was some kind of dog; its outline was beautiful and sleek.

"Marj! Look out!"

She swung her gaze forward, just in time to slam on the brakes as another large animal raced in front of her truck.

This creature was as black as the first, but much larger and more muscular, with denser fur. As the animal gave a quick glance toward the headlights, its eyes glowed with a blue sheen. It bared its fangs in a snarl, then bounded away, following the other animal almost faster than the eye could see.

"That's a wolf!" Patrick shouted.

"Yeah," she agreed, her heart hammering in her chest. "That was a wolf."

In the backseat of the cab, her chocolate Lab, Taffy, lifted his head and whimpered his agreement.

Marj drove the truck at a near crawl as the hard-packed dirt road ascended a steep, curving hill. The first animal had been terrified. The wolf had been furious. And it had *looked* at her, almost in outrage, as if it was demanding that she *help*.

Help with what?

Pat touched her arm. "Are you okay?"

"I'm fine."

"You don't sound fine."

Reverend Patrick Muller was new to Kennedyville, and Marj was giving him a ride home from a dinner party where friends had tried to hook them up. She supposed Alice meant well in trying to draw her out of the shell she'd been in since her father died. She wasn't sure she really appreciated it, though.

The one person who'd understood her was gone, and it would take a miracle to cure the loneliness that had closed in when he was gone. Still, because Alice had accused her of trying to be a Scrooge and ignore the Christmas season, she had made the effort to be sociable through dinner at Alice's house. It had drained her incredibly, and she was glad to be heading home.

Reverend Pat was nice; he'd made intelligent conversation over dinner, even persuaded her to participate in a charity function at the high school in a couple of days. And he wasn't at all bad-looking. No doubt he was going to be an asset to the community.

As agreeable as he was, though, she certainly wasn't going to tell him about her "special" ability.

When she was a kid, she'd assumed everybody could do

it. It had taken her painful years to realize that it was anything but normal, and to learn to control it. It had taken even more years to learn how to hide it from the rest of the world. Most of the time.

"I can't believe I almost hit a couple of animals," she told Pat, after she'd been silent maybe a little too long.

"They ran in front of the truck. It wouldn't have been your fault," he said comfortingly.

"But the animals would still be dead." The truck was laboring up the steep rise, and she put her foot on the gas.

"And we could have been injured, as well. Even as large as this truck is, hitting something as big as that wolf could have caused a lot of damage."

They rounded the curve and reached the top of the hill, and all hell broke loose.

There was a big white van parked sideways across the road, its headlights shining out onto the landscape. A pair of men stood in front of the van. One held a rifle up to his shoulder and fired twice, just as the second man saw Marj's truck.

She slammed on the brakes and came to a stop inches from the van, just as a wave of pain hit Marj in the back.

NO! Run! Save yourself!

Her spine arched, and dizziness shot through her, even as the wolf's voice inside her head faded.

She might have fallen forward, unconscious across the steering wheel, if Patrick hadn't grabbed her by the arm and shook her. She heard his concerned voice. She couldn't respond to it, but she did react to Taffy's barking in her ear and the nudge of his wet nose on the back of her neck.

That was her, all right. She didn't respond much to people, but animals . . .

There were animals in trouble out there. One was terrified, the other was hurt.

Can't move. Getting dark.

Marj knew she had to *do* something, but for a moment she had no idea where she was.

As she looked up, the second man grabbed the shooter by the arm. He shouted something, and pointed at them. The man with the weapon whirled around, the rifle still poised on his shoulder.

For a second, she thought she was going to be shot again. *Again?*

But the other man grabbed the shooter's arm and pushed him toward the van's open sliding door. The second man got into the driver's seat and barely took the time to slam the door before he roared off up the road.

Marj was out of the truck before the van's taillights disappeared around the next curve. Taffy jumped out after her. It was a few seconds before Pat Muller followed. She was pacing along the rocky edge of the road by the time he reached her, Taffy trotting beside her, his nose to the ground.

"What are you doing?" Pat asked. "I don't think it's safe to be out here." He plucked at the sleeve of her shearling jacket. "That man was shooting at something."

"Not us," she answered.

"What if they come back?"

Marj stared off into the cold, clear December night. "There's something out there."

Pat peered into the darkness, then looked worriedly at her. "What?"

"Whatever he was shooting at."

He'd hit it, too. She'd felt it; more than felt it, for a moment. She'd *been* the animal. Its thoughts had been hers. The awareness had been so strong that, for the first time in her life, the emotions and images she normally picked up had been experienced as words. Words from a—

"The wolf!" Pat exclaimed. "He must have been shooting at the wolf."

"Yeah."

Pat rubbed his jaw. "Maybe they were trying to shoot it as a protective measure. It wouldn't be good for a wolf to be running loose in the desert."

"Why not? There used to be Mexican red wolves running around here all the time." She glared at him. "Until we humans came along and hunted them to extinction in the wild."

Pat backed a step. "Yes, but—you saw that animal. It was huge! It would be irresponsible to allow that thing to run loose."

"Yes, it would," she agreed. "That's why I'm looking for it."

"You?" He sounded horrified, and looked around anxiously. "Marj, I think we better get back in the truck." He took a cell phone out of his jacket. "We should call animal control."

"I *am* animal control in this neck of the woods," she told him.

"You're a vet, and you run a shelter, but you're no match for a wolf."

"An injured or dead wolf."

"What if they didn't hit it?"

The wolf had been hit. She couldn't tell Pat how she knew because she was aware of just how crazy it would sound.

"Why did they run off when they saw us?" she countered. "What were they up to?"

"I better call the sheriff."

"Don't bother trying. Your cell won't work out here."

She had to find the wolf; it needed her. But where to start? She couldn't feel it any longer. She prayed that it wasn't dead.

A lot of desert stretched below, where the hill fell into a wide valley. Even with the moon nearly full, she could barely make out nearby scrub brush and the silhouettes of boulders and a few cacti. Mountains loomed dark on the skyline in the distance. There was a lot of ground to cover.

Injured or dead, she *needed* to find it. But how?

Taffy began to bark. Startled, Marj jerked around and saw that he'd moved downhill. His stance was stiff and tense, and he was barking at a shadow lurking deeper in the shadows.

Out of long practice, Marj set her own emotions aside and concentrated. Though she couldn't make out the shape of the creature cowering in the darkness, she recognized the animal's fear.

"Poor thing," she murmured.

Pat looked wildly around. "What?"

"Shh. Stay here," Marj whispered, and moved cautiously forward.

She put a hand on Taffy's head when she reached him, silencing him instantly. The big dog sat, and stayed alert but still while she moved forward. Within a few steps, she made out the shape of the first animal that had crossed her path earlier. More importantly, she reached its mind with her own questing feelings.

She absorbed the fear and sent out calm. When the urge to run tried to take over her limbs, she suppressed it and managed to keep the animal from bolting in renewed panic. She went down on one knee and held a hand out toward the dark shape. She sensed that the animal was a dog, but one that wasn't that used to people. Domesticated, but not a pet?

"It's okay," she murmured. "You can come to me."

The dog whined piteously and bunched its muscles to run, the one thing it really knew how to do.

Marj tugged it toward her with a mental command, and reinforced her will with a stern, "Come."

The dog slinked closer, and she saw that it was a long, lean greyhound. It was as dark as the night, her coat black satin in the moonlight. Her sides were heaving with fear and exertion, but she let herself be touched.

She was worried, very, very worried; maybe even more worried than she was afraid.

Marj rubbed the greyhound's head, caressed its soft ears, and concentrated on finding out what troubled the animal. "You want me to help, don't you?"

She sent out a gentle mental probe, and was soon flooded with images and sensations.

After a few seconds the dog bounded off. Marj surged to her feet, knowing that the dog knew exactly where to look.

As she turned to follow the greyhound, she ran into Pat. He reached out to steady her, but Marj dodged around him and raced downhill after the dog, Taffy loping at her side.

After a few seconds, she heard Pat working his way through the brush behind her. "Where are we going?" he called.

She couldn't answer and still concentrate on following the greyhound's mental trail. Fortunately, she didn't have far to go down the hillside before she literally stumbled onto the wolf.

She tripped and landed on a big body; hard muscle covered with thick, soft fur. She rolled off the prone animal as quickly as she could and knelt beside it. The dogs kept their distance. Taffy barked, not liking the smell of the wolf and unhappy at her being so close to it. The greyhound settled down on the ground to rest, exuding satisfaction in having performed its duty, along with continued nervousness.

Marj sat back on her heels, took a deep breath, and closed the barriers of her mind to the dogs. Now she had to concentrate on the wolf.

"Is it dead?" Pat asked, coming up behind her.

"No." She knew that in her bones. She ran her hands expertly over the big, warm body, probing through the heavy fur for signs of injury. "Ah," she said, when she found what she was looking for.

"It has been shot, hasn't it?"

"Yep." She tugged one of a pair of darts out of the wolf's back. "Tranquilized. He's not dead, but he is sound asleep."

"Good. That's one huge, dangerous animal."

There was nothing wrong with being dangerous if it was part of your nature.

She patted the sleeping wolf on the head. "He's not dangerous now. Isn't he beautiful?"

"What are you going to do with him?"

"Take him home." She was glad that it wasn't too far to her truck. "Fortunately, my biggest kennel cage is still in the back of the truck. Come on, Pat—help me carry this big boy up the hill."

2

 HARRY SUPPOSED HE WAS DREAMING. Either that, or the mattress truly was stuffed with cedar shavings. The aroma overwhelmed his sensitive nose, but wouldn't have been nauseating if not for the hangover of monumental proportions.

He couldn't remember feeling like this since college. He'd been smart enough never to get drunk since then; it wasn't healthy for the rest of the world when his kind lost control.

In fact, he couldn't remember how he'd gotten this way. *Had* he been drinking? He'd been feeling lonely, especially at having to be away from home so close to Christmas. He had gone into the only bar in the one-horse town to check out the locals, but . . . ?

He groaned. This wasn't just a headache. He had aching, strained muscles, and he was cold. He was naked, yes, that was it, and the room wasn't heated. He was naked, facedown on a thin mattress that smelled of cedar.

At least there wasn't a woman in the bed beside him, so whatever he'd done—

But there *had* been a woman.

An image of wide eyes in a heart-shaped face flashed

across his memory. A small woman behind the steering wheel of a big truck.

And he was naked because . . . ?

He'd been in wolf form, he remembered now. He remembered being changed, and sensing the woman through his werewolf senses.

And there'd been a dog, right? The poor thing had been in trouble.

Okay, yeah, now he remembered. He'd been out for a four-legged roam after being in town. Intending to get to know the territory, he'd come across this dog being chased by a pair of guys who didn't smell right. The dog hadn't felt any connection to them but fear. So Rin Tin Tin had come to the rescue, getting between the dog and the men.

Then he'd gotten shot? Harry remembered the impact, but felt no pain. Drugs, then. He'd gotten all woozy, and the last thing he'd done was think something at the dog like, *Go get help, Lassie.*

And maybe that *was* just what the fool critter had done.

Despite the drug hangover, Harry lifted his head and took a deep breath. Without the aroma of cedar masking other scents, he could make out animals, medicines, cleaning fluids, and disinfectants. It smelled like a vet's office. He'd been in wolf form, and the dog had gotten the woman to bring him somewhere safe. Now he'd morphed back to human. When he took his attention off the headache, he became aware of the deep ache in his limbs, spine, and ribs. It was much easier on the body when the change was under conscious control.

He opened his eyes and saw that he was surrounded by a metal cage.

"Oh, good God," Harry muttered.

It was a good thing the wolf had been asleep when he was captured. Even now, anger roared through him at the bars between himself and freedom. But he was in man form, and a man thought—even with a headache from hell.

And what did the man think? That he was on a case, and didn't want complications and questions that might interfere with his work. Or, worse, threaten his carefully guarded secret.

He reached out and touched the cold metal, fighting the urge to mindlessly shake and tear at the bars. While his animal part swore vengeance on whoever had done this to him, he looked around, found the cage door, and the simple latch that kept it closed.

Harry laughed.

Though his inner wolf was having a hissy fit, he was only being held in a kennel box, though thankfully a big one. He supposed he was lucky he wasn't wearing a flea collar.

He flexed his fingers. "The man thinks that he has thumbs, and getting out of here isn't going to be a problem."

Except that he heard footsteps approaching.

He was still too groggy to make the change back to wolf quickly. He fell facedown onto the cage floor, pretending to still be out, and thought, *Go away, go away, go away.*

That and, *You really don't want see a naked man's backside. Or at least be polite enough not to look.*

Marj's steps slowed as she approached the back door of the building. There was a voice in her head warning her to go away. The sensation wasn't frightening, but it was very compelling. It took some doing, but she brushed the strange impulse aside, not about to ignore the needs of an injured creature.

She'd spent much of the night tending to the greyhound. Its injures hadn't been accidental. The poor thing had several small but deep cuts, one on the back of the neck, one on the left ear. Marj figured that the beautiful animal was stolen, and the thieves had removed any identifying markings—a tattoo on the ear and an implanted ID chip in the neck.

She'd been worried about the wolf all night. Yet here she was, standing out in the December cold, hesitant about checking on the animal. The drugging could wear off at any time. The wolf would be agitated, which wouldn't be good for it, her, or the other animals. Besides, it was her back storeroom, she'd go in if she wanted to.

Maybe she should have left the wolf in the back of the truck, or in the barn or the kennels, but she wanted to keep the wild animal away from the cats, dogs, and other animals she sheltered on her property. Fortunately, she'd had Pat to help her wrestle the cage into her dark, narrow storeroom, even though he'd worried about her having a wolf on the premises.

"He'll be behind bars, in a locked room," she'd pointed out, but she'd thanked the minister for his worry. She wasn't used to having anyone worry about her, and she didn't like it. She appreciated having his physical strength, but when it came to emotional strength, she was used to going it on her own.

Marj concentrated on opening the door. The very act of turning the knob was tiring, as if she were pushing against some invisible barrier. Pushing the door itself open was almost an act of courage.

What, she was afraid of the big bad wolf?

Go away, go away, go away.

Marj shook her head and stepped inside.

It was barely dawn, so there was little light coming through the small window set high in the back wall. But there was enough to make out the sight of a naked man's bare buttocks.

"Good Lord almighty!"

He was asleep in the wolf's cage, his legs drawn up beneath him, and he was naked. Big and broad-shouldered, with a hell of a fine ass, muscular thighs, and—naked. Really, really, made-to-be-looked-at, built-like-a-god naked.

"Ohhh, my."

It had been a while since she'd been this close to a naked man, and never to one this impressive. Though the sight was shocking, she came to her senses, and demanded, "What the hell are you doing in there?"

The man didn't move. An arm covered his head, blocking his face. She took a step closer to the cage—and heard the phone ringing in the office in the front of the building.

Answer the phone!

She let it ring only twice before crossing the storeroom and hurrying to answer the call. She had a sleeping man where the wolf was supposed to be, which made for some serious questions that needed to be answered—but there might also be a veterinary emergency on the other end of the phone line. She'd deal with the caller first. The naked man wasn't going anywhere.

*   *   *

The instant the woman left the room, Harry sat up and turned to the cage door. He had to make his escape quickly, while she was occupied. He shivered. The temperature in the already cold room had dropped like a rock when she opened the door. It was also a reaction from all the energy he'd just burned clouding her mind. It annoyed him that she'd blocked most of what he'd sent her way; her resistance made his headache worse.

That wasn't supposed to happen!

While his stiff fingers worked the latch, he heard her voice in the distance, her tone calm and professional.

It only took seconds to open the door, then he crawled out and stretched his cramped muscles as he stood. Harry was not a short man, and being able to stretch out to his full height caused him to let out a sigh of relief.

Though he couldn't believe she'd heard him, suddenly the woman became silent. He could *feel* her listening, *feel* her stillness. It was like there was some kind of connection between them.

A connection Harry certainly didn't have time to explore. What he had to do was get out. The extra few minutes had given him more energy, even if he'd paid the price in embarrassment, and he was turning back into wolf form even as he leapt out the back door.

Now covered by a thick, warm coat of fur, Harry was delighted to be out in the brisk early-morning air. All his senses had shifted and sharpened along with his shape. Colors took on new depth, scents sparkled in the air, and his hearing became far more acute. It was good to be a werewolf, and he wanted to throw his head back and howl in delight. Impulse control could be tricky while in were-form, but that was because the impulses were good, strong, elemental ones. Control, however, was essential to survival.

A howl would bring the woman running, and he needed to get away cleanly before she even realized he was gone.

But one deep breath stopped him. There was something lingering—a faint, old scent—maybe. There were a great many animals in this place, which would make it harder to ferret out a trace of what *might* be there. But he had the best nose in the business.

Harry padded silently forward. Might as well have a sniff and snuffle while he was here.

"Just bring the kittens over, Mrs. Braem," Marj said when she couldn't take any more of the woman's complaints about strays and how bad animals were.

Mrs. Braem had found a mother cat with a trio of kittens in a shed in her backyard and wasn't at all happy about it.

"All right, then. I'll come pick them up," Marj said when the woman protested bringing them in.

"When?"

Marj thought about the mystery of the wolf, the greyhound, and the man in the storage room. "Later on today."

"Oh, no, you're not getting out of this. I want them off my property right now, or I'll drown them."

Fury shot through Marj. "Where's your Christmas spirit, Mrs. Braem?"

"What's Christmas got to do with animals?"

"Oh, I don't know—the manger and the stable, perhaps?" *Don't get sarcastic,* Marj warned herself. *Don't jeopardize the animals' safety.* "Never mind, I'll be over as soon as I can."

"This morning, Marjorie Piper."

Mrs. Braem had been her fifth-grade teacher and would just call her sassy if Marj reminded the old woman that she was Dr. Marjorie Piper these days.

"Yes, Mrs. Braem," she said.

She hung up and hurried back to the storeroom. When she saw the empty cage she skidded to a halt.

She hadn't known what she was going to do about the naked man in a cage in the first place—although her libido had suggested a few erotic things before she could stop it. The whole situation was worrying and confusing, not to say downright bizarre.

She'd had a lot of questions—like what had happened to the wolf, and why had he taken its place? And now he was gone.

How the devil did he escape?

Marj laughed. She definitely spent too much time with animals if she was surprised that a human had simply unlatched the door and crawled out.

But . . . where had he gone . . . undressed like that?

She walked to the open back door and looked around. The numerous buildings of Piper Ranch were perched on the crest of a hill. The land stretched out below in a long, barren slope down to the flat valley of a little river that was dry this time of year. She couldn't see any movement. The man must have bolted as soon as she'd left to answer the phone, and was long gone. She had a lot of dogs, so if he was snooping around the place, there'd be an unholy racket of barking to warn her.

Now both the man and the wolf were gone. She supposed she better call the sheriff and—

Her train of thought was derailed as the ringing phone

startled her once again, and she swore silently all the way to her office.

"What?" Marj demanded when she picked up the phone.

"Did we get up on the wrong side of the bed this morning?"

It was her friend Alice.

"I've barely been in bed," Marj answered.

"Oh?" The small word held a very loaded question. "Veterinary emergency? Or did you and Pat—"

"The Reverend Muller is a gentleman."

"I know, I talked to him this morning. But I have hopes for you two."

Don't. Marj looked at her watch. "What do you mean, you've already talked to him? Do you know how early it is?"

"He called me. He said he was worried about you being alone with a wolf. Are you alone with a wolf, when I set you up with a perfectly nice minister?"

Marj laughed. "Not that kind of wolf." An image of the hard-muscled stranger flashed through her mind and warmed her all over.

She pushed her erotic reactions aside as Alice continued, "You have no business being alone with a dangerous animal. Are you going to be okay? How did you end up with a wolf?"

"Didn't Pat tell you?"

"Something about men in a van and tranquilizer darts, and you acting really strange. Marj, you've got the man thinking you're Dr. Doolittle."

She'd heard the comparison before. She tried to be careful, tried not to give any evidence of being a crazy woman who talked to the animals. It wasn't so much that she talked to them, but that they talked to her. And it wasn't even really talking, but a kind of emotional communication.

Except the wolf. The oddest thing was, the wolf had actually spoken to her. That had to be her imagination.

"Promise me you won't tell anyone about the wolf, okay?"

"Why not?"

"Because—" Marj started to explain that it had escaped, but quickly thought better of it.

People had a lot of misconceptions about wolves. The chances were quite good that the locals would mount a hunt for the animal if the news that it was roaming free got out.

A wolf was a predator, and there was genuine reason for concern for livestock, but only if the wolf was desperate and starving. A wolf without a pack would be far more likely to go after prey like rodents than attack someone's cattle.

But her neighbors weren't going to listen to an educational campaign when it was easier to get out their rifles. Better safe than sorry, they'd say.

Better cautious, than a dead wolf on my conscience. Marj didn't know what had happened to the animal, or how the naked stranger was involved. She figured she'd better find out, and quickly, and keep quiet about it while she did.

"I have to go," she told Alice. "Mrs. Braem is threatening to drown some kittens. You'd think a widowed retired schoolteacher would take in a basket of adorable kittens, but will our Mrs. Braem succumb to the cat lady stereotype? No."

People could be so cruel to animals. Marj saw it all the time, and it soured her on her fellow human beings.

Alice knew this, but Alice was an optimist. "Bring the kittens to the Holiday Fete," she suggested. "Bring a bunch of your critters."

"Why?"

"You could set up an adoption booth, and you can auction them off or something. People are bound to want pets as Christmas presents."

Marj wasn't sure she liked the idea, but Alice was a force of nature not to be argued with. "I'll think about it. But right now I have to get over to Mrs. Braem's."

Then spend the rest of the day wolf- and naked-man hunting, she added to herself.

chapter

3

KENNEDYVILLE'S SMALL GROCERY store smelled strongly of fresh paint and sawdust. Marj nearly coughed when she stepped in out of the crisp winter air.

"Don't make a face like that, Marjorie Piper," Sam Murphy called from behind the counter directly across from the door. "I know it stinks, but it's a clean stink. Remember what the place was like a few months ago."

A wildfire had roared through during the summer, but the resilient people of the small town were putting their town back together. The high school, where tonight's celebration was being held, had been the first building restored.

Murphy's store was one of the last businesses to reopen. It was just four aisles of shelves, with freezers and cold cases along the walls. Not much, but having a local grocery store cut out the long drive to bigger towns to buy supplies.

Alice said that it helped make Kennedyville home, trying to remind Marj that she was part of the community. Marj hadn't been in town much for a while, and wasn't sure she even wanted to *belong*. She did take pride in being useful to the town, though, even if she did it more for the animals than the people.

She forced herself to be cheerful, and told Sam, "You could keep the door open to let a little fresh air in."

"There's probably a Health Department rule against it," he answered.

"Why would you have to worry about the Health Department?" she asked, closing the door behind her.

"I wouldn't," Sam answered, a little too loudly.

He glanced toward the freezer cases along one wall. Marj followed his glance to see a tall, dark-haired stranger in a brown leather jacket in front of the small dairy section.

Marj noticed that he had a strong, square jaw, and a high-arched, elegant nose. The man stood with his head cocked to one side, studying the milk selection. But the store owner looked with narrow-eyed suspicion on the man. It seemed he thought the man was listening to them.

Marj couldn't help but smile. Okay, maybe the folk around here were a bit insular, and most strangers were of the passing-through sort. Outsiders generally didn't go beyond the motel on the edge of the town or the truck stop diner across the road. For an outsider to come in for a few groceries was unusual.

Which aroused her suspicions, since she'd had some pretty weird encounters with strangers recently. There wasn't anything particularly familiar about the man by the milk case, but she hadn't seen her intruder's face. Any distinguishing marks that might identify this man as him were covered by clothing. Besides, he looked too tall to have been stuffed inside the kennel.

She guessed that the stranger had tried to strike up a friendly conversation with the shopkeeper, not knowing that Sam Murphy was the most taciturn person alive with anyone he hadn't known for at least a decade.

"Are you going to be at the high school tonight?" she asked Sam as she stepped toward the dairy case herself.

"Not if there's going to be animals there."

"Murphy, you are such a grump." She noticed that his only concession to Christmas decorating was a string of tiny multicolored lights hung on the front counter. "I'm giving away kittens."

"I thought I heard something about that. Heard about the wolf, too." He did not sound at all happy. "Did you bring it for show-and-tell?"

"No," she answered quickly. "The wolf is safe."

She hoped that wherever it was, it was indeed safe. She hated that the news had spread, and she'd had a few worried, and rude, phone calls. But so far no one had driven up to her place and demanded a look at the "dangerous vermin."

Well, there'd been a few demands, but she could be as stern and forbidding as they came. And she hadn't hesitated to point out that as the only local vet, they needed her.

"You better get rid of that animal," Murphy said.

"You sound just like Mrs. Braem."

"That's because we're going steady."

Before she could answer, the door opened again, and the store owner greeted another customer. Marj reached the dairy case, and tried to step around the stranger in front of it. He was lost in thought and seemed totally unaware of her.

"Excuse me," she finally said.

The man didn't move, but focused intensely arctic blue

eyes on her. "What's wrong with him?" he asked. "Doesn't he like animals?"

So the outsider had been eavesdropping! Looking into those bright, curious, compelling eyes, Marj couldn't be annoyed, and she was shocked by the flash of attraction that went through her.

She wasn't known for being outgoing and friendly, but she couldn't help but answer in a confiding whisper, "You can't blame Sam. He's been bitten by just about everything—snakes, scorpions, dogs. Scratched by cats. He even got pecked by a dove once. My Taffy's about the only critter that's ever liked Sam, but he's too lazy to dislike anybody."

The stranger smiled, which added to his attractiveness. He had deep dimples, and lines around his eyes crinkled. This gave him a mischievous air. "Taffy sounds like a gentleman."

Complimenting her favorite pet was a good way to get into Marj's good graces, and she smiled at him. It didn't hurt that the stranger exuded confident masculinity, was good-looking, and had a deep, sexy voice.

As they smiled at each other, they shared a long, lingering look.

"You like animals, I take it?"

There was now a distinct twinkle in his eyes. "You could say that. At least none have ever bitten me—unless it was consensual," he added, looking straight at her.

A *zing* went through her, and Marj went hot all over.

Which made her feel guilty, since she had a date with Pat tonight to go to the Holiday Fete and potluck dinner, and she was a firm believer in dancing with the one that brought ya.

Pity.

Not that she and the stranger were really flirting, but they *were* standing awfully close together. And his smile was making her feel all tingly and warm.

She hadn't been involved or even vaguely interested in anyone in a long time, and now she was going to a party with one man and having a hormonal rush over another. Not that she was was going to *do* anything about it; the rush simply proved she wasn't dead.

Suddenly she found herself wondering how long they'd been staring at each other, and why the tingling was stronger and the room warmer. And were they even closer, almost touching? The world seemed to have just gone away.

"The world does that, sometimes," he said.

It was as if he knew exactly what she was thinking, and Marj wasn't prepared for this, at all. Even if she was used to this sort of thing going the other way—but not with people. She'd probably spoken out loud, and the embarrassment of having done that shot a bolt of irritability through her.

"You're in my way."

Marj took a step sideways, but he moved with her, still blocking the dairy section. She ducked around him when he opened the case. She saw what she wanted, and there was only one; a yellow quart carton sitting between rows of chocolate milk and lactose-free milk.

She and the stranger reached for the eggnog at the same time. Their hands met inside the cooler.

The electricity that arced between them was as tangible as lightning. All of Marj's nerve endings short-circuited. Her head went haywire, and she jumped back with a gasp.

The man looked stunned as well and cleared his throat. Then he reached for the eggnog again, and Marj got her senses back.

"Excuse me," she said, "but I need that."

"So do I," he said. "I have to go to a party tonight, and I'm told I should bring something."

"Me too."

He looked down at her from a height of at least six-foot-three. She generally wasn't aware of being only five-foot-one, but this man made her feel small. She didn't like it.

"You're hogging my eggnog."

"And you're expecting me to be a gentleman and let you have it." He shook a finger at her. "I touched it first."

"You distracted me."

"I touched your hand." He gave her a cocky grin. "I admit I'm devastating, though."

She didn't know whether to laugh or be annoyed at this masculine self-confidence.

She turned her head and called to the storekeeper. "Do you have any more eggnog in the back, Sam?"

"With the Holiday Fete at the high school tonight?" Murphy called back. "What do you think?"

"Everybody can't be bringing eggnog."

"Take some chips and salsa," the stranger suggested. "Or potato salad. That's always a hit at a party."

"Eggnog is more festive. And I brought cookies to go with it."

"But not everybody likes eggnog."

"Taffy does."

Marj winced, realizing that she'd just admitted to catering to the tastes of a big, slobbering retriever.

The stranger laughed, and handed her the last quart of eggnog. "I'm a sucker for animal lovers."

She smiled her thanks and hurried to pay Sam. She found it oddly hard to walk away from the stranger, and was sure she felt his gaze on her the whole time.

Harry liked her. He wasn't sure if he should, and he wasn't going to let liking her get in the way of solving his current missing person case, if she was involved in any way. But he liked her—and he desired her.

He liked the way she walked; he liked the way she talked. He liked her dark red hair, her big brown eyes, and her heart-shaped face. He liked the way her shapely bottom was nicely molded by the khaki slacks she wore. He liked her voice, and the way she smelled, and the roundness of her breasts beneath the teal sweater, and the way she had hips like a real woman and a slender waist.

That sharp chin indicated a lot of stubbornness, and there was sorrow deep in those brandy brown eyes. She was a human, but he didn't hold that against her. He was human himself most of the time. And Dr. Piper had a little extra psychic energy that definitely appealed to the animal in him.

He was certain that he was going to bed her before he left town.

Though she didn't know he knew it, he knew a lot about her. Along with his nose, and an ability to ask questions, he had a laptop, and knew how to use the Internet.

After catching the scent of one of the missing kids at her ranch, he'd done a little digging with his laptop. Dr. Piper was single and wealthy. She'd been born and raised here, though she'd gone to school in California and practiced there for a while. Then she'd returned home and lost both parents within several years of each other. First her mother, to heart failure, then her father to cancer a year ago. She ran her animal shelter with private funds and kept to herself.

What was her connection to one of the missing teenagers Harry was hunting? And why hadn't she told anyone about him—in either his wolf or human form? Not that she'd recognize him in either form, since he'd spent a lot of energy projecting *you've never seen me before* at her in the store.

He also wondered how soon he would see her again and how soon he could get her alone. He'd like touching Marjorie Piper, and wanted to do a much more thorough job of it the next time.

But for now, it was time to get to the party at the high school. He'd told his kinsman he'd meet them there, as soon as he bought something for the potluck. And it looked like it was to be salsa and chips.

chapter
4

"MAY WE JOIN YOU?"

Marj was surprised at shy Annette Fennick's request.

Terry and Annette Fennick made her look like a social butterfly. They kept to themselves, home schooling their teenaged son, Phil. Over the years, Marj had seen far more of Phil than she had of his parents. It was from Phil that she'd learned about a new baby sister arriving six months ago. They must have found a sitter tonight, because here they were, with Terry standing diffidently just behind Annette, his hand on her shoulder.

Marj had been sitting alone with Pat for nearly an hour, and the conversation wasn't getting any more interesting, no matter how hard they tried. She smiled at the couple, and said, "Sure, join us."

She didn't look at him, but she could practically feel Pat Muller's frown at the intrusion. Well, maybe he'd been more entertained than she was, but she didn't think she'd been exactly scintillating.

The Holiday Fete was being held in the gym, with round tables and folding chairs set up in one half and a line of long tables for the auction of crafts and such on the other side of the room. Red paper tablecloths alternated with green ones and there was a potted poinsettia as a centerpiece on each of the dinner tables. The food for the potluck meal was heavy on decorated cookies, fruitcakes, and boxes of candy. She wasn't the only one to have brought eggnog, and there was also a bowlful of punch and an urn of coffee. Fortunately, Pat and Alice had made sure there was turkey, mashed potatoes, and other real food, so the guests weren't subsisting solely on a sugar-and-caffeine buzz.

Marj had left Taffy, the black greyhound, a pair of mixed breed puppies, and the rescued kittens in kennel crates behind one of the tables across the room. A sign reading NAME THE GREYHOUND hung over the black beauty's crate. Taffy was there to keep the greyhound company. And Marj had hopes of finding homes for the kittens and puppies before the evening was over.

Unfortunately, many of the dinner tables were only half full, or even empty. Not a lot of the population of Kennedyville had shown up for this holiday event. It was sad, really, and Marj was beginning to think that maybe there was something to Alice's repeated statements about how they were a "town in crisis."

"The fire should have brought us together; instead it's torn us apart," Alice's had proclaimed, and they organized this get-together with the new minister's help. Though she'd badgered everyone within fifty miles to come, the turnout was pretty disappointing.

Across the gym, Alice was now frowning furiously at the Fennicks for interrupting Marj and Pat's tête-à-tête, and Marj had to grin. Alice was seriously into matchmaking mode.

Marj's smile disappeared in surprise as the tall stranger from Murphy's store strode up behind the Fennicks.

"Hey, cousin," he said, putting a big hand on thin, sharp-featured Terry's shoulder. Then he held a chair out for Annette.

Quite the gentlemen, Marj decided.

Annette blushed and looked quite flustered at this gallantry. Terry took a seat beside his wife, and the stranger settled into the folding chair next to Marj. He reached a big hand across the table toward Pat, and said, "I'm Harrison Blethyin, but everybody calls me Harry. Nice to meet you."

The whole time he spoke, Marj couldn't help but notice that he was looking at her. And she couldn't help but look back. She wasn't sure what to make of it, and the amused twinkle in his blue eyes was—disconcerting.

It made her want to snuggle up close to him, unbutton his shirt, and start doing things that it was best not to think about while sitting across from the minister. She also had the feeling that Harry Blethyin knew exactly what she was feeling, and it was exactly what he wanted from her.

"Hello, Marjorie Piper," Harry's smile widened and his eyes turned hot. "It's good to see you again." His look implied that he definitely hadn't seen enough the first time.

Marj went hot all over but managed to say calmly enough, "It's only been an hour."

"You two know each other?" Pat asked.

"How's Taffy?" Harry asked, as though it was the most urgent thing in the world. He put his big hand over hers on the tabletop. "Did he enjoy the eggnog?"

"We do not know each other," Marj answered Pat. Yet she didn't pull her hand away, though there was no reason for allowing Harry's familiarity.

"It was the eggnog that brought us together. And Sam Murphy, of course."

"You are being inane," Marj told Harry. She looked at the Fennicks as Harry's fingers twined with hers. "How's the baby? And how's Phil? I haven't seen him for a while." *And who is this man, and why is he with you?*

"I'm a distant cousin," Harry said. "I've come for the holidays."

Marj didn't believe him. She didn't know why. Maybe because it felt like he'd plucked the words out of her head. It was as if they could silently speak to each other, which shook her. This was an intimacy far different than the empathy she'd always shared with animals.

"Welcome to Kennedyville, Mr. Blethyin," Pat spoke up.

"Call me Harry."

You should be called dangerous, Marj thought. She could sense it, beneath the good looks and the easy charm. He shrugged out of his brown leather jacket, rolled up the sleeves of his white shirt to bare muscular forearms, and sat back in his chair, looking like he was simply enjoying this small-town social function.

But there was something watchful about him. An aura that said he owned whatever space he was in. Everyone was looking at him. He knew it, expected it, and paid it no mind. The man filled the room, and this being a gym, that meant he took up a lot of emotional space. He was alpha to the max, even just sitting there, smiling.

Marj didn't think she liked his overwhelming *maleness*,

but it certainly was compelling. She'd bet every woman in that room felt a bit flushed and more female because of Mr. Blethyin's charisma.

The deep, inner wolf part of Harry didn't like it that Marjorie Piper was with another male. He must be more attracted to her than he'd thought, or he wouldn't be having this reaction. And he wouldn't want to be touching her above all else. Touching was a very important part of the mating ritual.

He was here to work, he reminded himself, not to start a ruckus with another male over the right to possess a mate. Especially a male like Patrick Muller. It was beneath his dignity; it wouldn't be fair to pick on someone who was so obviously a beta.

The first thing he'd noticed when he entered the gym was Marjorie Piper sitting alone with the man, looking bored. He'd been tempted to cross the room and take her away immediately. But since he was here on business, he'd sent his kinfolk to make sharing this table seem ordinary. He hated having to use the Fennicks. They were worried parents and wary of being around their human neighbors for any length of time. But they'd volunteered to do anything they could to help, so he took them at their word.

"So, you know my young cousin, Phil," he said to Marj, getting down to business. "He's grown a lot lately, don't you think?"

"I don't know about lately," she answered. "I haven't seen him for a couple of months."

The scent he'd encountered at her ranch *had* been an old one, and it hadn't been just the scent of a young werefox. There'd also been a werecat of some sort, cougar, maybe. The scent had been faint, and carefully masked. The kids had used the animals on the ranch to cover their own trail, and he hadn't been able to follow it, even though he had the best nose in the business. He didn't like being thwarted. Surely, this woman had some information that could set him on the right trail.

He felt Annette Fennick straining to ask about her boy, and he put a hand gently on her shoulder for a moment, letting the quick touch both reassure her and remind her that he was in charge.

"A couple of months? What was he doing at your ranch?" he asked Marj.

She gave him a suspicious look. "Did I say he was at my ranch?"

Her challenging tone made him bristle, instinctive alpha behavior, but he didn't let it show. She felt it though. He could tell by the way her brown eyes dilated and her body chemistry shifted, that she was aware of him, as a female. Across the gym, he heard a faint growl from her protective dog.

"I assumed," he said to Marj. "Perhaps I shouldn't have."

"Phil did stop by back in October," she said, looking at Annette. "He showed me a photo of the baby. She looks a lot like Terry, doesn't she?"

"A lot," Annette agreed.

"Was his friend with him?" Harry asked.

"Clark?" Marj nodded.

So, it was the werecougar. He was the ringleader of the crazy, little runaway group.

"What do you do for a living?" Patrick Muller spoke up.

"I'm a private investigator," Harry answered. No reason not to be honest with these people, but lots of reasons to be very cautious.

"That's a pretty macho profession," Marj said, not admiringly.

"I was a police detective in San Diego." he said, looking at her sternly. "Now I work on my own, specializing in missing persons cases." He touched the arch of his nose. "I've got the nose for it."

Annette gave him a worried look, as though he'd just given something away about his olfactory talents. She and her husband were werefoxes, and they had no sense of humor about the way weres and humans could interact.

It's a silly joke, he thought at the werefox woman.

Marj blinked and shook her head. Then gave him a very suspicious look.

That she was picking up on his thoughts was very disturbing. And sexy. This touching on many levels was deeply sensuous, but it wasn't the time or place to explore it. Later, when minds as well as bodies could share, the experience would be explosive. He'd heard it could be addicting, too. He'd have to watch out for that.

Before he could say anything else, a pretty blond woman came up to the table. She was smiling, but there was disappointment in her eyes as she looked from him and the Fennicks to Marjorie and Muller.

"Hello, Alice," Marj said. "This is Harry. Alice organized all this," she told Harry. *And you've spoiled her matchmaking, and she's probably really pissed.*

But there wasn't really anything to spoil, was there? he thought back at her. She'd just pretend her imagination was being overactive, because humans always looked for sensible, logical explanations when weird stuff happened to them.

"I'm sorry." Marj gestured around the sparsely populated gym. "I know you hoped more people would come."

"But it was an almost spur-of-the-moment celebration," Pat added. "Next year we'll plan it better."

Alice sighed and pulled up a chair. "This is not going too well," she conceded. "Maybe you should have brought the wolf, Marj. People would have shown up to see that."

Angry, Harry had to look down sharply and make a conscious effort not to let his fangs grow.

"I don't exhibit dangerous animals. They don't belong in cages," Marj said sternly.

Her words went straight to his heart. He almost kissed her then and there. As it was, he was barely able not to give her a grateful look. He wasn't here to fall in love, but to find some missing teenagers.

If those teenagers had been human, this wouldn't be such a hazardous assignment. But he had to be more than doubly on guard to protect the secret of all his kind. Involvement with a human could be a costly, dangerous distraction. Oh, he intended to have sex with her; he was too alpha to deny himself that pleasure. He just had to watch out for emotional involvement.

But right now the most important question was, what was her *emotional* involvement with the wolf?

"What are you going to do with this wolf?" he asked.

"Where did the wolf come from?" Alice asked at the

same time. "You said it was shot by the men in the van, but—"

"Does the sheriff have any information about them yet?" Muller wanted to know. "Was the greyhound stolen?"

Harry willed Marj to answer him first. He got the strong sense that she didn't want to talk about it at all.

chapter 5

MARJ HELD UP HER HANDS, and said, "I don't know where to begin."

The group around the table waited. She was intensely aware of Harry watching her, *willing* her to concentrate only on him. She fought off the almost overwhelming urge to do so and deliberately addressed Pat. "I'm fairly certain that she's a racing greyhound."

"How can you tell?" Pat asked.

"She's a gentle princess, but she doesn't have a lot of social skills."

"Never been housebroken," Harry said.

Marj nodded, without looking at the P.I. "And she has no concept of how to go up and down stairs. A track dog wouldn't know how to live in a house." She glanced over to where the greyhound lay, with Taffy resting beside her. "I figure she was stolen from a track, since the bastards cut her to remove all identification marks."

"Why would anyone do that?" Alice asked.

Marj shrugged. "I've made calls and sent e-mails, but I haven't heard back from anywhere about a missing racer yet."

She rather hoped she didn't. She knew it was selfish of

her, but Taffy and the black lady had bonded instantly. She hated the idea of her dog finding the love of his life, then losing her to the hard world of dog-racing tracks.

"They had the dog and the wolf in the van, and the animals somehow got away," Pat surmised. "What do you think they were doing with a wolf, too?"

"They were probably going to sell it," Harry spoke up. "Wolves might be endangered in places in the wild, but there's a huge trade in them as pets."

Alice gasped. "You're kidding!"

"He's right," Marj concurred. "People actually breed and sell wolves."

"They're dangerous animals."

"That's right, Alice," Harry answered. "And when people who buy wolf pups to raise as pets find out that their adorable puppy grows up wild at heart, things generally don't turn out well for the wolf."

Marj heard his bitterness and absolutely agreed with it. "You know whereof you speak."

His gaze caught hers. "I've done a lot of volunteer work with wolf rescue and rehabilitation at a wolf center in Colorado."

"Really?"

Marj tried hard to hide her sudden eagerness as an idea occurred to her. But she was sure he recognized that a lightbulb had gone off over her head, by the look in his eyes, and the slight smile that lifted the strong curve of his lips. That look also told her that whatever she wanted, it wouldn't come for free.

Fair enough.

She needed to talk to Harrison Blethyin, and she needed to talk to him alone.

Marj stood, and said, "Alice, it looks like everyone's finished eating. Why don't we get on to the craft fair and raffle part of the evening?"

"Wolves mate for life, you know."

A chill went through Marj at Harry's words, followed by a swift, hot, confusing rush of longing.

Mating for life. With who? Him? God, what a thought!

She gave her head a swift, hard shake.

He loomed above her, looking dangerous and unpredictable. There was a wild glint in his eyes. He'd unbuttoned his shirt collar, rolled up his sleeves, and a strand of black hair had fallen across his forehead, adding to the undomesticated look. He brushed it back with a quick, graceful gesture. For a moment she couldn't breathe, staring at his large, capable-looking hand.

"What?" she finally asked. She could barely get out the word.

Those eyes told her he was perfectly aware of her stunned, visceral, reaction to him, but he pointed behind where she sat. "And what are dogs but wolves that know they have a good thing? Those two are in love."

She'd been playing with the basket of kittens set on the table before her, dangling a green Christmas ribbon for them to bat at. Now, she turned to look where Harry was pointing, knowing that she'd see Taffy and the greyhound lying side by side. The old black metal folding chair creaked as she moved.

She'd let the dogs out of the big cage so that they could stretch their legs, and so that everyone could get a better look at the elegant greyhound. She had no trouble keeping them quietly well behaved. Being able to communicate with the animals was also calming for herself after spending several hours in the company of people.

She just wasn't used to humans anymore. Being around the locals she'd known all her life was hard enough, and Harrison Blethyin was downright disconcerting. Being with the dogs and cats, and having the slight distance of the table between her and others, soothed her.

She had found a home for one tabby kitten, and a brown-and-black puppy of dubious ancestry. She'd urged children to write down a suggestion for a name for the greyhound and put their slips of paper in the fishbowl on the table. She was going to draw one of the folded pieces soon and award the winner of the Name the Greyhound contest a prize.

The greyhound was sitting on her haunches, her huge eyes gazing upward. She looked something like the image of an ancient Egyptian statue of Anubis with velvety furled ears.

Taffy was lying next to the black dog, and he had eyes only for her. His tongue was lolling out, and he was drooling, which wasn't something he did very often. Never dignified, right now he was downright ridiculous.

"Yep," she said. "It must be love."

"He's totally smitten."

Marj jumped in surprise and realized that Harry was now standing beside her. And it was at Harry that the greyhound's worshipful gaze was directed.

Marj could feel the waves of emotion the animal directed at the man. The feelings weren't complex, but strong, and hard to put into words—gratitude? Love? Something that wasn't quite fear, but close—wary respect?

"I think Taffy might have competition for her affections," she said. "Are you thinking of taking her home?"

And I think she recognizes you, but from where?

Harry laughed. "Oh, no, not me."

For a moment, Marj wasn't sure which of her questions he was answering. There were more important questions that she wanted to ask him, too.

"Have a seat," she offered.

He'd already pulled up another of the folding chairs and set it very close to hers. He settled his big form onto the seat, then leaned close to her.

"All right," he said, affable, but hard-eyed. "What exactly do you want from me?"

Anger bubbled through her. She had the temper that went along with her red hair, and she fought not to let it get the best of her now. She couldn't afford to snarl at this man, to tell him he was arrogant and far too sure of himself.

A lost animal needed help, and it was up to her to provide it.

So she whispered when she wanted to shout. "I'm looking for a wolf, Mr. Blethyin."

"You've found one," he whispered back.

She sighed and looked around to make sure they were not overheard. "I did find a wolf—but I lost it."

He lifted one dark, heavy eyebrow. "Lost?"

"It escaped," she corrected. "And I'm afraid it's not going to survive out there on its own."

Harry wanted to take Marj's hand and tell her, *There, there, the wolf's just fine.* Actually, he wanted to take her hand, then take the rest of her. Her concern for his wereself touched him, and it turned him on.

"What makes you think your wolf won't survive?"

"He doesn't have thumbs. Which means he can't shoot back when ranchers shoot at him. He probably doesn't have a license to carry a gun, either."

Oh, I wouldn't bet on that.

She blinked. "What?"

"Wolves don't carry concealed weapons," he said. "Claws, fangs, and muscles have served them well for thousands of years."

"They're endangered now," she reminded him. "They don't exist well in the same areas that people live."

"That's right," he agreed. "And you're telling me you have a wolf loose in the environs of Kennedyville?"

She nodded and gave him a very anxious look. "Please don't tell anyone."

"And you haven't informed the local authorities?"

She gave him a faint smile. "Of course I have."

"Meaning—that you are the local authority." She nodded. "And why are you asking for my help?"

He was half-tempted to tell her that to find her big black wolf, all he had to do was look in a mirror. This was scary, because being tempted to reveal anything to a human was far more than was safe or sane for his kind. Such honesty was only possible when a were took a human mate, which rarely happened these days.

At least, it wasn't *supposed* to happen these days. He believed one of the reasons the teenagers had gone missing was because someone in the group had trespassed that unwritten taboo.

"I want to hire you to find the missing wolf for several reasons," she answered, once again looking around furtively.

"We're alone," he said. He moved closer to her, reveling in her warmth and scent. "Your boyfriend is glaring at us, but he's stuck dancing with that little old lady." Somebody had brought in a boom box, and instead of Christmas music, some of the townspeople were dancing to an OutKast CD. "Life is truly strange," he murmured.

"And Pat's a long way from being my boyfriend," Marj answered.

"I know."

He took her hand and experienced that electric contact between them once more. He managed to pull away from her just in time—before taking the kiss he desperately wanted.

Harry cleared his throat and forced his mind back to business. "You have other reasons for wanting to hire me?"

Blushing, she got back to business. "You're a professional investigator, and you said you've done volunteer work at a wolf sanctuary." She touched his arm. "Will you help?"

That jolt went through him again, but Harry had himself under control. "For a price."

"Of course I'll pay you."

"That's not what I meant. I want to make a bargain with you."

Her suspicion soared. The emotion was strong enough to attract the attention of her dog. Harry gave Taffy a hard look, and the dog grunted and put his head back down.

"I should explain why I'm visiting the Fennicks," Harry told Marj. "We are distantly related, and that's why they called me when their son ran away from home."

"Phil ran away from home?"

"Three months ago."

"But—I saw him—back in October."

"So you said. For helping you with the wolf, I want your help finding him."

It was a one-sided bargain, but who said a werewolf had to play fair protecting his kind from humans? If he didn't find those kids soon, humans were going to catch on to what they were. They were too young, stupid, and idealistic not to give themselves away.

"How can I help you?" Marj asked.

People were heading their way. "I'll let you know," Harry said.

Feeling wary and puzzled, Marj put on a smile as Alice shepherded all the kids up to her table.

"Time for the name drawing!" she announced.

Marj put on a wide smile. "Sure."

Harry brought the greyhound forward. It jumped up on the table for him, while Taffy followed and bumped his big head into the back of Harry's legs. Marj stuck her hand into the fishbowl and brought out one of the folded scraps of paper.

"Dennis Cooper wins the prize!" she announced. "And our greyhound princess's new name is—Noel."

"NOEL'S A GOOD NAME," Marj told the greyhound, which was lounging on the green-and-
black plaid dog bed in one corner of her huge
kitchen, Taffy lying nearby on the tiled floor.

She poured herself a fresh mug of hot chocolate and sat
at the table, her thoughts returning to earlier in the
evening. "But I don't know why Dennis's mom wouldn't
let me give him a kitten as a prize."

They settled on ten dollars for naming the dog, instead.

There'd been a scattering of applause, then everybody began to quickly pack up to go home. Alice looked
very unhappy, disappointed that her effort in bringing
the community together had been a lukewarm affair, at
best.

Before Marj could say anything to comfort her friend
Harry took her by the arm, and said, "I'll help you with
the critters."

Marj was riveted by his gaze, which concentrated
intently on her. She was drawn to his large, very masculine
presence. Her throat tightened, heat pulsed through her,
and she licked her lips. She found herself staring at his
mouth and wanting very much to be kissed.

Stunned, she pulled herself together enough to say, "Sure. Thanks."

She moved in a daze as she put the kittens and puppies back in crates and took them out to her truck. Harry followed her out to the rapidly emptying parking lot, carrying the larger cage. Noel and Taffy trotted along behind them and hopped into the back of the cab.

Then it was just the two of them, and Harry moved very close to her as she stood by the truck door, her keys dangling in her hand. Their breath frosted the winternight air.

He put his hand up to cup her cheek and ran his thumb across her bottom lip. The touch seared her, burning away any trace of cold. Their gazes locked. Her knees went weak, she dropped the keys, and his other hand settled on her hip.

Harry started to pull her closer.

And the Fennicks walked up behind them. Annette gasped, which drew Harry's attention. He glared, and Terry cleared his throat.

"We have to go now," Terry said.

Harry growled, then walked away with the Fennicks without saying a word.

It took Marj a few seconds to get herself together. When she did, she wondered why the Fennicks had looked so disapproving. Maybe because Harry was supposed to be looking for their son? No doubt they wanted him to keep his mind strictly on business.

They were right, she told herself an hour later in her kitchen. Harrison Blethyin did need to keep his mind on business first.

"Too bad."

Not only had she looked forward to being kissed, Marj also wanted to talk more with Harry. But he'd been swept off by the Fennicks before she had a chance to get a cell phone number. And the Fennicks didn't have a telephone. She and Harry needed to discuss when he'd look for the wolf, and how. Even more importantly, she was worried about Phil Fennick. Of course she wanted to help. Why had the Fennicks kept the news about their son quiet?

Well, they were very private people, and they *had* called in professional help. But Phil was only sixteen, seventeen at most. Didn't the authorities have to be notified about a runaway minor?

She knew a lot more about animals than she did about people. Maybe, sometimes, that wasn't such a good thing.

A disturbing hint of longing and loneliness threaded through her. Not only did she want to see the handsome, confident stranger again, she *desperately* wanted to. There was something challenging about him—and, oh my, he was so very sexy

"Sexy, which can be defined as *trouble*. What do you guys think? Do I want that tall, dark, and dangerous kind of trouble?"

Oh, yes, her body responded.

Marj wasn't exactly alone in the room, so technically she wasn't talking to herself. Besides the newly christened Noel, Taffy lay on the white tiled floor munching on a chew toy, and the puppies and kittens slept in boxes in opposite corners. There was a relaxed buzz of animal contentment, but right now the emothional background noise didn't soothe Marj's restive mood.

She felt suddenly weary, and a glance at the digital

clock on the microwave showed her it was later than she thought.

Late or not, she had chores to do before she could get to bed. She was glad that she didn't have any sick animals in the clinic, so she only had to check the kennel building. The animals had been fed hours ago, but she always made sure they had plenty of water. And she always took the time for some petting and to communicate with her rescued animals.

She grabbed a worn old pea coat off a hook by the back door, and went out into the December night. Stars burned brightly overhead, and the cold, dry air was crisp and tangy in her lungs. Though the outside lights weren't on, the long, low kennel building next to the barn was easy to make out in the silvery moonlight. She could have found it simply by following the emotional charge surrounding the place though. All the animals inside were waiting for her evening visit.

There was a soft and sentimentally sloppy part of her that was always tempted to move all of her rescued animals inside, to let them have the run of her home. But that way lay disaster. Then she'd be tempted to make every abused, lost, unwanted dog, cat, llama, ferret, and whatever else landed on her doorstep into a personal pet. The goal was to find homes for the rescued animals, not to turn into an eccentric old lady with dozens of "babies" underfoot. To adopt them herself would be to deny a lot of fine animals homes with people who needed to love them and to be loved by them.

So, Taffy was her only official pet. She shouldn't have let Noel inside—especially since the racer was undoubtedly used to living in a kennel—but Taffy had insisted.

Not that he was spoiled, or anything. And he wasn't the one dealing with housebreaking his newfound love.

Sometimes it was not such a gift to be able to talk to animals.

She was almost to the kennel door when all the dogs inside began to bark. And not the scattered barks of welcome that always accompanied her visits; they were baying a warning, and she heeded it.

She ran for the switch inside that would turn on all the floodlights. Coyotes came around at night sometimes, and if the light didn't scare them off, she had a rifle stored in the building.

Just as Marj reached the light switch inside the door, and the night turned bright, a heavy body plowed into her. She went down hard on the concrete stoop. Pain shot through her hip and her head, and the breath was knocked out of her.

"Where is it?" a voice asked from inside the kennel. "Is it in here?"

The man who'd tackled her dragged Marj to her feet on the stoop. Her ears were ringing, and she was dizzy. The dogs were barking wildly, and their concentrated excitement hit her even harder than the blow on the head had.

Her attacker held her close to him, her arms forced behind her back. "I don't see it," he replied.

"She'll know," the other one said. "The animal couldn't be anywhere but here."

"Move." Her attacker pushed her toward the interior of the building.

Just then, the dogs stopped barking.

There was a moment of tense, expectant silence.

Then a deep snarl rumbled outside.

Marj's captor twisted around, taking her with him. And a huge, dark body came rushing through the doorway. She caught a glimpse of fangs. And eyes. Ferocious eyes that glowed bright blue neon.

There was a shout. Someone screamed.

And the wolf leapt.

Soft fur brushed her cheek as the wolf jumped at the man behind her. The hands gripping her let go. Marj stumbled forward and fell, her head hitting the concrete again. She was vaguely aware of a struggle behind her, and a pair of boots flashed by close to her face as the world faded to darkness.

"Taffy, you're a hero."

The dog thumped his tail on the kitchen tiles when Harry spoke to him. Harry patted the chocolate Lab's head, watching out the open back door as the sheriff drove away with the two prisoners.

The last couple of hours had been nothing if not interesting, and Harry felt a certain satisfaction at the way things had gone.

He'd been sneaking around Marj's ranch for perfectly innocent reasons when the ruckus started. After he'd dropped the Fennicks off at their place, he'd gathered several sets of clothing and taken them to leave at various out-of-the-way places on Marj's property. The one disadvantage in shifting from human to animal shape was that nakedness was required. Oh, one could go were while fully dressed, but then you'd have to claw your way out of the restrictive cloth. That was uncomfortable, took precious time that could prove dangerous, and ruined the clothes in the process. Better to strip down and have clothes waiting in a convenient spot when it was time to become human again. To maximize one's options, more than one spot was best.

He'd been upwind of the kennel on the farthest side of the property when the dogs began to bark, and his reaction had been stronger and more visceral than he'd ever experienced before. He had instinctively responded to threat of danger to the woman by morphing and racing to the rescue in wereform.

And she'd seen him!

As had her attackers. Once he'd secured the men and made sure Marj was safe, he went to work on them. He called the sheriff, as well. By the time she arrived, bringing the local nurse practitioner with her, Harry had used his kind's hypnotic gift to convince the intruders they hadn't seen a huge black wolf. They believed that the animal that rushed out of the night to protect Marj was her brown Labrador retriever, that's what they'd told the sheriff. At no point in the evening had anyone mentioned anything about any wolf.

Thus, Taffy was the hero. People were far more likely to accept a logical explanation.

The men had also admitted they'd broken into the kennel, and attacked Marj, to find a racing greyhound they'd stolen that had escaped from their van. Having gotten their confessions to several crimes, the sheriff packed them into the back of her SUV and drove away. Harry hadn't used his hypnotic talent to coerce the truth out of the men. The pair were none too bright and had babbled their story freely, each trying to implicate the other more deeply than himself.

The nurse, who turned out to be Marj's friend Alice, was still in Marj's bedroom.

Harry closed the back door and headed toward the bedroom to see how Marj was doing. Alice met him in the hallway that led to the front of the house and put a finger over her lips, to tell him to be quiet. Then she took his arm, and escorted him back to the kitchen. Harry disliked being led around by anyone, but for the moment he curbed his alpha urge to do exactly what he wanted to do.

Once they were in the kitchen, Alice asked, "What on earth are you doing here, Mr. Blethyin?"

He'd realized at the high school that Alice was one of the community leaders, and he figured what she knew, the town knew. It wouldn't hurt to circulate a story about his and Marj's connection that had nothing to do with wolves, or werewolves.

But first, Harry asked, "How is Marj? Will she be all right?"

"She's asleep."

"Is that good, if she has a concussion?"

"I don't think it's a concussion. But I'll take her to the clinic in Paloma tomorrow to have her checked out."

"Can I see her?" he asked, to make it sound like she was in charge and he was cooperating. He fully intended to have a look in on Marj, but he'd wait until he'd gotten Alice out of the house.

"She needs to rest." Once again, she gave him a curious look. "What are you doing here?"

He could tell she would have preferred it if the mild-mannered Reverend Muller had been the man standing protectively in Marj's kitchen. It made him wonder how well Alice really knew her, for if ever there was a woman who needed an alpha male, it was Marjorie Piper. Like called to like, and she called strongly to him.

He made sure Alice was looking into his eyes, and bent all his will on making her believe him when he said, "Marj and I were—together—back when she lived in California."

"She never told me about—"

"Of course she told you about me. I'm the cop she dated for a long time. We broke up, then she moved back home before we could reconcile. I don't want to go through another Christmas without her." He willed her to *believe* that he was in Kennedyville solely to win Marj back.

"But—I thought you were visiting your cousins . . ."

"I am. One of the things Marj and I discovered we had in common is our connection to this area. I used the visit to Annette and Terry as an excuse to see Marj."

She blinked slowly. "Oh." She sighed, and looked pleased. "That's so romantic. Marj has been so lonely since her father died. And—"Her expression grew a little suspicious again. "But why are you here now?"

"To be with Marj, of course. She shouldn't be alone on this big place. She needs a man. She needs someone to take care of her." He said each word firmly, placing them into Alice's thoughts. "You want her to be happy. You know I'm the one who'll make her happy."

After a short silence, Alice nodded. "You'll make her happy. I'm so pleased for her."

"It's late," he said. "You're tired. I'll see to it that Marj gets to the clinic tomorrow." *Give us privacy,* he thought at her. Besides, Alice did look tired.

Duty warred with his persuasiveness for a moment, then she said, "Okay."

He could also tell that she was also eager to spread the word about Marj's newfound long lost love. He used that eagerness.

"And now you want to go home." *And you have calls to make.* "It's late," he added. He took her arm and guided her to the door. "Good night, Alice. Merry Christmas."

As soon as she was gone, Harry went to wake up Marj. After all, he had to tell her all about Taffy's heroically rescuing her—and make her believe it.

MAYBE IT HAD BEEN A DREAM, but when she woke up Marj couldn't stop thinking about the wolf. She looked up at the ceiling as morning light poured in her bedroom window, and tried to ignore her aches and pains. She remembered that she'd been tackled and manhandled, and bumped her head when she fell—and that Taffy had come to the rescue.

She could feel him lying next to her now, his big, warm body stretched out along her side. He was taking up more room than usual in the bed, but she figured her furry hero deserved a little more spoiling than usual. She fumbled a hand out from under the twisted covers, and reached over to pet his flank. All the while she was thinking about the wolf.

In the dream, the wolf had blue eyes. Which proved that it was a dream, because wolves didn't have blue eyes. Maybe some Arctic wolves did, but she didn't think so.

Well, she couldn't lie abed much longer. A shower would help the aches, and she had chores to do. Besides, Taffy was scratching on the door to get in, so—

So, if Taffy wasn't in her bed . . .who—or what—was?

Marj cautiously patted the body lying next to her again.

"That feels good," Harry Blethyin said, his lips close to her ear.

Marj would have shot up off the bed if his hand hadn't held her down.

"Careful, you might have a concussion. I'm here to make sure you're okay," he added. "Don't worry; Alice knows I'm here to look after you and that my intentions are mostly honorable."

If Alice knew it, everybody knew it. She glared at him. "Mostly?"

Even as she spoke, she noticed that he was lying on top of the covers, fully dressed in a black turtleneck and jeans. Only his shoes were off. She was wearing plaid pajamas, and remembered Alice helping her into them the night before. It was all very—chaste. She slapped away a feeling of disappointment. A smug glint in his blue eyes told her he was aware of it, anyway. He kissed her on the cheek, then his lips brushed very gently across hers.

She almost groaned in frustration when the brief contact ended.

Out in the hallway, Taffy whined loudly. Harry got up and let the dog in, then leaned against the door frame.

She remembered that he had that told her about Taffy's saving her last night. Funny thing was, she had no memory of taking Taffy to the kennel with her. Still, she hugged the dog when he jumped up on the bed and let him lick her face a few times. Before she could push the Lab away, Noel came in and jumped on the end of the bed. Taffy immediately stretched out beside the languid and imperious greyhound, his big pink tongue lolling foolishly.

"He is so in love," Harry said.

"I know—and he looks so stupid."

"Yep. Love'll do that to a man."

"To anyone."

She and Harry shared a quick glance, then looked away even as sparks flew between them.

Marj sat on the edge of the bed, while Harry crossed his arms, looking composed but for his tousled black hair. "I suppose I should thank you for last night . . . but what were you doing here?" she asked.

"I came to talk to you about my case," he answered.

"And finding the wolf?"

He nodded. "How's your head? Alice wants you to go to a clinic."

"I have chores."

He smiled. "Already done. All creatures great and small have been fed, watered, and petted. You'll find I'm useful to have around."

She eyed him critically, from his smiling, handsome face to his broad shoulders, lean hips, and farther down. She liked the scenery. "Coffee made?" she asked.

"Not yet."

"Well, then—"

He turned toward the hall. "Take a shower. It'll be done by the time you're dressed."

"What about that clinic visit?" Harry asked, when Marj joined him in the kitchen.

She had one bruise in the middle of her forehead and another on her left temple. It infuriated him all over again to see her injuries; made him wish he'd bitten and clawed up her assailants. Sometimes he regretted that his kind imposed such restraints on their animal natures these days. Sometimes it was just no fun being a werewolf.

Marj thanked him for the mug of coffee he offered and the plate of buttered toast. She looked good despite the bruises. Her auburn hair was still damp from the shower, and slicked back it revealed the angles of her heart-shaped face. He caught the warm, female scent of her, along with almonds and cinnamon from her soap and shampoo, and he thought he could spend the whole day breathing her in. Desire for her curled inside him.

"I'm fine," she asserted, after taking a gulp of coffee.

You sure are.

"Are you sure?" he asked quickly.

It was really odd, how their thoughts connected so easily. He wasn't used to this kind of connection with a human. Marj wasn't like anyone he'd ever met, shape-shifter or not. She did things to his emotions, made him want to protect her, almost as much as he wanted to make love to her.

Have sex, he corrected. Lots of sex. The word *love* implied an emotional commitment he couldn't afford.

Harry poured himself a fresh cup of coffee and sat down opposite her. He noticed that she was looking past him, and turned his head to see that she was looking at the battered and scratched-up back door.

"Thinking of leaving?" he asked.

Marj brought her gaze quickly back to his, and he caught a flicker of suspicion before she managed to mask it. "I have to get to my office soon." She ate a piece of toast.

"You need a lot of help around here."

"I have a part-time hand who comes in once a week. Except he took December off. And my vet tech quit. The local teenagers know I'll pay them for help."

"Phil's mom told me that he used to do chores for you

sometimes. He'd already left home when he was here in October with his friend."

She absorbed this for a moment. "His friend's a runaway, too."

He nodded. "I've traced a connection with Clark and four other missing teenagers to Phil Fennick. It looks like they hooked up in an Internet chat room and decided to run off and start a commune in the mountains around here."

This was essentially the truth, leaving out the part about five of the kids being shapeshifters of one kind or another.

She looked worried. "They're living up in the San Jagos in December?"

He nodded. "From everything I've found out, that little mountain range is rugged, inaccessible, and exactly what this little back-to-nature group is looking for. They want an isolated, peaceful place to live together in harmony."

"Do the authorities know about this?"

"Of course," he lied, then added truthfully, "but the authorities' missing persons resources are always spread thin, and at least two of these kids are legally adults. I'm the best there is at finding people, and I've got a personal stake in this hunt. These kids' families want them home for Christmas. I plan to see they get their wish."

She glanced at a wall calendar that featured a photo of kittens. "Then you've got fourteen days."

"It'll be sooner than that. In fact, I figure Christmas is what's going to bring the kids down out of the mountains. And it's going to be easier for me to find them outside the wilderness than in."

Normally, that wouldn't be true—at least with tracking

humans. But shapeshifters knew lots of tricks to mask their presence. These kids were deliberately hiding from their own kind, and at least one of them was a genius at disguise. Harry was actually thinking of hiring the kid once he got past the rebel-without-a-clue stage and made it to reasonable adulthood. The fact that Harry had picked up a faint scent of the werefox and werecougar at Marj's had been his only lucky break recently.

"Christmas?" Marj asked.

"Christmas presents," he clarified. "Christmas food. Christmas parties. These kids are going to want to celebrate the holiday. I figure Phil and some of his friends will show up here, to earn money for presents for their girlfriends."

"So, you're going to hang around here waiting for them to show up?"

He nodded. "That's a big part of the plan."

"What if they don't have any Christmas spirit?"

He shook his head. "Who can resist Christmas?"

"Me," she answered.

He didn't believe that for a minute, but her expression told him that she didn't want to talk about it. She also seemed skeptical of his plan.

"And while I'm waiting for the kids to show up at your door, I'll also find your wolf."

This drew a smile from her. He liked making her smile.

"More toast?" he asked.

She shook her head, and winced when she did. "I need to get to the office." She stood. "You go wolf searching."

Three hours later, Marj's headache was finally gone. She had two e-mail responses the to the ad she'd placed for a vet tech three weeks ago, one response the first week, and one just yesterday, and she'd sent off e-mails setting up appointments. She'd also answered several phone messages, and was catching up on a recent professional journal.

The whole time she'd been doing these tasks, her thoughts had been on Harry and the wolf.

Sometimes when she looked into Harry's eyes, she thought she saw the wolf looking back at her from them. An odd thought, but then, she could communicate with animals. Certainly there were things in the world odder than that, weren't there?

And she just couldn't get the dream about the black wolf rescuing her off her mind. She knew that the dream was somehow about Harry. When she tried to remember exactly what had happened when she was attacked, she got a confusing double image of Taffy superimposed over the black wolf. When she thought about it too hard, the headache began to throb in her temples again. So she put it out of her mind for now and went back to wondering how her kitchen door had gotten so badly scratched up if Taffy was outside with her, rather than trying to get out to help her.

Taffy couldn't have opened the door on his own.

Before she could pursue this thought further, the phone rang and the outside office door opened. Harry came in as Marj picked up the phone.

The call was from the sheriff.

Harry perched on the edge of the desk during the short conversation, and asked, "What was that about?" as soon as Marj was off the phone. "Yes, I'm nosy," he added. "It's one of the reasons I'm a detective. That call was about Noel, right?"

She nodded.

"Her owner's been found? Does she have to go back to the dog-racing track? Are you going to break Taffy's heart like that?"

"Will you let me get in a few words?" she countered. "Yes, her owner's been found," she said, after Harry grinned and mimed zipping his lips closed. "Sort of."

He tilted up an eyebrow in question.

The gesture made Marj laugh as she tilted back in her chair. It gave her more distance from Harry, but also a better angle to look up at the big man who towered over her, even while sitting down. The look of eager curiosity made his features even more handsome.

"The thieves told the sheriff what track they stole Noel from. They wanted to use her as breeding stock with another racer they just happened to acquire. I get the impression they're involved in some sort of illegal racing circuit. When Sheriff Murchison contacted the track the greyhound was stolen from, she found out that Noel's owner died of a heart attack a week ago. So, then she hunted down the guy's heirs."

"Who are coming to pick up Noel any minute now?" he asked anxiously. "You aren't going to let her go are you? She deserves a better life than living in a cage."

His passion on the subject was touching. For all that she agreed with him, Marj had to be practical. "I wouldn't have a choice." His look of disappointment pained her. "Fortunately—well, unfortunately, considering that the man who owned her is dead—we don't have to worry about turning her over to his heirs. They have no interest in racing greyhounds and have already turned his other dogs over to a greyhound rescue group. The sheriff was told that they don't care what we do with Noel."

Harry bounced up off the desk, looking as happy as if he'd just been given a marvelous Christmas present. "You're going to keep her!"

Marj rose from her chair. "I didn't say—"

Just then, a car pulled up outside, and Marj had to go to the door. Karen Montgomery and her two kids got out of the car as Marj came out of her office. Harry followed her out and walked across the yard toward the house.

Karen Montgomery's gaze followed him for a moment, and she grinned and briefly fanned herself when she turned back to Marj. "Hi," she said. "The kids have decided they want a pet for Christmas. Is that greyhound you had at the Fete available?"

A proprietary shriek silently went through Marj—both at the question and at the way the woman had looked at Harry. She put a professional smile on her face and briskly stepped forward. "She's not housebroken yet," she said, guiding the family toward the kennel. "Why don't I show you all the well-behaved, adoptable dogs that are available?"

An hour or so later, the Montgomerys drove away with a happy German shepherd in the back of their SUV, and Marj headed for the house.

Harry put his arm around her waist when she reached the porch. "I see you didn't give Noel away. You're going to keep her. Taffy will be pleased."

She relaxed against him. Despite the difference in their sizes, they fit together very well. "I didn't do it just for Taffy." She gave a resigned sigh. "Once I let something into my house, I have trouble letting it go."

"I'll keep that in mind," he said, then turned her toward the door. "Come on, I have something to show you."

"HAVE YOU BEEN WOLF HUNTING TODAY?"
she asked, as he closed the door behind them.

"I'm saving that for tonight," Harry answered.
"Today I worked on my case. Come on, I'll show you."
Keeping his arm around her, he led her down the hall to
the living room. Taffy and Noel tagged along behind
them.

When he'd explored the house that morning, he'd
found that the living room had a very unlived-in feel to it.
In fact, but for the kitchen and Marj's bedroom, the whole
place felt abandoned. Everything was clean and neatly in
place, but there wasn't any life to this house. Maybe it was
just too big for one person. Maybe Marj's office and the
animal shelter were the places her heart called home.

"Now, you're going to wonder what relevance what
you're about to see has to luring the kids out of the mountains. I'll explain, but first close your eyes."

He watched to see that she obeyed, then put his hands
on her shoulders and guided her to the center of the living
room. He positioned her so that she'd see the corner
between the living room window and the fireplace.

"Okay. You can look now."

Her body stiffened beneath his touch when she opened
her eyes. He'd suspected that she be briefly annoyed at his
presumption, but he hadn't expected such deep anger. Or
the almost physical wave of pain and grief that washed
over her and into him.

"Marj?" He pulled her back against him to wrap his
arms protectively around her.

"What have you done?" she demanded. "What right
did you have—?"

"It's Christmas," he pointed out. "A house needs a
Christmas tree."

He'd found the boxes in a closet. One contained the
pieces of an eight-foot artificial pine tree. Other boxes had
held Christmas ornaments, candles, lights, and decorations. He'd spent an hour moving some furniture and
assembling the tree in the best place to be seen through the
window. He'd placed gold and red candles on the coffee
table and mantel, then lit them and a fire in the fireplace.

"I put a few of the ornaments on the tree," he told her,
"so it would be pretty when you first saw it." She continued to stay stiff and very still in his arms. "You don't like it,
do you?"

"You had no right." She choked on a sob. "No right."

"I didn't think you'd mind."

"I *hate* Christmas!"

"That's not true. You wouldn't have been at the
Holiday Fete if you did."

"Alice made me."

"Nobody makes you do anything," he scoffed. "You're
too alpha to do as you're told."

"Christmas is okay for other people," she conceded. "I
wish them well."

"You give your Taffy eggnog. You named the grey-hound Noel."

"That was luck of the draw. I'm indifferent to the holiday for myself. Please take down the tree."

"I want to use it to lure the kids out of hiding."

That stopped her. "How?"

"They'll see it through the window when they come looking for work, and it'll be a reminder of what they're missing."

"That's cynical."

"No. It is a reminder of what they're missing. And it's a reminder for you, too. You need to come back from being so alone and aloof—or you wouldn't be reacting so strongly."

"Let me go."

He cradled her gently instead. Sometimes people needed contact, whether they thought they did or not, whether they were psychic or not.

The connection between him and Marj was stronger than he'd thought. Her grief, and her effort to bury it, rocked him. He turned her, so that they were facing each other, he cradled her head, and guided it to rest on his chest. "Cry if you need to."

"I don't want to." Her words were muffled in his shirt.

"Then tell me all about it. Do whatever helps."

"I hate Christmas." She lifted her head to look up at him, tears bright in he eyes. "I just do."

"Because your father died this time last year."

"He died at the end of November," she answered, a catch in her voice. "How do you know about it?"

"Research. I've read over a year's worth of the town's

newspapers since I started on this case, including obituaries."

She accepted the explanation with a grudging nod, and a tear spilled down her cheek. "I don't want to go through—the memories. Christmas—it just reminds me—last year was—Christmas sucks."

"Christmas sucked last year," he said. "This year it's time to start over. Christmas is about birth, beginnings, hope, light in the darkness—all that good stuff. And presents. Don't you want presents? And parties? And lights and music, and trees and all the good stuff."

"You sound like Alice."

"She's a soprano, I'm a baritone. But if she's trying to get you back into the world, she's right." Harry loved life, he loved the world. He ached to show Marj that the world was beautiful again. "Hiding is only a temporary refuge."

"Who says?"

"Me. You need to remember you're alive."

Then he kissed her. There was simply nothing else he could do. What surprised him was the passionate hunger of her response and the way her mouth opened eagerly beneath his. The salt taste of her tears was on his tongue, her lips soft. The heat of her body and the scent of her skin went to his head.

His hands moved down her back, caressing and drawing her nearer. He sensed her surprise at her own reactions, that a part of her was fighting to gain control.

Oh, no, what this woman needed was a good loss of control.

What *he* needed was her.

He broke the kiss long enough to literally sweep Marj off her feet. She was so much smaller that holding her in his arms was easy. And cradling her against his chest was the most natural thing in the world.

"What the—"

He swung around and started out of the living room. "I'm not making love in front of the dogs," he declared.

Taffy and Noel were standing nearby, gazing at them with the sort of enthusiastic doggy attention that said they wanted to play, too. He almost regretted leaving the living room, with the romantic holiday air he'd created with the tree, the soft candlelight and cozy fire. But they could make love there later. Right now, he wanted the comfortable intimacy of her big, wide bed.

Harry carried her all the way to her bedroom, and Marj was shocked at herself for not protesting once. This man was little more than a stranger! Yet his kiss did something to stem the aching loneliness. She desperately needed his kisses, and more.

She's spent a year in hell, and somehow, Harry held out the promise of heaven.

She shouldn't want him so badly that her body ached with the need. But she'd wanted him since she'd first seen him in Murphy's.

Everything female in her had woken up and caught fire at the first sight of his eagle-nosed profile, the heavy lock of hair falling across his forehead, the sexy slash of his mouth, the wide shoulders and narrow hips. His smile, his confidence . . . his hands. Good God, what gorgeous, big, competent hands! She'd noticed them from the start. And wanted them on her from the start.

She wanted them on her now.

When he closed the bedroom door and set her on the

bed, she pulled him down beside her. He came with a smile, and a burning kiss that left her breathless.

"Touch me," she said, placing his hand on her breast. "Here. Everywhere."

"I will," he promised.

He stroked her then, and slowly peeled her clothes away. His lips followed where his hands explored, and she caressed him. His hard-muscled body was a wonder to her. It was a long time since she'd been with anyone, but even if she'd been more experienced, Harry was still a revelation. She was amazed at how bold she could be with him, how greedy she was to touch and taste and claim every inch of him. She took great pleasure in exploring his body, loosening his clothes as she went. His turtleneck came off first. She liked his chest, with its well-defined muscles and pattern of dark hair that arrowed down in a vee to his flat stomach.

"You work out," she said, and traced her hands over him.

"Nope," he answered. "You are so beautiful," he told her. "I work out. Well, I lift a lot of bags of animal feed."

Then they kissed for a long time, bodies and mouths melded together for a long, arousing time.

When Harry got up to shed his trousers and underwear, she leaned up on an elbow to watch him strip. It felt deliciously decadent, really, watching a big, gorgeous man taking off his clothes for her.

He turned around, and she had the pleasure of studying his bare backside while he searched through his dropped clothing.

"Ah," he said. When he came back, he was holding a condom packet.

Marj moved beside him and stroked his erection, loving the weight and heat filling her hand, wanting that same feeling inside of her.

Within moments, Harry leaned her back on the bed. He caressed the insides of her thighs, and higher. His fingers danced and teased over her inner folds and clitoris. When she moaned and arched her hips upward, his mouth came down on her. His tongue drew more than moans from her; an orgasm pulsed through her almost instantly. She cried out, and her fingers stroked through his hair.

He moved up her body, sliding skin on skin, then he came inside her. His hardness filled her, the fit completely perfect. They moved together slowly at first, setting up a gentle rhythm, savoring each other, letting the pleasure rise and build.

It wasn't long, though, before his strokes became deeper, faster, and she rose to meet them with a hard-driving need of her own.

The passion building to overwhelm her was more than just physical. He was inside her, their bodies joined, but there was another joining, something wonderful between them that went far beyond physical release. They were—

Mated.

She felt it as well as thought it, and the word and the feeling belonged to both of them. This was a passion that was deeper, richer.

Roaring, rushing sensation overtook her, an explosion so wonderfully intense that she was consumed in long, lingering brightness that faded slowly back into the real world.

"Whoa," was the most coherent thing she could manage after she finally came back into herself.

"Ditto." Harry was a hot, heavy weight on top of her, and his lips were near her ear. He nibbled on her earlobe, sending little lightning flickers of renewed desire from her head to her toes.

"You're good," she said.

He gave a satisfied sigh. "I know."

What might have seemed arrogant and irritating to her before just made her laugh now, a low, breathy, downright dirty laugh.

He kissed her throat just beneath her ear, then moved slowly down her neck, her cheek, her eyelid, her jaw, her shoulder. Each quick, tender touch sent pleasure through her. His hand found her breasts, and her nipples were instantly hard and sensitive against his palm. His lips soon replaced his hand on her breast, and his hand moved down between her legs.

She'd thought herself completely satisfied, sated, melted with happy exhaustion. But within only a few moments, she was alive with desire all over again.

"I'm good," he said. "You're better."

Then they made love all over again.

chapter 9

"You hungry?" Harry asked, as they shared the shower. He was washing her hair and taking great pleasure in the fact that Marj was practically purring.

"Hmmm?" She sighed in utter contentment. Her back was pressed against his chest, and he felt the sigh all the way down his body. Just that small movement was enough to arouse him again.

"Hungry?" he asked over the rush of warm water. "For supper?" Not to make love again; not just yet.

He had to keep his head. The night was young, and he still had work to do.

"I'm starving," Marj said, slowly coming up out of the fog of sensual pleasure. She sighed, with resignation this time. "And the animals need taking care of."

"You need to hire some help."

"Don't think I haven't tried."

They maneuvered around so that she could duck under the showerhead and rinse the cinnamon-scented shampoo out of her hair. Cinnamon was perfect for her, Harry thought, with her dark auburn hair.

They climbed out of the shower, and within a few minutes they were dressed. He helped her with chores, and when they went back to the house, he rummaged in the pantry and the refrigerator and made a cheese omelet while Marj sat on the floor, playing with puppies and kittens. Taffy and Noel demanded her attention as well, and Harry took great pleasure in the amount of affection Marjorie Piper had to give.

The more he knew about her, the more time he spent with her, the more he wanted to know, and the more he wanted to be with her. Which was terrifying.

He had to find those kids soon and make his escape, or this was only going to get worse. He was werewolf, she was human. It hardly ever worked out. There were physical risks to consider, cultural problems. Family pressure alone kept most matings between were and mortals from really having a chance.

One of the reasons the adolescent group was missing was that a werecougar boy had hooked up with a human girl. Of course his parents, and his entire clan, were utterly opposed to the relationship. Harry's job was to bring the boy home.

He's just a kid, Harry thought. *He'll get over her.*

Just as Harry would get over Marj. They had something special, something he feared he'd miss terribly. But he'd get over it.

Marj looked up, sniffed. "Is the omelet burning?"

Harry quickly turned his attention back to the stove. A few minutes later the meal was on plates, and she'd put the tired puppies and kittens back in their crates.

"Hope I find them homes by Christmas," she said as she took her plate from Harry.

"Speaking of Christmas . . ." he said, and led the way back to the living room.

The candles and fire had burned down a bit, but the place still had a nice holiday glow to it. She gave the tree an almost tolerant glance. She did smile, at last, at the array of candles, and turned that smile on him.

His head was reeling from it as they sat down next to each other on the couch. This position left them vulnerable to two tall dogs, but they fought off Taffy's and Noel's begging, and laughed together while racing to finish eating before the dogs wore them down.

"Do they get to lick the plates?" Harry asked when they were finished.

"No."

"They should, because it's almost Christmas."

"Don't spoil my dogs," she admonished. She got up, and he followed her back to the kitchen. "You cooked; I'll clean. Want to dry the dishes?"

This domesticity was far too much fun. "I'd love to, but I have to go wolf hunting now." Harry took his leather jacket off the coat rack by the kitchen door and shrugged into it. "I think it's best if I conduct this search mostly at night. Not only will the animal be more active at night, but the less the locals see someone skulking around the area, the less suspicious they'll be."

She accepted his explanation and offered him a kiss before he left. He enjoyed the kiss so much that he almost confessed that he *was* her wolf, so that he could keep on kissing her and wouldn't have to leave.

In the end, it was Marj who nudged him toward the door. "Good hunting," she told him.

The words caught at his heart. She didn't know it, but

she'd just said the same words a werewolf's mate did when sending him out into the night.

He had to swallow hard around the tightening of his throat before he could say, "Thanks," and walk out the door.

I know that butt.

The thought came to Marj as she was reaching toward a cabinet to put away a plate. The memory was vivid, and overwhelming. The dish crashed to the floor out of her numbed hand. Taffy yelped, and jumped away.

Marj was so stunned that she had to hold on to the edge of the counter with both hands to keep from sinking to her knees as the memory washed up out of her subconscious. She'd only encountered the naked man a couple of days ago, yet all thought of him had been pushed out of her mind.

It felt like it had been deliberately nudged away, overlaid, covered. Her awareness of the process was almost tactile. As if someone as psychic as she was had used his mental ability to rearrange her thinking. Or at least to try. She knew how strange this seemed, but she didn't doubt the truth of it.

He had done it.

"I *know* that butt."

She closed her eyes, and the memory of watching him move around her bedroom in all his glorious nudity was superimposed over the image of the naked man lying inside the wolf's cage.

They were one and the same.

She remembered thinking that Harry was too big to have been trapped in the cage, before she stopped thinking about the naked man at all. Had Harry put the thought about his size into her head as a diversion?

She settled cross-legged on the tiled floor, amid the debris of the broken plate, and rubbed suddenly aching temples. With her eyes closed, she once again called up the memory of how Taffy had rescued her from her two attackers.

Once again, the image of Taffy superimposed itself over the sight of the wolf's glowing blue eyes, the softness of its fur brushing her face, its solid weight bearing her down.

The image of the loyal Labrador retriever made perfect sense. But she knew in her gut, and in her extra senses, that that wasn't what had happened.

As Taffy came up and sat down next to her, Marj reached over and put her arm around his neck. She felt his concern, and the constant love for her that was so much a part of him. Becoming aware of his emotions made her realize that Taffy might have his own memories of what happened that night.

What good was having the ability to talk to animals, if she didn't call upon it when needed? She didn't normally try to pick up more than an animal's current emotional state. Actually, she didn't generally try, it just happened. But she could pick up images and memories if she concentrated hard enough and the incident was sufficiently traumatic to stick in the animal's mind. She could only hope that the attack registered deeply in Taffy's mind.

And when she was finished with her him, she had an entire kennelful of witnesses that she could interrogate.

Harry was aware of the cougar's scent on far western side of the ranch even before he made the shift to wolf form.

He took deep breaths of the cool, dry night air as he took off his clothes, folded them, and tucked them between a bush and the base of the large boulder at the entrance of Marj's long drive.

The cougar prowling out in the darkness was no ordinary one, either: there was another shapeshifter in the vicinity. Harry hoped it was one of the missing kids, but somehow he doubted it. Because he thought that the reason he was having so much trouble tracking down his quarry was due to the camouflage talent of the werecougar youth.

Harry stretched his hands over his head and arched his back before dropping down onto hands and knees. He ignored the sharpness of the winter wind on his bare skin and let the change come slowly, let it be a sensual pleasure rather than a rush of necessity. Making love with Marj had put him in the mood for all the sensual pleasure he could get.

The distant scent became even more obvious when Harry was in wolf form, and easily recognizable. Harry was annoyed at the delay in his search, but he couldn't put off tracking the other were, since it was his client, Mr. Losimba.

He was glad that the trail led quite a distance across the rocky valley, away from the buildings on Marj's hilltop. The last thing he wanted was the Losimba kid's family marking up the territory Harry was using as bait.

When he found Losimba, the werecougar was perched regally on top of a rock outcrop, his gold fur frosted by moonlight. Harry came to a halt and took a moment to appreciate the pose.

Then he switched from wolf to human form. All werefolk were telepathic, but it was easier to communicate mind to mind with humans than across forms. Wolf to wolf, or any other canine type, was natural for him, but canine to feline was just—wrong.

Harry ignored the sudden blast of cold, along with a natural distaste for cats, and said, "You're lovely. But if a rancher gets a look at you up there, you're going to get shot."

The Losimbas were as urban as most shapeshifters these days. Normally, when werefolk went out into the wild to take on their animal forms, they did so on large tracts of wilderness property owned and guarded by the Council of Clans. If you wanted to run free, you paid an annual fee for the privilege.

Losimba snarled at Harry, then shifted in a blur of gold from cat to human form. He remained seated on the flat rock perch, looking no less proud and regal as a man than as a mountain lion. Instead of snarling, he sneered.

"There are many reasons I have no use for humans. Their lust to murder all predators, including each other, is only one of them."

Losimba was very much a political animal, and an arch-conservative one, at that. The last thing Harry wanted, especially since it was freezing out here, was to get into philosophical discussion.

"Yeah. Well. Whatever. What are you doing here?" Harry asked. "Other than interfering with my investigation."

"I want results." Losimba jumped down, light and graceful, from his perch. "I want my son back."

"And the other kids?"

"Yes. Of course." Then he sneered, "Except for the human. Something has to be done about her."

Harry disliked the ominous tone. "The Council asked me to find them, that's all. No violence is intended toward that girl."

"She can be made to forget, if enough pressure is applied."

"If the boy's mated with the human—"

"It doesn't bear thinking about," Losimba cut him off sharply. "My breed doesn't associate with that kind." He sniffed disdainfully, "while you obviously enjoy wallowing in the human sewer. There's human stench all over you."

Harry caught himself growling deep in his throat and longing to rip the werecougar's throat out. He didn't let himself rise any farther to the bait, though. Losimba was famously old school in his attitudes. Except that the anti-human attitudes were really only the product of the last couple of generations. What had started out as a way to avoid extinction had turned into prejudice and snobbery in many werefolk. Those were games Harry didn't play.

"Why aren't you searching for the children?" Losimba demanded. "What progress have you made?"

Harry understood a parent's worry, but he didn't like Losimba's arrogance. He also didn't like the fact that the other were was here. When he took on a case, the area of the hunt became his territory. There wasn't room in his territory for another alpha, never mind the other shapeshifter's breed.

"Did the Council send you to oversee my methods? Or are you trying to screw this up on your own?"

"Why aren't you doing anything?" Losimba demanded. "You've had weeks—"

"And in those weeks, I've tracked the kids down to this area." He pointed back toward the buildings far away on the hilltop. "To that place. All I can do now is watch and wait. If this was a human missing person case, I could use these more." He tapped his nose, then touched an ear. "Our kind are harder to track than humans."

"We're better than humans."

"Our senses are slightly different, and some humans come close to us in their physical and psychic abilities. And this isn't the time or place to discuss breed differences. I don't know about you, but my balls are freezing off."

"You damn lobos are sentimental fools. You'll let the humans domesticate you and drag the rest of us down with you."

Once again, Harry fought off the urge to mix it up with this guy. He reminded himself that Losimba was worried about his kid. People under that kind of stress often lashed out because it was the only way to deal with their frustration. Or, Losimba was just a jerk.

"Stay out of my way," he told the werecougar. "Even better, go home."

"I want action! I want news."

"I've told you all I know, and all I'm doing. This kind of hunt takes patience."

Losimba suddenly looked sad, and tired. "I promised his mother I'd have him home by Christmas."

Harry didn't bring up the fact that Christmas was a *human* holiday, even though the celebration was one of the things that united werefolk with their shape-challenged cousins. Harry wondered what kind of miracle it would take to get that peace on earth, goodwill toward others thing going between the different sides of the evolutionary divide.

He was tempted him to ask Losimba if he'd welcome a human daughter-in-law into his home for Christmas dinner. But the answer might be a not-too-flippant *as* Christmas dinner; and then Harry really would go after the werecougar, tooth and claw.

"Go home," he said to Losimba. "Don't interfere. I will get those kids home."

Still tense, Losimba glared at Harry for a while out of tawny eyes. Then he shifted from man to cat with such graceful fluidity that even Harry had to admire his shifting abilities. All admiration was off, however, when Losimba then snarled at him once more and stalked proudly away.

Harry studied how Losimba managed to fade his scent to barely a trace as the other were disappeared from sight. Any information he could get would help in his hunt for the kids. The blocking was of a psychic nature, sending out a mental camouflage signal aimed specifically at the thought processes of other shapeshifters. It was a variation on how shapeshifters mentally influenced humans not to notice anything out of the ordinary they witnessed.

"He's good," Harry acknowledged. "But his son's better."

Then he changed back into a huge black wolf and went for a run, reveling in the power, the speed, the sharp senses of his animal form. Most importantly, he took huge pleasure in being warm.

But after a while, a new sensation caught hold of him and made him turn his steps toward the hilltop. Something called him back toward Marj. After only a few hours away, he was already lonely for her. Instinct told him he was going home—and that bone-deep belief scared the conscious part of him to death.

He found the boulder on the edge of the drive with no problem. He also had no problem detecting Taffy's scent, or Marj's. She and the dog had been here while he was gone. He supposed that she'd taken the dog for a walk, maybe hoping to spot the wolf, or him in human shape. Maybe Taffy had gotten a whiff of the clothing left by the boulder and come over to investigate. It was probably all perfectly innocent . . . and it filled Harry with dread. His misgivings grew worse when he couldn't find his stashed clothing anywhere near the boulder.

The instinctive part of his mind told him to *Run! Now!* Any little breach of normal safety precautions triggered a fight-or-flight response in his kind. But the logical part, which should have been agreeing with the instinctive part, was telling him he needed to talk to Marj. That he needed to explain to her. That he just needed Marj.

Okay, he needed her. But he wasn't going to show up at her door either as a wolf, or naked as a jaybird. He had left two other sets of clothing, identical to the ones he'd lost, secreted around her property in case of any emergency. The first thing he was going to do was head to the barn, to don the clothes he'd left under a stack of feed bags.

He crossed the yard silently, clinging to shadows. The area was full of the crisscrossing scents of animals and of Marjorie, of himself, and other people from many different days and times. He could detect no immediate danger.

He was at the barn door and getting ready to change to human so he could open it, when he realized it was a trap. He felt Marj's anger and whirled around. Following the direction of her emotions, he spotted her sitting on top of the cab of her pickup truck. With a tranquilizer rifle aimed at him.

She fired even as he sprang toward her, then fired again.

Two spots of pain blossomed along Harry's side. He went down hard on the cold ground. As the world went dark, his last thoughts were, *Oh no, not again!*

chapter 10

"Tranquilizer darts."

"Yep," Marj answered

"That's the second time this week, dammit."

Marj watched warily as Harry sat up from where he'd been lying on the concrete barn floor, wrapped the red blanket around his chest, and glared at her. She was sitting on top of an old trunk, her legs tucked beneath her and an old quilt covering her lap. All the overhead lights were blazing, and the wide doors were closed and locked. It was just the two of them, as she'd left Taffy and Noel locked in the house. There was no way she was risking her dogs' safety around a wolf.

She also noticed that he gauged the distance between them and looked at the rifle she cradled on her lap. Harrison Blethyin was not a happy camper.

"How's your head?" she asked.

"Pounding. Brutally, viciously pounding."

"I can do something about that."

"You've already done quite enough."

She guessed she had, but she'd dragged the wolf in out of the cold and kept him warm with a blanket while he slept off the drugs and turned slowly back to the shape of a man. And she hadn't used as strong a tranquilizer as the men who'd shot him. She had questions about those men, and Harry's involvement with them. But there was another matter to deal with first.

"You're a werewolf," she said.

At first his expression was a mixture of wariness and anger, but gradually he began to look a little bit annoyed. Maybe it was just the headache. Eventually, he said, "Don't get all hysterical about it, or anything."

Well, at least he didn't try to deny it. What did he expect from her? Did he think the appropriate response would be to scream, to panic? To call the tabloids?

"I could exchange the darts for silver bullets, if it would make you feel more threatened," she suggested. "Besides, I had hysterics when I first figured it out. Should I have videotaped it for you?"

"You sound bitter," he said, as though it concerned him. "I don't know what you have to be bitter about."

"You lied to me."

He rubbed his jaw, dark with stubble at the moment. He slowly got to his feet, still wrapped in the blanket. He kept his gaze on the rifle, and moved slowly toward a shelf stacked with twenty-pound bags of animal feed. "I'm going to get dressed now."

"Your stuff's not there."

He dropped the blanket as he turned around, looking annoyed.

She just looked. She already knew he was gorgeous. After all, she'd seen him naked in a cage, and in her bedroom. She'd watched the slow, graceful transformation from wolf to human form while he was unconscious. Perhaps that should have disturbed her—but it had been beautiful; like a kind of art. And here he was naked again, and looking at her with angry sparks in his blue eyes. Sparks went through her, as well—she couldn't help it when she was around him. She wasn't going to try to deny how much physical attraction she felt for this—man? For the man-shaped part of him?

"You found my clothes in here, too? How?"

His angry question refocused her attention. "Taffy found the clothes out by the drive. Then I showed them to Bailey. He's a beagle/bloodhound mix. Once I told him what to look for, he had a ball."

"Once you *told* him?"

She found it odd that he sounded suspicious and skeptical. Then, again, why did she assume he knew everything about her? It seemed like she'd known him forever, but that wasn't true at all. And most of what she did know was false.

"Are you going to let me stand here and freeze to death, woman?"

"Are you going to turn into a wolf and attack me?"

"Of course not!"

His indignation slapped against her psychic senses, and she believed that he believed what he said. Which would have to do. His folded clothes were lying next to her on the trunk. She flipped back the quilt and tossed shirt, pants, socks, and shoes to him.

She continued to watch him closely while he dressed, and when he pushed aside some of the bags and perched on the storage shelf.

"Now what?" he asked.

"Now you tell me what's really going on."

He stared at her, his expression blank. But she could

feel his thoughts teasing and tickling around hers, trying to get into her head and change what she believed and remembered. She didn't like his reasons, but she welcomed the connection. She'd never shared this kind of communication with a human before. Heck, if there wasn't a wolf part of him, maybe she wouldn't be able to do it.

Stop that! she finally told him, and conjured up a mental image of her smacking the big, black wolf on the nose.

Harry blinked. Then he threw back his head and laughed. "You're not afraid of me, are you? Not one little bit. I'm a werewolf, you know," he added seriously.

"And I'm Dr. Doolittle," she answered.

She's not scared, Harry realized. *And she's not freaked.* She was, in fact, incredibly accepting of the fact that he was a very different type of being than she was. It didn't bother her that he could turn into a dangerous animal. She accepted him for who he was, and knowing that she did filled his heart, and his head, with—her.

He could also tell that her knowledge and acceptance of his *otherness* did not stop her from being really pissed off at him.

"You want explanations," he said.

She settled the rifle back across her lap. "How can you tell?"

As he was faster and stronger than a human, he could take the weapon away from her at any time. But he wasn't going to strip away a prop that made her feel safe. He didn't blame her for not trusting him just yet.

Harry rubbed a sore spot over his ribs. "I really hate getting shot."

"At least I only use tranquilizers. My neighbors wouldn't be so humane."

"You were worried that a rancher would take a shot at me?"

"Of course. That's why I hired you to find—you," she finished with an annoyed grimace. "I suppose you found that really funny?"

He shook his head. "No. I found it sweet. And useful," he admitted. "I have been using you, but for the very best of reasons. I really am a missing persons—"

"Werewolf."

"Which gives me the perfect skills for the job. But it's my being a werewolf you want to know about first. I can *feel* your curiosity. You want explanations, assurances, background—all that stuff that's supposed to be secret. Stuff that has to be secret," he added. "We only have two choices in dealing with humans that learn it."

He waited for her to ask what those two choices were.

"Tell me about werewolves," was all she said.

She was not paying attention to consequences. Harry didn't understand that, because Marj struck him as the sensible sort. He supposed that learning that the myths and legends of the supernatural world were real could shake even sensible people into reckless behavior.

She knew he was a real shapeshifter, and had proved that he couldn't make her forget. That left him with those two choices—and he already knew that he wasn't going to kill her.

He sighed. "Okay. You know all the ancient tribal stories about shamans taking on animal forms?" She nodded. "Well, a long, long time ago those shapeshifting abilities were a well-known and accepted part of the world. I'm talking prehistoric times. We evolved as humans, among humans. We were people with psychic gifts that could also be manifested with the physical ability to take on the form of certain totem animals—wolves, bears, foxes, tigers— just about any mammalian predators. The ability to turn into wolves has always been the most prevalent. But as humans stopped living in small tribes of hunter-gatherers and settled into farming communities, they didn't have any need for predators in their midst anymore. The were-folk were driven out. We ended up banding together into our own tribes and mating only with our own kinds. So, what was originally a rare mutation for a specific psychic gift turned into dominant traits in our offspring."

"So, you have to be born a werewolf? What about the legends of people being becoming werewolves by being bitten by one?"

Harry shrugged with discomfort. "Yeah, well, unfortunately that can happen. None of our scientists have been able to figure that out yet. But we've only really had the ability to study the infectious properties of—"

"Werewolves have scientists?" she interrupted.

This was not the time to explain to her that most of the real research into the scientific aspects of supernatural phenomena was being carried out by vampires. Information about his own kind would do for the time being.

"There are werefolk involved in the research. We go to college," he added. "We're not animals, you know."

Marj laughed. "Don't get your tail in a twist. Go on."

He laughed, too, delighted to hear such a common werewolf joke from this human woman. Of course, it was probably a common sort of joke for a vet who ran an animal shelter, too. Either way, it reinforced the connection between them.

"I wonder," he said, "if you would let me make love to you right now, knowing what I am."

That wasn't what he'd meant to say, but suddenly it was very important for him to know. He was almost scared to look at her, afraid of seeing disgust openly on her face. Or, even worse, her trying to hide it.

But she looked at him steadily, thoughtfully. Her emotions rippled around her. He picked up brief, overlaying shades of surprise, curiosity, anger, impatience, and lust. Harry especially liked that deep, rich ribbon of lust that wound through everything else Marj was feeling.

"So, you still like me," he said. "I can feel it, even if you won't answer my question."

"Because it's not a relevant question for the moment. It's a matter of trust," she said. "Liking has nothing to do with whether or not I should trust you."

"I'm very trustworthy."

"You didn't tell me you were a werewolf." She made a face at her own words. "Okay, if I were a werewolf, I wouldn't spread the news around, either. The world isn't safe for the radically different. I'm not forthcoming about my own—peculiarities."

"There is nothing at all peculiar about you, lovely Marjorie."

She waved off his flattery. "Tell me more about werewolves—or should I say werefolk?"

"Werefolk. We are separate breeds, but we all answer to rules set up by an elected group Council. The Council is very conservative. For the last fifty or sixty years they've made it the priority for all memory and belief in werefolk to be wiped out of human consciousness. It'll be safer for us if people don't believe we exist."

"People *don't* believe werewolves exist."

"See, it's working."

She didn't even crack a smile. "It would be dangerous for your kind if you were discovered. Everybody knows the legends, and the horror movies and books about how people get bitten and turn into bloodthirsty monsters during the full moon. That sort of bad publicity could get real werefolk killed."

"Precisely."

"Do you turn into a ravening monster during the full moon?"

Harry curbed his indignation. "Not my style," he told her. "But the legends have a basis in reality. People who are bitten by weres do change physiologically. What's normal for someone born as a were manifests more like a disease—at least initially—with someone who's been bitten. While a natural-born werewolf can change almost anytime, without pain or difficulty, a bitten develops a monthly cycle that forces the change. The process is not only painful, but it makes them crazy. The animal self takes control, and it's vicious, hurting, and terrified. Eventually, most bittens will get control of their minds and bodies and blend in to normal shapeshifter society. If they're protected and cared for from the first, the transition is an easier process."

"So, you're saying that the stories of werewolves as monsters are strictly about people who've been bitten and gone on a rampage?"

"There are good and bad people in every society. I will say that *most* of the legends of violence come from the bittens. We're trying to kill the legends, which is why the council has encouraged closing off our society to outsiders. There's been a long moratorium on taking human mates. Biting has been forbidden." He shook his head. "It's helped keep our secrets, but it's been hell on our gene pool. Some of the younger people are getting rebellious about it. Which brings me to why I'm looking for the runaways."

Good Lord, what had he just said? It was all very right to tell Marj some basic stuff. But he had no right to give away information about anyone else. Confiding in her came way too naturally.

Marj heard Harry's mental *OOPS* loud and clear. She believed he was searching for something, and he claimed it was runaways. Runaway what? Werefolk? If that were true—

The realization came to her with a start. "Phil Fennick's a werewolf!"

"Werefox." Harry gave a deep sigh. "I've already told you too much, but I do want your help to get the case closed safely, and soon. The kids I'm looking for are a pretty mixed bag of radical hippie kits, kittens, and cubs."

"Radical hippies? Uh, the sixties were over about thirty years ago. Hippies have grandchildren now."

Her parents had actually met at some rock concert back in the sixties, and they'd traveled around the country in a VW Beetle. She'd seen photos of them in long hair, bell-bottoms, and fringed vests. They had ended up as very successful lawyers, then retired young to raise the only child they had late, out in the clean, open, independent West. And they'd raised *her* to be independent, to respect the environment, to celebrate rather than to fear the differences among people, to follow her love of animals wherever it led her. They'd certainly encouraged her to develop her psychic gift and never to fear it.

Marj supposed that qualified them as clinging to their original hippie ideals. And how she missed them! It was a pity that they'd never lived to see grandchildren. Not that she was likely to produce any, in any case. Because the one man she was insanely attracted to had turned out to be werewolf. And Harry had already told her that werewolves didn't take human mates.

One-night stands, as she already knew. Brief liaisons. But not lifetime partners.

Damn.

"You know the generation problems humans went through back then?" Harry asked, drawing her out of her reverie.

She pulled her attention back to the present, because moment to moment was all she was going to experience with Harrison Blethyin. "Yes."

"That kind of upheaval is what's going on among my people now. I have to find the kids before they do something stupid—like out themselves. Or freeze to death up in the mountains."

"Freeze to death? Can't they stay in animal form and survive in the wild?"

He threw back his head and laughed. "Modern kids? I don't think so. I meant what I said about their being lured out of hiding for Christmas presents and parties. Everything I told you about my methods of finding them is true." He tapped his long, elegant nose. "This is not much good in trying to track down my own kind."

They sat across from each other in silence as Marj absorbed everything he'd told her. She couldn't help but believe that he was essentially telling her the truth. But she was still confused and suspicious.

"What about Noel?" she asked. "What about the men who stole her? Why did they shoot you? What have you got to do with them?"

"Not a damn thing," he answered. "I was just out for a run that night. The same way you were just coming home from a party." He hopped down from his perch on the shelf, stretched, and yawned, then held his hand out toward her. "Look at it this way: without those jokers, we never would have met. It's late. Let's go to bed."

Marj considered how easy he was about continuing to fit into her life. What should she do? Tell him to go? Where, back to the Fennicks? To the motel in town? It was too late for him to go banging on either door.

"There are four bedrooms in the house besides mine," she said, getting to her feet. "Go pick one while I lock the rifle back in the kennel."

chapter 11

HARRY WOKE UP the next morning feeling resentful at being exiled from Marj's bed, no matter how comfortable the one he'd chosen was. He'd slept in a second-floor bedroom at the back of the house, directly over Marj's first-floor bedroom.

At least she hadn't made him sleep in the kennel. Or brought the rifle into her room with her. She wasn't afraid of him, and that was heartening. He'd tried to bolster her trust by keeping away from her, when he wanted to do anything but. He'd been aware of her nearby while he tried to get to sleep, like any male could feel his mate, and it had been difficult to stay all platonic and safe.

Alpha called to alpha, dammit! And that woman called to him, even while she slept. When he finally got to sleep, she called to him in his dreams. He hoped she hadn't slept any better than he had.

The dogs were waiting outside the bedroom when he opened the door. Taffy's tail thumped enthusiastically on the floor as Harry appeared. Noel stepped forward and butted her soft head against his thigh.

Harry paused to give them a friendly pat and scritch. Then he suddenly recalled some things Marj had done and said about her own relationship to animals. His curiosity piqued, he settled down on the worn hallway carpet, the dogs surrounded him. He continued stroking Taffy and Noel while he connected with them on a deeper level, asking their opinions of Marjorie Piper.

"You really are Dr. Doolittle."

"You've been talking to the animals—about how I talk to the animals," Marj answered.

She was standing by the sink with a mug of coffee cradled in her hands. She hadn't heard him enter the kitchen, but she'd felt his presence, had anticipated his arrival more with each step he took. She was looking out the kitchen window at a faint dusting of snow covering the landscape below. She loved the view down across the valley. The jagged peaks of the San Jago Mountains rose in the distance, densely covered in pine and aspen below the snowline.

It was a beautiful, sunny winter morning, yet her usual pleasure in the view was tinged with loneliness. The world was so very wide and empty to her today.

Then Harry spoke, and her heart sang.

He put his arms around her waist and pulled her back against him. For a moment she lost all awareness of everything but his warmth, his size, his presence. The world stopped being lonely, or empty, and she leaned back against him. She closed her eyes on a heartfelt, contented sigh.

"You listened in on our conversation upstairs?"

"Not exactly. I felt a kind of buzzing excitement coming from Taffy's direction. It's hard to explain."

"I know. Do you know how wonderful your talent is? How special it makes you?"

His words went to her heart, but she answered, "I know how weird it makes me to other people."

"Not to me. That smells good."

She didn't mind when he reached up and took the coffee from her hands. It was her second cup, anyway. And she wasn't weird to him. That was worth far more than a cup of coffee.

She couldn't, and wouldn't, let the moment last. But she let it go on for a while. He smelled good, and he felt good, very male. She felt very protected. She told herself that enjoying this sensation was detrimental to her independence, but didn't try to deny the arousal that built second by second, with sweet, steadily growing heat.

"I'm making your bones melt, aren't I?" he asked after a few minutes.

She tilted her head back to get a look at his face, but mostly got was a view of his strong, square jaw. "You are so very sure of your effect on women, aren't you?"

He set the empty mug on the counter and turned her to face him. "Yeah."

"Animal magnetism?"

"I'm just a hot guy."

"Yes," she agreed.

He grinned, and for the first time, she noticed he had dimples. He was so attractive that it hurt, which was why she decided that the moment was at an end, even as he bent his head to kiss her.

When she moved sideways, he straightened and let her go.

"I made oatmeal," she said. "Do you eat oatmeal? Or are you strictly a carnivore?"

"Oatmeal's fine. I don't do the Atkins thing." When she

reached into an overhead cabinet for a bowl, he stepped up behind her. "Let me get that."

She sat at the table while Harry served his own breakfast. After setting his bowl down at the table, he went back to the counter and brought mugs of coffee back for both of them.

When their hands touched as she took the mug, he said, "You know I'm going to kiss you eventually, don't you?"

"Eat your breakfast." She glanced at the cushions in the corner, where Taffy and Noel were now lying side by side. "Or I'll feed it to the dogs."

"Okay," he said, and pulled her up and out of her chair.

The next thing Marj knew, they were holding each other tightly, and their mouths were pressed hungrily together.

The kitchen, her worries, all the world went away. All that existed was where they touched, and where they touched they blended in a flash of shared desire.

Marj had no idea how long they'd been kissing before she became aware of Taffy barking.

The dog's excitement finally got through to her, his emotions translating to *Here! Here! Someone's here!*

Just as this registered, a loud knock sounded on the back door.

Harry spun away from her, and swore.

Marj leaned her hands on the kitchen table to steady herself. Her body raged with need, her head spun—and the knock sounded again. She pulled herself together enough to psychically tell Taffy to shut up. Then she crossed the kitchen and flung open the door.

A pretty, nervous-looking girl stood on the back porch. "Dr. Piper?" she asked.

Marj stared at her. "Yes?"

"I'm Heather Adams. You had an appointment to see me this morning. About the vet tech job?"

Marj had completely forgotten about the job interview. She forced a smile now. "Of course. My office is just across the—"

"Come in, Heather," Harry said, stepping up behind her. He put a hand on Marj's shoulder. "I think Heather would be more comfortable talking to you in the living room." He maneuvered Marj away from the doorway and ushered the young woman inside. "Here. Let me take your coat."

Marj didn't think the young woman noticed him holding the fleece jacket close to his face and taking several deep breaths before he hung it on the coatrack. Marj was briefly surprised, then she remembered who he really was and what he was here for. He was barking up the wrong tree, though, if he thought a job applicant would be one of his runaways.

Then she almost laughed at the look he gave her, realizing that he'd caught her *barking up the wrong tree* thought.

Living room, he thought at her. *Christmas tree. Warmth. Coziness. Longing for home.*

"Come on into the living room," she said to Heather. She smiled at Harry. "Why don't you bring us some tea and cookies?"

"That went well," Harry said, after Marj returned from showing Heather around the property. When Marj gave him a slightly annoyed look, he gave her a reassuring smile.

"Lucy, you got some 'splaining to do," she replied.

He heard the girl's car start and drive away, and fought down the hunter's urge to start the pursuit immediately.

He held his hands up in mock confusion. "What?"

"Why were you in the living room while I was talking to Heather?"

"I finished decorating the tree," he answered. "It needed to be done. Besides, did you see how wistfully she looked at it? That girl is going to go back to her boyfriend and tell him she wants a real Christmas."

"That girl isn't a werewolf—a werefolk."

"Oh, and how can *you* tell?"

"Because the dogs barked. I've noticed that animals stay quiet when you're around. Heather's one of the people who e-mailed me about the job."

"You're an observant woman, Dr. Piper," he said proudly. "But do you think werefolk don't use e-mail?"

"Not if they're hiding out in the mountains."

"We live in a wireless society, Marjorie. Modern kids might want to live free and furry, but they're going to have their laptops and PDAs with them. Or maybe she saw your ad pinned on the bulletin board at Murphy's store when she came in for supplies and used the Internet connection in the motel lobby to apply. I didn't expect them to let their one human member come into town."

"She seemed quite independent to me," Marj said. "I don't think anyone *lets* her do anything."

"We werefolk males are always attracted to strong women."

"Why wouldn't they want Heather to come into town? And are you really sure she's involved with your runaways?"

He chuckled. "There's werecougar scent all over that

girl. You know what cats are like when it comes to claiming what's theirs. Like this." He drew her close to him and rubbed his cheek against her throat and shoulder.

She leaned into his touch. "Keep that up, and I'm going to start purring."

"We'd be more than purring," Harry said, and reluctantly made himself step back. He did stroke her face with the back of his hand one more time, enjoying the way they so easily aroused each other. "I have to go."

He felt her wanting to reach for him. But she also understood that he had a duty to perform and a need to hunt.

"Where?" she asked. "Following Heather? I thought you said you couldn't—"

"She's human. I can follow any human scent, and she's leaving me a trail that will lead straight to her boyfriend and all the others. Gotta go." he said.

He gave her a swift kiss, and was out the door.

It was only after he was miles away from Marj's place that it occurred to him that she hadn't asked him if he would be back, and he hadn't told her that he would be.

He hoped that wasn't a big mistake.

chapter

12

 "How does he think he's going to get those kids home?" Marj said as she rubbed the ears of Bailey, the bloodhound/beagle mix. They were long ears on his short body, and helped make him look silly, and funny, and cute. She couldn't understand why she hadn't been able to place him in a home yet—though she'd miss him when he was gone.

She was going to miss Harry when he was gone, too. She missed him already.

That was one of the reasons she was in the kennel, giving the animals some TLC. She had affection to give, and these lost, unwanted animals were quick to appreciate it. A more practical reason for spending time holding, petting, and playing with them was to socialize them, of course.

But she wasn't feeling practical right now. She was upset, and being with the dogs and cats was comforting. She'd taken them out of the pens one by one for exercise and play. She was sitting on the concrete floor in the center of the kennel, with the excellent tracker Bailey on her lap.

Marj had been worrying and wondering about Harry's dilemma since he left a couple hours ago. It was all very well and good for him to track the kids down to their lair, or commune, but then what?

Not that it was any of her business, she supposed. She had her own worries, her own responsibilities.

But—

What was Harry going to do when he found those kids? Talk them down out of the mountains? Handcuff— or possibly leash—them? And what would being rounded up like that do after they were carted off home? Why, make them want to run away again, of course.

"You can catch more flies with honey, can't you?" she asked Bailey, who was more interested in her continuing to scratch his belly than in inane questions from a human. "I bet those teenagers would rather have honey than lectures."

An idea occurred to her, and she turned the dog back onto his feet. "Bailey, old boy," she said, thinking what she wanted at his doggie brain as she spoke. "Remember how you helped me find Harry's things before? You know his scent. He can't track werewolves, but you can. You and I are going to find Harry."

But first she was going to go to Murphy's store to do a little shopping.

"Hi, there," Marj said.

Still in wolf form, Harry had heard her and the dog coming, but he'd kept his gaze on the shack, tent, and SUV occupying the hollow below this stand of trees. He was very glad that to be upwind of the hollow, especially when he became aware of the approaching human and dog.

Since he couldn't do anything but growl or howl at her in his current form, Harry closed his eyes and willed himself back into his human shape. He could have used telepathy, but it was so much more satisfying to vent annoyance vocally.

He turned his glance briefly to her when she came up beside him, and whispered, "What are you doing here?"

She had a large pack hoisted on her back and was carrying a canvas bag. "Brought you some stuff, including some clothes," she said, looking over his naked form.

It was cold up here, with an icy wind already cutting into his naked skin. His feet sank uncomfortably into snow-covered pine needles. Marj was wearing a heavy parka, heavy boots, and gloves. She was obviously comfortable in the winter climate.

"Thanks," he said, and quickly put on the clothing she'd brought in the bag. When he was dressed, he asked again, "What are you doing here?"

"This was your idea," she answered. "I'm just here to help execute it."

"I have no idea what you're talking about."

He was both irritated and surprised that she'd followed him, and happy to see her. He looked at the dog she'd brought with her. Not her trusted Taffy, but a short mutt with loose skin around its head and long ears. "Don't tell me you used *that* mutt to find me?"

She nodded. "You can track humans, but not werefolk. Did it ever occur to you to use dogs to track werefolk?"

"Of course I wouldn't use dogs to—!" He almost sputtered with indignation, and had to struggle to keep his voice low. "That's insulting."

"Even Taffy picked up your scent. And Bailey, here, is much better at it than Taffy."

"But—"

Harry was an expert tracker, and being stumped by the runaways had hurt his professional pride. But if he stopped taking it personally, he saw how Marj's actions made sense. Marj's actions had worked. And hers was a solution that wouldn't have occurred to him because, well, because he was a werewolf.

He chuckled softly and touched her cheek. "Okay," he said. "You found me. But you still haven't told me why you're here."

"To help you lure them back to the real world," she said.

She peered down the hill, shrugged out of the pack and handed it to him, then set off down the slope toward the cabin. The dog ran ahead of her. Neither of them were moving quietly. Upwind or not, the young people down there were bound to notice Marj soon. There was nothing for Harry to do but follow after.

He caught up to her quickly, and they heard the shouting coming through the thin walls as they got closer.

"I am so taking the job!" The voice was Heather's.

"No, you're not! You're my mate, and you do as I tell you!" a male voice shouted angrily.

"Don't take that tone with her!" another woman spoke up. "We didn't come here to be dictated to by males."

"We came to live the old ways," another male said. "That means the males of the pack—"

"Do what the females tell them," the second woman cut him off.

"Maybe in your home pack, Alison, but—"

"We need the money!" Heather overrode them. "And this is our home pack."

"What do we need money for?" yet another male asked. "We can survive in the wild."

Marj turned to Harry and whispered, "The last one's Phil Fennick."

"I want—things," Heather declared. "I need—"

"You want to go home," the first male declared.

"No! I love you, Clark. I want to be with you!"

"Then what is it you need?"

"Christmas!" Heather shouted back. "I need Christmas."

Harry grinned at Marj. "See? I was right."

She nodded. "And that's our cue."

With that, she stepped up onto the creaky porch, and knocked on the door. Harry, close behind her, realized that she was humming "Santa Claus is Coming to Town" under her breath.

The door was flung open dramatically by Heather. She stared at them for a moment, while the other people in the cabin gathered behind her. Finally, she said, "Dr. Piper? What are you doing here?"

"See what you've done?" Alison accused Heather. "She followed you here."

Clark stood behind Heather with his hands on her shoulders, protective as he glared at Harry. "Interesting company your Dr. Piper keeps."

"I like to think of her as my Dr. Piper," Harry said.

He moved forward, nudging Marj ahead of him, but not taking his gaze from Clark Losimba's the whole time.

He'd been playing the dominance game for twice as long as the werecougar boy had been alive. Besides, he was an Alpha lobo, which was the top of the food chain in the werefolk world. Harry didn't think Clark was even aware of stepping back as he advanced into the shack with Marj at his side.

Once he and Marj were inside, Harry kicked the door

closed behind them. That didn't help the temperature much, as the small woodstove in one corner wasn't any defense against the frigid air let in through the thin walls. The place had only one room with a small window, a bare floor, and no visible amenities. The room held three cots and an assortment of cardboard boxes. The mingled scents, physical and mental, of fox, cougar, wolf, and human was strong, with all six of the runaways crowded into the one-room shack. With Harry and Marj inside, too, there wasn't much room to move.

"Not exactly five-star accommodations."

"We don't need to live like humans, lobo," Alison spoke up. She was werewolf, as well.

He sensed that this young female was trying hard not to be alpha of this communal group and welcomed being able to turn the aggression she tried to suppress on someone who could stand up to it.

"I do," Heather chimed in.

Clark broke eye contact with Harry to turn a challenging look on the other woman.

"Which is why we let you have all the blankets," Alison said. She smiled at Clark. "We take care of each other."

Clark swung his attention back to Harry and Marj. "We don't want you here."

"We won't stay long," Marj answered.

Harry was aware of how determinedly cheerful she was being, and that she wasn't going to be intimidated by a bunch of teenagers, no matter how tough and dangerous several of them thought they were.

"I brought you some things." She gestured to the pack, and Harry handed it to her. She, in turn, put it down on the nearest cot. "I saw your parents the other night, Phil," she went on. "At a Christmas party at the high school. It was a lot of fun; too bad you missed it. There was dancing." She continued to speak as she took items out of the pack and placed them one by one across the cot. "Pattie Corbett brought her whole CD collection. Didn't you used to go out with Pattie, Phil?"

"Yeah, but—"

The kids were drawn to gather round her as Marj laid out her treasures.

"What's all that, Dr. Piper?" Heather asked.

"I smell chocolate," Alison said.

"Candy. Some cookies. There's hot chocolate mix. I brought fruitcake, too. What's Christmas without fruitcake?"

"Better for everyone," one of the kids spoke up. There was laughter.

"I like fruitcake," Alison declared.

"I'm sorry I couldn't carry too much with me," Marj said. "But I thought you'd like a taste. There's plenty more to be had at my place. I'm in the mood for baking a lot of Christmas cookies this year."

"I remember your baking cookies," Phil said. "I could smell them from miles away—but you didn't make any last year."

She smiled at him. "I'll make up for the lack this year." She gestured at all the teenagers. "It's going to take a lot of baking to fill up a crew this size."

"What are you talking about?" Clark demanded. "Who is this human?"

"You did some chores for me back in October, don't you remember?"

"She's my friend," Phil spoke.

"Your *parents*' friend," Clark said.

"No," Marj said. "I know Phil much better than I do his folks. If you'd like to come back to work for me, Phil, I could certainly use the help. You too," she added to Heather.

The dog had staked out one of the kids for attention, and was being held in the arms of a girl, who was looking wistful. Marj was handing out candy and other treats to the runaways, one by one, and talking to them about how she planned to spend Christmas in her big, warm house. Most of them were listening avidly. The kids were really homesick, Harry concluded happily.

"What's going on?" Clark demanded, his attention fully on Harry while the others concentrated on stuffing down candy bars and fruitcake. "Did my father send you?"

"Are you from the Council?" Alison spoke up.

Harry noticed how she was regarding him wolf to wolf, and told her, *Don't think about it. I already have a mate.*

Alison glanced between him and Marj. *A human?* Far from being appalled, she suddenly looked at him with respect. "Then you can't be from the Council."

"But I am," he said. "I'm also not completely on their side. I've been looking for you, but to see that you're okay." Harry took a step back, and said, "Listen up." When their attention was on him, he went on, "My name is Harrison Blethyin. Some of you might have heard of me."

Alison and Clark exchanged a quick glance, which told him they knew who he was. These two were the oldest of the shapeshifter group, not technically runaways. At nineteen, Heather Adams was also legally an adult, and human—so, technically, none of Harry's business. But seeing how they were living in this isolated icebox of a shack, he was determined to get all of them back to a more civilized and safe place.

"You're the tracker," Alison said.

"You work with humans," Clark Losimba said. "Helping them. My dad thinks you're a freak," he added, but he was smiling at Harry when he did. "My dad's a jerk."

"Jerk or not, he misses you, Clark. And Council or not, no one can make you go home or back into our world."

"It's not *our* world," Alison asserted. "We left because everything's messed up with werefolk. All werefolk *do* is hide from the humans. We're told we can't mate with humans, that we can't bring humans into the breeds. They don't even like us to associate with breeds other than our own. That's not living!"

"I agree with a lot of your complaints," Harry said.

"But you can't change a world by hiding from it," Marj said. "And your parents and grandparents aren't always going to be the ones who make the rules. If you really want to change the system, work to get the power to do what you think is right."

"You don't know anything about it!" Alison shouted.

Marj calmly faced the young werewolf female without a flicker of annoyance or intimidation. Though she didn't realize it, Harry knew that Marj was asserting that she was the alpha female.

"You're right," she said. "But I do know that Phil's family misses him. And so do all the other families you've left. Even if you don't go home immediately, you could at least let them know you're safe. And while you're thinking over what you want to do, why don't you come stay at my house?"

"What?" Phil asked, with a betraying eagerness in his voice. He looked around hopefully at the others. Even though he'd been the one arguing for living off the land when Harry and Marj came up to the shack, a taste of home had quickly changed his mind. "Could we do that?"

"I've got plenty of spare bedrooms," Marj said before anyone could call for a vote. "And plenty of work if you're looking for jobs. So don't feel like you're being offered charity."

"And there's the Christmas tree," Harry said. "And decorations and lights, and music, and a big, warm fireplace." Get them off this mountain first; then work to get them home. "And you'll love Marj's cooking," he persuaded. "You probably miss decent food."

"Christmas," Heather said, looking pleadingly at Clark. "We could at least stay at Dr. Piper's for Christmas." She placed her hand protectively on her abdomen.

"I'd be delighted to have you," Marj told them.

Harry had known Heather was pregnant the moment she appeared at Marj's door. And Marj wasn't at all surprised by the girl's revealing gesture. Smart woman, his Marjorie.

So smart that she came to him, took his hand, and said, "Why don't we leave them alone to talk it over?"

He nodded. "The decision is yours," he told them. He took the dog from the kid's arms, and they turned to leave.

They hadn't even gotten to the door when Alison called, "Wait. Maybe we could come down to your house. For a night or two."

chapter
13

"IT'S A BEAUTIFUL EVENING," Marj said, when she heard the kitchen door open.

She was gazing up at the sky from the back porch as purple dusk faded, and the stars came out, but she was more aware of Harry coming up behind her than of anything else.

She wanted his company. She wanted it more than anything in the world, but she'd deliberately walked out of the kitchen to be alone while the kids cleaned up after supper. She needed to be alone, to prepare herself for his leaving.

She'd known Harry only a few days, but it seemed like a lifetime, and everything had changed and . . .

"Your job's over," she told him.

"Not quite yet," he said. He came up beside her and put his arm around her shoulders. She automatically leaned into his warmth and strength. "But it's a good sign that Clara called her family the minute we got back. And that Phil trotted off to visit his folks."

"He did?"

"Yep. He changed to fox form and snuck off a few minutes ago. I don't think he wants Alison to know how homesick he's been. Not that that crush can ever come to anything."

"Why not?"

"She's a wolf, he's a fox."

"And it's forbidden for them to—"

"Not as long as they stay in human form. But we can't stay in human form—not permanently. Besides, Alison hasn't even noticed his interest."

"Poor Phil. Then again, he's sixteen," she added. "Very few people find true love at sixteen."

And what about those who found true love in their thirties? A love as impossible as a fox falling for a wolf? With the death of each parent a bit more feeling had been drained from her, but since meeting Harry, feeling had rushed back. She was fighting not to drown in the flood.

She wasn't prepared for the desire that shot through her when he leaned down and kissed her cheek. It was a simple, affectionate gesture, yet it *ruined* her.

"You're a good woman, Marjorie Piper."

Marj made herself get her breath back and her emotions under control. She thought her voice was quite calm when she answered, "I seem to have an ability to take in strays."

"It's a gift," he answered. "One that I—Who's that?" he asked, as a vehicle's headlights came into view up the long drive.

"Somebody with a sick animal, maybe," Marj answered.

She wasn't in the mood to deal with a patient, or someone bringing her an unwanted animal, but she didn't exactly have a choice when duty called.

She tried to shrug away from Harry, but he wouldn't let her go. "I have to get to my office," she said.

"I don't think so," he said, and touched his nose. "I only sense humans. And two more cars just turned off the road."

"That's Alice," Marj said, as the first car pulled up.

Harry came with her, as though they were attached at the shoulders, when Marj moved off the porch to greet her friend. Behind them, Taffy and Noel began to bark, and Marj was aware of Taffy's joy at seeing Alice. The usual racket began out in the kennel as more and more vehicles parked in the yard and people began to get out. Greetings were called, and food aromas began to perfume the air.

"What's going on?" Marj asked, when Alice approached with a large casserole dish in her hands. Alice's husband, Mark, carried another large dish, and Pat Muller got out of the backseat. He came up holding a huge cookie tin.

"We're having a celebration," Pat announced. "Congratulations," he added to Harry. "I do believe the best man won."

"Thanks," Harry answered. "I appreciate that, coming from you."

Alice leaned close to kiss Marj's cheek, and Marj got a delicious whiff of Alice's famous macaroni, cheese, and ham casserole. It wasn't that long since she'd had supper, but suddenly Marj was hungry all over again. And more than hungry, she was totally puzzled.

"Alice, what—?"

"I've been thinking about those kittens." Mrs. Braem came up holding a tray of her equally famous candied apples. The scent of warm cinnamon was like perfume in the air. "Maybe I was hasty to give them up so quickly. I like cats."

"I'm glad to hear it," Marj answered. "But what are you all—?"

"I'll be taking them and their mother off your hands when I leave tonight, Marjorie. But right now, let's party. You! Young man, come help me with these."

Marj turned her head to see that Mrs. Braem had spoken to Clark. He and the others kids had come out onto the porch to see what was going on. Taffy had come out with them and was weaving around people's legs as the citizens of Kennedyville made their way into the house.

"I'm so happy for you two," Alice said, when Marj looked back at her. "Not just for you, either, but for all of us." She risked spilling the casserole when she used one hand to make an extravagant gesture that took in the crowd. "Since the fire we've gotten so insular and inward, just worrying about our own problems. I thought the holiday party at the school would pull us together, and you saw how that flopped. Then, when everyone I told was so happy at the news about you and Harry, I realized that what we really needed was a new beginning to celebrate. Your coming marriage is a symbol that we all survived, that we're moving on, that the community is growing. So we're having a combination Christmas and engagement party. Surprise!"

"This is a Christmas present for all of us," Pat added.

"It is?" Marj managed, overwhelmed by Alice's assumptions.

"It is." Harry squeezed her shoulders, then kissed her temple. "Marj is the best Christmas present I've ever had. Believe me, Reverend, I'm grateful."

Tears blinded Marj's eyes, and tightened her throat. *Stop that,* she thought at Harry. *Don't make this worse.*

Make what worse? He thought back. *You've given these people something to be happy about, and I love you for it.*

You what? You can't—

Can't you feel it?

"We need to talk," he whispered, "but let's get this party started first."

Fine for him to say. He wouldn't have to live with them once they discovered there was no engagement.

How had Alice gotten the idea she was engaged?

When I hypnotized her, Harry confessed. *I must have implied more than I intended. I think a lot of it was her own wish fulfillment.*

"Let me help with that," Harry told to Alice, taking the large dish from her. "Let's get inside and get warm."

Harry hustled everyone inside, and Marj followed.

It was several hours later before he took her hand and led her back out onto the porch. The pleasant company had lulled her sense of dread and confusion, but it rushed back again once they were alone. Inside there was more laughter than she'd heard in a long time, and people were singing Christmas carols.

Harry put his arms around her and drew her close. Being near him was delicious and heart-wrenching at once. "Harry . . ."

He cocked his head to one side, and listened for a moment. "They're having a good time."

"At our expense," she muttered.

"Nice and noisy," he went on. "Gives us a chance to talk without being overheard." He drew her to the porch steps, and they settled down side by side at the top. "What's your problem, sweetheart?" he asked her, when they were huddled close together.

She wanted to cry. "I've finally met the one man in the world who understands me, the one man I'm comfortable with, the one man I need in my bed—and I can't have him."

"Would that one man be me?"

She glared at him. "Of course it is!"

He kissed her. After her bones had just about melted, Harry said, "I'm not going anywhere."

"But—your people don't mate with humans."

He put a finger over her lips. "Sure we do," he whispered. "Look at Clark and Heather."

"Yes, but, you said . . . Didn't they run away because it's forbidden?"

"It's not forbidden, and they ran away because his dad's a jerk."

"Harry, I got the distinct impression that your Council forbids fraternization between you kind and mine."

"It's never been forbidden, just strongly discouraged for a couple of generations. Besides, you can't forbid people to marry their true mates. And you're mine."

Hope flared to life. "I am?"

"Didn't you recognize it the moment we first touched? We found our life partners at Murphy's dairy case. I didn't want to recognize it at the time, but it happened. And here we are."

"What do you mean, you didn't want to recognize it?"

Harry laughed softly. "We guys get notions in our heads about not giving up our carefree bachelor days. It's a macho crock, really. I'm no lone wolf, Marj. I need to mate, with you, for life. I'm not saying it's going to be easy," he went on. "My people can't forbid it. We don't have laws so much as guidelines. They can strongly discourage human and werefolk unions, and certainly do. Our people have gone along with this policy, but you've seen how dissatisfied the younger generation is. But times are changing, and you and I can live here, away from all the Council politics."

"You can't abandon your own kind. Not for me."

"I don't intend to abandon anyone, but a mate is always more important than anyone else. My family will accept you into our home pack, though we're going to have some trouble with your in-laws at first."

"I'm going to have in-laws?" Even if they didn't want her, she liked the idea of having family again.

"Besides, if anyone complains about our mating, there are traditions I can call on to counter any protests. Remember when I told you that there are only two ways to deal with humans who find out about shapeshifters?"

"No."

"I did bring it up. Actually, there are three ways to handle humans knowing about us. One is to make the human forget the knowledge permanently. But that won't work on someone with your psychic gifts. The second is, and I'm sorry to admit this, to kill the human. But we only do that if the persons intends us harm, and after a trial. And the third . . ." He kissed her again, then repeated. "And the third—"

And once again they were interrupted by a car pulling up to the house, an expensive sports car that Marj didn't recognize. This time, the dogs didn't set off their usual racket.

"Werefolk," Marj said.

"Yeah," Harry agreed, as he and Marj rose to their feet.

A handsome, platinum-haired male got out of the car and strode arrogantly forward. There was something very familiar about his looks.

"Lucius Malfoy?" Marj asked Harry.

"Clark Losimba's dad."

She recalled Clark's comments about his father. "That could be worse."

"Yeah."

She wondered if she should get the tranquilizer gun from the kennel. Harry must have caught the thought, because he gave her a smile.

Then he turned to the newcomer. But before he could speak, the back door opened and Clark came rushing down the stairs.

"Dad—"

That was as far as he got before his father swept him into a fierce hug. Clark hesitated, stiff with tension, but only for a moment, before he hugged back just as fiercely.

"I missed you so much, Clark."

"Me too."

Then Heather came out of the house and walked toward the men. Clark broke away from his father and held his hand out to her.

When she joined him, he said to his father. "This is my mate." His tone and look dared for there to be any argument. "And the mother of your grandchild."

A number of expressions crossed the elder male's proud features while the young couple stood before him with their arms around each other, completely calm and sure of themselves. Finally, his features settled on stiff resignation.

"I see it's a fait accompli. Do you expect me to be gracious about it?" he asked Clark.

"Yes, we do," Heather said. "Merry Christmas, Mr. Losimba."

Losimba looked at his son, then at Heather, and smiled. "A grandchild." The couple nodded. Losimba's shoulders slumped, but he kept smiling. "That is quite a Christmas present."

Heather held a hand out to Losimba. "It's cold out here, come in with us and join the party."

He gave a stiff nod. Marj could tell he wanted his son back, even if it required compromise. Compromise was a good beginning.

"All right," he said, and went along with the young couple.

"That went well, I thought," Harry said. He whirled Marj around, and back into his embrace. "Where were we?"

"Could we get back to kissing? It warms me up."

"Me too. I'm going to more than warm you up, when everyone's gone and the kids are tucked in. Anyway," he went on. "I was about to tell you the third way werefolk keep our secrets safe from outsiders."

She smiled. "How?"

"Why, we marry them, of course."

Marj's heart soared, and she held Harry even tighter. She never wanted to let him go, and she didn't intend to. She threw back her head and laughed. "I love you, Harrison Blethyin!"

"I guess that means you accept my proposal."

"I have to. We're already having an engagement party."

"Then it will be a very merry Christmas." And he kissed her.

POCKET STAR BOOKS
PROUDLY PRESENTS

I HUNGER FOR YOU

SUSAN SIZEMORE

Available in paperback Spring 2005
from Pocket Star Books

Turn the page for a preview of
I Hunger for You. . . .

"Looks like we have a robbery gone sour. Maybe we can work with their demands."

The negotiator's voice, heard through the earpiece of member Colin Foxe's headset, sounded relieved.

"Do you want us to hold?" the team leader questioned.

After a considerable pause, the negotiator said, "Get your team in place, but wait for a go."

They already knew that there was an officer down inside; a cop who'd noticed something suspicious while driving by. She'd called it in, then gone inside. Shots had been fired. The situation escalated quickly after that.

Colin could smell the wounded officer's blood drifting on the evening breeze through a bullet hole in the office window. He could also sense the faint flutter of her heartbeat. She wasn't dead, but she didn't have much time. He couldn't see inside, since curtains had been pulled across the wide windows at the front of the building, but his heightened senses picked up a tangled mixture of physical markers and high emotions.

It was everybody on the team's job to stop this situation, but he took it very personally. He'd taken vows, made promises to protect and serve humanity that were far stronger and more binding than even his oath as a Los Angeles police officer.

He and his S.W.A.T. team were here to see that the hostages and injured cop were saved. It was a great team, well-trained, well-coordinated, well-led; he was proud to be a part of it.

Dressed all in black, he moved in line with the rest of the team. Crouching low, they had formed a circle that was stealthily closing in on the one-story building. Their target was the small publishing company located in an office park on a quiet side street. At least four armed men were inside, holding a dozen hostages.

A cloudy night covered the team's movements as they left behind the police vehicles that filled the street and dodged carefully around the cars in the parking lot. To focus on their objective, they used night scope goggles—all but Colin, who'd left his up on the brim of his helmet. He could easily see in the dark.

Though he was outwardly calm, the excitement of the hunt burned through him, as it always did at times like this. The extra senses he normally reined in were fully focused. He could smell fear, and taste it, as well. The threat of violence hung around the office building like a pall of smoke.

One touch of anger scratched across his senses like nails on slate. He didn't think the fury was coming from one of the perps. It was one of the hostages, and she—yes, that was definitely a strong sense of femaleness—she was royally pissed off. In a hostage situation, it was better to be scared than angry. Scared people were more likely to keep their heads down and do as they were told, increasing their chances of survival. Colin didn't like this, it added risk to the situation. If this woman did something stupid . . .

Telepathy wasn't his strongest sense, and using it might distract him from the team effort. But he did risk sending one thought toward the perps and hostages alike.

Calm down.

I am calm, came the immediate reply.

It took all his training to keep the surprised Colin from rising out of his crouch. She'd heard him! And answered! And the brief touch of her mind on his made him red hot.

Suddenly shouts erupted from the building, followed by shots. And screams.

"Go!"

He was up and moving even as the command came.

Colin was the first one through the door, rushing in just in time to see the flying side kick that knocked away the gun of the man who would have shot him.

"Hey!" Colin shouted at the woman who'd disarmed the shooter.

"Thanks for the distraction," she called back. She jumped and kicked again, straight up, taking the bad guy under the chin. He dropped like a rock.

Colin grabbed her by the waist as she came back down, and pushed her to the floor.

"Stay put," he ordered, as the rest of his team came boiling in through the door he'd broken down.

Big brown eyes looked up at him, full of shock and fury that sizzled all the way through him. He motioned for her to get under a nearby desk, and turned to take out another gunman. There was already a third man down. No doubt the Karate Kid had gotten him, too—which was probably why the shooting had started.

Farther back in the building he heard shouts and screaming. Members of the team were heading that way at a run.

"You could have gotten everybody killed!" Colin yelled at the woman.

"Well, I didn't!" she shouted back.

This was no time for an argument. Colin quickly joined his team and got into the well-practiced rhythm of a rescue operation. But even as he went about helping to secure the rest of the bad guys, part of him was still aware of the impression of soft, warm flesh over hard muscle he'd gotten in the moment he held her. Her skin held the scent of ginger, and her psychic signature was pure heat, as if her blood was laced with chili peppers.

He couldn't let it go, and marched back to the front of the building as soon as the place had been secured. By this time she was out from under the desk, and one of the medics was arguing with her. Colin noticed that one side of her face was badly bruised, and she was cradling her left hand with her right.

Anger shot through him, and a hot, possessive protectiveness. "Who hurt you?" he demanded.

She looked around, and her dark brown eyes locked with his. "I'm fine."

"That doesn't answer the question."

Her gaze flickered to an unconscious perp on the floor, then back to Colin. "I took care of it."

Her response only served to redirect his annoyance at her. He ripped off his helmet and headset and glared at her. "You had no business doing what you—"

"Hey!" she interrupted him. "I saved your ass."

"No, you didn't."

"He was going to shoot you when you came through that door."

"He wouldn't have." He took the woman by the shoulders, and was instantly and intimately aware of the warmth of her skin. "My job is to do the rescuing."

Her anger was incandescent. "You were a little late. Those men held us hostage for four hours. Where were you?"

"Organizing a *safe* rescue." Everything about her burned him, but he liked it. She infuriated him, needed to be tamed, and he liked, that too.

"Did you stop at Starbucks for a few lattes on the way?" She jerked her head to where the medics were working on the wounded officer. "She could have died. We *all* could have. Somebody had to do something."

"So you decided to play hero? Bad move, sister."

Her head came up sharply, brown eyes flashing.

He could have kissed her then and there. "I am not your sister."

"And you're no hero, either," Colin shot back.

"Officer," the medic cut in. He put a hand firmly on Colin's arm. "Officer."

The Prime part of Colin almost turned on the medic with bared fangs, as if the man was challenging him for a mate. It shocked him that the instinctual impulse was triggered by a mortal, and it took him a moment to get the vampire part of himself under control. He closed his eyes, took a deep breath—and let the woman go.

"Ms. Luchese's injured," he heard the medic say. "We need to get her to the ER."

"I told you I'm fine," she said.

Colin looked at her. "Luchese, you always think you know best, and never do what you're told, right?"

She smiled. It was wicked, and edgy, and that lit a different kind of fire in him.

"Yeah," she acknowledged.

"Go with the medic," he told her. She would have protested further, but he sent a stern command into her mind. *Go.*

Then his team commander called his name, and Colin went back to work without another glance.

Several hours later he met the woman in the ER as she came out of a treatment room. Despite the frantic hubbub in this part of the hospital she spotted him instantly, as if she was as drawn to him as he was to her. She looked at him, then looked away. He felt her consider walking past him and out the door. Her left arm was in a sling, and a shiny cream covered the bruises on her face. Her shoulders had a tired slump to them but she consciously straightened when she saw him. Apparently she was ready to do battle all over again.

"You look beautiful," he said, coming up to her.

Her eyes went wide in surprise. She thought he was making fun of her, and asked, "Officer, are you supposed to talk like that?"

"I'm off duty."

"You're not here to—take a statement, or something?"

"Didn't an officer talk to you already?"

"Yeah. He told me everyone got out okay. So why are you—?"

"I wanted to check on you." He couldn't help but run a hand up her uninjured arm, and felt her shiver. "How are you feeling?"

"Nothing's broken, just a sprained wrist," she answered. "I don't need the sling, but I promised the nice intern who looked at it that I'd wear it until I'm outside the hospital door." She took a deep breath, and made a wry face. "I'm sorry I yelled at you. You risked your life to save us. Thank you."

He gave a slight shrug. He was there to take care of her kind. Mortal life was precious and it was an honor to protect the helpless—even if Luchese here didn't think *she* was helpless.

"I was scared," she went on. "That made me—testy."

"What were you doing out in the front office with

your captor? Why weren't you tied up in the back with the others?"

"I thought you weren't here to ask questions?"

"Not officially; I'm curious. You were up to something, weren't you?"

"They were making ransom demands," she answered. "They were incompetent idiots with guns. They—"

"Had the wrong building," he filled in. "We know that from questioning them. By the time they figured out they'd screwed up, the officer had called the robbery in. But what were *you* doing?"

"Trying to split them up, so I could take one down and get his weapon. They were demanding a lot of money, and threatening to kill people if they didn't get it. So I told them I was an heiress, and if they'd let me call my family, they'd be rich. I got one of them to take me up front so I could use the receptionist's phone, while one of the others was occupied talking to your negotiator in the back. It worked." Then she laughed, the sound a little shaky. "And I was only there to pick up a friend for lunch."

He shook a finger under her nose. "Luchese, that was very stupid of you. Brave, though," he added, as a flash of annoyance went through her. He touched the tip of her nose, then found himself tracing the outline of her lips. Soft, full, warm lips. A wave of hunger crashed through him. He was going to kiss those lips, soon. The smoldering look she gave him told him she knew it, too. He was going to taste her. But this was not the place.

He made himself take a step back. "My name's Colin Foxe," he finally introduced himself. "You have a first name, Luchese?"

"Mia," she answered. "Mia Luchese."

Mia. A short, pretty, uncomplicated mortal name. Nothing like the complex, beautiful names of vampire females. And even though someday he would bond with a vampire female, right now, he wanted this human woman.

He reached out and took her uninjured hand. "I'll take you home."